Knowledge is everything to the powerful.

The Last Leviathan
ANACOSTIA MILLER

HOT TREE PUBLISHING

THE LAST LEVIATHAN
THE GUARDIANS OF FARLIGHT ISLES
BOOK ONE

ANACOSTIA MILLER

HOT TREE PUBLISHING

THE LAST LEVIATHAN © 2024 by ANACOSTIA MILLER

All rights reserved. No part of this book may be used or reproduced in any written, electronic, recorded, or photocopied format without the express permission from the author or publisher as allowed under the terms and conditions with which it was purchased or as strictly permitted by applicable copyright law. Any unauthorized distribution, circulation or use of this text may be a direct infringement of the author's rights, and those responsible may be liable in law accordingly. Thank you for respecting the work of this author.

THE LAST LEVIATHAN is a work of fiction. All names, characters, events and places found therein are either from the author's imagination or used fictitiously. Any similarity to persons alive or dead, actual events, locations, or organizations is entirely coincidental and not intended by the author.

For information, contact the publisher, Hot Tree Publishing.

WWW.HOTTREEPUBLISHING.COM

EDITING: HOT TREE EDITING

COVER DESIGNER: BOOKSMITH DESIGN

ARTWORK: LEO @LEO.NOR_ART

E-BOOK ISBN: 978-1-922679-81-9

PAPERBACK ISBN: 978-1-922679-82-6

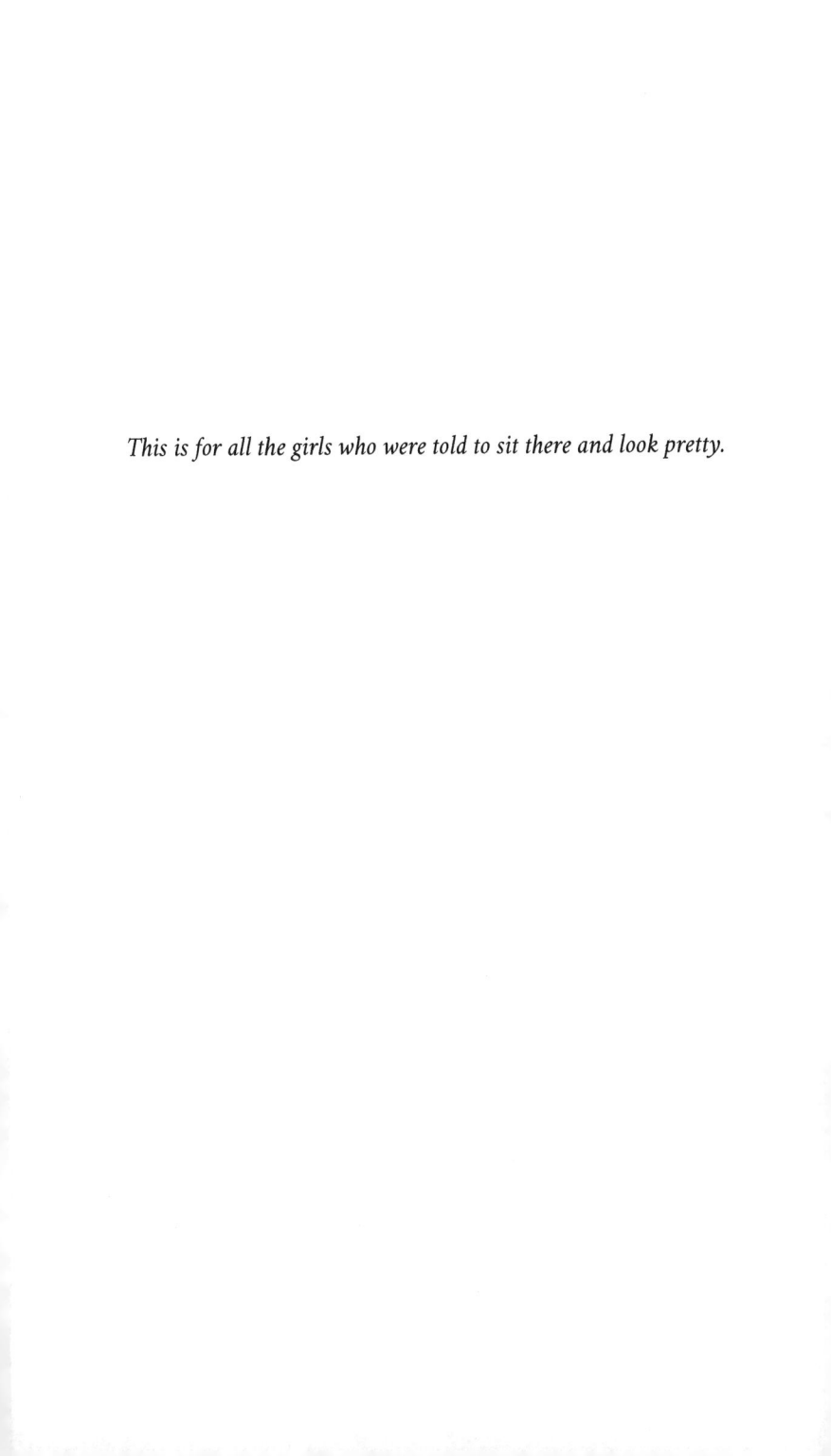

This is for all the girls who were told to sit there and look pretty.

- Farligh
- Violetta Silver's Haven
- The Wilds
- Fisherman Gully
- Bliss Thatcher's Colony
- The Fae Occupied Gullies

The Isles of Farlight

- Farlight Keep
- The Ivory Keys
- Pike Estate
- West Algar Sea
- Shipwreck Bay
- Lucky Bartram's Outpost
- Anchorage Cove

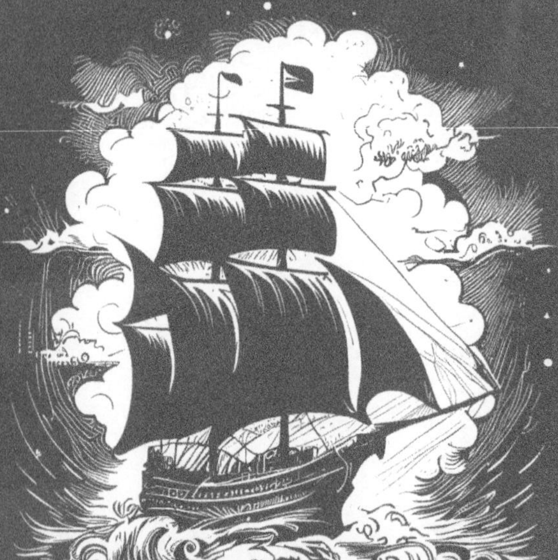

1
MAEVE CROSS

My life ends today.

That was the only thought in my mind as the moon shone into my bedchamber from my balcony door. In less than a day, I'd be stuffed into a dress, my father's arm keeping me tightly in place as he dragged me to the altar to marry a man I *hated*.

Nathaniel Pike—Lord of the Ivory Keys.

At least I could spend my last night staring at the harbor. Watching the light twinkle off the surface of choppy waves and wondering what it would be like to be free. Not shackled to my royal obligations.

Wind in my hair as I breathed in the thick, briny breeze.

The ocean called to me, but I could never answer.

Thickness formed in my throat as my father's voice echoed in my head.

"Oh, don't make a fuss, Maeve. It's only marriage. He's a rich man. He'll give us what we need."

Burn in the Nine Hells!

I wanted to see how my father fared when he was stripped of his voice and privileges.

It wasn't *only* marriage. It was the rest of my life saddled with an egotistical man who viewed me as something shiny to use for his pleasure. But, oh no. I couldn't say anything about it without seeming *hysterical*. A word weaponized to keep me in my place.

A silent, pretty piece of meat.

Tears dotted my bedspread and wetted my nightgown. Hopelessness swallowed me.

There was a swift knock on my door. I perked up, using my palm to wipe away the tears.

No one should be at my chamber at this hour.

Unless....

Hope swelled in my chest.

Maybe, just maybe, it was my father. Perhaps he had finally seen reason and was coming to tell me he'd called off the wedding. But when I swung my door open, my hope solidified and sank deep into my belly like a heavy stone in water.

My mother.

The absent figure in my life stood in my doorway, dressed in nothing more than a nightgown and carrying a lantern in one hand and an elixir in the other. My lips flattened into a straight line, trembling slightly as I fought off tears.

There was a frantic gleam in her eyes, but I couldn't find it in me to care.

"What?" I warbled, swallowing my raw emotions.

She didn't ask for an invitation as she sidestepped me, forcing me to take a step back while she looked down the hallway both ways and then closed the door behind her. "You know I can't get you out of this, Maeve."

"Why not?" I put up a stiff lip, but I couldn't hide the damp tracks down my face.

"When your father wants something, no one can stop him," she said quietly, as if she was afraid someone would hear her. My entire life, she had always been distant, so her sudden appearance in my bedchamber was odd to say the least.

"But I'm sure you could—"

"I *can't*, child." She outstretched her hand that held the tonic. "I need you to take this. I can't save you from this wedding, but I can buy you time."

Desperation colored her tone, an emotion I'd never heard from her before. My mother wasn't numb or intoxicated. In fact, she looked stone-cold sober.

I looked down at the shimmering liquid, but I didn't take it.

"I can't stay, Maeve. Please."

My tears had dried, and a flare of anger bubbled to the surface.

Of course *now* she decided to be present.

Only now.

Hours before I was sent away forever.

Not during my twenty-two years of life where she'd been drunk and absent. Emotionally unavailable. I didn't know how to feel about it, so I pushed those feelings down and asked, "What is it?"

"A wedding tonic," she answered. "It will prevent pregnancy for three months. Not forever. But you'll have more time."

"More time for what? I'll be trapped." The words came out like a snarl as I snatched the tonic from her hand.

She didn't answer, and I caught a glimmer of... was that regret flickering in her eyes?

Good. I hoped it ate her alive.

"Just drink it. I need to go," she said, voice thick. She

turned on her heel, opened the door, and closed it behind her without another word.

Without another explanation.

Just like during my childhood, no one ever answered my questions.

I held the smooth glass vial, chilly from the liquid inside.

And drank it.

MY LIFE ENDS TODAY.

The cream-hued lace over my face could've been a hanging rope. It would probably feel the same. A cascading train of pearl-laden embroidery followed my gown with every step, a pool of fabric pulling me down into a deep, endless trench like the seas surrounding the Isles. I feared I would never escape.

The haze of lace obscured my vision as I struggled down the crimson trail to my soon-to-be husband. Blurry visuals of the common folk gawking at me from open windows. Nobles in the pews watched as I marched toward my fate.

That would be my legacy—Nathaniel Pike's *pretty wife*. My voice would be smothered.

I never had much of a voice anyway. Not as the Princess of Farlight. My life would always end like this. Groomed to be a wife. An arm piece.

A bargaining chip.

A tool to use to get my father his army. He never cared for my happiness. No matter how much I objected to this engagement, I had no power of my own. I could rip my veil off right now and yell to the high heavens, but what good would that do?

I dragged my feet in silent indignance, but my father

pulled me along, ignoring the fight I put up, like I was a petulant child. It would never be more than a temper tantrum to him.

I glanced up at my father. He wasn't looking at me.

What can I do to make you see me?

A white-gold crown adorned the top of his grayed hair, curled around the metal as if he'd slept in it. He never took it off. He *lived* in it. A glimmering black stone containing flecks of blue like the depths of the ocean sparkled in his amulet. He never took that off either. It was always shined and polished to the nines.

Leviathan draconite.

The mere sight of it caused bile to rise in my throat. A purely visceral reaction that I had no control over, similar to the disgust that crawled under my skin whenever Nathaniel touched me.

My father and I both wore our family crest proudly—the moray eel coiling through a dragon skull, indicative of our history.

My crest was in the form of a brooch made from draconite as a goodbye gift. It had been pinned to my corset that was peeping over the extravagant white dress.

I hated how it felt on me.

I didn't want it.

My father's crest was woven into his surcoat with golden embroidery.

He curled my arm around his elbow as the music played behind me. All eyes were on me. Commoners. Nobles. People from both the Ivory Keys and Farlight watched the union of His Lordship, Nathaniel Pike of the Ivory Keys, and me, Maeve Cross—the princess hidden under lock and key far up in my tower with only the harbor to gaze upon for that elusive taste of freedom.

I should've leaped from that balcony.

Now only a few steps away, I could take in my soon-to-be husband's attire. Nathaniel was dressed in a manner that boasted of both his status and his military power, his elegant silver armor bearing the Pike crest of a barracuda. While he was only thirty-four, he had influence that far exceeded his age. His reputation matched his coat of arms.

All teeth.

It wasn't hard to notice him dragging his light eyes up my dress from my petticoat to my tailored corset designed to show off the valley between my breasts. His gaze felt like the stroke of a freshly sharpened blade.

The officiant stood beside Nathaniel, dressed in all red and holding a holy book in his hands.

I'd heard stories of the Reaper. A black cloak. A scythe to whisk away souls. But now, I truly believed the Reaper was a man in crimson holding a holy book as he placed coins on my eyelids. This officiant didn't know what he was doing. Or he didn't care. I'd hedge my bet on the latter.

My father and I reached the steps. I held my head high. I would not give Nathaniel the satisfaction of a subservient wife.

Never.

The music petered out, but I was barely aware of it. I'd tuned almost everything out, numb to it all. I could've screamed from the highest tower how badly I didn't want this, but what power did I have?

"Do you, King Varric Cross, give your daughter, Princess Maeve Cross, to Lord Nathaniel Pike?" the officiant asked, looking only at my father. Not me.

Because they don't give a damn how I feel.

"Yes," my father answered as he gestured for Nathaniel to take my arm in his place, just as we'd rehearsed.

My throat bobbed, but I didn't argue. I couldn't embarrass my father. As horrid as everything was, I couldn't bring myself to disappoint him.

The lord stepped down to my level, replacing my father as he went to his seat.

Sickness crept up my throat, my skin crawling as he touched me. It didn't matter how many times we'd rehearsed this, my reaction never changed. Physical contact didn't usually bother me, but Nathaniel's touch tore this reaction from my bones.

I dug my heels into the rug, making him work extra hard to haul me up the steps. Those cold eyes met mine, and I didn't look away. I wished that only once, someone would look at me and feel fear rather than dismiss me as nothing more than a foolish woman who didn't know what she wanted.

I knew exactly what I wanted.

The ocean.

The breeze.

Freedom.

Unfortunately, that wasn't what had been chosen for me. If that didn't piss me off enough, Nathaniel loved to tell me all the ways he could use me. Yes, *use.* Like I was a replacement for his left hand.

Every time he got a moment, Nathaniel would lean over and whisper how he couldn't wait to see how wet a virgin could get.

Rehearsal dinners.

Luncheons.

Wedding preparations.

If my parents heard him, they didn't say anything.

And meanwhile, I had to politely smile and fight the *overwhelming* urge to tell him how dry he made me.

I'd rather bed a fish.

But here I was, getting handed off like some buttery hors d'oeuvres at a celebratory party. Or perhaps like a basket of bread at dinner. I knew they'd devour me until nothing remained.

But I was determined to leave a bitter taste in his mouth.

A smirk pulled the side of Nathaniel's mouth. His jaw was freshly shaven, and his icy blue eyes felt just as cold as their color. I knelt in front of the altar, and he followed my example. His armor creaked, the draconite-imbued sword on his hip brushing the floor.

The officiant read phrases and paragraphs from his holy book that didn't apply to this situation at all. We weren't in love. My father was simply passing off the keys to my irons.

Nathaniel pulled on my sleeve when it was time to rise. I took my time, clearly annoying him when he dragged me back up to my feet. When the officiant asked for objections, the chapel was silent. That didn't surprise me, since there was no one to speak up for me. I didn't even have any bridesmaids. Or friends. A cold pit opened up in my stomach.

I was alone.

The officiant let Nathaniel know when it was time to pull my veil back, and I let him. Nathaniel wasn't an unattractive man. Not even for being twelve years my senior. Blue eyes pinned mine as a satisfied grin curled the corner of his mouth. His gaze slid down to the exposed skin of my chest. It sickened me.

He looked so damn smug that I had to curl my hands into fists to stop myself from striking him across the face. Instead, I looked at him like I smelled something putrid.

Oh, he didn't like that at all.

A tic formed in his jaw, offense written across his mouth. Satisfaction flickered through me.

Oh, this is just a taste, my dear husband. I'm going to make your life burn like the Nine Hells.

He said the vows to me, and I soullessly repeated whatever the officiant said. My skin crawled as Nathaniel slid a ring on my finger, set with a massive stone to display my new status.

I hated status. The parties. The complete apathy toward anyone deemed *lesser*. The obsession with power. It turned men into monsters.

But I had to pretend to be happy. My lips twitched as I forced a smile, remembering that I should be putting on a show so I didn't embarrass my father.

"You may kiss your new bride!" the officiant announced.

The crowd cheered, and Nathaniel grasped my face, dragging me forward into a forceful kiss. I flinched, refusing to open my mouth as his tongue came out to lick at my lips. The urge for violence buzzed in my chest, and I needed to repress the impulse to bite him.

When I wouldn't play along, he drew back, his grip on my face going tighter only for a moment before he released me. It was the first time he'd ever shown aggression toward me.

Fear flared inside me. My heart dropped into my belly, which was churning with bile.

"Come now, *wife*."

We walked out and into the Great Hall, where servants were waiting to serve our reception dinner. When we sat at the head table, he leaned over, pinching my side harshly while our guests came filing in.

A reminder to behave.

"Next time you refuse me, you'll regret it. Don't forget who you belong to." His hand drifted down to where he'd be touching my thigh if it wasn't for the layers of fabric.

Choosing my words carefully, I widened my eyes as if I

didn't understand what he was saying. "But *husband*, we needed to keep it chaste. Otherwise, it would've been indecent."

He removed his hand, gaze softening as he stroked my jaw with the back of his hand. I shivered, nauseous. "Play up your innocence while you can. I'll deeply enjoy ridding you of it."

Ugh.

I repressed the urge to gag, a shameful rouge brightening my cheeks. I wriggled uncomfortably, gulping down the taste of vomit.

Nathaniel grinned, visibly enjoying my discomfort while the servants brought over the first platter of food. "Go ahead. Eat. No one will save you tonight. I'll have what I'm owed."

I don't owe you anything.

But could I say that?

No.

Smile and nod. Cross your ankles. Don't eat too fast. Don't talk. Your purpose is to please your husband.

I gazed at the guests, all of them gathered for my father and Nathaniel. I didn't have anyone here for me.

No one will save you.

My father took a seat next to my husband and immediately began discussing armies and strategy. Taking advantage of his new freedoms while he stripped me of mine. *Bastard.*

"Have you rid yourself of that pirate problem yet? I don't want to share the port with scoundrels," Nathaniel asked, gulping down wine while I refused to touch my glass.

Maybe if he drank enough, he'd forget me.

My father sighed. "Pests. Kill one and two take their place. But with your resources, perhaps I can finally hit them at their source."

Pirates. Now that was the life. No man telling you what to do. I'd heard stories of women taking to the high seas despite the naval armies refusing to recruit them. They clawed their way out from under the thumb of those who believed themselves superior.

It was a shame that the age of pirates would be coming to an end.

I'd recently overheard my father saying so in his study. It was a rare opportunity, but when I did manage to eavesdrop, I clutched on to the information. Knowledge was *everything* to the powerful. The ultimatum my father proposed echoed in my head.

"They can join our army or hang."

The idea churned the sickness in my belly.

"Maeve!" Nathaniel jabbed me in the ribs to get my attention.

I winced, whirling around to look at him. I bit my tongue and swallowed a swear. "Yes?"

"I was saying how you'll need to be careful at the harbor when we depart for the Ivory Keys. I can't have my new wife snatched before I've had a chance to—"

Thankfully, he didn't finish his statement, as my father cut him off. "You'll have to forgive my daughter. She's always been a daydreamer," he jested.

Nathaniel chuckled like I wasn't here. "Can't have her getting too many ideas, then."

The corner of my father's mouth twitched into a frown. "Maeve is quite bright. You could learn something."

My husband paled briefly before straightening up again.

I didn't reply, but warmth bubbled up in my chest before it became cold again. I was feeling a complicated myriad of emotions.

I spotted my mother on the other side of my father. She was practically a ghost, ignoring my existence as she enjoyed the food. She didn't say anything. Didn't object. The biggest female figure in my life… absent.

Aside from sneaking into my chamber last night to give me a tonic to temporarily prevent pregnancy. What good would that do? Three months down the line, I would still be forced to carry Nathaniel's heirs.

I really am alone in this place, aren't I?

"Nonetheless, you should take my escort to the harbor. The darker it gets, the more pirates take to the taverns. And the more sea beasties rise to the land," my father warned. "It's your responsibility to keep my daughter safe now. I can't have the sea claim her."

"Don't you worry, King Varric. I will take very good care of Maeve." Nathaniel tossed back the remainder of his wine. "We should be on our way to the Ivory Keys."

He held out his hand, and I took it. Powerless.

"It's a beautiful island. You'll love it," my father told me, standing to press an affectionate kiss against my cheek. "It's time you left your tower, darling. These stone walls are no place for you."

He drew back, and I wiped my cheek with my palm. "At least my new prison will offer a change in scenery."

"Maeve—" my father started.

I turned my back to him, crossing my arms while breathing heavily through my nose. I was trying so hard not to cry. I wouldn't give them that power over me. "Goodbye."

"Smile and wave as you leave, Maeve."

I whipped my head over my shoulder to pin my father with a withering stare. Hot tears welled in my eyes, but I blinked them away. I sucked on my teeth and forced a smile as I hooked my arm in Nathaniel's and let him escort me to the doors, a detail of guards behind us.

But my eyes screamed, *"Go to the Hells."*

The cool coastal air greeted me as we stepped outside. The moon was high in the sky, and the water lapped nearby. I glanced back at the castle within its stone walls, its iron gate like a devouring maw.

As comforting as the air felt, that feeling was sapped out of me as soon as I stepped into the carriage. I scooted down as far as I could on the bench to put as much space between me and Nathaniel as possible. He climbed in after me, and the guard closed the door.

A faint clucking noise from the driver broke through the silence, followed by whinnying from the horses and the sound of grinding wheels sloughing through the mud as the carriage jolted into motion. I crossed my arms over my chest, tucking the long train from my dress under myself.

The harbor wasn't far away. Once I was loaded onto Nathaniel's ship, it would be over.

A hand reached across the carriage, heading right toward my breasts, but I slapped it away. "Did I give you permission to touch me?" I snapped, glaring daggers.

Nathaniel tilted his head to the side, a smug grin curling his lips. "It's sweet that you think I need permission."

I turned my body completely away from him, but he didn't let me escape. He grasped my arm and forcefully yanked me across the carriage until my chest pressed against his armor. My muscles whined, and a yelp fell from my lips.

"You think you're a stallion, but you're nothing more than a foal. A pathetic little creature who can barely use their legs. You will cry for me. You will bend for me. Refuse, and you will break for me." His breath fanned over my lips with every word.

"We've hardly been married an hour and you're already threatening me?" I hissed back. Perhaps it was foolish to bait a man nearly twice my size, but I wasn't going to roll over. I was going to give back as much as I was given.

His eyes glimmered with thinly veiled violence. He grasped my face as he'd done in the chapel, holding me in a vise grip. "Fight all you want, Maeve. Overpowering you is the fun part."

I bared my teeth, thrashing to pull myself back with a snarl. "Get your disgusting hands *off me*."

"I'll do something about that vile mouth."

He crashed his lips into mine, taking advantage of my parted lips to plunder my mouth.

Bile rose in my throat as his slimy tongue swiped my lips, my tongue. I gagged, then bit down on his lip hard enough to draw blood. The metallic tang of it flooded my mouth, and Nathaniel hissed, yanking me back, grasping my throat hard.

I shoved at him, panic rising and firing in my blood. It was no use. He was stronger than I was. I tried to gasp for breath as he closed his hand around my throat, black dots flittering across my vision.

I can't breathe.

Suddenly, the carriage came to a harsh halt. Nathaniel pulled away, shoving me into the corner against the door. He breathed hard, pale ivory skin flushed.

Relief bombarded me like a tap had been fully opened, and cool, refreshing water cascaded down my throat to soothe the awful pressure of his hands. My mouth felt swollen. My neck ached. I breathed hard, gulping in the air that I had just been deprived of. I felt like a cornered animal.

The danger of my situation became vastly clear.

Nathaniel wasn't above hurting me.

A knock sounded from the carriage door, and Nathaniel brushed his hair back. He opened the door and wiped his mouth, smearing blood from where I bit him.

"What is it?" he asked, not hiding his annoyance.

"I apologize for the interruption, milord, but we have a block on the ship. They are asking for your identification," the carriage driver reported.

Nathaniel sighed. "Fine." He looked over at me. "There are pirates all over this port. Stay here. I will be back, and I will protect you."

I nodded, desperate to have him leave. If even for a moment.

"Look at you. Already learning. Maybe you'll last longer than the others."

Others?

He grinned, then slid out of the carriage and away. It was like I could finally take my first breath.

The fear paralyzing me ebbed away bit by bit until I gained control of my muscles again. I reached up to touch the bruises forming along my throat, then whipped my head to look out the window. I could see Nathaniel in the distance speaking to the harbor watchman.

My chest rose and fell rapidly as I took in the numerous ships in the harbor. Some massive. Some small. Despite the number of ships, the pier was fairly empty with only a few sailors strolling up and down the wooden planks.

Nathaniel looked back over at the carriage, his cold eyes washing over me like the hot breath of a predator billowing down my neck. He would be back any moment, and I'd be nothing more than a bunny in the jaws of a python.

He'd swallow me whole.

My upper lip curled into a snarl.

I will not let him.

With one brave shove, I pushed the door open and scrambled out of the carriage on unsteady legs. As I was about to dart away, my lacy train got stuck in the carriage door.

"Princess?" The carriage driver's voice carried over from his seat on top of the carriage.

I ripped the train, making direct eye contact with him. He was coming toward me.

No. I wouldn't go to the Ivory Keys. I wouldn't be Nathaniel's wife.

I took my one chance at freedom and sprinted off toward the taverns lining the docks.

"No one will save you."

He was right. I had to do it myself.

2
MAEVE CROSS

If I hid on the island, Nathaniel would find me. He would use me up until I was a shell. No doubt by now, he knew I was gone.

My window of freedom was closing.

I pressed my back against the grimy wall of a tavern shrouded in darkness. The cacophony of rowdy men cheering, bountiful music, and excitement filled the air. I gulped hard, thinking over my options.

"I'm finished. This is it. I'm *done for*," I murmured to myself, eyes clenched.

Suddenly, hushed voices came around the corner. "...the shipment is ready for your captain."

"Excellent. I'll have my men bring in the coin," a woman's voice answered. She had an accent I didn't recognize. "Same place?"

"I'll bring it to the alley instead. Too many guards out tonight," the first voice offered before I heard one set of padding feet initiate the going of separate ways. I didn't hear the other pair of feet, though.

The alley. *Perfect.*

I'd stow away. It didn't matter where I was going as long as I was far from Nathaniel. After all, I'd rather walk a plank than share a bed with him.

My heart thundering with excitement, I ducked behind a large trash receptacle. The scent of moldy food was putrid, but I didn't have much of a choice. I tugged my large skirt up to my chest, tucking myself into a ball so I wouldn't be noticed.

The door from the tavern to the alleyway burst open, and I heard heavy crates being placed on the cobblestone. Again and again, more crates were added to the stash, the men grunting and huffing as they laid down the goods.

Then silence after the door slammed shut.

I waited a few beats until I was sure they wouldn't be coming back. Then I came out of the shadows, heart in my throat. Shouts in the distance caught my attention.

"Where is she?"

"I d-don't know, sire."

Nathaniel. He was looking for me.

I kicked off my heels, leaving me with only my stockings as a barrier between my feet and the cobblestone.

Without much thought, I opened the lid of a crate big enough to fit me. It was filled with various supplies from gauze and bandages to pots and pans. The noise of men trotting to the alleyway had me climbing inside the crate. I closed the lid over myself and tucked my dress between me and the supplies.

I held my breath, shut my eyes tight and willed my heart to slow down.

It didn't take long for the crate to be lifted, my body jostled side to side as a man from outside grumped, "Have supplies always been this heavy?"

"Maybe you're just getting weak," another man teased.

"I'll show you weak."

Nerves bombarded my body, a cold sweat trickling down my forehead. Boots hit wood, the men grunting and huffing as I was carried up an incline.

I couldn't tell which way was up or down, but I could hear the lapping of waves hitting the hull. Wherever I was going, it was a big ship. Crewmembers were chattering and cheering among themselves. Then there was a loud thud and all the jostling stopped as my crate thumped onto the wooden planks. I could only assume that I was finally put down.

"Ha, call me weak now, you sonuvabitch," the man laughed, the voice diminishing as a door clicked shut. "Come on. We're leaving port."

Thank the Gods. Take me far away.

I should've been nervous.

After all, I didn't know where I was, if I was on a military vessel or a pirate ship.

I hoped for the latter. Nathaniel had a reputation as a pirate hunter, so no pirate would want to be within twelve nautical miles of him. That's what I was counting on, at least.

And that, in and of itself, filled me with insurmountable *joy*. I beamed, tears welling in my eyes as I curled up inside the crate.

Is this freedom?

A soft sob fell from my lips as I cupped my throat, the touch of my fingers reminding me how bruised it was. I stayed put, hidden in the crate. We needed to be on the open ocean before I climbed out.

I didn't go through all this to be left in the port.

Even though my surroundings were cramped, I didn't feel as claustrophobic as I had in the carriage. Even the supplies jabbing into my legs didn't dull my spirit.

When my eyes closed, I allowed myself a moment of peace. The boat swayed on the water, and the movement told me that we had left the port. The ship rocked me into a shallow slumber. I drifted between being incredibly alert to relaxed until I wasn't sure how much time had passed, but it had to have been a few hours. I could hear talking and laughter from nearby, but it sounded like it was in a different room. It was probably safe.

I reached for the lid, opened it a crack, and looked around at my surroundings before I pushed it off. I snapped my head from side to side, taking in the scent of earthy vegetables. The wooden shelves were filled with jarred goods and emitted a pleasant aroma of cedar.

This must be a pantry.

I slung my legs over the top of the crate, wobbling as my feet touched the floor. My dress felt suffocating. I had to get it off. The itchy sleeves. The fluffy petticoat. I shed the layers. As I tore each tier of lace from my arms, liberation surged through me as if a weight had been lifted off me. I unlaced my petticoat and all the layers of my skirt. I had forgotten how heavy the dress was.

My underthings—a corset, chemise, and bloomers—provided enough coverage. Right now, I needed mobility. I glanced down at my corset, noticing my brooch.

Damn. I needed to hide that. If anyone knew I was the princess, they'd ransom me, and I'd be back in Nathaniel's grubby hands. Pirates lived for the coin, and enough of it would get them to weigh the danger. I couldn't risk thinking their fear outweighed their desire for coin.

As soon as I touched the stone, I felt sick. But I gulped it down. My personal feelings about the crystal didn't matter. It was about survival now. I unfastened the brooch from my corset and pinned it on the inside of my bloomers. No one would see it, but I would still have it in case my situation became dire. I didn't know what I was walking into, and I needed to be prepared for anything.

The door to the pantry creaked open, and I gasped, throwing myself behind a crate for cover. Maybe they hadn't seen me.

Shiiiing—the sound of a cutlass whistled through the air. "Who the fuck are you?" a feminine voice spat out. I recognized the accent. She was the woman from behind the tavern.

I winced, taken off guard by the vulgar language.

Right. Sailors. They were known for their vulgarity.

I remained silent. Hiding.

She let out a frustrated sigh. "I saw you jump behind the crate, lass. Show yourself."

My throat bobbed with a thick gulp. I put both my hands up to show I was unarmed and stepped out from my cover. "Uh... good day."

Piercing green eyes pinned me from beneath a wide-brimmed hat. Dark auburn hair cascaded over her shoulders, several tendrils either braided or locked. She was taller than I was. There was a dark violence in her eyes. Light from the lanterns glinted off her cutlass as she pointed it at me. "Who are you?"

"I'm Mae," I gulped, nearly squeaking, deeply intimidated.

"What are you doing on *The Ollipheist*?" she demanded.

"Is that the name of this ship? I haven't heard of a military ship named that."

Two crimson brows came together, bringing out the blue veins that showed through her translucent skin. "That's because this isn't a military ship, love." Her eyes darted to the white lace discarded on the floor, then up to the red marks that now decorated my throat.

Pirates. Scoundrels. My ticket to freedom.

"I… I had to get away," I admitted, my cheeks flaring with warmth under her intense stare. "I hid in the crates."

She put up one hand, silencing me before I could ramble. Her pale, freckled hands were adorned with scars. Calluses. The hands of someone who worked for everything she had. She sheathed her sword within a sash under her long coat. "Save it for the captain. Come. Walk in front of me."

I had to obey. If I didn't, I could be thrown into the ocean. Or worse, they could turn around and take me back to Farlight. I nodded, using my wide brown eyes to my advantage. The red-haired woman pushed the door of the pantry open, and I walked out in front of her.

"Up the stairs," she ordered.

As I stepped out of the pantry, I saw what seemed to be a mess hall full of sailors playing cards and having loud conversations. If I didn't know any better, I'd think they were celebrating. One of the sailors did a double take, the cheerful atmosphere diminishing as they noticed me one by one.

The crew's gazes followed me and the redheaded woman. More and more sailors caught my eye along the hallways leading to steps going to the upper deck. The silence gave way to the clapping of waves against the hull. Nervousness pricked the back of my neck, my hair standing on end.

Then I heard a familiar voice whisper, "I told you that crate was heavy."

I wobbled with every sway of the ship. It was a miracle I didn't tumble to the ground.

I could sense eyes on me and instantly wished I were wearing more layers. My underthings were too thin, making me feel too naked. While most of my skin was covered, the cool breeze felt indecent. I noticed every groove of the wooden planks under my feet.

Surprisingly, my stockings didn't catch on any loose splinters. The floor was smoothly sanded, and as I stepped up the stairs, I could see why. Most of the crew was barefoot, wearing baggy trousers tied off at the calf, linen shirts, short navy blue woolen coats, and variously colored sashes housing their gear.

I gulped down my nerves, my heart hammering in my ears.

But even my nervousness wasn't enough to keep my head down. The ship moved under my feet, and I struggled to keep my wits about me. Meanwhile, some of the crew hung off the rigging above me, while others were standing on the half wall that was the only boundary preventing us from falling into the ocean.

How in the Four Kingdoms are they keeping their balance?

"Keep walking, lass," the red-haired woman said behind me.

I looked up, noticing another woman near the helm, her black hair in locs and adorned with golden jewelry that complemented her rich reddish-brown carnelian skin. She was talking to the helmsman, pausing only when she noticed me as we continued walking toward her.

We were probably headed to the captain's quarters right behind the helmsman.

My heart thundered in my chest as nerves took hold of me again.

My cheeks warmed, and I looked down at my hands, at the ridiculous ring perched upon my finger. It might as well have been a dog collar.

A flare of anger welled up inside me as I pulled it off, glaring at its expensive stone before I launched it into the sea. It didn't even make a noise when it hit the water, taking its smothering weight with it.

"Stay," the red-haired woman ordered.

I stopped as she commanded me to, twiddling my thumbs.

"Boats, get the captain for me."

The dark-skinned woman nodded.

Her name was Boats. *What an odd name.*

Boats stepped away from the helmsman and knocked on the cabin door. The man who appeared in the doorway looked a lot like Boats, only instead of locs, he wore a red bandana around his head. He had a radiant smile.

Was that the captain?

He looked too kind to be a captain.

"Yeah?" the man asked before he noticed the red-haired woman behind me, and then his eyes finally settled on me. Both eyebrows went up, and he released a deep sigh. He tucked his head back into the captain's quarters. "Levi, Wraith has someone for you."

I turned to the woman in the wide-brimmed hat. Her name was *Wraith*? That was somehow even odder than Boats.

Heavy boots hitting the wooden planks drew my attention back over to the doorway of the captain's cabin as another man stepped out. He was taller than the first man and wore a white pirate's blouse unlaced halfway down a rather impressive chest. A leather surcoat hung across his wide shoulders, emphasizing his brawny frame. A brightly colored sash carried his gear—a well-cared-for cutlass and pistol.

He had the appearance of a man who knew how to throw his weight around. He wore a leather tricorn hat with golden detailing, lowered slightly so at first, I could only see the shape of his mouth.

Dark stubble accentuated the mauve color of his lips.

My heart jumped into my throat as I started to feel warm

everywhere. Part of me was worried it would leap out of my mouth and run away from me.

The captain lifted his hat slightly and pinned me with an intimidating gaze. He had black hair that cascaded down his shoulders and eyes that were somehow even darker. I tilted my head to the side, meeting his gaze with a curious one of my own.

He was younger than I'd expected. Older than me, but he had to be in his early thirties.

His eyes had a reflective quality to them that literally glimmered in the moonlight.

Interesting.

I shifted from foot to foot, nearly forgetting about everyone else. I could only feel his eyes on my face, sensing none of the other crew who watched from the sidelines. If that wasn't confusing enough, my nervousness ramped up tenfold.

"Who's this?" the captain's voice rumbled.

Good Gods. More heat mottled my cheeks. Why was I so nervous?

"Stowaway, Cap. I found her in the crates. Runaway bride by the look of it. Her dress is still in the pantry. She also just tossed her wedding ring into the sea," Wraith reported.

He didn't seem pleased by that. "Give her the treatment of any stowaway. Throw her in the pit," the captain said before turning on his heel to go back into his cabin.

Everything inside me stiffened. I didn't know what *the pit* was, but it didn't sound pleasant at all. My lips parted to say something. Plead my case. The words died on my tongue. I didn't know what I was going to say. Or how I was going to keep his attention.

"Uh, Levi," the man in the bandana interrupted and reached out to tap the captain—*Levi*—on the shoulder. Not a very strange name in comparison to Wraith or Boats. He leaned in to mutter something in the captain's ear.

Levi's massive shoulders moved up and then down as he released an annoyed sigh. "Are you fucking serious?"

The man in the bandana gave him a sheepish smile but nodded. "I'm afraid so."

"Ugh. Fix it." Levi looked at me from over his shoulder and grumbled, "We will not be throwing you in the pit."

The crew watched as he turned completely around to look me up and down before walking down the few steps until he was right in front of me. My eyelashes fluttered as my eyes climbed him to meet his.

I arched my neck to look up, trying to seem less nervous than I felt. But it was difficult with this large man looming over me. He stared down at me along the bridge of his nose in such a condescending way that I fought the urge to push him backward out of my personal space.

"Since I can't throw you in the pit and forget about you, you're going to answer my questions. If you don't, I have no reservations about throwing you overboard. Understand?"

My first instinct was to argue. Tell him that he had no right to speak to me in such a threatening way. That he had some nerve demanding anything of the *princess*.

But I needed to remind myself that I wasn't a princess. I was a stowaway on a pirate ship who was fleeing her horrible husband. If I played my cards right, this man was going to give me my freedom.

My throat felt tight as I uttered, "I understand."

3
MAEVE CROSS

"Who are you?" Levi asked, his eyes not once leaving mine. It was as if he was searching for lies. Searching for answers in my face. I felt trapped under his gaze, fighting the urge to fold just to escape it.

A flare of danger and excitement whorled in my belly.

Good Gods, those eyes were intense.

Unfortunately, I was a horrible liar, and I knew that the moment I lied about something, he'd know. But I could lie a little, right?

My name is Princess Maeve Evelyn Cross. "Mae."

"Just Mae?" He arched a thick, dark brow.

"Does the rest matter?" I retorted.

He narrowed his eyes, leaning down even closer but still not close enough to touch me. His proximity began to annoy me. "Out of all the ships in the harbor, why did you choose *The Ollipheist* to stow away on?"

"Convenience."

"Why did you flee your wedding? Did he not do it for you?" That *condescending* tone. I hated it.

I breathed hard through my nose, annoyance coloring my

features. "Look at my throat. You look smart enough to figure the rest out."

His eyes didn't leave my face. Perhaps he'd already noticed the bruises. "Tell me your husband's name."

Well, *damn it*, I couldn't do that. Lord Pike was a very public figure. As soon as I said his name, they would instantly know who I was. Especially with all the royal wedding decorations littered around the port.

Think, Mae. Think!

My eyes darted around the deck before landing on the hilt of a cutlass. "Cutl…er…." I searched for something else. "Cutler Helms…worth."

I didn't think I could've come up with a worse lie if I tried.

Several of the crewmen laughed and muttered among themselves. My cheeks flared with heat, and I looked away from Levi's intense gaze.

He sucked his teeth. "Okay."

He took a step back from me, and I could breathe again. That didn't last very long, because the ship hit a hard wave and I wobbled, trying to keep my footing right. I made a noise of surprise as I tried to keep from falling. Unthinking, I grabbed his arm to steady my legs.

The cool leather felt worn and lovely under my fingertips. But I could feel those damn dark eyes on the crown of my head. He didn't move, didn't push me away, just stood perfectly still as I struggled to regain my balance.

As soon as I realized what I was doing, I shoved myself back, face absolutely *boiling*.

I folded my arms across my chest, feeling even more naked in my underlayers than I did earlier. Falling on my face would've been less embarrassing than clinging to a man's arm.

"All crew aside from night crew, get to the lower decks. Get your meals from Butcher and turn in for the night," Levi ordered.

Their cook is called Butcher? *What did I get myself into?*

My eyes were glued to the planks as the noise of stomping feet retreated down the stairs to the lower deck. I could see the crew out of the corner of my eye, and I slowly started to go in their direction, hoping he didn't notice me.

Maybe I could blend in.

"Not you," Levi said, and I knew he was talking to me. "You're not crew, and we're not done."

"But what if I'm hungry?" I asked. I wasn't, but I would do anything to get away from him. I didn't like how my belly fluttered whenever that baritone voice washed over me.

"Then too fucking bad."

I stamped my foot down on the planks, huffing as I turned around to see Wraith watching me closely. "What are you looking at?"

The corner of her mouth twitched, but she didn't say anything to me. Instead, she looked over at her captain and said, "Good luck."

Rude.

He waved her off as Boats joined her, and they walked off to the lower levels by themselves. Wraith cupped the small of Boats's back in a manner that seemed way too affectionate to be by accident.

"Do you want me to stay, Cap?" the man in the bandana asked, coming down the steps to stand next to him.

"No. I'll take care of this. I'll see you in the morning," Levi said, and in just another few moments, all the other noise started to go quiet. Only a handful of crew remained now, making me feel Levi's presence even more. "You. Come here."

"Go into your cabin with you? No," I grumbled, the words

flying from my lips before I could catch them. "You could be a scoundrel for all I know."

He arched a brow at me, and something that sounded suspiciously like a laugh fell from his lips.

My cheeks darkened, and I could feel the heat on the tips of my ears.

"You stow away on a pirate ship and then accuse me of being a scoundrel?" He laughed to himself again before saying, "I don't like to repeat myself." He climbed the steps toward his cabin, clearly expecting me to follow him.

I ran my tongue over my teeth, knowing perfectly well that I didn't have much choice in the matter. But I didn't have to be happy about it. A sharp breath left my nose, and I dragged my feet, holding on to the railing of the steps so I didn't fall down when we hit another wave.

The helmsman nodded respectfully at the captain, and he nodded back, holding his cabin door open for me.

Hesitantly, I entered the dimly lit room, belly churning as I found myself within the intimate surroundings.

The smell of salty air and musky cedarwood enveloped me. My thighs started to tingle, the scent nothing short of delightful.

Not only was the captain pleasing to the eyes, but he also smelled nice.

Mounted bookcases adorned the walls, and there was a large window to overlook the ocean and see the stars. In front of the window sat a small table with two chairs and an open bottle of rum.

Two unused glasses.

I also spied a desk with an oil lamp and scattered papers and logbooks.

I turned to the side, somewhat surprised that it was so spacious. My eyes grazed a half-made bed adorned with furs and pillows. I had to fight the urge not to imagine the captain underneath those sheets. What did he wear when he slept?

My throat bobbed, and I tried *so* hard not to think about it.

I bet we'd look good in that bed.

Gods, where did *that* come from? *Focus, Mae. Focus.*

"I know you're lying to me, Mae," he said, closing the door with a soft click.

"I have no reason to lie," I lied, voice breaking midsentence.

"Uh-huh. All right. If that's how you want to play this." He passed me, walking a direct line to his bottle of rum. He shrugged off his leather jacket and hung it on the back of the chair, then plucked his hat off his head to place it on the table. "Sit." He gestured to the seat across from him.

"I'd rather stand." I eyed the thick band of muscle around his arm that was no longer shrouded in that jacket. He poured a glass of rum for himself and then another into the second glass.

He hummed, taking a sip of his drink. "What did I say about repeating myself?"

I placed a hand on my hip and muttered, "I don't remember." I was baiting him, and unfortunately, he knew it.

"You can either sit down or I can sit you down myself, sweetheart."

With narrowed eyes, I sauntered through his cabin and sat down across from him. I crossed my arms, folding my legs one over the other.

"Good choice." He gestured to the second glass of rum. "What I don't understand is *why* you're lying. It's not like we're a military vessel. We don't care if you have a warrant. But how about you have a drink? Loosen your lips."

I glanced at the golden liquid with disdain. At twenty-two

years old, I'd never once had a sip of alcohol. Not even a glass of wine at dinners. There was no way in the Nine Hells that I'd start in the company of a strange man. "I'd rather not."

"Then start talking." He took another sip, and I regretfully watched his throat bob when he swallowed. "What is your husband's name?"

"I told you. It's... uh... Cutter Helms...thing," I answered confidently.

"I thought it was Cutler Helmsworth? Seems odd for you to forget the name of your beloved," he stated dryly.

I took a deep breath, several beats passing between us. I refused to meet his eye, my mind churning with both lies and truths. But if I started lying again, all I would do was confuse myself. After another moment or so, I sighed, hesitantly looking over at Levi just as he finished his glass of rum.

"Listen, the reason—"

He slammed his glass down onto the table. "I'm done listening. Save your fucking sob story for someone else."

A gasp slipped from my lips, my hand pressing reflexively into my chest. "Excuse me?"

"I gave you several chances to tell me who you are and what you want. I even waited until I finished my drink. But instead, you've proven to me that you're not above lying. Which you are terrible at, by the way. I can't trust you. I certainly don't trust you around my crew."

"Now, wait a minute—"

He pinned me with a withering stare. "I don't know why you think I owe you my time. I don't know why you're acting like the world owes you a favor. Guess what, *sweetheart*. Pirates don't do favors."

This was going south *fast*. I knew how I needed to play it. Slowly, I batted my eyes, letting them water like I was about to cry. This worked on my father. It worked on Nathaniel. It would work on any man to get what I wanted. I looked up, giving this captain my biggest doe eyes.

"It's really cute how you think that'll work on me."

I huffed, getting to my feet. "You're a brute! A young woman comes aboard with bruises, and you treat her like a criminal!"

He kicked his feet up onto the table and poured himself another glass, quietly watching me.

"Aren't you going to say anything?" I hissed, nearly pulling my hair out with how frustrated I was.

"I will once you get this little temper tantrum out of your system."

"Temper—" My voice started to get shrill, and both of his eyebrows went up in a way that told me I was proving him right. I grasped on to my temper, pushing it down as hard as I could. "I needed to get out of Farlight."

"And how is that my problem?"

My mouth fell open when I didn't know how to answer that question.

He put his feet down and leaned over the table, propping his chin up with his hand. "How do I know you're not one of King Varric's assassins?"

"I assure you that I'm no assassin," I replied, scoffing at the ludicrousness of the accusation.

He hummed. "That's exactly what an assassin would say."

"Then what's stopping me from assassinating you, huh? Captain Levi?" I propped my hand on my hip.

"You call me *Leviathan*. Only my mates call me Levi."

Leviathan? What was with all these ridiculous names?

"And as for the assassin bit, that is an excellent point. Nothing is stopping you from assassinating me," he stated as he suddenly stood up and crossed his cabin.

I watched his back flex as he moved, an annoying heat welling in my belly.

Damn him and his nice back.

But the fact that he turned his back at all was proof that he didn't see me as a threat. I pulled my mouth to the side, now angry that he wasn't intimidated by me.

He opened a chest at the foot of his bed and retrieved something. Then he turned back and came right toward me. My cheeks flared, and I didn't realize what he had until he grabbed my wrist. "Unhand me, brute!" I shouted.

"I already know I can't trust you around my crew, so how can I be sure that you won't assassinate me while I sleep?"

He pulled me over to a ballast across from his bed, but no matter how hard I fought, he was too strong for me. "Release me!" I squealed rather undignifiedly when he hooked the handcuffs he'd retrieved around a thick rope, easily locking them onto my wrists. I thrashed and pulled at the rope, but it wouldn't give.

My eyes flashed over to him, rage bubbling inside me. *How dare he cuff me!*

"Not my favorite use for these, but it'll do for now, won't it?" He gave me the smuggest, cockiest grin. The two dimples on either side of his mouth took me completely off guard.

It disarmed me, my mind going blank as I stared at his mouth for a solid beat or two before I finally got my wits about me again. I threw my leg out with every intention of kicking him.

But the bastard sidestepped it.

"I'll scream!" I threatened.

Leviathan turned away from me, completely unbothered, and all that did was make me angrier. "Go ahead. It wouldn't be the first time I brought a woman into my cabin to make her scream."

I gasped. "I knew you were a scoundrel! Torturing defenseless women."

A bark of amusement left his lips. "A type of torture, I suppose."

My face turned numerous shades from pink to tomato red when the meaning of the remark finally dawned on me. I kicked my legs. "Pig."

He sat on his bed and took his boots off. "Be careful who you're hurling insults at. I have half a mind to keep you tied up the entire journey. We'll be at sea for a month."

His threats seemed empty. There was no way he'd keep a woman chained up in his cabin the entire time. *Unless he would.* I breathed hard through my nose. "Captain *Leviathan*, would you please release me?"

"No."

"My arms hurt."

"Don't care."

I snarled, pulling hard on the cuffs. "Burn in Hell!"

"Which one?" he asked, crooking an eyebrow. "If you're going to threaten me, at least be more specific."

I didn't have a good answer, so I thrashed and shouted a curse I'd rarely ever used before. "Fuck you!"

"You certainly have the mouth of a sailor, don't you?" He chuckled to himself and pulled his shirt over his head.

I hated the way my eyes locked on to his naked skin, my mouth watering at how *good* he looked. From the roped muscle of his arms to the blue-inked tattoo of a sea serpent that curled around his chest, partially hidden under a sparse sprinkling of dark chest hair. It wasn't faded in the slightest, not like the other, subtler one wrapped around one of his biceps. I couldn't get a good look at it from where I was cuffed.

Twenty-two years of my life, and the first time I see an attractive half-naked man is in this situation.

I gulped hard, screwing my eyes shut to tamp down the foreign sensation of heat welling inside me.

No.

No.

No.

This man is holding you captive!

"Keep your clothes on, you bastard!" I demanded, my cheeks so red, it was a miracle I hadn't set myself on fire. "You have some audacity to lock a lady up and then undress in front of her!"

He waved me off. "Forgive me for getting comfortable in my own bed. You're lucky I'm keeping my breeches on."

I gasped. "You… you…."

"Cat got your tongue, hm?"

"*Ugh!*" I huffed with annoyance.

He ignored me, twisting the dial on his oil lamp until the flame went out. My face felt hot. I was angry and embarrassed all at once. His mattress squeaked as his shadowed form climbed onto it. "Get some rest, sweetheart. The real work starts tomorrow."

"Work?" I asked quietly, feeling oddly at ease in the dark. At least I couldn't see him anymore, and he couldn't see the mortification mottled all over my face.

Leviathan's voice carried through the darkness. "Pirates don't do favors, but we reward hard work. You want a favor, you gotta work for it. Impress me enough and maybe I'll give you a bunk of your own."

"That easy?"

"Nothing about it is going to be easy."

I slid down to the floor, and the rope I was attached to

came down with me. I tucked my knees into myself and rested my head on folded arms.

Take a breath, Mae.

I could hear Leviathan settle in his bed as I mulled over what he'd just told me. I held my temper in check, refusing to let it run away from me again.

"Pirates don't do favors, but we reward hard work."

If I could work for a bed, then I could work for my freedom too. This was my chance to finally make a name for myself without the expectations of my crown.

This was *my* chance.

Then all at once, I felt the anger melt away when everything else came up to the surface.

All the exhaustion. All the running and shouting and hiding came back to me. My body felt tired, my head heavy. My arms whined at the odd angle, but I was too tired to fight the lull of sleep. Not as the ship rocked beneath me and I could hear the breathing of Leviathan across the room.

My eyes drifted closed, and for once, I was excited to see what tomorrow held for me.

4
MAEVE CROSS

The dreamless sleep was a welcome break from my usual nightmares. Blood and screams frequently permeated my subconscious, haunting my dreams. I didn't understand where the nightmares came from, but they tortured me nonetheless.

But that restful sleep was ripped from me the second freezing-cold ocean water was dumped over my head.

I shouted, my head lurching back, wildly searching for the source as I tried to break out of my sleepy haze.

The bucket clanked onto the ground next to me.

My mouth flapped open and closed as I fought for the words to express the *rage* bubbling inside me first thing in the morning. I looked up at Leviathan, and all that anger boiled over. "You prick!"

I thrashed at the restraints, damn near snarling at him like a rabid animal.

"Not a morning person, I see," he said. He was completely dressed in leather boots, a scarf across his forehead, and a tricorn hat on top of that. A red sash was tied around his waist, housing a cutlass and pistol close to his body.

But I could still see his eyes peering down at me. Last night, I thought the glimmering blue speckles could be a trick of the light, but even in the morning, they still glittered like crystals.

Sunlight shone in from the large window, illuminating the entire room. "What in the Hells did you expect?" I retorted, leaning down so I could use my shackled hand to wipe the salt water beading along my brow.

As irritated as I was, it was quite freeing to swear as much as I wanted. Whenever my father heard me curse in the past, I was "rewarded" by having an extended guard detail assigned to me. My extracurriculars were taken away, and I was confined to my room like a misbehaving child. It didn't matter that I was an adult woman with my own opinions. I had to remain subservient. I would only have my things given back to me when I agreed to smile and nod and curtsy and pretend to be the docile little girl they expected.

"No man will marry you if you have a foul mouth."

When I argued with my father, I might as well have been speaking to the stone walls. He never heard a damn thing I said. Our relationship deteriorated even more when Nathaniel came into the picture, and it became clear that my father had no qualms about selling me off for something he wanted.

An army.

The corner of Leviathan's mouth turned up, revealing one disarming dimple. "It is quite amusing to see a noblewoman speaking like a sailor."

My blood turned to ice. "Noblewoman? Whatever gave you that idea?"

"Look at your hands, sweetheart."

"Stop calling me that," I muttered under my breath,

glancing at my hands. I didn't know what he was getting at. "What's your point?"

"Your hands are dainty. Soft like a child's. You've never lifted a finger in your life, have you?"

My mouth went dry, my face heating up again. Thankfully, my belly rumbled, breaking the silence and giving me something else to talk about. "You denied me dinner. Will you deny me breakfast as well?"

His lips parted to say something, but a knock at his door interrupted whatever snarky response he had. "Come in," he called out.

The door opened, revealing the dark-skinned man in the bandana from last night. However, he wasn't smiling this time. A dark blue wool jacket adorned his shoulders, reaching midthigh, and he had on a pair of nice-fitting brown breeches. Just like his captain, he wore a sash holding his weapons.

His golden-brown eyes locked on to me, noticing how I was tied up. I pulled at my restraints again, making a show of how uncomfortable I was.

I groaned in exaggerated discomfort, wriggling in an attempt to gain a little pity. In all honesty, I was actually surprisingly comfortable. My shoulders ached a little, and my corset cut into my ribs, but it wasn't intolerable. "I'm *so* uncomfortable. Your brute of a captain kept me tied up *all night*."

Leviathan rolled his eyes. "Save it."

The eye roll combined with the dimple in his cheek gave him this odd boyish charm. I didn't like it one bit. I scoffed, halting my movements. "Fine."

"This is Howler, my first mate."

Howler? Their names just keep getting stranger, don't they?

Howler dipped his head in a polite hello. At least one of

them had manners. Then he straightened his posture and gave Leviathan a cautious side-eye. "You're putting me on babysitting duty, aren't you?"

Leviathan smirked at Howler before shifting his gaze over to me again. "If I leave her here, she'll just bellyache, and no one will get any work done. I'm supposed to study merchant routes with Wraith."

Howler sighed. "What do you want me to do with her?"

"I really don't give a fuck. Put her to work."

I huffed through my nose. *It's like I'm not even here!*

Howler glanced over at me with the most skeptical expression on his face. "I don't think she's made for this type of work, Cap. Just look at her."

A blaze of indignation shot through me. "I can work twice as hard as anyone on this blasted ship!" If there was one thing I hated more than being undermined, it was being treated like I was fragile.

Howler's eyes went wide at my outburst, but Leviathan laughed. "Aw, that's the spirit, sweetheart." His condescending tone got under my skin.

I seethed at the pet name and muttered a curse under my breath. He might as well have patted me on the head like I was a well-behaved puppy.

"Make her scrub the deck or take her to the gunnery for all I care. Assuming she knows how to use those pretty hands. Just be back in time for the meeting." Leviathan tossed Howler the keys to the cuffs. "Feed her first. She gets testy."

Oh, piss off. I'm not a tabby cat.

Even though it was tempting to tell him off, I bit my tongue. I slowly got to my feet, wriggling the rope and the restraints up the ballast with me. Howler unlocked the irons and tossed them over to Leviathan.

"Come now, lass. Let's get you some breakfast," Howler said politely, gesturing to the door.

He didn't need to tell me twice. I was desperate to get away from Leviathan and his piercing gaze. That irritating curve of his mouth and charming dimples—

Why am I thinking about his mouth?

I shoved the thoughts away as I stepped out onto the main deck with Howler. There was a man at the helm, comfortably steering the ship. Like Howler, he wore a bandana over his forehead, probably to shield himself from the beating sun in the cloudless sky.

Young men were scrubbing the deck, using mops and scrub brushes to scrape up all sorts of gunk. Gods, it looked dirty. Up on the sails, a few men and women hung from the rigging, making minuscule adjustments to catch the wind.

Most everyone seemed to be wearing baggy rolled-up breeches and waist-length jackets. No tails. No adornments. Nothing like the naval uniforms I'd been used to seeing at the castle. And oddly enough, the women were dressed exactly like the men—in breeches, not a corset in sight.

I was always told it was indecent to wear breeches or to bypass the discomfort of a corset and that women couldn't do the same jobs men could, but one night here had proved all that wrong.

Like the cogs of a wheel, everyone seemed to have their job and looked content doing it.

"Morning, Plankwalker," Howler commented to the man at the wheel, who looked over his shoulder and gave the first mate a big grin.

Plankwalker. That couldn't be a real name. Who would name their child that?

"Mornin'." He glanced at me. "And mornin' to you, too, Mae."

It felt nice to be greeted politely instead of having water dumped on me. "Good morning, good sir." I crossed my ankles and curtsied because I felt like he deserved it.

Plankwalker chuckled. "Look at the manners on her. Can't believe this is the same lass who was bickering with Cap all morning."

My cheeks flared, and I stood once more.

Never mind. I'm not going to curtsy to any other person on this ship. They're all awful.

I looked away and noticed Wraith leaning against the half wall with Boats standing between her parted legs. The two seemed deep in conversation, standing unusually close together. Wraith reached up to brush a few locs over Boats's shoulder, her hand lingering against the other woman's neck.

Both of their jackets were longer, like Howler's. Perhaps they were officer jackets?

Narrowing my eyes, I observed their dress, getting the idea that it was somewhat of a uniform. Suddenly, Wraith's eyes flashed over to me. She glared at me with a seething gesture to *piss off*.

Boats pulled on Wraith's sleeve, her mouth curling into a repressed smile. My cheeks flushed, and I looked away as Wraith gave Boats her full attention again.

I rubbed my arms and reminded myself that people generally didn't like it when I stared.

I stepped down to get to where the workers were scrubbing gunk off the deck, wobbling every other step as the ship hit a few waves, causing me to grasp the handrail for dear life.

I really hoped this clumsiness would subside soon.

All this rocking from side to side was getting tiring, as was clinging on to anything or *anyone* nearby for support. I gathered my feet together, took a deep breath, and focused on not falling on my face.

"Good Gods, you haven't got your sea legs yet." Howler stepped next to me and offered his arm. "Grab on. I won't think any less of you."

I ignored him, stubbornness beading up inside me. "I can do this myself."

"If you fall on your face, everyone will take the piss. Why do you think Cap let you hang on to him last night?"

Heat bloomed in my cheeks as I imagined all fifty sailors on the upper deck stopping what they were doing to laugh at me. That somehow seemed worse than taking Howler's help. Hesitantly, I reached over and grabbed his jacket. It was made of sturdy wool or perhaps fustian. Good-quality fabric.

Curiosity frothed up inside me as I looked at the sailors. I hadn't been on many ships. The few I'd been on were navy vessels, and while the crew seemed to work just as hard, they looked vastly different.

"Is it customary to work in such little clothing?" I asked, holding on to Howler's arm to abate my clumsiness.

He shrugged. "Don't want to get tangled up in the rigging or dragged to the ocean floor when your garments soak up water."

"I thought pirates dressed extravagantly."

He gave me a dazzling smile. "We love to dress up for port, but not here on the ship. I wouldn't want to get my nice clothes filthy."

"I suppose that makes sense. What about the women?"

He paused, arching a brow. "What do you mean?"

"I always heard it was bad luck to have a woman on a ship. Women could never join the navy in Farlight."

"That's a load of bullshit," he stated. "We're all sailors. Women. Men. In between or neither. We're all the same creed. I see no difference. Anyone who says otherwise is benefitting from making a distinction."

My eyes widened, and it took me a few moments to respond. "I like that point of view."

He chuckled. "Glad to hear it. As far as our clothing is concerned, we dress to make our jobs easier, not to uphold an image or a standard. It's not like we're trying to impress anyone."

Howler opened the hatch to the lower deck as numerous sailors made their way to the upper deck, mouths full and chewing loudly around a slew of "Good mornings."

Howler leaned in. "And trust me, no one here is worth impressing," he muttered under his breath.

My mouth crooked into a half smile. "Certainly not."

We descended the staircase and followed the noise of loud laughter and clacking wooden cups. If I didn't know any better, I'd think this was a celebratory dinner and not a casual breakfast.

It was a fairly small dining area with tables between stowed cannons. Sailors were moving in and out about twenty at a time. They ate quickly before getting to work.

"How many sailors do you have?"

"Nearly 175. Three shifts."

My stomach churned with nerves as I gazed across the mess hall, looking for someone I knew.

It seemed foolish, considering there was no way I'd know any of these people.

Howler also seemed to be looking for someone as he guided me inside the mess hall and sat me down at one of the tables. "Sit tight. I'll be back shortly."

I reeled back in surprise when Howler jumped on my table. All the sailors fell silent and waited for his announcement.

He shouted, "Attention! For those of you who don't know, this is Mae. She's our resident stowaway. Be nice."

A chorus of "Hi, Mae" came from all around me. I sank down in my seat, my cheeks flaring.

"Where's Gunny?" Howler... well, *howled.* Was that why they called him Howler?

Finally, it dawned on me.

I'm such a fool. Those are nicknames.

Pirate monikers.

How did I not understand that the moment I heard *Boats*? Or *Plankwalker*?

Why did I think someone actually named their child *Wraith*?

Out of nowhere, a lean man popped out of a corner. "Here, Howler."

He was completely covered in soot and grease; his hands were the only part of his body that wasn't filthy. Even through all the dirt, he seemed younger than Howler. Only a few years older than me.

Howler jumped off the table and made a beeline directly toward Gunny. "You're in charge of her."

Now I felt like the scraps no one wanted after a big meal.

Gunny looked down at me. "Do you know how to load a cannon?"

Do I look like I know how to load a cannon? "Erm... no."

"Prepare pistols?"

"No."

"Sharpen swords?"

"No."

Gunny hummed, and his mouth pulled into an utterly delighted smile, showing off a crooked tooth. "Then you have a lot to learn today." He looked at Howler from over his shoulder. "Go on, git. I have a lot to teach this little birdie."

Howler rolled his eyes so hard, it looked like he was about to burst a blood vessel before his gaze settled on me again. "I'll retrieve you later."

Please don't leave me with this strange man. I was just getting used to Howler's company, but I gave him a small nod. I needed him to like me. That could save me with Leviathan in the long run. I gulped and uttered, "Thank you, Howler."

He didn't reply as he turned tail and left me alone in a room full of strange, loud sailors.

Those words felt odd. I couldn't remember the last time I thanked anyone, but that was going to change. I didn't have to like Leviathan, but what he said last night stuck with me.

"Pirates don't do favors, but we reward hard work."

So be it.

5
MAEVE CROSS

"Butcher makes good porridge," Gunny commented as he put a steaming bowl in front of me.

The gray slop looked... unappetizing to say the least. But my stomach grumbled nonetheless. I needed fuel to get through the day. While this breakfast didn't consist of pastries or some kind of smoked meat, it was enough to warm sailors' bellies. It would be enough for me too. Gripping the tarnished spoon in my hand, I braced myself for the taste of slop.

Gunny plopped onto the bench next to me and tipped the bowl he was holding to his lips, drinking down the paste like it was nothing. "It ain't gonna bite you, birdie."

"I know," I muttered.

Gunny tilted his head, watching me poke at it with a spoon. The corner of his mouth twitched, his upturned brown eyes glinting. He pulled a soot-covered handkerchief from his pocket and wiped his mouth, revealing tawny-tanned skin otherwise hidden under grime.

"He even used that butter we got from port," he continued. "Salted it just right so that even spoiled lassies like you oughta like it."

My eyes darted over to him. "Spoiled?" My voice turned shrill like it had on Leviathan last night.

He snickered, then brought the bowl up to his lips and swallowed down the rest of his porridge.

I'll show him spoiled.

Setting the spoon down, I cupped the bowl, bringing it to my mouth just like Gunny had. Tipping my head back, I poured the porridge into my mouth, trying to drink it down before I tasted it.

Then I felt incredibly foolish. It warmed my belly, satisfied the gnawing hunger, and pleased my tongue. Delightfully salty, smooth, and creamy, made with both butter and oats.

It didn't take much effort to finish the bowl.

I placed it back on the table, wiping my mouth with my hand. My cheeks were warm when I glanced back at Gunny, and he gave me a knowing smile, showing off a twisted canine.

"It was quite tasty."

"I like your spirit," he commented. "You'll learn this fast, but Butcher is a great cook. Everything tastes great even if it ain't pretty."

"I think I understand that now," I replied, my cheeks still pink.

He slapped me on the back once he got to his feet, taking the wind out of me. "Onward, birdie. We got work to do."

I winced and rubbed my shoulder. "Where are we going?"

He scooped up our dishes and stacked them onto a growing pile. Young sailors—cabin boys, maybe—were collecting the dishes and taking them down to the galley.

"Why, the gunnery, of course!" Gunny replied, moving

quickly out of the mess hall and into the series of long hallways connecting various rooms.

I chased after him, passing crewmen napping in hammocks and sailors moving supplies around the decks.

It was a struggle to keep up, and I had to brace myself against the wall as the ship swayed back and forth. "I thought we were just in the gunnery. I saw all the cannons!"

"The cannons I need to prime are out this way," he called back.

He turned a corner, and I just about ran into a wall as he guided me to the front of the ship. Sunlight greeted me as I turned into an offside room with open portholes and cannons in the process of being prepped.

"Aye, Gunny!" one of the sailors greeted, looking back at him as I came tumbling into the room behind him.

Gunny looped an arm around my shoulders and enthusiastically said, "We have a freshie. We gotta show her the ropes."

As I waved, my heart thundered nervous tremors in my chest. All the gunnery sailors were dusted with a thin coating of grease and gunpowder. Gunny proceeded to rattle off the names of all the sailors in the room, but I couldn't repeat them. He spoke fast with a thick accent that made his words jumble together even more.

"Nice to meet you all," I said.

The sailors waved back at me before returning to their duties.

Gunny spun me around and sat me on a barrel. "Sit here, birdie. Imma get you working on sharpening cutlasses."

I raised both my eyebrows. "You trust me with a cutlass?"

He laughed deeply. "Not like you know how to use it."

"Like it's *so* difficult," I rebutted. "You wave it around and stick them with the pointy end."

Gunny shook his head, chuckling under his breath. He turned and stepped over to what looked like a small armory, various cutlasses mounted behind chains. There were a few revolvers too. The curved sword made a whistling noise as Gunny pulled it from its mount before placing it across the table in front of me. It was rather short and stout, not long and thin like the ones I'd seen.

"You're talking about infantry swords. These are cutlasses. A curved blade designed for slashing, not for *sticking them with the pointy end*," Gunny explained, using what looked like a rectangular stone to scrape down the curved blade. Then he lifted the rock to repeat the motion from hilt to tip.

"Why use these and not the infantry ones, then?" I asked, observing him. I knew I would be expected to duplicate his actions. Sparks ignited as he ground down the dull edge.

"Infantry swords aren't particularly good at cutting ropes in an emergency situation. They also aren't ideal for close quarters. Very unpractical for our lifestyle," he stated.

I hummed. "How is it you became so versed in weaponry?"

"It's my job. I'm the head gunner."

That's why they call him Gunny. "Head gunner? But you're so young." He couldn't be older than twenty-six.

Gunny showed off his twisted canine when he smiled. "I ain't know much, birdie, but I've always known weapons. Always came easy to me."

"Well, consider me impressed, Mr. Gunny."

He chuckled and passed the sharpening stone to me. "Give it a whirl."

With confidence, I took the stone and duplicated his actions. He made minute corrections for me to follow, but he seemed pleased as I took his instruction. "Like that?"

"Aye." He nudged me playfully. "Maybe you ain't so spoiled after all. You're a quick learner."

"Good teachers make good pupils," I replied with a polite smile.

He released a belly laugh. "Flattery works wonders, but it won't work on Cap."

I rolled my eyes. "I doubt much works on him."

Gunny shrugged. "Eh. Makes him a good captain." He stood up and took the cutlass away from me.

I ignored his comment. "What are all these weapons here for?"

"Maintenance mainly. These are the communal weapons for battle. Only the officers and the vanguard are completely armed at all times."

"Vanguard?" I asked, trying to think hard about any other sailors I'd noticed who were fully armed.

Gunny hummed. "You won't see them much. The officers work sunup, but the vanguards are on night crew. Trained warriors to keep watch when most crews sleep. Most of the crew isn't armed, aside from knives and gear associated with their jobs. We only have a handful of vanguards. Indispensable in battle."

Another group of people to avoid.

He took a few pistols from the wall and passed them off to his crew.

"I can help with the pistols too," I stated.

"I'm not letting you shoot your toes off, lassie. You get to polishing and sharpening." He grabbed another cutlass to place on the table in front of me. "Do a good job and I'll let you shoot off a cannon later."

I reeled back. "A cannon?"

"Aye. The best way to keep a cannon in tip-top shape is firing 'em," he said with a wink. "Now, get to work!"

And I did. As far as jobs were concerned, I felt like this was the least laborious of any of them. But by the time I finished sharpening about fifteen to twenty more swords, my fingers were cramping. My hands were covered in gray dust and smelled like metal.

But when I got my own cutlass, I would now know how to maintain it. The thought amused me. The Princess of Farlight toting a cutlass like a true warrior. My father would have a heart attack.

Gunny disrupted my thoughts. "Put the sword in the armory there and get over here."

I hopped off my barrel and grasped the hilt of the cutlass.

Heavier than I thought.

I slid it behind the chains and onto the mount. Thankfully, I didn't fall on my face and impale myself the moment the boat swayed. Balancing seemed more manageable than before. I wasn't grasping every surface to steady myself.

Gunny and a handful of other sailors whose names I couldn't remember were crouched around a cannon. Except for Gunny's second-in-command, who had a spider tattoo on his neck and was called Spider. His name was easy to remember.

A thick chain looped around the back of the cannon to keep it in place. The shaft of it had a canvas covering.

Spending time with Gunny was interesting. He rattled off information left and right, telling me that even a six-pound cannon still weighed about twelve hundred pounds, and if I ever saw a *loose* cannon coming toward me, I'd best get out of the way until it was roped back into place unless I want to be flattened.

"Watch closely, lassie. Then I'll have you help load it."

I gulped, but excitement flared beneath my breastbone.

There was no way in the Four Kingdoms my father would've ever let me do this.

"A woman shouldn't do men's work."

Watch me.

I observed the sailors as one of them shined the cannonball. Gunny told me it was to remove dirt and debris that would cause preliminary sparking. Another sailor used a long stick with a sponge to clean it out before they put the gunpowder into the barrel.

The gunpowder was premeasured in canvas sacks. They tamped it down with the sponge stick. After that, they had something called a *wad* fashioned from linen scraps from ruined clothing or potato sacks to make the cannonball fit better into the barrel.

"Put the cannonball in," Gunny ordered me as a sailor handed me the shined ball.

Gods, this thing is solid. I struggled to lift the ball, rolling it into the barrel carefully. Then the sponge stick was used to shove it down into the barrel too.

"Fire in the hole!" Gunny shouted, and all the sailors yelled it back to him as they jumped away from the cannon.

I followed suit, plugging my ears with my fingers as it was lit, hissing before *booming* across the ocean. The cannon reeled back powerfully, held in place with the ropes and chains to keep it from exploding into us.

My eyes were wide, a gleeful giggle pouring from my lips. My heart pounded with the adrenaline circulating through me.

"That was exhilarating!" I commented, getting another playful nudge from Gunny.

"Then let's do it again," he ordered.

By the time we had fired off all the cannons that needed

priming, my hands were coated in grime, and there was soot on my cheeks and staining my white undergarments.

Did sailors bathe? Did they have fresh clothes?

How did that work here?

Good Gods, I'd never gotten this filthy in my life. One of the gunnery assistants passed me a stained towel to get some of the oil off my hands.

"I certainly hope you logged all that gunpowder, Gun, or I'll load you into one of those cannons and shoot you into the big salt."

Wraith's voice caught me completely off guard. I jumped, the sound of it sending chills down my spine. She always seemed to appear out of thin air!

Gunny seemed unbothered. "Aye, aye. I logged it all just for *you*."

Wraith's intense green eyes drifted over to me. "Looks like it's you and me, love. Let's get you cleaned up."

My throat bobbed as Wraith turned on her heel, clearly expecting me to follow her. Gunny stopped me. "This was fun, birdie. Come visit me down here sometime. I could always use the extra hands."

I beamed, feeling a sense of accomplishment. "I might take you up on that. Bye for now."

He waved at me as I went after Wraith, not tripping as the boat swayed from side to side.

6
MAEVE CROSS

Wraith didn't say much to me.

She took me to the officers' quarters at the back of the ship, under the captain's cabin on the upper deck. It was more modest than the cabin above us but much nicer than the crew's quarters below deck.

Bunk beds were mounted against the wall on either side, and there was a bench table in the surprisingly spacious area between them.

"Do all the officers eat here?" I asked, gesturing at the table.

Wraith sat on a bunk personalized with a few drawings carved into the wooden posts. She hummed to herself, never once taking her hat off. "Aye."

Getting Wraith to talk was like pulling teeth. I twiddled my thumbs as she went through a chest attached to the foot of her bunk.

"You should fit into Boats's clothes just fine," she said so quietly that I didn't think she was talking to me until she threw a few garments over to me.

"There's no corset here," I mentioned, catching the clothing before it hit me in the face.

The intense redhead waved her hand dismissively. "What for? You don't have anything that needs bindin'."

My cheeks flared. She wasn't wrong. I was fairly slight. "Isn't it indecent not to wear a corset?"

Wraith laughed suddenly, the noise startling me because it sounded just as scary as she was. I hadn't realized a laugh could sound intimidating. "Don't make me laugh, love. You also consider it indecent for women to be sailors. I heard all about your conversation with Howler earlier."

"I didn't mean it like that." I crossed my arms, still feeling grimy and disgusting from my day with Gunny. "I just… never mind. Answer the question."

Wraith took off her long officer's coat, rolling her eyes as she debated whether or not to answer me. "Sailors with large busts wear supports. Others wear nothing. You needn't worry about it. We don't much care for decency."

I glanced at the clothes, worried my greasy hands would stain them. "Wouldn't it bother Boats that you took her garments?"

"It shouldn't. I borrow my wife's clothes all the time whenever I want something more colorful," she replied.

"Your wife? I don't see a ring," I commented, gesturing to her hands.

She shrugged. "Jewelry gets tangled in rigging. Rips fingers off. Besides, our relationship is worth more to me than any piece of jewelry. Now, let's get you cleaned up." She stood up, almost silent as she walked across the cabin to a small room tucked to the side.

I followed her.

"After all, you'll be staying in the officers' quarters for the duration of this trip. Can't have you scumming about the cabin with your filth."

A sense of relief came over me. "I won't be in Captain Leviathan's cabin?"

"No. But he doesn't trust you to be with the rest of the crew," Wraith explained, opening the door to the side room.

Thank the *Gods* I wouldn't be handcuffed to a ballast in his quarters, watching him undress before bed. Just thinking about it pinkened my cheeks. His impressive physique. The way he moved with a sense of grace. Even for a brute.

Even the mere thought had my insides tangling in knots. It really wasn't fair.

He had no right to look like that.

Wraith interrupted my indecent thoughts. "Pay attention."

My face was still hot when I focused on her. "Right. Continue."

She grunted with annoyance before getting back to whatever she was saying. "We're one of the few ships that filter water as we sail. We have Seabird to thank for that."

"Seabird?"

"Our surgeon. Brilliant woman. If you're lucky, you'll never meet her. She doesn't take kindly to little stowaways like yourself."

"I see." I tucked my head into the room, noticing a wet room equipped with a toilet and waterspout high on the wall. "I have to say that I'm surprised. I didn't think pirates bathed."

Wraith found no humor in my comment. "Filthiness creates sickness. When you're on a ship for weeks or months at a time, you learn to stay clean. Illness spreads like a plague in close quarters."

Plague. Something I never wished to experience firsthand, but it seemed like Wraith had.

"Leave your clothes in the basket, and I'll show you how we clean laundry," she ordered, placing the fresh clothes for me on the bench. "I will not be cleaning your clothes for you."

Before she left, she showed me two knobs. One was extremely filtered water meant for drinking, while the other was just desalinated for bathing and cleansing purposes.

The water was incredibly cold, but I didn't know what I expected. In the castle, my baths were always warmed for me.

I could get used to cold baths. A small price to pay.

I scrubbed myself with the provided soap, working extra hard to wash the soot and gunpowder from my skin. After a minute or two, the water didn't seem so cold. Soon enough my skin and hair were finally clean.

It felt odd not wearing a corset. *Is this what full breaths feel like?* I buttoned the shirt all the way up, maintaining as much decency as I could before wiggling into undergarments and breeches.

These undergarments were much shorter than bloomers, stopping midthigh but made of the same material, offering a nice barrier between me and the scratchy wool trousers. I couldn't remember the last time I dressed myself, considering my outfits were chosen by my parents and I was fastened into them by my chambermaids.

My father would shout at me if he saw me in breeches, but I felt so mobile in them. I smiled to myself, enjoying one more layer of freedom.

The bruises on my neck were gone, and so was the feeling of Nathaniel choking the life from me. I stroked where the marks used to be, and I couldn't help the smile that curled my lips. Relief soared in my chest; I felt hopeful as I looked at the woman in the mirror, knowing I had a future doing what *I* wanted. Not a life of service but one of adventure.

I hoped I never saw either of those awful controlling men ever again.

Hair still wet, I stuck my head into the officer's quarters to see Wraith taking her hat off, her gorgeous red hair over her shoulders. The tips of her ears poked through the hair and extended into exaggerated points.

Oh my Gods, she's an elf!

"You're an elf!"

Wraith gave me a seething look as she perched her hat back on her head.

"Are you from the Gullies?" I asked, referencing the small fae colonies south of Farlight.

She scoffed, getting up from her seat. "No."

No? Where else could she be from?

I followed her as she walked out to the stairs leading to the upper deck. "Then where are you from?"

Wraith stopped in her tracks, turning on her heel to glower down at me. "It's none of your fucking business."

I reeled back, pressing a hand to my chest.

"You're lucky we didn't toss you overboard the second we saw you. Harass me with more of your inane questions and I will knock you off the half wall."

My heart hammered beneath my hand. "O…kay."

"I'm not interested in being your friend. In fact, I have better things to do than babysit you, but here we are." Wraith paused, her eyes burning as she looked at me down the bridge of her sloped nose. "You will follow me. You will keep your questions to yourself. And you will *not* slow me down."

I gulped thickly, my mouth feeling gummy and dry. "Okay."

Without another word, she turned back around and ascended the stairs.

Plankwalker, always at the helm, got Wraith's attention, showing her a section of parchment that looked oddly like a map. I inched closer to get a good look at it, but Wraith purposefully got in front of me.

"This marker is wrong. Should be a lighthouse, not a watchtower. Fix it."

"Aye, ma'am." He took an implement out to adjust something on his map as I followed Wraith across the ship.

The elven woman didn't make good company at all. Clearly she was upset that I asked about her origins, but I didn't think that was a rude question. Nonetheless, I had to be careful. I was in no position to disrespect the people who could kill me in a heartbeat.

Apparently, Wraith was the quartermaster, which meant she was in charge of inventory, ordering supplies, and making sure all sailors got the appropriate cut of treasure, and was second mate after Howler. Perhaps that's why she was so callous. Lots of responsibilities.

She guided me down to the livestock area full of chickens, pigs, and goats. The scent of farm animals was pungent in my nose. I tried not to make a face.

An aging man fed the pigs scraps from the galley. He looked like an old farmhand nearing the end of his career, with braided white hair, eyes that crinkled, and jowls that dipped past his chin. The olive-hued skin on his face and hands gave way to a peachier pale tone where his shirt was rolled up. After a lifetime of hard work on the high seas, he had sunspots in the high points of his face to prove it.

Wraith took inventory of the chicken eggs and bid the old man a friendly hello.

Well, friendly for her.

Not much more than a grunt to anyone else.

While she did her job, I offered to help him feed the animals. I'd never been in such close proximity to farm animals before, but I was determined to be useful.

Can't throw me overboard if I'm useful.

Granted, I wasn't thrilled to get my hands dirty in pig slop, but I would do whatever I had to. It helped that the pigs were quite adorable, snorting with excitement when I plopped slimy goop into their pails.

It was humbling. These creatures were so grateful for everything they got. One of the pigs stuck its pink snout out at me, and I gave it a hesitant scratch across its wiry chest. It snorted with contentment, making me release a little giggle.

I patted a few of the goats, and they seemed equally excited for their dried pebbles.

The shepherd thanked me for the help—speaking in old sailor jargon, of course, so I had no clue what he was actually saying. But it sounded like a "thank you," so I decided it was safe to assume that was what it was.

I couldn't believe my first day was almost over, but when Boats came to retrieve me for dinner, I felt a sense of accomplishment. I'd done so many things I never had before.

What else will this journey hold for me?

7
MAEVE CROSS

Night fell, a full moon high in the sky visible from the windows in the officers' cabin. It reflected off the waves, glimmering like jewels in the sea. The serene visual settled the restless part of me.

What lay just beneath the surface? What kingdoms lived in the depths?

The sea called to me, beckoning me to explore. It shouldn't. I didn't know how to swim, much less dive. But the idea of submerging myself gave me an odd sense of peace.

Like I've returned home.

My eyebrows came together in deep thought. It didn't make any sense to me. I'd lived my life in the castle, so why did the sea feel like an old friend? Familiar?

Behind me, I could hear the officers—Howler, Wraith, and Boats—having dinner. Laughing and joking with one another. They were strangers to me, but I liked how natural it felt to be near them. Even after only a day.

The brooch pinned to the inside of my waistband irritated me, reminding me that it was there. Reminding me who I was.

I gazed at the officers for a moment longer before turning my eyes back to the waves. They could never know who I was. If I got too comfortable, it would be dangerous. It offered too many variables. No matter how I felt, I could never forget that they were pirates. They'd turn me in for a bounty.

After all, everything was always about coin.

The evil that made the world go round.

I sat on my bunk, hypnotized by the waves.

A light tap on my shoulder pulled me briefly from my thoughts. Boats stood next to me with a bundle of fabric in her arms. Behind her, Wraith and Howler were drinking rum. As usual, Wraith was giving me a dirty look.

"Yes?"

Boats gave me a friendly smile, looking just like Howler when she did, and placed a coat and blanket on my bed. "It gets cold. Can't have you getting sick."

"Oh, thank you."

She had kind eyes. "You'll be on ship crew with me tomorrow. I'll be your CO for the rest of the voyage."

"CO?" I inquired.

She blinked a few times. "Commanding officer."

"Oh." I paused, nibbling on my lower lip. "I'm not familiar with ship talk. This is all new to me."

A moment passed, and she squeezed my shoulder. "You'll get there." She gestured to the table behind her. "Drink?"

I shook my head. "I'd rather not." Just like when I was with Leviathan, I didn't want alcohol to blur my inhibitions. That would be too risky for me.

"I'll leave you to it, then." She returned to the table where the other two officers were sitting and rejoined their conversation like old friends.

I envied them, wishing I had friends like that. But maybe I was doomed to be alone.

The door opened, and a heavy set of boots came through the doorway. My entire body went rigid as I shot my gaze over to the door.

Sure enough, Leviathan had walked in. My mouth became dry as cotton when I raked his open shirt with my eyes. Heat flushed my face, shamefully coiling in my belly. He was just as attractive as he had been that morning.

The way my skin prickled was absolutely reprehensible. What was worse was that I couldn't seem to control my mouth around him. I could be perfectly respectful to his mates, but the *captain*? Arguably the one person I should respect above all others, but no. I resorted to name-calling.

My cheeks darkened even more as I thought about all the insults I'd thrown at him simply because he got under my skin.

I couldn't keep doing that.

I needed to get myself under control.

But unfortunately, my eyes had other ideas as I looked him up and down. Heat welled between my thighs. The sensation was downright foreign to me, and that in and of itself was irritating.

I squirmed in my bunk the moment those intense eyes met mine. I fought the urge to look away. Leviathan's presence filled the entire room.

It took my breath away.

But I didn't look away. Instead, I held his gaze and stood up from my seat, jutting my hip out with indignation.

I didn't know what it was about him, but he enticed my inner anarchist.

"Oh, you're still here? I forgot about you," he commented.

Asshole.

"I'm afraid you didn't leave much of an impression either," I rebutted, seeming unable to stop the words from leaving my mouth. But I did receive a little surge of satisfaction when the corner of his mouth twitched upward. Just for a moment, I got a glimpse of his dimples.

His tongue pressed the inside of his cheek as if he was repressing a grin. He sat down next to Howler—

I'd completely forgotten that his mates were in the same room with us. And they had just watched me mouth off to their captain.

Thankfully, no one said anything. If I didn't know any better, I'd think Wraith was chuckling under her breath as she poured Leviathan a glass of rum.

"So, how is my favorite stowaway?" he asked, eyes never drifting very far from me.

I tilted my head to the side. "*I'm* the favorite? You must not get very many."

"Most are smart enough to avoid *The Ollipheist*," Leviathan said. "Not you, though."

I narrowed my eyes, a spear of anger shooting through my chest. *Did he just call me dull?* I sucked my teeth. "Could you repeat that? I didn't hear you the first time." I batted my eyelashes a few times, baiting him.

He still knew it, though.

"We've been through this, Mae," Leviathan commented, taking another sip of his drink.

The way his throat bobbed when he swallowed should be grounds for imprisonment. The image of me sliding my tongue across his golden skin infiltrated my mind, making my mouth absolutely water.

I hated it.

That was when I noticed the mates watching us, but Leviathan in particular. Howler gave him the strangest expression before Leviathan finally stood up, grasping the bottle of rum. "I have a set of bones in my cabin. We don't have to use yours."

Howler followed. "Good, but you still lost one of my pieces."

Leviathan waved him off. "I'll find it."

"Bones?" I murmured, mainly to myself. I didn't know what they were talking about.

Wraith followed suit, standing to join them. "Deal me in. You good here, Boats?"

Her wife nodded. "Always, love."

Wraith dipped at the waist, taking her hat off to press a loving kiss against Boats's lips. She murmured something in a language I didn't understand before her green eyes flashed over to me as if daring me to try something.

Unlike Leviathan, I had no problem looking away. His threats seemed empty, like he simply enjoyed the banter. Wraith, on the other hand, I fully believed would gut me before I could cry for help. I gulped thickly, trying not to imagine how easy it would be for her to kill me.

For goodness' sake, she hardly made any noise when she walked! I'd never see her coming until it was too late.

I didn't need to look at him to feel Leviathan's gaze briefly land on me once more. The three of them left, leaving Boats alone with me in the officers' quarters.

Her presence felt much more pleasant. She gathered the dishes and placed them outside the door for the cabin boys to collect when they did their last rounds. My attention returned to the windows and the thrashing water. We hit an aggressive wave that rocked the boat back and forth before it settled again.

"Do you ever wonder what's out there?" I asked quietly, glancing over at Boats on her bunk across the room, a book opened on her lap.

She can read? I thought pirates were illiterate. Or at least, that was what I'd been told. My father made a point of telling me that pirates were uneducated. That's why they resorted to crime. The longer I stayed here, the less I believed that.

Boats hummed, looking up from her book to me. "All sorts of sea beasties live under the surface. Sirens. Kraken. The kuru. Giant sharks and devil whales. Some say even leviathans still swim in these waters."

The boat rocked again.

"I thought all the dragons had been hunted," I commented.

"The sea is still vastly unexplored. You never know. Why do you ask?"

The ocean beckoned my eyes again. Gods, it was beautiful. I could stare out at it forever, never tiring of its mystery. "I've never been on the ocean before. Never out of port."

"It's a fascinating place to be."

It was. A question gnawed at me as Boats sat there reading. "Where did you learn to read?"

Her dark eyes drifted to me, eyebrows rising far up into her hairline. "Why wouldn't I be educated?"

My cheeks warmed. "I heard many rumors. Stereotypes, I suppose." I went quiet, realizing just how offensive my statement was. It wasn't my business.

Boats sighed heavily. "If you must know, Seabird taught me. She taught most of the crew. While illiteracy is a stereotype to an extent, it's never a choice. The aristocracy has done its damnedest to keep its working class uneducated."

"I... I don't understand."

Boats tilted her head to the side, watching me closely.

"Then you haven't been paying attention. Ignorance is a choice too."

Never in my life had I ever considered myself ignorant, but I was sheltered. Kept out of the plain eye. Everything I knew came directly from my tutors. Or my father. I took everything he said as truth, but who was to say he didn't lie to me to keep me how he wanted me?

Subservient.

She's right. I am ignorant.

Her clothes were suddenly itching my skin. I was overcome with the realization that she worked for everything she had, while it had all been given to me. The guilt bore down on me—even more so because she'd been so nice to me.

I didn't deserve it.

But at the same time, all the things my father had done, from limiting education programs to funneling the guard down to the port, had driven people to this life of piracy—and then he hanged them for it.

Just like he drove me into the arms of an abusive man to get something he wanted.

My belly churned, and a bout of rage welled up before flittering away.

"They don't teach that in Farlight, do they?" Boats asked, not unkindly.

I shook my head. "No."

"I'm originally from Farlight Harbor," she added. "Howler and I were a shiphand's children. We're no stranger to how the nobles treat the lower class."

"Howler is your brother?"

She grinned from ear to ear. "My twin. I'm sure our resemblance is uncanny."

"It is." I chuckled quietly. A moment passed, and then I said, "Thank you for sharing that with me."

Her eyes softened, but she didn't reply, just opened her book again.

My mouth became a tight line. Now that I knew this, I'd never forget it. I knew my father had profited for quite some time off the backs of others, but I never heard any story but his. It felt wrong in my ears.

What else didn't I know?

I'd learned more in one day than I had in twenty-two years in my father's care. I'd never trade it for anything.

"What's bones?" I asked.

"A game with carved bone pieces. You count the dots for points. Levi likes to play it after a long day, while my brother likes to drink every time he loses." She paused. "Maybe we'll let you play it with us sometime."

I smiled. "I'd like that."

Bloodcurdling screams. Arms grabbed me. Blurry faces. Panic laced in every motion. Tears ran rivers down my face. My small body didn't move. I was frozen in place.

"Run! Get out of here! Find the dra—"

A guttural, wet scream ended the sentence. Warmth splattered across my face. In my eyes.

Everything blurred red.

My breath came out in sharp, dizzying gasps. My fingertips turned numb, my legs collapsing out of pure carnal fear. Different hands grabbed me.

I was terrified.

My heart jumped into my throat as I wailed, afraid I would be next.

No, please.

Please.

No.

The glint of a knife poised against my face. A big hand holding my face still.

Don't take—

My eyes flew open to see Wraith looming over me, grasping my shirt as she jostled me awake. "Wake up. You're okay."

I panted, a cold sweat all over my body as the familiar nightmare moved through me like a poltergeist. "I-I-I...." Words escaped me.

Her eyes pierced me, not as cold as they usually were. "You don't have to speak."

"I-I'm sorry. Did I wake you?" I ground out, still overcoming my nightmare and embarrassed that I had caused a scene. I looked past her at the other bunks, where Boats and Howler were still sleeping soundly.

"I'm a light sleeper. They sleep like the dead."

I expected Wraith to turn away from me and go back to her bunk, but then she sat beside me.

"Do these nightmares happen a lot?" she asked.

I ignored the question. They happened more often than I cared to admit. "I'm sorry. I won't do it again. I didn't want to disturb you—"

"I'm no stranger to nightmares, lass. We all carry something with us. Some worse than others...," she trailed off, lost in thought as she rose to her feet. "Go back to sleep. You have an early morning."

When she sauntered back to her bunk, I felt oddly comforted.

The nightmares didn't come back that night.

8
MAEVE CROSS

AFTER A FEW DAYS, I found my favorite place on *The Ollipheist*.

A bright, humid greenhouse protected by a wall of glass filled to the brim with greenery. Tomato plants and herbs. Celery and carrots. Easy crops to meet the nutritional needs of sailors. Not to mention that it felt nice to see green among all the blue.

I could only get there by walking out onto a balcony near the galley at the bow of the ship. During dinner, the occasional sailor would mosey out to smell the plants. Shipwreck Bay, the pirate safehold, was lush with plant life, and the greenhouse helped when they would start getting antsy or homesick.

I understood the appeal.

There was only one small bench in the greenhouse, and whenever I walked in, I'd see an older woman reading there. She had blonde hair with white streaked through it and faded smile lines around her mouth. Her skin was almost as light as her hair, looking as if she'd taken great care to avoid sun damage.

Was that Seabird?

I glanced down and noticed she was wearing a leather glove on only one hand. An injury, I realized. She was missing her pinkie and ring fingers on her left hand.

She hadn't looked up at me yet, but I also didn't want to bother her first thing in the morning.

Don't stare, Mae. People don't like that.

I went to the opposite side and looked out at the ocean. Butcher had enlisted me to gather some fresh produce for breakfast, but I didn't want to miss out on the view.

Butcher was quite the character. An old sea dog, as Gunny would say, with only one eye and one leg. He had a boisterous laugh and a thick accent. So thick that I almost never knew what he was saying, but I liked him.

Apparently, he was a butcher before he took up piracy, and that's why they called him Butcher. A frightening nickname for such a delightful man to be around, but he seemed to enjoy it.

I was starting to settle in with the crew, always thrilled when they gave me a new job. Something new to learn. It made me feel useful. I craved the work.

And the company.

During long stretches without work, some of the sailors taught me to play cards. They regretted it soon after because I kept winning. I assured them it was only beginner's luck. Still, I enjoyed myself.

When night came and I lay in my bunk on the cusp of sleep, I'd hear a violin echoing through the ship. Expert playing. I'd lose myself in the music and allow the sweet serenade to lull me into a peaceful sleep.

I didn't care who was playing. I never wanted it to stop.

I should get those vegetables before Butcher comes looking for me.

Not long after I completed Butcher's task, Boats sought

me out, letting me grab a boiled egg before joining the shiphands up top.

I disposed of the shell in the compost bin before following my CO. "What are you having me do today?" I asked.

"Nothing too strenuous. Just need an extra pair of hands to send tools up the rigging."

Rigging—meaning the ropes and chains that support the masts and control the sails.

"Can I climb the rigging instead?"

"Love the enthusiasm, but no. You're not trained for it."

"Fine. Fine." I finished my boiled egg as Boats opened the hatch leading to the main deck.

Instantly, I was met with the sounds of cheers. Pained grunts. Hard hits. Flesh hitting flesh. We crested the stairs, and I searched for the source of the sound.

Are those sailors brawling?

Two sailors were wrestling, throwing punches, and drawing blood. A larger group of sailors surrounded them, tossing coins to Gunny and shouting about who they thought would win.

Huh. Another thing to pass the time, I saw.

The fighting ring intrigued me. It definitely shouldn't. I knew nothing about fighting, but something about it was exciting. I loved to think I could teach them a thing or two, but I'd only end up with a black eye and Leviathan pointing and laughing at me.

Probably.

Gods, the man got under my skin. I'd see him every now and again, but thankfully we hardly said a word to each other. It certainly didn't stop him from visiting me in my dreams every once in a while.

I mean....

No. I was mistaken. It was nothing more than a break from the nightmares. I'd sooner dream of entangling myself in the fishing line than entangling myself with—

"Mae," Boats said sharply, interrupting my thoughts. "Pass up the bucket of tools on the pulley system."

Right. I had better things to do than imagine how far Leviathan's dragon tattoo went. Or if he would keep ridiculing me if I shut him up with my mouth. What would I have to do to render him speechless for a change?

Good Gods.

Enough of that.

I tied the bucket of tools to the rope before threading the other end of it up through the pulley and sent it to the sailor dangling from the main mast. The noise of the brawling wasn't too distracting as a sailor sent down what they didn't need, and I sent up whatever Boats told me to.

Boats went back and forth, managing all the sailors on deck.

Damn it.

I could feel Leviathan's presence before I saw him. Instantly, I started to feel warm.

I'm only warm because of the sun. Nothing to do with him.

But even so, I couldn't help myself as I looked at the brawling ring again. My throat bobbed. Was he taking to the ring? I watched him across the deck as he took his shirt off excruciatingly slowly.

Now that was plain unfair.

He complained that I'd be the reason he'd never get any work done, but there he was distracting *me*. What a hypocrite. One of the many things on my growing list of reasons why I couldn't stand him.

His dark hair was pulled up and out of his face. Equally dark hair peppered his chest, shrouding the blue ink of a dragon tattoo. I gobbled up the visual of Leviathan entering the ring with a fellow sailor.

With my eyes, I traced the muscles bulging on his arms. The veins threaded through the skin. The bunching of his back.

Unfair. Completely unfair.

He took a fighter's stance, moving gracefully around each hit, carefully timing his strikes to catch his opponent off guard. Sweat beaded across his brow, sliding down his face and neck before welling in the notch between his collarbones.

I gulped, my insides curling.

The sun was hotter than usual today.

"Mae!" Boats dragged my gaze away from her captain. "Focus, or you'll be swabbing the deck with the cabin boys!"

"Right!" I turned completely around. I couldn't be distracted if I wasn't looking at him. I pulled another tool up along the contraption.

I snuck a glance over my shoulder, my heart thundering hard when Leviathan looked directly at me. The corner of his mouth pulled into an overtly arrogant smirk, a dimple puncturing one of his cheeks, before he took his opponent out without even looking away from me.

My lips parted; a wild, rapturous warmth slid down my entire body.

How is that the sexiest thing I've ever seen?

But he couldn't know that. I'd never admit that out loud. So instead of letting him think I was fawning over him, I simply shrugged like I'd seen better.

That smile fell off his face, and I felt a twinge of satisfaction. But then it suddenly came back, that intense gaze darting over to the side of the deck. Even his dimples looked like they were up to something.

I followed his gaze over to Boats.

Damn it.

9
MAEVE CROSS

No wonder the cabin boys complain about this.

I scrubbed back and forth, up and down, the water turning a revolting gray from how hard I was scouring the stains. They cleaned this damn thing every day, so how in the Four Kingdoms did it get so *filthy*?

I grumbled to myself as my fingernails turned black. My—Boats's—pants were soaked. Thankfully, they were already navy blue, so the stains wouldn't be too noticeable. I could feel raw patches forming on my knees from crawling around from stain to stain. The thick material felt thinner around the knees, but at least it offered some protection.

Talk about dirty work.

"You sure you do this every day?" I retorted to one of the cabin boys, mimicking his motions against the deck to hide the fact that I'd never mopped anything before.

The cabin boy was probably around eighteen, his face still round with baby fat. His pale, almost translucent skin was flushed pink all the way down his neck. He was tall and narrow without an ounce of fat anywhere else on his lean physique. I wondered if the poor thing had eaten breakfast yet.

He was saturated in sweat as it dripped down his brow. Gods, he looked a mess. With a glance my direction, he huffed, "E'ry mornin'."

"It's still filthy," I commented, wiping the sweat off my forehead with the back of my hand.

"'Course it is. Salt coats e'rything."

I hummed. "So scrubbing helps the longevity of the vessel."

"I suppose. Salt'll eat it."

I looked over at Boats, who was shaking her head at me while discussing something with Leviathan. My guess, probably something about me doing this disgusting job again tomorrow. I moved the scrub brush in circles while another cabin boy splashed water across the deck and a third one mopped up all the salty grime.

Why couldn't I have been given a mop instead of a scrub brush? I squeezed the wooden handle that sat awkwardly in my hand. My palms felt raw too. Roughened by hard work.

I stole a glance at Leviathan.

Tell me I have a child's hands now.

As exhausting as this job was, I was satisfied by the progress. Here I was, getting dirty, working my ass off. It gave me this sense of pride I'd never gotten during castle lessons.

We had to have been scrubbing the deck for over an hour with the sun beating down on our backs. But this job was just as important as the others. I couldn't imagine cutting my bare feet on sharp chunks of crystalized sea salt on the planks. Or having it soften the wood so it was unstable.

It didn't matter how much I complained—I was being useful.

The cabin boy next to me looked the worse for wear. His face was bright red. He looked like he was struggling but was afraid to stop his ministrations.

"How long have you been on *The Ollipheist?*" I asked him. Maybe some conversation would help distract him a little.

He shook his head. "Um… a few months."

"And what's your funny nickname?" I continued. Gods, I didn't know why I pitied him. Perhaps because he reminded me of my tutor's son. My tutor was a real piece of work, but her son was always nice to me.

The cabin boy tilted his head, finally looking back over at me. "I haven't earned one yet. You can call me Luther."

Earned? "Well, nice to meet you, Luther. I'm Mae."

He laughed under his breath. "Oh, we all know who you are."

I paused my scrubbing. "What is that supposed to mean?"

"You're the one who lied to the captain's face and kept your tongue," Luther said.

"And that's unusual?" The words came out exasperated… and much louder than I intended.

The young boy gave me the most serious look. "Captain Leviathan is not a man you lie to. He's done worse for less."

A chill ran down my spine, and I stole another look at Leviathan standing next to Plankwalker and Boats. And to make it worse, he was looking right back at me. His mouth haunted me, making my belly feel warm again.

I went back to my work. "Perhaps I caught him in a good mood."

"Lucky you."

"What else do you know about the captain?"

He paused. "No one knows much about him. No one asks either. He's a very private man. If you have any questions, ask one of his mates. They've known each other since they all started pirating together."

That piqued my interest. "All of them?"

"Well, Leviathan and the twins. Wraith came later, but she's tight-knit with 'em now."

My curiosity satisfied for now, I shut my mouth. I nodded and scrubbed more firmly, determined to get it done. If I had any questions about Leviathan, I should ask the twins. Wraith would never tell me anything, but Boats... I could get something out of her.

Luther grunted as we made our way over to a wall to clean the baseboards. His arms were shaking.

"Are you all right, Luther?" I asked, concern ebbing into my voice.

"Aye... f-fine," he answered, his own voice warbling.

He'd gone from bright red to white as a poltergeist in about ten minutes. "No, you're not," I said. "Come on." I stood just as we hit a rough patch of sea. My heart rate spiked as I bounced, nearly falling backward into the water.

That was close.

"Be careful over there!" Boats shouted. "We're hitting rough water!"

"Aye!" I shouted back, turning my attention to the clammy boy still hunched over on the floor. I offered Luther my hand. "You need a break."

"I'm fine, lass," he insisted.

"Don't jest," I demanded. "Come on. Let's get you out of the sun."

After a long moment, he took my hand and stood on shaky feet. Instantly, he fell limp as the blood left his head, fainting under the sun. I could barely support his weight. He might be a scrawny thing, but he was heavier than he looked.

Shit.

He jolted back awake, shoving me as he came to. I lost my footing, and he passed out again against the deck.

We hit another rough patch of water, and my unsteady legs combined with a shaky boat knocked me back. My heart jumped into my throat as the feeling of falling enveloped me. A scream left my lips as I plummeted into the water.

The impact ricocheted through my entire body, freezing my arms and stiffening my legs. I clawed toward the surface, desperate to get out of the darkness swallowing me.

I can't swim.

I can't swim!

Panic consumed me.

Beneath me, there was nothing but darkness. A horrible nothing that could've been hiding any of the sea monsters I'd read about.

Reflexively, I opened my mouth to inhale.

Burning salt water filled my lungs, causing every inch of my body to convulse. I fought the waves, but they overpowered me, throwing me against the hull of the ship and churning my body like a meat grinder.

It's pointless to fight the sea.

My back hit the hull of the ship again, and the sensation of barnacles slicing into my skin felt like razorblades. But then everything was numb.

I couldn't see.

I couldn't feel.

My heart felt like it would burst. It was as if I had swallowed fire instead of water. I wanted to cry and scream for help. Everything started to blur as the pain crested inside me, reaching a peak of agony before becoming nothing.

Will Death come for me?

My limbs were getting heavy, everything sinking and pulling me into the deep. Now I was becoming a part of the same sea I'd loved while spending hours staring at it from my balcony.

I'm going home.

My eyelids started to close, the sense of calmness overcoming everything else. I gazed forward at an odd light coming toward me. Blue flickering eyes. Before darkness swallowed me completely, I reached toward those eyes.

I was no longer afraid.

10
CAPTAIN LEVIATHAN

I never accounted for Mae.

No last name.

A fake husband.

Nothing she would divulge.

I supposed it didn't really matter. She was willing to put in the work, so I was willing to let it go. The woman had a mouth on her. Every curse or insult she threw at me was nothing short of hilarious.

Luckily for her, she never mouthed off to me in front of my crew. My mates didn't count. We'd known each other long enough that a mouthy woman wouldn't change our dynamic that eight years of captaining and twenty-five years of friendship had created.

But if Mae were to be adamantly disrespectful in front of the shiphands, I'd be forced to reprimand her.

For now, I allowed myself to enjoy the banter. It felt different. A breath of fresh air, even. When we reached Shipwreck Cove, I'd let her go so she could find her way. With her determination, I was sure she'd fare just fine.

I stole another look at her scrubbing the deck with the cabin boys.

I almost expected to see her complaining like a noblewoman. Doing a shitty job like she'd never lifted a finger in her life. I hummed under my breath, surprised to see her smiling from ear to ear, her face speckled with gray sludge from the deck.

Her loveliness never ceased to strike me with the vigor of a fist.

Dark locks piled on top of her head, unruly and all over the place. Wide doe eyes that she tried to use to get her way every chance she got. Those eyes could bring a man to his knees, but they didn't work on me.

If I buckled every time a pretty lassie made eyes at me, my crew would have mutinied by now.

Mae stood up, her knees filthy, and looked down at a cabin boy. She held out a hand, red and raw.

My lips parted to tell her to back away from the lip of the ship as we hit a rough wave. Then my heart jumped into my throat. She was jostled but didn't fall over. Boats shouted the warning, and Mae looked over at us, nodding like she understood.

A sense of unease yanked in my chest. Mae wasn't listening. My eyes darted down to the choppy waves as she reached out a hand to pull up the dehydrated cabin boy.

I started moving toward her, Boats close behind me.

He was going to faint. I'd seen it time and time again. Glassy eyes and shaking muscles as the sun beat down on their backs. They weren't used to the labor yet.

He's going to faint.

Mae needed to get back from that edge.

But she seemed to have no care for her own well-being as she pulled him to his feet.

Before I could get another word out, the cabin boy fainted, then immediately came to and flailed right out of her arms. That coupled with another rough wave against the hull knocked Mae off her feet, sending her tripping over the lip of the half wall and falling backward into the water.

Motherfucker.

"Shit," I breathed, instantly breaking into a run.

My crew surrounded the edge, muttering among themselves in a panic. They wouldn't survive if any of them jumped in. Not in these waters. Not with the predators that scoured the depths.

Howler ran over to my side. "You're not jumping in there after a stowaway, are you?"

"Move," I ordered sharply, my sailors making a break in the crowd for me. "You know I have to."

I'd jump in after any of my crewmen. Not even a stowaway deserved to drown.

"Levi—" Boats started to say.

"I'm going." I dropped my coat before untying my sash and handing Howler all my gear. I kicked off my boots.

Howler shook his head. "You dragons can't help yourself around an innocent in danger, can you?"

Without saying a word, I gave him a knowing look. He already knew the answer.

I dove off the deck into the water like I had many times.

The dragon tattoo under my skin bubbled to the surface as I allowed a partial shift. My hands became webbed, my eyes sharp in the darkness. Gills formed in the sides of my throat, leaving me fully capable of breathing underwater.

I searched for her, and it didn't take long to see her churning within the water, thrown into the hull of the ship. Barnacles split the skin on her back. The blood was luring sea beasts up from the depths.

But I was also in the water, and they would sense me too.

The music from sirens and the clicking from the kuru dissipated the moment they sensed me. Even the goddess of the sea—Cliohde—wouldn't stand between a leviathan and something they wanted.

I cut through the water, not as efficient as I was in my fully shifted form but still better than the average swimmer. Mae wasn't kicking or trying to break away from the sea's grip. Her skin was pallid, not bright and lively as it was earlier.

That didn't sit well with me at all.

But I could've sworn she reached out to me as her eyelids fluttered closed. I looped an arm around her waist, pulling her flush against me. My other hand found her face as I pressed my mouth against hers in an attempt to give her the breath of life.

My tattoo glowed, offering oxygen to bring her back from the brink.

Nothing.

Fuck.

She'd taken in too much water. Snatching the rope my sailors threw out for me, I dragged her up to the surface. Like a finely oiled machine, they pulled us back up onto the ship. Mae was limp in my arms, damn near turning blue.

"Out of the way!" I ordered, laying Mae on the deck. I knew she wasn't breathing, and I needed to get oxygen circulating. Enough time had been wasted already.

I placed the heel of my hand over her heart, topped it with the other, and started pressing two inches deep. Blood seeped from the wounds on her back, saturating the wood beneath her. Everyone on deck was silent, watching as I attempted to bring Mae back from the dead.

"Howler, get towels. Now," I huffed, pausing my chest

compressions to give her a rescue breath. Her lips were cold. Body freezing.

More chest compressions. *One. Two. Three.* Pause. Breathe.

"Come on, Mae. You didn't come out here to drown," Boats said, keeping the crewmen back to give me some more space. "Make yourself useful!" she shouted at her shiphands. "Get Seabird. Now!"

Numerous crew members darted down to the lower deck.

One. Two. Three. Breathe.

One. Two. Three. Breathe.

Again.

Again.

Again.

Don't do this to me, Mae.

She was too young to die like this. To have all the opportunities stolen from her. But life was a cruel bitch.

My family knew that better than anyone. Especially my mother.

With one more rescue breath, Mae lurched forward, spitting and coughing up seawater against the deck—and all over me, but I'd overlook that. She inhaled greedily, the powder blue of her lips already pinkening again.

The remaining crew cheered.

"Oh, thank the Gods," Boats murmured, completely turning away, overcome with relief.

Mae looked lazily at the crew, her chest rising and falling. Color returned to her cheeks as she noticed me sitting next to her before she lost consciousness again. Her hair was plastered all over her face. I pushed it back reflexively and noticed a thin scar on the top of her ear.

Faded.

Barely there.

A matching one on top of the other.

Before I could inspect further, the cabin boy from earlier —Luther, if I remembered correctly—pushed past the sailors. "Is she okay? Is she okay? I'm so sorry. I-I-I—"

I glanced over my shoulder at the young man, pushing Mae's hair back over her ears. "Go to the lower deck."

He visibly gulped but obeyed just as Howler was coming back with towels.

Mae trembled uncontrollably. We needed to get her warmed up before she succumbed to hypothermia.

Howler covered Mae with a towel, hiding her translucent blouse. I hadn't noticed, but I was relieved that he took her modesty into consideration. I scooped Mae up into my arms as she teetered between consciousness and sleep.

She pressed her cheek against my soaked shirt, completely exhausted.

Her back bled steadily, but it already seemed to be slowing. Faster than I'd expected it to.

"Get everyone back to work," I told Howler before glancing over at his twin. "You come with me."

Boats gathered my jacket, boots, and gear from the deck without me having to ask.

Howler nodded. "Aye, Cap." He turned back to the crew and howled, "You heard the captain! Back to work!"

The crew scattered back to their jobs.

"Are you taking her down to the infirmary?" Howler asked.

I didn't like the idea of leaving her someplace where I couldn't keep an eye on her. "No. Send Seabird to my quarters."

My first mate raised an eyebrow but didn't argue. "Aye."

Boats followed and held the door open for me as I carried

Mae into my cabin. I rested her weary body on top of the furs adorning my bed. Her clothes were still soaked, as were mine. But I didn't care about my bedspread as much as I cared about Mae being cold.

"Close one today, hm, Levi?" Boats commented, placing my gear on my desk.

"Seems that way," I replied, going to the chest at the foot of my bed to dig up something Boats could change Mae into. "This will do." I tossed a clean shirt near Mae's sleeping form. "I want you to change her clothes."

Boats dipped her head, expecting that.

A knock sounded on my cabin door before Seabird let herself in. I walked over to her and pressed a fond kiss against her cheek. "Good afternoon, Mama."

She smiled, ruffling my hair like she did when I was a boy. It didn't matter that I was much taller than her now. She looked past me at Mae curled up in a ball on top of my bed.

My heart slammed against my ribs when I noticed how small she looked there. Her back was still bleeding, but once Boats changed her clothes, Mama could get a better look at it.

"That must be the stowaway," she stated.

I scoffed. "The infamous stowaway, but we just call her Mae."

My mother shared a laugh with me as we both stepped away so Boats could change Mae's clothes. Relief welled in my chest.

Mae was in good hands now.

Sailors died on the water all the time. Our lifestyle was destined for a violent end one way or another. But for someone as young and bright as Mae, it wouldn't feel right to have that light snuffed out so soon.

Not if I can help it.

11
MAEVE CROSS

"Don't cry, little girl. We can't hurt you...."

Blood saturated my fingers, sliding and pooling across the soil wedged between my toes. My eyes hurt from how hard I'd been crying. My throat felt caked with it. A hand curled around my ankle, drawing my gaze to the body of a woman who took care of me.

Her skin was greasy with pallor. The only color of life was crimson. Crimson everywhere.

I couldn't remember what she looked like. Her face was a blur.

Her hand fell limp as her killers lifted me, taking me away. Far away.

I beat the man's chest with my little fists as I sobbed, confused. My heart ached. Fear swallowed me whole. I didn't understand what was happening.

Slowly the blur started to ebb away. Bodies tossed into fire. The smell of burning flesh filled the air, making me sick.

"Don't fight or you'll join the pyre. It'd be a pity to put you to waste," the familiar man's voice said.

I shook and cried but stopped fighting.

I leaned my head against the glimmering black amulet sparkling with blue—

I awoke with a start, panting hard, my eyes wild. It took a moment for the pain to sink in. As soon as I jolted up, my entire back throbbed. My ribs compressed and expanded with greedy breaths, each one more painful than the last. My skin prickled with the cold, and I grasped the furs tighter, trying to calm down.

Just breathe.

Breathe.

I closed my eyes tightly as I took slow breaths through my nose, willing my heart to slow. Many times, I'd awoken after a nightmare in my bedroom, alone. I'd have to soothe myself in the moonlight. Gods, I was so lonely.

I didn't have anyone.

No one is going to save you, Mae.

I didn't need the easy way out. I didn't need to be soothed. No. I had myself. That would have to be enough.

My heartbeat slowed, no longer pounding in my ears. After the adrenaline from my nightmare petered out, the pain set in.

Damn it all to the Hells.

With a groan, I fell back onto the bed, my back aching something awful. My throat felt sore. There was a raw sort of pain in my bones.

Where am I?

I looked around.

Why am I in Leviathan's cabin?

Then it hit me. The potent scent of a salty sea breeze and musky cedar wood. The smell was stronger in the furs on Leviathan's bed.

Wait.

Why am I in Leviathan's bed?

The furs tickled my bare legs. My cheeks turned red as I slowly realized what I was wearing.

Why am I wearing Leviathan's shirt?

What in the Hells happened?

Wait....

I fell into the ocean. I drowned.

Oh Gods. No!

I threw the furs off me and searched for my clothes. My brooch. The coat of arms that was always pinned to the inside of my waistband.

Oh no. Damn it!

It was gone.

Which led me to two options.

It was possible that it fell out and sank to the bottom of the ocean. I sincerely hoped that was what happened. The other option was that Leviathan or another crew member now had it.

I'm done for.

I couldn't let them ransom me off to Nathaniel. I'd rather drown.

Before I could panic even more, the door swung open. I recognized Leviathan's footsteps; I didn't even have to look to know it was him. I yanked the furs back over my bare legs, suddenly feeling incredibly hot. I felt even warmer surrounded by a smell that was so recognizably *Leviathan*.

"So she lives," he commented, coming to the foot of his bed to gather some clothes from the chest. He was visibly damp, his hair held back with a bandana across his forehead. His shirt clung to his body, leaving *nothing* to the imagination.

Glowing orange light came in from his window, bathing

him in the soft light of dusk. Gods, the sight of him caused a lump to form in my throat.

My face felt hot. "Is Luther okay?"

"You drown, and that's your *first* question?" He didn't look at me as he pulled out a shirt, chuckling to himself. "He's fine. For now, at least."

I sat up, my body positively *aching*. I gritted my teeth, trying to ignore the searing pain in my back. The bruising all over my ribs. How every breath hurt. "Don't punish him. It was an accident. I was too close to the edge."

"You don't give the orders here, sweetheart."

A soft cry fell from my lips as I pressed myself back against the headboard. I ground my teeth together, fighting another wave of agony.

Leviathan arched a brow, tossing a change of clothes onto his desk. "I wouldn't be moving so much if I were you. You took quite the beating when you fell."

My eyes flared with indignation. I didn't want to lie down. I wanted to argue.

"I'm only going to say this once. *Lie the fuck down.* You're mucking up the bandages Seabird put on your back."

With a grumble, I obeyed. "Where is she now? Her company has to be better than yours."

He rolled a shoulder, the corner of his mouth twitching up. "Excuse the poor woman for getting dinner."

"Well, don't you have anyone else to babysit me?"

He chuckled. "Why? Can't stand the sight of the man who saved you?"

"Not if you want something for it." The words came out tight, angry. I blamed the pain.

He paused as if deeply considering how to reply. "This isn't a charity, but I suppose I can give you one thing for free. Go diving off the deck again and I'll ask for a kiss."

I gaped, my face deepening to another shade of red as I looked away. The image of him curling his hand in my hair and tugging me into a passionate kiss enraptured me. My mouth went dry. "I'm a biter."

"Of course you are. I'd expect nothing else from that sharp tongue," he replied, laughing quietly to himself. "But you have nothing to fear from me."

"I'm wearing your clothes," I pointed out.

He shrugged. "I'll make sure to let you get hypothermia next time." He pulled his wet shirt over his head.

Oh, damn. I'd seen him half naked numerous times now, but I seemed to forget how it made my belly tighten. How I felt unbelievably warm every single time.

This time I couldn't blame it on the sun beating down on me.

I swallowed, seeking out the coil of his dragon tattoo that appeared to wrap around his entire body. "So what's the story behind the tattoo?"

He pulled another shirt on, effectively hiding his physique from my gaze. "My pirate moniker is Leviathan. Might as well lean into it." He dropped his hands to unbuckle his belt, and I looked away completely.

"Can't you change your breeches elsewhere?"

"Excuse me for changing my clothes in my own bedroom." He sighed after my face turned a few more colors. "Fine. If it makes you so uncomfortable, I'll go into my side room. But don't pretend that you weren't eyeing me up a moment ago."

My face boiled, but I still replied, "Don't flatter yourself."

"Whatever you say." He shook his head, disappearing into a side room. A few more moments passed, and then Leviathan reemerged wearing a fresh pair of breeches… and a cat sitting comfortably on his broad shoulder.

I almost didn't see it considering it was completely black aside from two wide green eyes.

"Where did that thing come from?"

He sat at his desk, and the cat jumped down to curl up on a few papers while he gave it an affectionate scratch under the chin. "Show some respect, Mae. Lieutenant Commander Lazlo is a higher-ranking sailor than you are."

"This cat is my commanding officer?" I asked, fighting the curl of my mouth at the absurdity of the comment.

He glanced over at me, expression stone-cold serious. "Yes, he is."

"Okay. Apologies, Lieutenant Commander Lazlo."

As soon as I stated the cat's title, he hopped up on his haunches, giving me his full attention. Suddenly, he waggled his rear and hurled himself onto Leviathan's bed, right next to me.

The giant long-haired black cat collapsed onto his back, revealing its big, fluffy belly. I couldn't help reaching forward to ruffle his inviting stomach.

"Stop," Leviathan said, making me pause my advancement. "Usually, I'd just let Lazlo claw up anyone foolish enough to scratch his belly, but you've been injured enough for one day."

"What?"

"Only scratch his ears and chin. Anything else and he'll slice you to ribbons."

The cat gave me the most mischievous look, and I was inclined to follow Leviathan's advice. I scratched the cat's chin, and he started purring, rumbling with contentment. A small giggle bubbled past my lips, and I continued to scratch Lazlo to his heart's content.

"You're such a handsome kitty," I commented, glancing

over at Leviathan, who was watching me with his interesting eyes. "I have to admit, I didn't think you were a cat person."

"What kind of person do I seem like, then?" he asked, kicking his feet up onto his desk.

I shrugged. "Not a cat person." I paused, rubbing Lazlo's ears. "I know why you have farm animals on board, but why cats?"

"Ships are notorious for harboring vermin. Cats eliminate vermin. They also work wonders for the injured. Nothing lifts spirits like a purring feline."

"I'll say." I grinned, giving Lazlo one more scratch before he hopped off the bed to crawl into a small space between a bookshelf and the floor.

"Break time is over," Leviathan chuckled.

I relaxed into the furs, the pain still throbbing, but it didn't hurt so bad when I settled in. "I have a question for you."

"Go ahead."

"How does someone get a pirate moniker? The cabin boys don't have one."

"Why are you interested? Want to join life on the high seas with a crew of scoundrels?" he asked, his eyes locked on me. He leaned on his palm, giving me his full attention.

His eyes could've been the feathery touch of his fingertips, and I wouldn't have been able to tell the difference. My gaze fluttered down to his mouth, the curve of it puncturing a dimple into his cheek.

Those dimples gave him this boyish quality that made him look that much more charming.

My belly felt tingly, like a swarm of butterflies had been released inside me. "Just curious."

"Ah." He made this throaty noise that made my belly feel

even stranger. "I suppose I can indulge your curiosity. You see, a pirate moniker serves two purposes. One, it upholds a reputation, a legend. Two, it protects us. If we were to use our legal names everywhere, there is a higher chance of us getting turned in for a bounty."

I nodded, pleased I was getting a real answer out of him for a change. "How do you get one?"

Suddenly, Leviathan laughed. "If you were to get a moniker, Mae, it would probably be Doe Eyes or maybe Bunny."

A frown pulled my lips down. "No, it wouldn't."

"Definitely, sweetheart. No one is ever going to take you seriously with that face. You look too sweet to be cutthroat."

And we're back to him being an asshole again.

"Stop calling me *sweetheart*. I don't like it."

His mouth pulled into the biggest, cockiest, shit-eating grin I'd ever seen. And that said a lot for Leviathan. Even his dimples didn't soften it. "I don't think I will. It suits you."

I was about to tell him to stop being so rude when there was a knock at the door. It opened, revealing a woman I recognized as Seabird. She wore a custom glove on her three-fingered hand. Her fair hair was pulled up, and wrinkles aged her face in a way that made her look experienced, not old. There was nothing frail or fragile about Seabird. She appeared fierce, but her eyes were kind.

Leviathan got up to meet the woman at the door, where he leaned down to press a kiss on her cheek while she fondly ruffled his hair.

They spoke to each other in hushed tones before Leviathan gave the older woman a charming smile that looked nothing like the grin he'd given me and left the room.

"I'm glad to see you awake, Mae," Seabird stated, striding toward the bed. "Let me get a good look at you."

I expected to feel nervous with a new person in the room, but something about her soothed me. She didn't feel as fierce as she looked. She felt safe.

My guard softened a bit in her presence.

12
MAEVE CROSS

Seabird slowly unwrapped the bandages taped to my back to inspect the slices I'd sustained from being thrown against the barnacle-laden hull. I winced when she applied a salve, using a gentle touch to smooth it into the wounds.

"They're healing faster than I expected," Seabird commented as she laid fresh bandages.

"Is that a bad thing?" I asked, catching on to the strange tone in her voice.

"Not at all. I would expect them to be infected or still bleeding, at least." She hummed. "But they only seem to be leaking sebum. You're lucky."

She moved away, and I settled back onto the bed. I groaned, sore all over. "I don't feel lucky."

"Injuries will do that to you, but it could be worse. Can I inspect your ribs?" she asked, not moving the furs until I nodded.

While I was only dressed in Leviathan's shirt and my teeny undergarments for the bare minimum of modesty, I didn't feel embarrassed to have Seabird look at me. She had a gentle touch, as if she'd soothed away many aches in her lifetime.

I wanted to ask her about her hand, but even I knew that it wasn't appropriate to question a woman about a severe injury upon first conversation. So I settled for a broader question. "How long have you served on *The Ollipheist*?"

Seabird blinked at me, her eyes rising from my pale bruises up to my face. I'd never gotten a good look at her eyes before. They were as blue as the sea. And now that she was closer, I noticed several more streaks of white through her blonde hair, which was fine and long like cornsilk.

Nearly every inch of her skin was covered with a thin jacket and leather breeches. It only added to her intimidating frame. But while Wraith would probably kill me if she had the chance, I didn't feel that way about Seabird at all.

She was like a mother bear. Fierce, but nurturing.

I'd never had that before. My mother liked to pretend I didn't exist. I theorized that my father had me with someone else during the war and then brought me home to an angry wife. Of course, I could never ask them that outright. But I'd never learned the real answers either.

She lowered my shirt to cover me back up. "Your bruises heal remarkably fast too. You were black and blue only a few hours ago."

I gave her a sheepish smile and said, "Lucky, I guess."

"To answer your question, I believe I've been here about fifteen years. Captaining until Leviathan took over for me," she said smoothly.

"You were a captain?" I asked. "How exciting."

Seabird cracked a smile. "Leviathan thought so too. He's got the guts for it."

I wanted to ask more questions. Pick her brain. How did she become a pirate? What did it look like when she was captain? Why did she stop? Then the door to Leviathan's cabin slammed open.

The entire atmosphere of the room changed. Seabird straightened up instantly, the smile falling from her face as a more serious expression took root.

"Get out," Leviathan barked sharply. A tone I'd never heard before.

All my hair stood on end as I fought my aching muscles to sit up all the way. I'd never seen him like this before. Eyes blazing. Face flushed.

Infuriated.

"What is this about?" Seabird asked, crossing her arms to take a firm stance in front of me.

"As your captain, I'm ordering you to leave."

A tense moment passed as I looked between Seabird and Leviathan. "Aye," she said before obeying and leaving me in this room alone with an angry man.

I know what happens when men get angry.

I swallowed, every muscle tensing. I'd run if I had to. I'd fight if I had to. I would not let myself be handled by an aggressor. Never again.

Leviathan closed his eyes, his chest rising and falling wildly. He was fuming, and when his eyes opened again, I could feel the blazing heat of his rage. For the first time since I'd met the man, he *scared* me.

He withheld his temper, grinding out between his teeth, "I'm going to give you one more chance to tell me who you are."

My blood ran cold. "My name is Mae. You know that already. Everything else is unimportant."

"I disagree."

My heart was in my throat. Pounding in my ears. "Then I don't know what you're talking about."

"Do not lie to me." He reached into the pocket of his jacket and pulled out something small, then tossed it so it landed directly next to me.

An eel slithering out of a skull engraved on my brooch.

"Why do you bear this coat of arms?"

Fuck.

"I… I was a servant f-for the crown." I stumbled over my words, unable to keep eye contact through my lie.

His teeth ground together. *"Bull-fucking-shit.* They don't give draconite to commoners."

"I stole it." Another lie. If he was this livid just from my brooch, I didn't want to know what he'd do if he knew who I was.

Leviathan dragged his hands through his hair. "Stop *fucking lying.* You don't have the hands of a servant."

I shrank underneath his tone, my heart pounding. Fear shook my hands as I grasped the furs. I felt trapped. Nowhere to go. Nowhere to hide. "I-I'm not."

He drew his cutlass, and the rest of my body went cold. "If another lie slips past your lips, I will slice you from navel to your lying mouth. I'll spill your guts for the sharks."

My fingertips stiffened as if frozen. My mouth turned gummy, and my throat thickened. His cutlass gleamed in the light of the oil lamps, sharpened to perfection.

If he cut into me, I doubted I'd feel a thing.

My mouth opened and closed. Every passing moment of silence only intensified Leviathan's anger. I didn't understand why he was reacting like this. Why he was so angry. I expected annoyance as well as greediness over the bounty I would give him, but never anger.

With one more dry swallow, I muttered, "My name is Maeve Cross. I'm the Princess of Farlight Isles."

The blaze in his eyes got hotter. "The Princess of

Farlight," he murmured to himself. He breathed hard through his nose, looking away from me as he released a dark chuckle.

To my relief, he sheathed his cutlass in the sash on his waist.

"Please—"

"I'm never going to escape your family, am I?"

I hadn't had time to ask him what he meant before he charged toward me, ripping me out of his bed with brute strength. A startled cry left my lips. I could feel his fingers around my arms leaving red marks from how hard he dragged me to the door.

"Let me go!" I hissed, my heart pounding. Fear ran like ice through my veins.

He kicked his door open, and all the sailors on deck turned to watch as Leviathan threw me down the steps and onto the main deck with only my hands to catch me. My body ached, and a whimper bubbled up from my chest as my knees scraped the planks. With no breeches to protect me from the wood, I felt every textured divot rough up my skin.

Tears stung my eyes, but I wouldn't give in and be small. I fought them, not letting myself cry.

The sun was lower now. It was almost dark, but I could still feel everyone's eyes on me. All the working crewmen came to a halt. Howler and Wraith were on deck. Seabird watched from the mizzenmast. Boats stood next to Plankwalker, looking guilty. I felt naked with my bare legs on display in the chilly wind.

I trembled, fighting the urge to hide. To cover myself somehow.

"We no longer have a stowaway. We have a prisoner," Leviathan announced.

Pushing myself to my feet, I shouted, "Let me explain!"

Leviathan gave me a withering stare. "The time to explain is over." He directed the next statement to his crew. "Not only do we have a prisoner, but we have a prisoner who will make us quite the bounty when we ransom her back to her family."

"No!" I cried out. "Just listen to—"

"Princess Maeve Cross of Farlight Isles," he said over me. "And she'll make us a great deal of coin."

I can't go back.

I can't go back.

No.

I won't *go back.*

Adrenaline spiked through my veins as I lunged at Leviathan with everything I had. He caught every poorly timed hit. He grasped me by the waist, and I made a move to grab his cutlass. His hands were hot against me. Goose bumps crawled up my arms when I felt his fingers touch my bare skin, then a bite of pain when he gripped my thigh.

The wind got knocked out of me as he tossed me backward again. Falling flat on my back, I swallowed down a cry as agony shot down my spine, the injury refreshed, nerve endings exposed.

"Don't fight me, sweetheart. You won't win," he sneered.

"Fuck you!" I spat, out of breath and in pain. Tears welled in my eyes, overfilling the corners.

He drew his cutlass as he came forward, pointing it directly at me. I'd rather die by Leviathan's sword than be Nathaniel's wife.

But I wasn't interested in dying.

I bared my teeth. "Get that blasted thing out of my face."

He held the cutlass there, barely an inch from my nose. I didn't know whether he was going to put it away or end me right then.

The crew was dead silent, not daring to interfere with their captain handling a *prisoner*.

"That's enough," Seabird shouted, severing the quiet. "I don't care who she was. Right now, she's an injured woman who's cold, terrified, and barely dressed. I did not raise you to act like this."

Raise him?

Leviathan blew a sharp breath out of his nose and sheathed his cutlass. "I want that cell fixed, and I want her in it." His blazing eyes met mine again. "I will send her back to the king in pieces if I have to."

I scrambled to my feet. "I'm not an item to buy and sell!"

"That's not how I see it, *Princess*. Mind your tone. Look around. You have no friends here. All I have to do is say the word, and my crew will cut you to pieces. We will *eat you alive*," Leviathan seethed.

I shook violently, realizing now how wrong I had been to view any of these sailors as my friends. They were my captors. Every last one of them. I was a piece of meat. A trophy.

An item to sell.

Nothing had changed.

"*Bastard*," I hissed.

Leviathan moved toward me, but Seabird got between us. She spoke in a hushed tone. "Cool off. I will handle her."

He practically bared his teeth as he uttered, "Fine."

Seabird turned, taking me under her arm to usher me to the lower deck.

"Back to work! All of you!" Leviathan snarled, and everyone instantly obeyed.

Even as I stepped down the stairs, I still heard the door to his cabin slam.

13
MAEVE CROSS

Seabird guided me to a hidden room near the officers' quarters on the middle deck. As she opened the door, I found comfort in her hand resting against my spine. It soothed the fiery pain scorching my skin.

"Sit," she said softly, letting me sit down on her bed.

This room was much smaller than the captain's cabin or the officers' quarters. But it was private, with a sliver of light coming out of a porthole window from the moon. Books lined her walls. Parchment and inkwells perched on top of her desk.

My entire body cried out in relief now that I was off my feet. I'd been throttled by the waves only a few hours ago. Exhaustion weighed heavily on my bones. As relieved as I felt, that didn't stop the overflow of emotion from coming out of the corners of my eyes.

"I've never seen him like that," I whispered.

Seabird gave me her back, opening a chest to find a pair of breeches. "You haven't known my son very long."

Her son? It made sense. How he took over for her. How he stepped back when she was involved. Even if one of his mates got between us, he wouldn't have lightened up. But he would for his mother.

"Only a handful of things garner that reaction from him. Mistreatment of his crew, brutalization of innocents, and the Cross family."

I took the breeches from her and pulled the oversized pants up to my waist. Seabird rolled the cuffs around my ankles, then did the same to the waistband to make it feel tighter. I was grateful she wanted to help me, not having the energy to do it myself.

"Has he always hated my family?" I asked, my voice still soft.

"We all hate what they've done to us" was the only thing she said before stepping away from me. Her stance was rigid. She clearly didn't want to talk about this.

But I needed the information. Anything to survive. "What have we done?"

It felt wrong to say *we*. I'd been trapped in a castle all my life, but I was a member of the Cross family. I was a part of it.

Seabird clenched her three-fingered hand, her eyes glazing over with an infuriated fire that matched her son's. But it was gone as soon as I saw it, melting away into pain. "I can't name the atrocities. Too many. Not a single member of this crew has been untouched. His soldiers have raped their wives. Killed their children. Hunted—" She stopped herself.

Rape? Murder of children? "I... I can't believe my father is responsible for that." My father took care of me. He loved me. There was no doubt in my mind—at least not until he married me off for an army. But even before that... some part of him scared me. I didn't understand it, but I felt it in my bones.

I started to feel very cold. I rubbed my arms, looking away from Seabird altogether.

"What you believe is irrelevant. What I need to know right now is why you're here."

There was no point in lying. I hesitantly looked back over at Seabird. Her eyes were ocean blue, like the flecks I'd seen in Leviathan's. But hers didn't glimmer like his did.

Stop thinking about Leviathan's eyes.

"I'd been forced into a marriage," I answered. "I ran."

Seabird wasn't satisfied. "Nobles get married off all the time. What else?"

I gulped. "It was to Lord Nathaniel Pike."

She stiffened.

"You know of him?"

"Unfortunately. Scourge of the Sea. You'd be his fourth wife."

Fourth? I didn't know Nathaniel had been married before me. What happened to them? An icy chill washed through my veins. There had to be a reason why my father never told me that.

"How do you know that? It's not common knowledge in Farlight."

The older woman gave me a sympathetic stare. "Pike has a reputation for going through wives. He's also incredibly well off. It wouldn't take much to buy silence."

I was quiet, feeling even more afraid of what would've happened to me if I hadn't run.

Seabird continued. "I wish I could say I was shocked, but considering Varric's history of treating people as if they were disposable, I'm not surprised he'd auction off his own daughter."

King Varric, I wanted to correct after how many times I'd heard it. But if he was responsible for so much pain, I wasn't sure he deserved the title. My voice shook as I said, "Nathaniel told me he planned on assaulting me that night.

He forced himself on me in the carriage, and I bit him. Then he wrapped his hands around my neck and squeezed."

A moment of silence passed between us until she finally said, "You did the right thing."

My shoulders sagged. "I didn't want to marry him. I didn't want to be my father's bargaining chip." My throat started to get thick. "My father wanted an army. He was going to do anything it took to get it." With a sniffle, I continued. "He'd sell his daughter to get whatever he wanted."

The mattress dipped next to me, and Seabird pulled me into an embrace. All that pain, everything I'd hidden, came frothing to the surface like seafoam brought in by a tide.

"An army?" she asked softly.

I nodded against her neck.

Seabird didn't say anything, but I felt how stiff the tendons of her shoulders were.

"I was alone. Nathaniel told me that no one was going to save me. He was… he was *right*. No one cared what would happen to me once I went to the Ivory Keys. I'd served my purpose. Everyone at the castle heard what he'd say to me… but *no one even tried to stop it*." My voice warbled as I started to cry.

Gods, it felt so good to cry.

"Let it out, Mae. It's all right," Seabird shushed, rubbing circles on my back. I felt like a little girl being comforted by a mother.

Another sob fell from my lips when I realized I'd never had that before. No one to comfort me. No one to tell me everything would be all right.

I fell limp and accepted the comfort, not knowing how badly I needed it.

When the sobs slowed and my tears ran dry, Seabird pulled away from me. "Thank you for trusting me."

I wiped my face with the back of my hand and gave her a weak smile. "No. Thank you. I needed that." I paused, thinking about Leviathan and all the crew. I thought about *how* Leviathan had looked at me.

Like I'd betrayed his trust.

I felt sick knowing that I had.

Finally, I was getting close. Finally seeing him under all the bravado he put up in front of his crew. Then those walls came flying back up again.

"What do I do now?"

"Everyone on this ship has been scorned by Varric one way or another. For now, you need to keep your head down. Mouth shut. I'm going to play negotiator, and if all goes well, Levi won't throw you overboard."

"Would he really throw me overboard?" I asked, ignoring the ache in my chest.

Seabird watched me closely. "In a heartbeat. But I won't let that happen. You put us in a bad situation. Especially if Pike is looking for you. The man is known for hunting pirates with nothing more than a spyglass and the scent of gunpowder."

I nodded. "I understand. I'm… I'm really sorry for causing so much trouble. I would've done anything to get away from him. I would rather die than be his shiny new wife."

Seabird rose to her feet, clearly pleased with my statement. "Good. You should never settle for that unless you truly want it." She paused, releasing a heavy breath while she adjusted her belt buckle. "Let me go get us dinner, lass. We can talk more when I return."

A symphony of music echoed down to the lower decks as it bled through the floorboards. A violinist was playing a raucous melody above me. The sailors in the mess sang along to it, chanting and humming, joining the music. I knew where the shanties came from but never discovered who was playing that melody.

"Who's that?" I asked.

"Stay put. I'll be back shortly."

She left, and all I could do was stare out the porthole window at the choppy waves and listen to the violinist play.

14

CAPTAIN LEVIATHAN

I SLAMMED the cabin door behind me. My hands were tightened into white-knuckle fists. I thought I could forget. I thought I had finally let it all go.

Heart throbbing in my ears, I gazed upon the brooch on my bedspread. It was carved from draconite.

Which one of my family died for her to wear it like a piece of jewelry?

She's a fucking eel.

I spiraled. Buried memories came back up to the surface. Old wounds torn open once more. Suddenly, it felt like I had lost my brothers all over again.

Like I was staring at my father's eyeless corpse across the room, two bloodied draconite gems attached to what was left of his eyes. I had known Varric was going to harvest mine next. I could feel paralysis in my veins. Even if I couldn't scream, I could still feel every sensation.

I thought I'd gotten better. The nightmares were gone. I didn't think about that night anymore. But now, it was back. All the pain. All the trauma.

It felt fresh.

My cabin door opened and closed. "You need to calm down, Levi."

"Fuck off, Howler."

"That's never going to happen. I didn't fuck off when you and Mama hid under Father's dock, and I'm not going to fuck off now." Howler walked over to my desk and pulled out a bottle of rum and two glasses. "You're my brother, and you're stuck with me."

I needed a drink.

"How'd you find out who she was?" he asked as he handed me the filled glass.

Taking a healthy gulp, I gestured to the brooch on my bedspread. "Boats found it pinned to the inside of Mae's waistband when she changed her clothes. She pulled me aside when she learned Mae woke up. I guess she didn't want me to smother the eel in her sleep."

Howler was quiet for a long moment, taking in the magnitude of our situation. Our stowaway was Maeve Cross, Lord Nathaniel Pike's wife. The wedding bells we heard at Farlight Harbor were for her.

Not only had she betrayed my trust by belonging to the family who brutalized mine, but she was the wife of a notorious hunter of both leviathans and pirates. Anything with a bounty. The Pikes had hunted the leviathans to the brink of extinction, selling and using the draconite behind their eyes to amplify their own magic and make war weapons.

My kind were pacifists—mutilated and used to fuel a war.

If there was anything I knew about Pike, it was that he never let anything go. He'd hunt Mae down and kill anyone who got between them.

Varric, on the other hand, was something else altogether. Something worse.

"Would you have?" Howler asked. "Smothered her?"

It was a serious question. "No. It doesn't matter how much I hate the Cross family; I'd never kill someone who couldn't fight back." I paused, finishing my drink. "I should've let her drown."

"But you didn't." Howler refilled my glass. "What are we going to do with her now?"

I don't fucking know.

"Ransom her. Maybe we can kill the whole lot of them when they come to Shipwreck Bay." I knew fair and well that was a terrible idea, but it did me a lot of good to hear Howler call me out on it.

"You're not thinking clearly right now."

"No, I'm not," I replied. "I'm really godsdamn angry, Howler."

"What can I do right now?" he asked. In my entire life, I could count on four people. The twins, my mother, and Wraith. As angry as I was, Howler would always be in my corner.

"You can leave me alone. I need some time to think."

He nodded. "Heard loud and clear. You know where to find me if you need anything."

I didn't say anything when he left, but my brother always knew how to take the edge off for me.

Not for a moment did I ever think that Mae would be an eel, but eels always hide their teeth. I thought of her doe eyes, the relief that filled me when I brought her back from the dead. How she felt when I scooped her up in my arms.

How much I liked it when she argued with me.

How soft her skin was under my roughened fingertips.

I ground my teeth together.

How long has she been playing me?

Did she know who I was? *What* I was? Was this all a clever play to infiltrate my ranks?

If he knew I lived, Varric would come for me. He'd bring his whole battalion for the chance to take my eyes. He'd kill my entire crew to get to me. Use me to murder more innocents than he already had.

I could never let that happen.

Shaking my head, I walked into my side room and grasped my violin. Whenever I spiraled, playing always soothed me. I tucked the violin under my chin, gliding the bow up and down the strings, then made a few subtle adjustments, noticing that they were slightly out of tune. Not enough for the casual listener, but I had the ear for it.

Then I let all my thoughts go, closing my eyes to pour all my ache into music.

After a few moments, the sailors on the underdeck joined my melody. Lutes, drums, and voices carried up to me. As tortured as I felt, I knew I was never alone in my torment.

Aside from my mates, my crew didn't know the history between my family and the Crosses. All they knew was that it was horrific. They didn't need the details.

I played and played, feeling every tense muscle relax as I started to let it go. Bury it back in the depths of my mind. Forget all about it. I was better when I forgot.

Then the door to my cabin opened again.

Would it kill them to fucking knock every once in a while?

I stopped playing, looking directly at my mother. She was obviously pissed. "Mama," I greeted, laying my violin on my bed.

"Don't *Mama* me like you've done nothing wrong," she snapped.

I scoffed.

"I didn't raise you to treat an innocent that way."

My eyes locked on hers. She was just as stubborn as me.

"Innocent? No Cross is innocent. Mae is an eel. Just as slippery as the rest of them."

Her jaw set. "*Ronin*," she hissed, using my birth name.

I stiffened.

"Mae wasn't even alive when the coup happened. She had nothing to do with it."

I stood up. "Why should that matter? She's benefitting off it all the same." I ground my teeth together as a buried memory flickered across my vision. All that blood. All that loss. Too much for a five-year-old to comprehend, but I remembered how it made me feel like it was yesterday.

All I want to do is forget.

Twenty-five *fucking* years, and I still couldn't forget.

"You weren't in that room, Mama. You didn't watch Varric carve out his eyes. You didn't *watch him die*," I nearly shouted, rage spouting up inside me like an overfilled pot boiling over a fire.

My mother looked away from me. Her throat bobbed as she gulped down tears.

All my pent-up anger evaporated. "I shouldn't have said that."

"I carry it with me." She was nearly silent. "I saw him there. I saw the fear in Martin's and Aiden's eyes. But you were the only one I could carry. You're not the only one who lost something that night."

"I'm sorry, Mama. I—"

She raised a hand to cut me off. "I don't want to hear it. My pain is not worse than yours. But I need you to remember that you're not the only one who hurts." She swallowed down the pain as she had for twenty-five years. "I can't go back. Neither can you. What we can do is move forward. I'm asking one thing of you. Hear the lass out. That's all."

"Why does this matter so much to you?"

"Because the man who mutilated children is the same man you will be sending Mae back to. Just sit down with her. Have dinner. *Listen*."

I was quiet for a few moments. I would do anything for my mother. This was no different. "Since this matters so much to you, I will."

"Thank you."

"But it won't be tonight. Or tomorrow night. I will have dinner with her whenever I damn well feel like it. Until then, we have a week and a half before we reach Shipwreck Bay. I don't give a fuck what you do with her. Just keep her away from me," I said, laying out my terms clearly. I wasn't in the right mindset to see Mae, much less listen to her.

She agreed before leaving.

It was time for dinner, but I couldn't eat anything anyway. Instead, I shed my clothes and turned in early.

My pillows smelled like her.

Like cinnamon and springtime.

Conflicted feelings warred inside me. Guilt from humiliating her in front of my crew. Throwing her down onto the deck and fighting with her. Nothing she could've done would've changed my mind then.

I was betrayed by her lineage.

Then I got so fucking angry when my crew got a glimpse of her freckled thighs revealed by how little she wore. My gut reaction made absolutely no sense to me. I put her in that position, and then I had the gall to be angry that my crew was *looking*?

I didn't have the energy to deal with my emotions anymore.

I wanted to lock them away and forget.

Just forget.

I'd already forgotten what my father looked like. What

my brothers looked like. I couldn't even remember my father's voice. Every good memory I had—forgotten. I had more memories of Howler's father than my own.

Whenever I thought of mine, all I could see was his cold, dead body, holes where his eyes should be. The rest of him was a blur.

That image haunted me.

Haunted my nightmares.

Haunted me during the day.

I'd never escape the Cross family.

15
MAEVE CROSS

I didn't understand.

Even as I sat on the bench in the greenhouse, staring out at the sea, I thought about Leviathan's reaction to my family crest.

What did my family *do* to him? It felt visceral. I could feel the rage roll off him, and I didn't know what made me feel worse: being ransomed back to the people I was running from or the fact that my father had perpetrated unspeakable acts of horror against so many people.

I stared out at the ocean.

A chill swept over my skin as I sat surrounded by the greenery and the sound of rushing water through the irrigation system.

"We aren't a charity."

Leviathan was right. He didn't owe me anything. He didn't have to do me a favor, especially considering what my family had done. Whatever it was, it was abhorrent.

Would I *let* Leviathan ransom me back to Nathaniel or my father? Not a chance in any of the Hells.

I refused to live my life attached to Nathaniel.

I would not live in a prison where the only reason I'd have to live was to sire his heirs. I would not be his servant nor be reduced into a pretty plaything. I would not absorb every strike because he felt like pushing me around.

I'd get my freedom even if I had to fight a ship full of pirates for it.

The way I saw it, I only had a few options.

Convince Leviathan to listen to me. He was the captain. He made the final calls. If he decided to let me go, no one would push back. I had to appeal to his humanity somehow.

Rippling waves rocked the ship side to side, but I didn't sway. Clouds shrouded the sun, darkening the skies. A rumble sounded off in the distance.

A storm was coming.

No land in sight. Nowhere to run. Not yet.

Fat raindrops splattered against the glass, drumming a melody along with the waves.

If I couldn't convince Leviathan to let me go, then I would fight him the second we hit land. I knew we were going to Shipwreck Bay, a pirate safehold. The center of their trade. There'd be places to hide there. Other ships to stow away on.

All things considered, the crew on *The Ollipheist* treated me well. I couldn't be sure another ship would spare me the same courtesy.

But what other choice did I have?

I didn't want to hurt anyone, but when it came down to it, I would.

"There you are," Wraith said, breaking my train of thought. "I've been looking for you, Princess."

Instantly, I stiffened. I hadn't even heard her footsteps. Wraith was a woman I never wanted behind my back. I searched for her, whirling around on my heel to keep my eyes on her at all times. "You found me."

She looked at me from under the brim of her hat, piercing me with her eyes. Droplets of rain deepened the brown of her leather coat. "Storm's brewing. You should get to the lower deck."

"I can't stay on deck? Help where needed?" I asked. If I made myself indispensable, then Leviathan wouldn't be able to get rid of me. Not easily, at least. If I couldn't get to Leviathan, I could get to his mates.

They'd do the hard work for me.

Wraith released a low, rumbly laugh. "Oh, please, love. You'd fall off the ship the second we hit choppy water. And this time, Cap won't save you."

No, he won't. "Give me something to do."

She tipped her hat back, arching a brow. The points on her ears were prominent with her hair tucked back. "It would be an easy night to have off. Especially for a princess."

"I don't care. I won't be useless."

In an instant, she moved soundlessly toward me.

My heart kicked up, and I took a step backward, my back hitting the raised plant bed.

"I know what you're doing."

I gulped thickly. "Then you know the stakes."

Her hand snapped out to my chin, grasping it hard enough to keep me still. The calluses on her fingers scratched up my skin as she slowly pushed my hair back, intense eyes flickering over my ears.

What in the Hells is she looking at?

"What are you doing?" I hissed, trying to withdraw, but she wouldn't let me.

Suddenly, she released me and took steps back to maintain the distance between us again. "What happened to your ears?"

My hands flew up to the tops of my ears. I felt the subtly rough skin there. My eyebrows came together. "Uh… birthmarks. I've had them as long as I can remember."

"On both?"

Her question caught me off guard. "Yes. Why?"

Wraith deferred the conversation. "If you want a job, go to Gunny. His crew bails the water out of the hull if we spring a leak."

"What about Boats?" I wondered.

"Boats and the ship crew are on top deck, manning the sails and rigging. We need to keep moving through the waves. Otherwise, the ocean would tear us into scrap." The rain started to fall harder. "Lower deck. I won't repeat myself."

"Aye," I agreed, leaving the greenhouse to go to the gundeck.

The rain splattered against the main deck as the storm brewed overhead. After Leviathan revealed my identity, I stayed in the room with Seabird for the first few nights. She wanted to make sure it was safe for me. I hadn't seen him since, and I felt relieved but also perhaps a little disappointed.

I'd been excused from my duties, but I got restless and helped Shep with the animals.

He never asked questions and never treated me any differently. Honestly, I think he liked the company. I got on with him really well. Shep was always nice to me, like Butcher was. They never made me feel like I didn't belong.

The first night back in the officers' quarters was strange. They didn't know what to do with me, but I wanted to work.

It was enough. I kept my head down and worked for the next week, ensuring that I was useful.

The other sailors weren't so cordial. I was often greeted with "Hi, Princess," like my title amused them. Oh Gods, I hoped that wasn't going to be my pirate moniker.

"Evenin', Mae," Luther said shyly from the mess hall doorway.

I paused, looking over at the gangly, red-faced cabin boy. "Good evening to you too." Even though he was the reason I fell overboard and upended my initial plan of freedom, I had no ill will toward him. It was an accident, and I knew he felt bad enough about it without me rubbing salt in the wound.

"Are you doing all right?" He rubbed his hands together like they were dirty.

"I am. Yourself?"

"Good, miss. A few cabin boys and meself have the night off. You're welcome to join us for cards," he offered.

It was a sweet gesture. I gave him a smile. "Thank you, but I'm going to help Gunny with bailing."

"Oh. Okay. Have a good night, then," he said, turning awkwardly and going back into the mess. I heard whispers from the other cabin crew. I couldn't make out what they were saying, but I did hear Luther reply, "I tried. She's bailin'."

Then noises of disappointment.

I almost cried. It was nice to hear that some of the crew still wanted to spend time with me. Maybe another time. Right now, what mattered was showing I could be useful. Get Leviathan to see me as something other than *Princess of Farlight Isles*.

"Oi! Princess!" I heard Gunny shout from the armory.

If his crew keeps calling me that, Leviathan will never forget my title.

"What're you doin' 'ere, birdie?" He sat at a table, playing bones with his assistant, Spider. The rest of his subordinates were sitting around the armory, playing cards, and eating some sea biscuits.

Waiting for orders, I realized.

Gunny waved me over to his table, and I had a look at the score.

Looks like Spider is winning right now. The gunnery assistant had a big smile, proving that he knew just how good he was at playing. He shook the bones in a cup before turning it over to reveal more high-scoring dots carved on the top of the knucklebones.

Gunny groaned, "Blimey! You're a cheat."

"Don't be such a poor sport," Spider teased.

I sat down on the vacant barrel. "Here for work," I answered. "Heard you need help bailing."

Gunny grinned, revealing that twisted canine. "You love gettin' your hands dirty, don't cha?"

For once he wasn't covered in grease or metal shavings. Without all the gunk, he could be quite handsome with his upturned friendly eyes and healthy tawny skin. A light sprinkling of stubble, though it was patchy.

His hair was cropped short, and he usually had a bandana wrapped around his forehead. It wasn't as brightly colored as what Howler wore, but it suited Gunny's personality.

"You know me, Gunny. I hate sitting still."

He nudged me with his shoulder. "Don' I know it." He tossed the bones into the cup and shook it a few times. "We patched the split from the last storm, but we're on standby in case it springs a leak. Already sealed all the deadlights too. Not much to do now." Gunny turned the cup over, revealing yet another terrible roll.

"Not your game, hm?" I teased, feeling comfortable enough around Gunny to give him a hard time.

"Lady Luck doesn't favor me today." He paused, scratching his chin before shooting me a dazzling smile. "How about you play a few turns for me, eh? Or would you rather go be alone in the officers' quarters?"

"I'll play. Though I'm surprised I haven't been thrown in the pit yet, or at least put down here with the rest of you," I said, taking the cup of bones.

Gunny shrugged. "I don't dwell on what Cap thinks. He's got his own reasons, and I'll leave it at that."

I rolled the bones before dumping them out. Gunny clapped when he saw that I rolled better than him. Spider, on the other hand, shook his head.

"Takin' the easy way out, ain't you, Gun?" Spider huffed playfully before he took the cup from me. "I prefer you in the officers' quarters anyway. More room for us down here," he said. "Besides, I like my hammock. Good for my back. And you look like you snore."

"I do *not* snore," I gasped.

Spider waved me off with an under-his-breath laugh. "You know, it's funny. We noticed all the wedding banners for a royal wedding in Farlight Harbor, but not once did we think that same bride would be on our ship."

"Small world," Gunny commented.

"It really is," I agreed, enjoying this moment of normalcy.

The storm raged above us, rocking the ship back and forth. The hole never sprang, and whatever leaked in from the rain was easily bailed out. I had a good time with the gunnery crew, and I didn't feel like an outsider with them either.

The only one who seemed to care where I came from was Leviathan.

16
CAPTAIN LEVIATHAN

"You were right about her ears." Wraith's voice carried over to me as she climbed the ladder onto the flat deck on top of my quarters.

I had a bottle of rum resting next to my leg, ready to be shared with my mates.

The stars were bright in the sky, glowing against the dark water. My mates and I liked to gather a week before we docked to enjoy the stars before the light pollution of Shipwreck Bay dulled them.

"Oh?" I said, encouraging her to continue.

"The marks on them are odd. If I didn't know any better, I'd think her ears were tipped," she continued, sitting down on the stool next to me. She grabbed the bottle and uncorked it with her teeth before handing it back to me.

"Why would the Princess of Farlight have tipped ears?"

Wraith hummed, keeping her voice hushed. "I'm unsure. But there's more there. It's possible she's a ward."

"Or she's a liar." She'd proven to me that she was not above lying, but also that she wasn't very good at it.

Unless that was her game.

Wraith shook her head. "I don't think she knows."

My lips parted to say something else, but Howler interrupted from the bottom of the ladder. "Eh! Levi! Got the good stuff?"

I lifted my bottle of rum. "Always," I replied, grinning to hide the seriousness of Wraith's and my discussion before dismissing it altogether. It would be kept between the two of us until I knew what to do with it.

I didn't want to think about the doe-eyed girl who'd dragged my crew into her marital spat.

Boats followed Howler up the ladder and took a comfortable seat on the deck between Wraith's parted legs. She leaned back, seeking comfort that only her wife could give her.

"Love," Wraith started, curling a frayed braid around her fingertips. "A few of your braids are unfurling. Do you want me to freshen them up?"

Wraith wasn't an affectionate woman, but if there was one person she was soft for, it was her wife. Boats nodded, falling slack the second Wraith gently undid a braid with a pick.

We passed the bottle of rum around, catching up on all the little things we didn't usually have time for early on in the voyage. And as usual when Howler had too much to drink, he started gushing about his wife, four daughters, and one little baby boy waiting for him back home.

Long voyages were hard on him and his family, but his wife, Isa, knew how much Howler loved the sea. She'd never get between him and his other love. Additionally, I was sure the coin helped keep food on the table for five rugrats.

Boats rattled off gossip she'd caught from the lower decks while Wraith silently braided her hair. She put the gold cuffs back in place to adorn the pretty braid and then moved on to the next one.

"The cabin boys have quite the crush on Mae," Boats continued, laughing heartily as she tipped back the rum before passing the bottle back to her twin.

Wraith chuckled. "Doesn't surprise me. She's pretty. Second-prettiest lady on the ship." She pressed a kiss on the top of Boats's forehead.

"Oh, hush, you," Boats muttered, reciprocating the affection.

"I'd rather not talk about her," I stated. I gulped down the golden liquid to numb the odd sensation twisting in my chest. Unfortunately, I had an abnormally high tolerance. I'd feel fuzzy but never drunk unless I really indulged.

I wanted to be drunk.

My mates looked at one another before focusing back on me. Howler silenced himself by taking another drink.

"Oh, she doesn't reciprocate any of their feelings, Levi," Boats jested, her cheeks flushing from the booze and bringing out the red undertones in her skin.

My eyebrows jumped into my hairline, and I tipped my hat back. "I wouldn't care if she did," I replied from between my teeth. I shook it off. "No, my mother requested that I have dinner with her. Hear her side of the story. I'm not interested in hearing what an eel has to say."

"You probably should hear her out," Howler said quietly, gauging how I'd react.

It was safe to say that I wasn't angry anymore, but I also hadn't seen Mae since my outburst. "I'm not going to listen to a liar," I argued.

"But if you told Seabird you'd hear her out, then you oughta do it," Boats tacked on.

I groaned, looking away completely to steal the bottle of

rum. I wanted to forget that Mae was even on the ship, forget how sweet her face looked, from those wide brown eyes to her petal-pink lips.

I needed to stop thinking about her mouth. It didn't matter how attractive I found her; it didn't change what her family did to mine.

"The girl is trying incredibly hard to impress you, Levi," Wraith said. "She takes on extra tasks every day. Jumps around to help Shep and Butcher. Doesn't even turn in until after she scrubs dishes. She's got the spirit."

My shoulders stiffened.

"What is it you always say? Hm?"

I knew where Wraith was going with this, and I wasn't happy about it.

She answered her own question. "We don't do favors, but we reward hard work."

"Throw her a bone, mate," Howler agreed. "Just get it over with."

I didn't reply.

"Unless…," Boats started, and I could hear the smile in her tone.

"Don't say what I think you're going to say," I warned, looking back at her to see the same shit-eating grin I'd normally encounter on her brother.

"What happened that night? The first night when she was in your cabin? Hm? Howler said she was tied to the ballast. And poor Mae didn't utter a word about it," Boats continued, waggling her brows.

"Do you honestly think I fucked her?" I crossed my arms, glaring daggers. I'd be lying if I said I hadn't thought about it. But fantasies were very different from reality. It didn't matter that I often wondered how she'd look underneath me.

Once I cooled off, my skin would tighten again, a heat

welling in my belly. The traitorous bastard in my trousers would press against the placket of my pants if I so much as smelled her hair on my pillows or remembered how small she looked curled up in the furs.

Would those wide eyes gloss over in wonderment if I found myself between her—

Enough.

An eel wasn't worth the fascination. Certainly not worth getting hard over. My cock, however, didn't get the message. I'd stripped my bed, washing all trace of Mae from my bedspread. But I couldn't seem to get her out of my head.

"Didn't you?" Howler asked.

"No!" I hissed. "Of course not!"

"Come now, Levi," Wraith said. "No one ever gets away with talking to you like she does. Someone with even one eye could see that you fancy her."

"Like I fancy ringworm."

Out of the corner of my eye, I caught the top of Gunny's head peeking over the railing. He popped his head up, cheeks pink as he muttered, "This seems like a private conversation."

"You tell anyone what you just heard and I'll feed you to the sharks," I threatened, the vein in my neck popping. Whether from embarrassment or irritation, I couldn't be sure.

"I would *never*, Cap. Never," Gunny promised, a grin in his voice. Then I heard him clamber back down the ladder, chuckling to himself as he disappeared under the deck.

"Fucking Hells. He's going to tell everyone." I pressed my face into my hands, then looked up, glaring at all the smug assholes I called my mates. "Can we just leave it?"

"So you do fancy the princess?" Howler commented.

"Do I fancy the woman whose family murdered mine while she waits in line to sit upon the throne meant for me?"

I tasted each word, and they tasted as ridiculous as they sounded. "Do you lot even hear yourselves?"

Wraith laughed under her breath, finishing another one of Boats's braids. "Then prove it."

"Prove it?" I spat back. "How do you suggest I do that when you lot and the rest of the damn crew have already made up their minds? Does everyone think I slept with her?"

"It's the steamiest gossip we get around here," Boats replied.

I waved her off, heat rising in my face.

Wraith shrugged, keeping her expression neutral. "Go have dinner with her. Get it all out of your system."

The second Wraith said *get it all out of your system*, all I could think about was gripping Mae's throat while I slid inside her.

Is she a screamer?

Fucking hell. The only reason I was thinking about it was because I'd been celibate for months. I've been in somewhat of a dry spell since the last woman I'd taken to bed robbed me before I woke up the next morning. Of *course* the next woman who got me going would be the heir to a *murderer*.

"Fine. Go get her. I'll hear her out right now," I just about snarled. "Give me that." I plucked the bottle of rum from Wraith's hands.

She laughed out loud. "You'll need it more than me."

Boats sat up. "Right now? It's the middle of the night. She's probably sleeping."

"Good. Then I'll irritate her as much as she irritates me. Maybe this time she won't lie to me."

Before any of my mates could respond, I went down the ladder and into my cabin. I could hear the three of them having a laugh at my frustration.

My friends were assholes.

I tipped back more rum, trying to distract myself from the unfettered excitement whirling in my veins.

Do I fancy her?

I huffed. No. Of course not.

Then why the fuck was I so nervous?

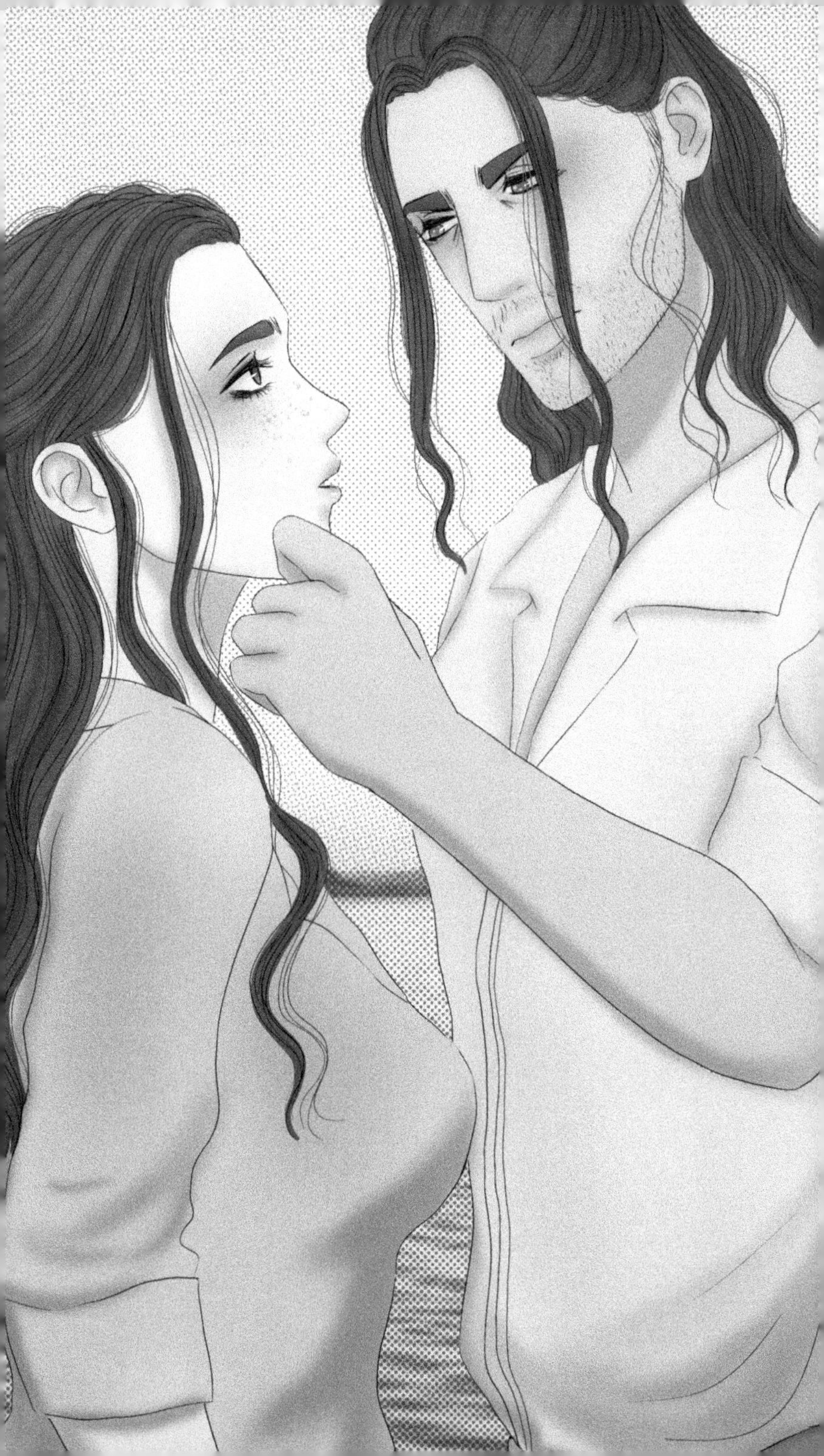

17
MAEVE CROSS

"Wake up, lass." Wraith's voice stirred me from a deep slumber. Two hands jostled me by my shoulders. My head lolled back and forth as sleep tried to drag me back under.

I grumbled something incoherent, blinking slowly, crusted slobber on the side of my mouth.

"Come now, love. Levi isn't going to wait all night for you," Wraith continued.

I shook my head. "Nuh-uh. Sleep now."

My back fell against my bunk, and my eyes rolled closed again.

Ah. Sweet, sweet sleep.

Wait.

Leviathan is waiting for me?

My eyes flew open, and I lurched upward out of bed. I turned my head to see all three of the mates staring at me. "W—" I looked between them. "Why are you three staring at me?"

"Does she always snore?" Howler asked.

"Every night," Wraith replied. "You just sleep through it."

I shook my head, too tired to feel offended by the snoring

comment. With the back of my hand, I rubbed away sleep sand from the corners of my eyes. "It's the middle of the night. What does he want?"

"He's ready to hear you out," Wraith answered.

"This can't wait until morning?"

Howler laughed, climbing into his bunk. "Levi is rarely in a listenin' mood. You oughta go while you can."

He had a point.

I groaned. "All right. All right. Is he in his cabin?"

"Mm-hmm, with a bottle o' rum to share with you," Boats tacked on, getting ready for bed.

With a bottle of rum? In the middle of the night?

My cheeks started to heat, goose bumps rising up and down my arms. Sure, I'd been alone with him before on several occasions, but the idea of sneaking into his cabin in the middle of the night caused all sorts of indecent images to flash across my mind.

I mean, I wasn't exactly *sneaking*, but still.

I shook them off. Last time I spoke to Leviathan, he threatened to kill me.

"If I don't come back, assume he killed me," I muttered, tugging on my jacket and socks. It was a cold night, and I didn't have the luxury of a fur blanket.

Howler snickered but didn't say anything.

Why did I have the feeling that they knew something I didn't? Not bothering to dwell on it, I tiptoed out of the officers' quarters and up the steps right outside. The hatch opened directly in front of the captain's cabin.

I climbed up, then closed the hatch softly.

The night crew were doing their rounds, taking a second to notice me, whisper among themselves, and go back to whatever they were doing. I crossed my arms, my heart galloping in my chest, eager to leap out of my mouth.

Why was I so nervous?

I gulped down my nerves and brought my fist up to knock on his door. The night helmsman chortled under his breath but didn't say anything.

A sailor I'd never met before eyed me up and down, armed with knives and pistols. A vanguard, I realized. They only ever worked nights.

The door opened, and I couldn't stop my cheeks from warming as I looked up at Leviathan. I felt tingly all over, my face on fire. As usual, his shirt was half unbuttoned, distracting me briefly before I uttered, "A little late for dinner, don't you think?"

The corner of his mouth twitched. "Not too late for a drink. Come. Let's talk."

I frowned, but I didn't argue. I wasn't in the place to argue. He stepped aside, and I went beside him. I felt it when he closed the door, his presence consuming me.

His cabin smelled like brisk sea air and cedar, a mouth-watering scent that never ceased to make my belly coil. Leviathan brushed by me, the light touch making me shudder.

During the night, it was significantly quieter.

No chatter from the crew on deck.

No shanties from the belly of the ship.

Just Leviathan and me with the roar of waves lapping against the hull.

He kicked his boots up onto the small table by the window as he took a seat, then gestured across from him. I trudged over to him as if my legs were made of lead.

"Do you want a drink this time?" he asked. "I know I need one to get through this conversation."

I glanced at the bottle of the golden liquid I'd been

curious to try but too cautious to taste. "What harm could it do?"

I didn't need to keep up with my lies anymore. He already knew my identity.

He poured two glasses of rum before sliding one over to me.

How did I not notice how big his hands were before?

Shaking my head, I lifted the glass, tilted it toward him, and then took a sip.

Oh holy Hells.

Ugh.

I couldn't hide my distaste as I sputtered, coughing loudly as the liquid fire scraped down my throat and burned my nostrils.

When I finally got my senses back, Leviathan was repressing a grin, but one of his dimples betrayed him.

"Can't handle your liquor, sweetheart?"

That *tone*. I hated that condescending tone! I kept direct eye contact with him, my nostrils flaring as I took one more grueling sip. I swallowed thickly. "You don't know anything about me. Don't pretend like you do."

"Oh, *forgive me*, Princess," he replied, still using that better-than-you tone.

I narrowed my eyes, running my tongue over my teeth.

"All right." He put both of his hands up in mock surrender. "Let's skip all the fucking pleasantries. Why shouldn't I send you back home?"

I chewed on the inside of my cheek, trying to think of the right way to say it. How could I make Leviathan understand my predicament?

He leaned forward over the table, those intense eyes searching mine. My mouth felt dry, my breath catching in the back of my throat. Gods, my heart dropped into my belly.

He was barely a foot away from me, and I could smell the rum on his breath.

For something with such a ghastly taste, I didn't know why it smelled so mouthwatering on him.

"If you don't want to talk, fine," he said, hot breath washing over my face. "Once we get to Shipwreck Bay, I'll send you on your way."

Every word brought him a little closer, and I tilted my head to the side, enraptured by his mouth. The sharpness of his jaw. A strong nose that had clearly been broken a few times. His pink lips seemed too full and soft to match the ruggedness of his face.

Then the corner of his mouth turned up, showing off one of his dimples. "After I collect on you, of course."

I reeled back, a bout of anger bubbling in my belly. I made a noise of frustration, my chair creaking as I stood up. I turned completely away from him with my arms crossed. Knickknacks lined his book-laden shelves. Some dragon memorabilia here and there. A folded piece of parchment covered with smudged ink.

At first glance, Leviathan didn't seem to be the type of man who had keepsakes.

But he was only human, like I was.

My stiffened shoulders relaxed as I accepted that there was no point in fighting. No point in trying to hide anything. He would make his decision on what to do with me. If I couldn't convince him, then I'd fight until my last breath.

Here goes nothing....

"Freedom matters to me more than anything," I murmured, severing the silence between us. I turned back around, goose bumps rising all over my skin as I met his intense eyes again.

"As it does to us," he conceded, gesturing for me to continue.

I took a deep breath, struggling with myself to get the words out. "My entire life, I'd been groomed to be a docile, subservient woman—"

Leviathan chuckled under his breath. "I don't believe that."

"Well, it's true. Don't interrupt me."

Both sides of his mouth curled up, revealing those dimples that haunted me. "Right. Continue."

I sighed. "My father reprimanded me whenever I went against his word. Which was… a lot. It doesn't matter. What matters is that I was married off to Nathaniel Pike because my father wanted his army."

"His army?" Leviathan asked, the smile falling off his face completely. The lilt in his voice turned dead serious. "What for?"

I didn't know whether or not I should be telling him, but I supposed it was necessary information. Maybe it would be my ticket to freedom.

"My father's study was next to my bedroom," I stated. "I assumed it was because he always wanted eyes on me. I was, after all, his bargaining chip. However, if I pressed my ear against the wall, I could hear his private conversations when he got impassioned."

"Go on."

"All I know is that Nathaniel would give my father his resources after we married. I'd be his pretty new wife, and he'd take the army to the pirate safehold and draft all the criminals. Join the military or be hanged for treason," I answered.

Leviathan blew out a heavy breath from his nose. "Of fucking course." He stood up completely as if he was no longer comfortable sitting down. He took several steps toward me, and I nearly buckled at the knees. "What does he want the army for?"

"I... I don't know," I replied honestly, averting my gaze. My father was private most of the time. I didn't know much about his plans aside from the snippets I'd overheard.

Leviathan's hand shot out to grasp my chin and tilt my head up. "Look me in the eye, Maeve."

My eyes snapped to his.

Leviathan has never used my full name before....

So when I heard it from his lips, it captured my attention completely. I gulped thickly, his proximity overwhelming me as my knees shook. The scratchiness of his calloused hand rubbed against my skin. His touch ignited warmth in my belly, my eyes going wide as the heat welled between my thighs.

"I-I don't know," I whispered again, losing myself in his intense gaze.

He kept me there in his grasp. I couldn't move away from him if I tried. I was trapped. And for a moment, I swore I saw his eyes flicker down to my mouth.

At that exact moment, I yearned to feel his lips against mine. To taste the rum on his breath. To suffocate in the scent of sea air and cedar.

I couldn't hide my reaction. My back arched, my eyes locking on to his lips before I met his gaze again. My breath accelerated. My blood roared in my ears. There was a tingling in my spine. My lips parted ever so slightly with invitation.

He released me, instantly moving away from me. I fell slack against the shelf, hot all over.

My cheeks mottled with mortification. *Oh Gods*, that's not

why I was here. There was no doubt in my mind that he recognized my reaction but didn't reciprocate it.

What in the Hells am I doing?

Leviathan maintained several feet between us, elongating his form against his desk. He crossed his arms as if blocking himself off from me. "I believe you. Continue with your tale."

I nodded, trying to get my wits about me before I spoke. "My father would do anything for that army. Including selling me off to an abusive man who would find another high tower to lock me away in."

"Those marks on your neck that first night," Leviathan started. "Pike did that?"

I nodded.

A tic formed in his jaw.

This was the moment that I expected him to share Seabird's reaction. Tell me that I did the right thing by running.

"That's a nice story, *Princess*. But that doesn't change a damn thing."

It took me a full moment to respond. "What? After everything I just told you, you'd still send me back into the arms of the men who... who...." *Who would hurt me.*

But Leviathan wouldn't care about that.

He slammed his hand onto his desk, and I caught the familiar glimmer of rage in his eyes. It was softer than the first time. Not as volatile. "The bottom line, sweetheart, is that you can be *my* bargaining chip now."

I went cold. "You're no different than they are."

A tendon in his neck strained. "I'm *nothing* like them," he nearly snarled. "This is survival. Nothing personal."

Traitorous tears welled in my eyes. I ground my teeth together, finding the anger inside myself. "You're a *monster*. Just like them."

In an instant, I was shoved hard against a bookcase. That same calloused hand that I'd leaned into moments ago fastened around my throat. I gasped, sandwiched there between the bookcase and Leviathan's brawny frame.

My hands flew up against his chest, torn between shoving him away and… I didn't know what. I just knew that I didn't completely hate being caged in if he was the one looming over me.

His body was painfully solid against my hands.

"That's not the first time I've been called a *monster*, and it won't be the last," he answered, eyes blazing. "Enjoy your freedom while it lasts."

I stared into his eyes with indignation, my upper lip pulling up as I hissed, "You'd sell an innocent woman to protect yourself?"

He closed the distance between us even more, and I could feel his breath fan my face. His smell filled my nose, and I hated the way it made me feel. I teetered on the line between being incredibly aroused and blazingly *pissed off*.

"Wrong," Leviathan answered, his voice incredibly low. The blue flecks in his eyes looked brighter. "I'd sell an innocent to protect my crew. I'd do *anything* to protect them from Varric Cross." His breathing accelerated. I could feel his heart slamming hard against his ribs. "If… if you *knew*—"

His voice nearly broke, and I got the first glimpse of an old wound that had healed poorly and ripped open again whenever something agitated it.

Me. *I'd* ripped it open.

A myriad of emotions assaulted me. Simmering rage. A coiling desire. Guilt. I didn't know what I wanted. I didn't know what to do. I didn't know why I *cared*.

His hand left my throat to press against the bookshelf beside my head. "We do what we have to for survival." His words sounded tortured. "You don't... you'll never understand."

I stared up at him and murmured, "*Make* me understand."

"I can't."

Leviathan was so close to me. A breath left his lips, and I watched the battle in his eyes. I wanted to understand. To know why he was acting like this. How could I possibly get through to him?

Before I could do anything—*say* anything—he pulled back, a strange expression in his eyes. He looked at his door, his entire body growing rigid.

"Stay here," he ordered.

I went to follow him, and he stopped, whirling around to glare at me.

"If I have to repeat myself, I'm going to cuff you to the fucking ballast again."

A lump formed in my throat as I stopped midstep.

"You'll know when it's safe."

Safe?

Leviathan didn't elaborate as he charged toward his door. He closed it hard behind him. Then there was the distinct *click* of his lock from the other side.

Before another moment could pass, I heard something I'd never heard before.

A warning bell.

18
MAEVE CROSS

Noise erupted outside the cabin door.

"*Move! Tie your safeties!*" Leviathan roared above the ruckus, cutting through the sounds of terror. "*Go! Go! Below deck! Now!*"

I could hear the urgency. The pure, guttural command of it.

Howler's voice carried just as far. I couldn't make out what he was saying, but I knew it was important.

Ding. Ding. Ding.

The warning bell rang with the same urgency that Leviathan had displayed. I heard the clattering of swords as if belts full of gear were colliding with the deck.

That's when I heard it.

The song.

A hymn of slow, hypnotic music. It clogged my ears. Shadowed my sight. Like a shroud of darkness looming over me. Blood filled my mouth as I bit down hard on my tongue. The music numbed me like the most potent anesthetic.

The song morphed. It became grinding. Like metal scraping metal.

Wrong.

It didn't sound beautiful. It sounded wrong.

Something inside me twisted.

Almost instantly, all my senses came back to me. I knew, deep inside with everything in me, that I couldn't stay in Leviathan's cabin. I didn't know why the effect of a siren song had suddenly gone away, but I didn't care.

Grabbing the door handle, I jiggled it, testing the sturdiness of his lock.

Damn it.

The song got louder. Splashing joined the cacophony of noise. Outside Leviathan's window, I could see shadowed creatures rising from the ocean. Multicolored fishtails in the moonlight. Smooth like sharkskin. Extended fleshy wings dragging their bodies up to the deck.

Move faster, Mae.

My heartbeat raged in my chest, my breathing accelerating as I found a heavy paperweight on Leviathan's desk. Small, made of iron, it didn't look important. Instantly, I threw it into the small window next to the door. The opening was just big enough for me to climb out.

I needed to help.

I wasn't going to sit there useless.

No way in the Nine Hells.

The glass shattered, the trinket bouncing back inside onto Leviathan's floor. I didn't have time to be safe about climbing out. I kicked a leg out, pants protecting my legs from the jagged shards.

I moved fast, almost on an instinct I didn't understand.

The song warped further, sounding like the screeching of birds. Down the deck, I noticed sailors attached at the waist to the mainmast, their arms extended toward the beasts like they were beautiful nymphs.

I scanned my surroundings, hair rising on the back of my neck. Where was Leviathan?

Dread sank its claws into me as a morbid thought rang through my head.

Have the sirens already taken him?

I tamped it down. If that was the case, then I... I was the only one not under the thrall of the siren song. It was up to me to stop this.

I didn't have time to be afraid.

A lever pulled inside me, and my hands squeezed into fists.

I have to do this.

Howler crouched over the hatch leading down to the lower decks, his hands shaking as he gripped his safety harness. He flicked the metal hook at the end, trying to attach it to the knot.

He was fighting the song.

But he was losing.

I saw the moment the hypnosis took root, his entire body going slack as he stood up completely. Beside him, another sailor had lost control over themselves. The vanguard's body dragged itself to the lip, where he tossed himself overboard. His hand was still on his safety, but he'd run out of time to secure it.

I didn't know what to do. Ice was injected into my veins as I watched Howler. No reaction on his face. The hypnosis was deeply ingrained in him as he... stood there. And watched.

A siren swooped up, talons from its hands hooked into the vanguard I'd seen earlier, hoisting him up into the air.

A waterfall of blood rained down on Howler as the siren feasted on the vanguard. His gear landed on the deck as his flesh tore with a horrible wet noise.

The siren made a crooning noise as it dropped the vanguard's corpse into the water for her kin to devour.

My eyes locked on to the discarded gear.

A cutlass.

A pistol.

Howler moved toward the song, ready to throw himself overboard.

"*No.*"

Before I could think, I sprinted toward him, throwing my entire bodyweight against Howler. It clearly took him by surprise as he flopped down like a fish. Howler lay there, moving blindly toward the song. Not even reacting to my weight on top of him.

I pushed him back down as I grabbed the hook on his safety and attached it to the knots securing one of the several sacks along the half wall. Howler squirmed but didn't try to undo his safety.

His kind dark eyes were glazed over. But underneath the glaze, I could see a sliver of realization. Like he knew what was happening but had no control over himself.

Thump.

Only a few feet in front of me, I heard the loud, wet slap of a tail. Something heavy landing on the deck. A shrill hiss.

My entire body went rigid.

But despite every single warning bell going off in my head and every inner thought begging me not to look—I rebelled against them.

I will not be afraid.

A hot breath left my nose as I slowly looked up, going eye to eye with the same beast who'd devoured a vanguard right in front of me. Blood streaked down her gaping maw containing rows and rows of teeth, like a shark.

There were no scales on her tail. It was entirely smooth. She looked nothing like the depictions I'd seen of sirens.

Beady black eyes. Long blonde hair concealing gills along her throat. A flat, inhuman nose that was nothing more than two slits in the center of her face. Her head twitched to the side as she eyed me closely. I stared right back, not daring to look away as she tilted her head back and *shrieked.*

It didn't sound like a song. More like the grating call of a bird. She swayed from side to side, almost serpentine, preparing herself to lunge. Her clawed hands were webbed, her extended wings the same oil-slick color of her body. Her skin stretched over thin fishbones. The shape of them wasn't birdlike at all but more like a bat.

She cawed again, but this time, it didn't sound like a bird. Her throat bobbed as she uttered the word "*Sentry.*" Her voice undulated with a sharp, skittering laugh.

I must've imagined that. Sirens didn't speak. Not like merrows.

How did I know that?

A flash of something came over my eyes.

The merrows in the Gullies. The matriarch would brush my hair. The shoal would play with me. Feed me grilled fish. Read me stories about Cliohde and—

A screech broke me from my thoughts. I dove for the vanguard's gear and yanked the cutlass free from the sash. I took a stance, moving exactly like how I'd seen Leviathan wield a cutlass—ironically, when he'd pointed it at me.

"You will not hurt my friends."

The siren looked me up and down before opening her throat and trilling in what I could only perceive was amusement. "*Watch me.*"

She slapped her tail against the deck, extending bat-like

wings toward me. Then she charged, slithering with massive muscles tensing in her tail.

I swung, slashing toward her wings.

But before she could come at me like a battering ram, she stopped in her tracks. Fear washed over her face. She instantly turned away from me, slithered off the deck, and dove into the ocean.

Confusion squeezed my eyebrows together as the song came to a sudden stop, the nighttime sounds of water lapping the hull of the ship replacing it altogether.

Suddenly, a massive huff of hot breath blew into my hair.

I jumped, spinning on my heel and meeting the eyes of a... a... *leviathan.*

The cutlass slipped from my fingers and clattered against the planks.

The massive head of the sea serpent was just above the water, looking directly at me. It had a mouth full of teeth that were bigger than I was. But I didn't feel afraid. Not when I saw dark eyes with speckles of glimmering blue within them.

Leviathan's eyes.

A hot feeling of shame welled in my belly at the thought that I knew, in detail, what his eyes looked like. The blue flecks were like crystals, shining brightly.

Like draconite.

A sickness came up into my throat when I realized that I could literally *see* the draconite in his eyes. The resource my father had murdered for. Guilt churned my stomach. How many of Leviathan's kind had my father murdered for their magic? How many had Nathaniel murdered?

I didn't know the answer to that question, nor did I want to. But I *needed* to.

I stared at Leviathan, completely overwhelmed.

His scales shimmered with iridescence, flickering from

blue to green under the moonlight. Golden horns curled around his head like a crown. My mouth felt dry as I stood there, completely speechless as the sailors around me started to regain consciousness one at a time and were groggily undoing their safeties.

The roar of water filled the air as the dragon hoisted himself up from the ocean, a massive wingspan blotting out the light from the moon. Water dotted my face as the webbed wings flapped once. Twice.

He was *magnificent.*

A glowing blue light encircled his body as if a spirit was being pulled forth, looping around him like an effervescent froth. When Leviathan landed on the deck in front of me, completely naked, the blue spirit slid back into its place under his skin—his dragon tattoo.

My mouth fell open, and he grabbed a pair of trousers from the pile of clothes I hadn't noticed. I could feel how wide my eyes were as I stared at him, unable to put anything into words.

Once he had the trousers on, he approached me, looking down at me in a way that had goose bumps rising all over my body. I shrank down, overwhelmed and completely in awe.

"I thought I told you to stay in my cabin."

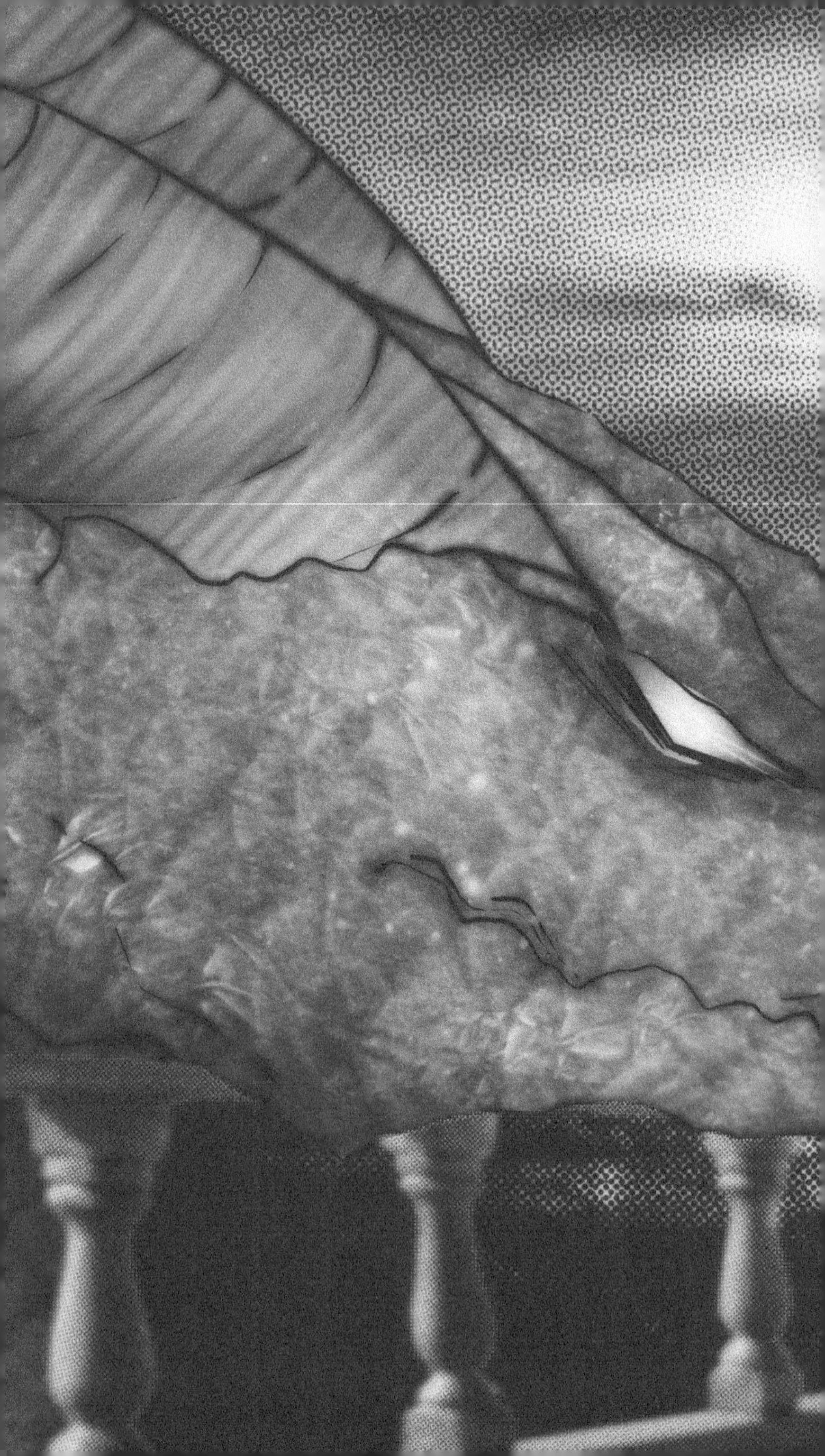

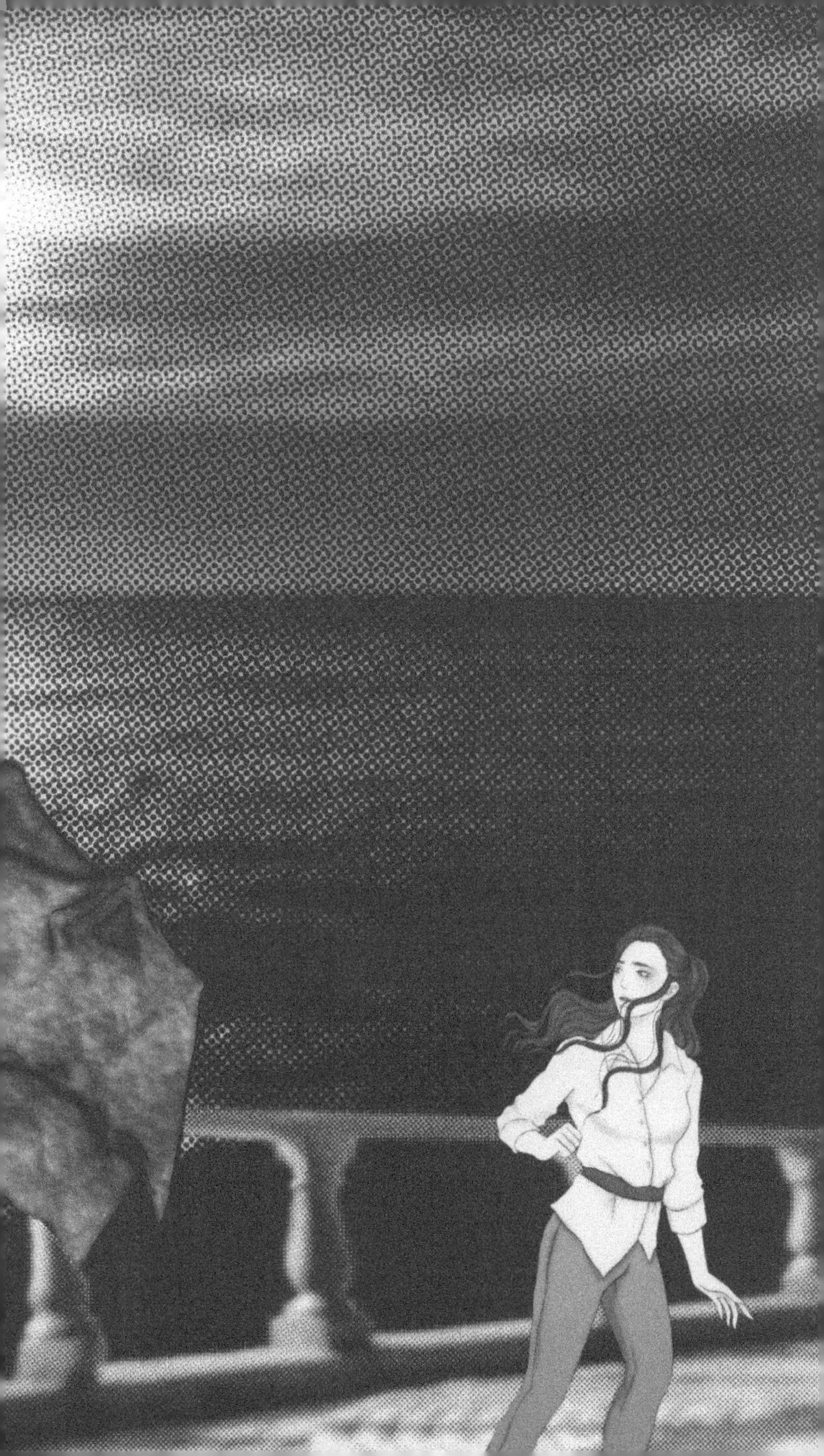

19
MAEVE CROSS

"You're... you're a—" I stammered, my lips refusing to release the words.

"Leviathan is a *leviathan*. Very original, I know," he scoffed. Then his attention wasn't on me anymore as Wraith came onto the deck, followed closely by Boats. Both of them were in their nightwear—oversized shirts and pants, not like their normal fitted attire.

Wraith fired off a question. "Where do you need me, Cap?"

Leviathan grabbed his shirt from the pile where his trousers had been. He shrugged it on but left it completely unbuttoned. "I need a head count. We lost some men in the water."

Wraith's intense green eyes met mine, her eyebrows furrowed with some emotion I'd never seen in her before. "Aye. What else?"

"Only barebones crew are allowed on deck," he continued.

"Do you think the siren clan will come back?" Boats asked this one, reaching over to squeeze her brother's shoulder.

Howler stood there, void of all color aside from the crimson running down his face and staining his white shirt red. He looked clammy. Still in shock. Completely silent with his eyes widened as far as they could go.

"I doubt it. I drove them down to the pits," Leviathan replied, noticing Howler's panicked demeanor. "Are you all right?"

Howler's throat bobbed a few times before he gave his friend a weak smile. "Close one tonight, Levi." He paused and took a deep breath. "We lost Will."

No need to use a nickname for a dead man.

The captain closed his eyes briefly. "Damn it." He addressed Wraith. "I want that head count tonight. Send any injured to Seabird."

"Aye." Then Wraith was gone, charging off into the distance and shouting orders at the men still on deck. As the unessential personnel went down to the lower decks, I couldn't miss the eyes on me. The whispers about me.

"Did Mae not react to the song?"

"How is that possible?"

"Even Wraith falls under the thrall."

"Boats, I need a damage report. I don't think they did much harm to the hull, but I don't want any surprises either." Leviathan gestured to the massive pool of blood that Howler couldn't stop staring at. "And a cleanup."

"You got it, Levi."

And then she, too, was gone.

Howler's hands were shaking, and I reached over to offer comfort. I grabbed his forearm, snapping him out of whatever worrisome thoughts he'd been drowning in. "Are you okay?" I asked softly.

He took a deep breath. "I will be. I've had close calls before, but never *that* close."

I nodded, but before I could tell Howler that I'd be there if he needed anything, Leviathan whipped around, his eyes sharpened on the two of us.

"Both of you, come with me."

He took us back to his cabin, closing the door behind us once we got inside.

Howler looked over at me, color returning to his skin now. "You saved me tonight, Mae. You… you didn't have to, but you did."

The complete genuineness of his comment caught me off guard. Of course I'd helped him. What else was I going to do? Let the sirens eat him the way they'd frenzied over the other sailors?

Howler turned to Leviathan, who was still leaning against the door. Arms crossed. Deep in thought. "She saved me, Levi. She fought a fucking siren. I saw. All the sailors saw. You can't ransom her after that."

I blinked. I'd forgotten about my problems. In that situation, it hadn't mattered. I didn't think—I just acted.

"I'll make that decision," Leviathan stated with cold absoluteness. Then he clapped a hand onto Howler's shoulder. "Go get some sleep. I'll have Wraith take over for you tonight."

The first mate dipped his head in understanding before his captain opened the door for him and he left, once again leaving me alone with Leviathan.

He closed the door, and his presence filled the entire room. The smell of sea air and cedarwood filled my lungs again, heat rising in my cheeks. Leviathan's back was to me as I watched his shoulders rise and fall.

Even in this form, his body didn't lack any power.

Moments of silence passed, and I felt uncomfortable. Squirming under the quiet, overwhelming presence

Leviathan radiated. It made sense. The loyalty of his crew. The fact that he kept to himself. The reaction he had when he saw my brooch... made from draconite.

Which one of his people's skulls did my father carve it out of?

"How are you immune to the song, Princess?" he asked, his voice dangerously low as if he was daring me to lie to him again.

"I'm not immune. I reacted to it at first, and then... then it went away," I answered, twisting my fingers together.

He whipped around, and I felt weak in the knees when he pinned me with his gaze. "What do you mean, *it went away*?" he demanded.

"I don't know. It just did!" I huffed, not once looking away. Not once shrinking. Sure, my knees felt weak, but if I could stand up against a siren, I could stand up to him.

Granted, he had the sirens retreating, but he wasn't a dragon right now.

He was a man.

"What about you?" I asked when he didn't reply. "You're a *sea dragon*!"

The corner of his mouth turned up in a scornful smirk. The blaze in his eyes rekindled, hot with a challenge. "No one will believe you."

I blinked, the words evaporating from my mouth.

"Do you know how much work I've done to establish my reputation? How much I've leaned into the legend? Hm?" His words were cruel. That old wound raw. "No one will ever believe that the great Captain Leviathan would ever be an *actual* leviathan."

Another moment of silence passed as I pondered what he'd said.

"Besides, your *daddy dearest* and your fucking husband

think they hunted us all to extinction." He released a humorless laugh full of pain. "Varric's gotten all the draconite his heart desires. But I doubt that would ever be enough for him."

Before I could stop myself, I stepped forward, my hand coming up to press gently against the firm planes of his chest. "I wasn't going to tell anyone."

Leviathan's eyes were locked on me. Then they flickered to my hand, but he made no move to back away.

I chewed on my lip nervously and murmured, "It was incredible."

His heart hammered underneath my palm, his eyes dipping down to my mouth before he pulled away completely. "Kind words won't change the fact that you're an eel. Slippery as the rest of them."

He brushed past me angrily, clearly noticing the glass shattered all over the floor where I'd escaped and the paperweight on the ground. With a heavy sigh, he picked up the small metal trinket. It didn't look like much, but he touched it like it was precious.

Leviathan returned the paperweight to his desk. He clicked the latch on the side so the compass sprang open. The glass inside was shattered.

Guilt churned in my belly. "Did I do that? I'm sorry," I whispered.

He shook his head. "It was already broken. The only thing I have left from my… old life."

"Old life?" I pondered out loud.

"You didn't think I was always a pirate, did you?" he returned, his eyes flickering up to me again.

My lips parted to ask another question.

"It doesn't matter," he said, snapping it closed. "Not anymore."

I tucked some stray hair behind my ear. "Does your crew know?"

"They don't know my real name, just my form."

"Do your mates know?"

"Yes." He paused. "They sometimes know more about me than I do."

The conversation seemed personal, like the walls Leviathan threw up were softening. I supposed, like me, he had nothing more to hide. "Are there more of you?"

He blinked once, a tic forming in his jaw. "No."

My entire body yearned to close the chasm forming between us. I didn't understand why. I just…. All the things he'd said to me, all the times he'd threatened me—they felt justified. My family was responsible for all the pain inflicted on him. How deep did those wounds go?

Is he really the last leviathan?

How lonely.

"I don't—" Leviathan started, his voice low and shaky as if he wasn't sure he should be saying it out loud. "I don't know how Varric figured it out. We didn't even know that draconite could amplify magic. Not until we were hunted for it."

I rubbed my hands together, sheepishly adding, "I don't know much about my father. He was usually either in the study next to my room or the bonus study under the castle."

Leviathan went completely rigid. His hands clenched into fists, bracing against his desk. The reaction was immediate, his eyes a million miles away. And I moved toward him.

I touched him again, just slightly brushing my fingers against his forearm. He jumped, eyes focusing on me once more.

"Where did you go?" I whispered. "Just now."

"It doesn't matter." He jerked his arm away. "Why do you care?"

My hand fell to my side. "I don't know," I admitted. "I just… I feel responsible."

"You should."

I couldn't hold his gaze as I twisted my fingers together. "I don't want to be ignorant anymore."

I heard his body turn until he was completely facing me. "Why did you help my crew, Mae? It wouldn't have affected you if you let Howler die. Let that siren feast on every one of them."

"I wanted to help" was all I said, my gut twisting at the awful visual of letting any one of the crew die. It wasn't an option.

"Look at me when I'm talking to you, sweetheart," Leviathan demanded, cupping my jaw and pulling it up to meet his gaze.

My cheeks flushed, a heat rushing down my thighs. Coiling in my belly.

Gods, his touch sparked inside me. Flint hitting steel.

"Why did you help Howler?" Leviathan repeated, holding me there, searching my eyes for a lie.

"I wanted to," I whispered. My throat bobbed, my nostrils flaring as I inhaled that intoxicating smell again. His eyes dipped to my mouth once more, their pupils eating up the irises.

His breath blew over my lips, his hand still on my jaw.

My lips parted. I could feel my face warm, and my breath came out all soft. I pushed myself into his grip, wanting more.

So much more.

The longer I stood there, the more my body reacted. My breasts felt heavy, their peaks beading under my linen blouse.

My thighs tingled, a throbbing sensation forming at their apex. The air around us thickened.

Leviathan seemed to realize what was growing between us and released me. He swore under his breath and started to pull away from me.

No.

Both of my hands flew forward, fisting either side of his parted shirt. I got up on my toes and pressed my lips against his.

The sparks took root, igniting the kindling in my belly. He groaned against my lips, looping one arm around my waist and pulling me flush against him.

Oh godsdamnit.

That kiss scorched me like an inferno.

20
MAEVE CROSS

A GASP FLEW past my lips as Leviathan moved us backward, our mouths consuming—*devouring*—the other. My back collided with his desk. I felt how hot and firm his body was pressed against mine.

My eyes fluttered closed, and I released a soft gasp when his tongue swiped along my lower lip. I fought for control over the kiss, but it was pointless.

Leviathan knew what he was doing. He *knew* how to kiss. I could taste the rum on his breath, sweeter than it tasted from the glass.

Gods, he tasted so good.

He *felt* so good.

My mind went numb, seeking sensation. I needed more. I needed to feel more. My lungs started to burn. Blood rushed in my ears, roaring like a storm. But I didn't want the kiss to end. I didn't want to breathe. I wanted to drown. Suffocate in his smell, his taste.

This wasn't the first time I'd been kissed, but it was the first time I'd wanted it.

I slipped my hands into his shirt, roaming the planes of his chest. The skin was hot to the touch, his heart hammering hard beneath my fingertips.

Excitement rolled in my belly. Between my legs, I felt myself throb. It was like I'd been drenched in oil, coated in gunpowder, and I… I *needed* to combust.

Leviathan pulled away, breathing hard, his pupils blown to oblivion. His mouth looked swollen and red, and I imagined I looked the same.

But I wasn't finished.

I curled my hand around the back of his neck, dragging him down for another fiery kiss.

He cupped my behind, earning another breathy gasp. He picked me up and sat me on his desk while he settled between my legs, taking just as much as he was giving. His hands roamed my body, and I didn't want to stop him.

His shirt slid off his shoulders, and I just about moaned, pulling him closer. I needed more. This fire had been lit inside me, and I didn't know how to put it out.

I wanted to let myself *burn*.

His big hands encircled my waist before moving upward to my breasts. I arched toward him in clear invitation. When his thumbs stroked the sensitive peaks, a jolt of pleasure rang through me as potent as a shock of lightning. A cry left my lips as I threw my head back, my eyelids fluttering.

"*Fuck*," Leviathan groaned, his gaze fixated on me as if he was absorbing every reaction.

His eyes were just as hungry as I felt, and seeing that—Gods, *feeling* it—sent excitement flooding into every fiber of my being.

It was then that he pushed closer to me, his hips meeting mine.

I whimpered. *He's so hard.*

I parted my legs farther, pleasure coursing through my veins as we rocked our clothed hips together. I started to get wet, a surge of pleasure I'd never felt so strongly before.

This haze of passion settled over us. Roaming hands. Panting gasps. Every rational thought left my mind as I sought out more of his body. All I knew was that I needed more.

Gods, give me more.

My entire body felt swollen, excited. Desperate, even.

Our mouths mashed together again, and he cupped my breasts as he once more circled my nipples with his thumbs. I imagined his mouth sucking softly, watching me as I came apart.

Something was building inside me with every grind of his body against my neediness. Each stroke of his fingertips. The taste of his mouth.

He pulled away to dip his mouth to my neck. Sucking. Kissing. Laving it with attention as his hips churned against mine. I could imagine how he'd move *inside me*. How he'd take me to the brink and back again.

Over and over.

It was almost too much. Dizzying. Overwhelming.

Oh godsdamn... I'm....

I'm....

"*Levi...*," I whimpered softly. "I need... I need—"

A knock sounded on his door, breaking the haze had settled over us.

"Get out," he muttered.

He broke away from me completely, and my entire body rebelled against me, nearly crying out in desperation. He leaned down to grab his shirt, pulling it on. He circled his desk, sitting in his chair.

My face blazed. Had I been about to—

Mortification settled over me, and I got off his desk. I stormed over to the door just after Wraith and Boats let themselves in. I didn't address them. I needed to get away. To hide.

I had just kissed Leviathan… but that description sounded tame compared to how it made me feel. How eager I was for his touch. I parted my legs for him. I rocked my body against his, chasing the heat in my spine.

How far would it have gone?

I was moments from pawing at his belt, needing nothing more than to feel his skin. I knew without a doubt that I would've had him on top of his desk. I had no care for anything else. I just wanted to know what his cock felt like.

I wanted to know what it looked like. I hadn't taken the chance to find out after he shifted back, but I wished I had.

How it would feel between my lips. How it would taste if I slid my tongue across it.

Could I make him as needy as I felt?

I wanted to know how hot his gaze would feel if I knelt between his thighs. If he spread me out underneath him.

If his kiss weakened my knees to pudding, what would his cock do to me?

Oh Gods.

My cheeks boiled. I wouldn't have been able to hide my desire if I stayed in his cabin. What was I doing? How did that even happen?

It was a mistake.

Leviathan knew it.

I knew it.

A lapse in judgment. A moment of weakness. That's all it was.

I went under the deck to the officers' quarters. I wasn't

surprised to see Howler down there, his face buried in his hands, a bottle of rum next to him. He was freshly clean in a new set of clothing. He wasn't wearing his usual bandana, his cropped hair carefully maintained in glossy black waves instead.

He looked exhausted but far from sleepy. I didn't think I'd be able to sleep right now either.

Howler didn't notice me walk in until I asked, "Need someone to drink with?"

He glanced up. His smile didn't reach his reddened eyes. "I'd like that. I need company right now."

I sat at the table with him, and he passed me the bottle. I wasn't the biggest lover of rum, I'd just discovered, but I felt like surviving a siren encounter was the best reason to drink. I took a swig, and it didn't burn nearly as bad as it did the first time, though I still coughed when I handed the bottle back to him.

We sat in silence, passing the bottle back and forth. It did wonders to help me forget about the incident between Leviathan and me.

At least until Howler asked, "So, what did Cap want to talk to you about?"

I was grateful for the darkness of the room. I think it helped hide my mottled cheeks. "He wanted to know why I wasn't affected by the song."

"Ah." He paused, taking another drink. "Personally, I don't give a shit."

"You don't?"

"Not one bit. All I care about is that I'll get to see my girls again." Howler sighed, leaning back on the bench seat. "And my little boy. Gods, the last time I saw him, he couldn't even hold his head up."

I hadn't known that Howler had a family. And by the way

his eyes shone when he talked about them, he missed them dearly. "Why don't you go home, then? Give up life at sea?"

"It ain't that easy. Five kids need to eat. I take the risks so they don't have to." Howler started to chuckle. "Gods, Isa would've dragged me from the grave just to kill me again if I didn't return home."

"Isa?"

"My wife." He looked up at the ceiling, that familiar beaming smile returning to his face. "She's so breathtaking. Not another lass in the world like her. I fall asleep at night to the image of her. Fuck, I'm going to put *another* baby in her the next time I see her. She always told me that we'd have enough to operate a man-o'-war."

I raised both of my eyebrows. "That's… that's a lot of kids, Howler."

He laughed. "I jest. Five is plenty. Enough to operate a ketch. Besides, I got snipped after our boy was born. I can't put my wife through another pregnancy. Last one nearly killed her."

We were quiet for a long moment.

"I'm useless without my Isa."

"She sounds lovely, Howler," I commented, taking a drink before passing the bottle back.

"I love my family more than anything. Even more than the sea. And the sea is one sexy mistress," he replied, pausing for a moment before the smile fell from his face again. "When I lost myself under the thrall, I thought that was it."

"Well, it wasn't," I pointed out. "You'll be seeing your family soon."

He put both his hands up. "You're right. You're right. But shit, it's throwing me a bit. That's enough about me. How are you doing?"

"Me?"

"Yes, you. I've seen people soil themselves at the sight of Levi's dragon," he replied, seemingly ready to distract himself from his own inner turmoil.

I shrugged, looking away to hide the way my cheeks brightened. "It was… kind of amazing."

Howler arched a brow. "Really? Okay. I wasn't expecting that response."

"I mean, I know a lot about leviathans considering…." I waved my hand.

"Your family. Yeah."

"But all the illustrations. All the lore. It doesn't hold a candle to actually seeing them in person," I answered, heat deepening the color in my cheeks up to my ears.

And then I kissed him and nearly let him have me in his cabin.

"Share with the class. What do you know about leviathans? From the royal perspective."

I was quiet for a moment, thinking about the knowledge I'd passively absorbed over the years. "Well, I know they'd been hunted for their draconite."

"And?"

"And they patrolled the waters for centuries. My father thought they were the reason we couldn't get to the continent of Algar from Farlight. But even without the leviathans, our ships weren't powerful enough to travel that far across the sea," I mentioned.

"The continent? The Four Kingdoms?" Howler added. "Why would he want to go there?"

"I don't know. He's always been fascinated with it." I rubbed my wrist. "Even when he discovered the king at the time was a Royal Leviathan. That the king ruled the land and controlled the seas. This was before I was born, but he revealed it to the other nobles, and they all turned on the royal family. My father had—still has—an amulet of draconite that allowed him to get the advantage. He wore it under his court sorcerer robes. Now, he wears it like a badge of honor."

My stomach churned.

"No one knew how he was so powerful." I buried my face in my hands, resting my elbows on the table. "Not much of it is public record. But Gods, it makes me sick to think about how long he was planning the coup."

Howler watched me intensely, his cheeks flushed from the alcohol. "He never talked about it with you?"

"*Psh*," I muttered, leaning back. "*Don't concern yourself with the conversations of men, Maeve. Just be pretty for your husband.*" I mocked my father's voice.

"Fuck. He sounds like a prick."

"The longer I'm here, the more I'm realizing that."

We were quiet for a moment, and Howler got up from his seat to circle around and clap me on the back. "Well, I'm off to bed. Good talk." He tapped himself on the neck, gesturing right to the place on mine where Leviathan had nibbled and sucked. "For the record, I'd pop up your collar. Hide that a little."

I gasped, my hand flying up to my neck. The skin there was still tender. I got up and charged over to the shower room to look at myself in the mirror.

Sure enough, Leviathan had marked my throat with a dark red love bite.

A reminder of what we'd done every time I looked in the mirror. Or whenever anyone looked at me.

No.

No.

A mistake.

It was a mistake.

I popped up the collar of my shirt, hiding it from view. There. If I hid it, I'd forget about it.

But my dreams surely wouldn't let me forget.

We couldn't get to Shipwreck Bay fast enough.

21
CAPTAIN LEVIATHAN

THE TASTE of Mae's mouth haunted me. The silky wet feeling of her tongue stroking mine. The way her neck arched back so I could taste her skin next. She was so responsive.

So *sensitive*.

Her sighs. Gasps. *Whimpers*. Those erotic noises destroyed me.

I thought about her more than I cared to admit.

Actually, she was all I thought about the next few days. How her warm brown eyes had widened, pupils devouring the irises with inky desire. Something inside me snapped when she'd kissed me.

I didn't kiss her.

No.

Mae kissed *me*.

Gods, the pink flush on her cheeks had spread down to the open neckline, and I found myself wondering how far I could trace her blush. Her loveliness struck me hard in that moment. It was like she'd never been touched before.

I'd reveled in the realization that she was offering a piece of herself to me. There was nothing I'd wanted more than to get to my knees. See if her arousal tasted as sweet as her mouth did. I would've licked and bitten her inner thighs. I would've devoured her until she begged me to take her.

And then I would've fucked her until she *screamed*.

But I'd want her to call me Ronin instead of Leviathan.

The thought of my real name gasped in her soft voice sent unwanted tingles down my spine. I'd tried so hard to fight my attraction to her. Pulled away whenever I'd felt inclined to indulge myself. None of it mattered because it was *Mae* who dragged *me* down for that rapturous kiss and mucked it up.

Now I wanted her more than ever before.

Damn it all to the Hells.

I buried my face in my hands, sighing heavily where I was sitting behind my desk while I waited for my mother to meet me for lunch. Shipwreck Bay was only a few hours away, and I wasn't any closer to an answer.

Do I sell Mae off like I told the crew I would? Collect a hefty ransom while I send her back into Pike's arms? My chest tightened. I didn't like that. From how Mae regarded him, from those bruises on her throat when I'd first seen her, it didn't feel right to give her back to a man who would surely *hurt* her.

And then there was the whole siren situation. If I wasn't sure her ears had been tipped before, I was certain now. No human was impervious to the song. Even the deaf or hard-of-hearing were susceptible to the unique vibrations. It would just take a little longer to take root.

Siren songs affected blood, vibrating through bone, the effects not explicitly auditory.

Wraith's elven blood could fight the song. The vibrations took longer, giving her more time to anchor herself down or help crew members, but she succumbed eventually.

Only fae blood could truly fight the song.

I didn't know what exactly Mae was or where she came from, but one thing was clear.

Maeve Cross is not Varric Cross's daughter.

I knew without a doubt that Varric knew this, but Mae believed she was his flesh and blood. But regardless of that, she was still his heir. His ward.

A flash of her came over my vision again. Her nervous smile. Her concern when her hand pressed against my chest, weakening my resolve. *Gods.*

She had *no right* being that lovely. I hated it. I hated that I was questioning myself. My crew trusted my callousness. They knew I'd make the right decision for them. They trusted me wholeheartedly.

But Mae is innocent. Innocent in the extermination of my family. Innocent in Varric's war crimes.

But she was also the only way I could possibly save my crew from Nathaniel's inevitable raid.

I could buy time. A trade-off. Freedom in exchange for his wife.

She was my bargaining chip.

And I *hated* that. Mae didn't deserve that. She deserved freedom as much as I did.

How pitiful.

The object of my desire was the heir of my reckoning and my chance at salvation.

This world wasn't fucking fair.

The door opened, and my mother walked in.

I shook off my thoughts as I got up and greeted her like I always did with a kiss on the cheek while she ruffled the top of my head.

"Hey, Mama," I said as I turned away to settle back in my seat.

When I looked back up at her, her arms were crossed, and there was a firm glint in her eye. She meant business today. "We're a few hours from home."

"Appears so," I replied.

A moment of quiet passed, and all I could hear was the tapping of her foot.

"Say what you're going to say," I urged, leaning back in my chair, my arms crossed just like hers. I had clearly gotten this stubbornness from someone.

"You can't sell her."

"And pass up on the ransom? You're not the captain anymore. I make the decisions regarding bounties." Even though my mother had passed the title to me, she didn't know how to step away. While she was one of my most trusted advisers, I got the distinct feeling that she didn't trust *me* when she butted into my decisions when I hadn't asked for her opinion.

A tic formed in Mama's jaw. "She saved Howler's life. Is that how you reward good work?"

I sighed. "I'm not going to fight with you right now. Did you know that Cross and Pike are planning a raid on Shipwreck Bay? I could buy us time by giving her over."

"Or you could give her over, and Pike immediately kills everyone on this ship for *kidnapping his wife*."

My mouth ran dry. "We didn't kidnap her. She stowed away."

Like Pike would ever care about that.

She raised one eyebrow, her lips curling in disappointment. I knew that look well. Like she was chastising a child. "You're not a fool. Men like Pike have no honor. Mae will be an excuse to not offer you a fair trial. Though instead of having her at our backs, she'll be watching us dance with Jack Ketch."

She'd be watching us hang, in other words.

I blew a hot breath from my nose. "Do you trust me?"

Instantly, her eyes softened. "Of course I do."

"We've been through this. You know how much I hate it when you barge in here like I don't know how to tie my shoes."

She knew she was overstepping. But once a captain, always a captain. She put both hands up and sighed. "Fine. You'll make the right decision. You always do."

"Then leave me to it." If I didn't make my boundaries clear, she'd push them. I didn't believe it was intentional, but it was incredibly irritating.

"All right." She turned, leaving me to stew after the door clicked shut.

My teeth ground together as I thought of Mae. Of the bruises around her neck that first night. The tender skin of her throat marred with red fingertips.

My belly tightened as a bout of anger sizzled in my blood.

Even if there were no other reason, I'd kill him for that and that alone.

I blinked. Once. Twice. I knew what my decision was.

THROUGH MY SPYGLASS, I could see the harbor at the edge of the horizon. It was about twelve miles away. As always, it was bustling. From fishing barges to trading ketches, ships came and went. While merchant ships were very much a prize in my line of work, pirates also did plenty of business with them.

Those we did business with were widely protected, as they broke the law to trade with us. They were one of us. That loyalty ran deep in our ranks.

I collapsed my spyglass. "We're clear," I said.

Plankwalker nodded and maneuvered toward the rear of the islands where our cove was nestled away in the mountains, close to town but hidden enough that we wouldn't get any unwelcome guests.

Glancing down from where I stood, I caught a glimpse of Mae with Gunny. My head gunner grinned widely, clapping her on the back and saying something that made her laugh. She was carrying something for him and was probably under his charge for the day.

Mae never complained about the work. She was eager for it. The first morning she was with us, she promised to work twice as hard as anyone on this ship.

I didn't believe it. I thought a prissy noblewoman would wither at the first sign of work, given her dainty hands and round eyes. Her petal-pink mouth and wide hips.

But fuck, had she proved me wrong.

I almost envied how at ease she seemed with Gunny.

She looked nothing like how she did with me.

With me, she was on edge. Not like I could really blame her either. Especially after I held her at knifepoint when I learned her identity.

At that moment, she was the enemy. She was an extension of Varric Cross, here to take this second family from me as violently as he had the first.

I'd hated her. I'd hated how I started to let her in. I'd hated how soft her mouth looked. I had hated the princess who benefitted from everything stolen from me.

But I don't hate her now.

I didn't see an adversary. I saw a hardworking woman who'd discovered a love for the sea.

A sailor hungry to learn.

Mae was the furthest thing from a demure princess.

She fit right in.

The corner of my mouth pulled up slightly as Howler called out, "Land ho!"

I noticed Mae's entire body instantly go rigid, her eyes widening with realization. As far as she knew, this was the end of the line for her. I'd said as much.

She turned her head, gazing at the shallowing water. Mizzenmasts protruded from the sea as reminders of the jagged rocks that lurked beneath the surface if you weren't careful enough to avoid them.

Retired sailors fished on the cove dock, waving at us as we closed in on the cove, instantly shaded by the massive cave walls. In the distance, up alongside the winding walkways, I could just make out the homes built into the cliff face. Sunlight streamed in from the mouth of the cove.

There were farms along the mountainside.

Lush green land meeting the rich cerulean of the sea.

My slice of paradise.

The families of my sailors waved at us as we approached, many of them flying down to the dock to greet their loved ones.

My crew came up from the lower deck, aware of their jobs to careen the ship, but that would come later. They'd been at work long enough; they'd earned a break before more work began. Their families jumped for joy on the dock, cheering loudly.

I couldn't help but smile. Despite whatever loss or hardships we endured during our voyages, we always came home to paradise.

I glanced over at our resident stowaway, and the guilt came back again.

Meanwhile, while my crew was blooming with excitement, I could see Mae get visibly more and more nervous.

She was rubbing her hands together, and she kept glancing at the half wall like she was debating jumping over it.

"Mae," I called out.

She startled, hesitantly looking over at me before her cheeks bloomed with the most endearing flush.

Instantly, I was hit with the reminder of pinning her against my desk. The sound of her voice as she murmured my moniker. Heat formed at the base of my spine, but I pushed it back. Or tried to.

How pink could I make her face?

Damn it.

"Come here," I ordered, maintaining my professionalism as Plankwalker expertly lined up the ship with the dock. Boats and her crew prepared to secure the ship and drop anchor.

Mae nodded, then handed Spider whatever she was holding and exchanged a few words with him. He said something cheeky, and she turned around and smacked him.

All I could make out was "It's none of your business!"

Her demeanor changed completely as she trudged over to me. She looked up at me and loudly proclaimed with clear defiance, "If you're going to send me back, at least give me a fair fight. I demand a duel!"

The corner of my mouth twitched. "Sweetheart, you wouldn't be able to take me in a fair fight."

"Even if I can't wield a cutlass properly, I'm still a hairpuller."

"Unfortunately for you, I like having my hair pulled" came out of my mouth before I could stop it. Plankwalker snickered while Howler coughed loudly. Thankfully, most of my crew was too distracted by their excited family members to notice the slip of tongue.

Mae looked so sweet when she blushed. I couldn't help my growing smile when that flush deepened.

"But fortunately for us both, it won't have to come to that," I commented.

Howler glanced over at me, obvious relief written across his face. "You've finally agreed to let her go?"

I shrugged. "A life for a life. Seems like a fair trade."

All at once, that tension left Mae's shoulders. The defiance in her eyes softened. "Oh."

Howler shouted in excitement. "You'll get to meet my wife and all my kids!"

The smile that curved Mae's face was downright disarming. "I can't wait."

The ship gently bumped into the pier as Boats and the ship crew placed the gangway. Like a roaring storm, my crew sprinted off the ship to kiss their partners and scoop children into the air. Squeals of delight and excitement followed.

The sailors on board who didn't have family chatted among themselves, stepping off the ship to enjoy their shore leave before the work started again in a few days.

Luckily, once the ship was careened, I'd offered them another two weeks of paid shore leave. Dirty, backbreaking work would always be rewarded with extra vacation and a bump in pay.

Careening was voluntary. Those who did it didn't have to restock the ship later.

When most of the crew had cleared out, I caught a glimpse of a handful of spouses waiting for their sailors on the pier. Sailors who would never come. After I delivered the news, I'd give them a few days to grieve before I handed over each sailor's effects and paid them for their loss. Of course, they could always stay at the cove, but few ever did.

That was probably the most difficult part of my job.

"I'll take it from here," my mother said after I'd broken the news, placing her hand on my shoulder. "I'll see you at Isa's later." She guided the widows and widowers away while I finished my duties.

As hard as it was, it was just the way of life here. This lifestyle was dangerous. We all knew what we'd signed up for.

But I sympathized with the new spouses the most. They were far too young to be widowed.

While my mates finished up their checklists, Isa and Howler's five kids clopped down the pier. The youngest girl, Ellie, who was about five, was tugging at her mother's skirt, saying, "Come on! Come on, Mama!"

"Babies!" Howler cried out as his kids charged across the gangway, nearly tackling the man to the ground. He laughed heartily, kissing each child on the nose, cheek, or forehead. "I missed you!"

Isa smiled warmly. Her face lit up when she saw her husband. She had her hair tied up in a scarf, a poof visible at the very top, and she carried a baby boy on her hip who was much bigger than the last time I'd seen him. His innocent eyes widened as he reached out two chubby arms to his father. Howler beamed with delight as he scooped the boy up and kissed him on his pudgy cheek.

"You've gotten so big!" Howler said. Then he stepped forward and kissed Isa on the lips, wrapping his free arm firmly around her waist. "Gods, I missed you, my darling."

Isa's round cheeks brightened the smallest amount, the hint of red barely noticeable under the deep, blue-toned umber of her skin. "I missed you," she murmured, pressing their foreheads together. She then reached over and squeezed his arm. She wobbled for dramatic effect, swooning excessively. "I forgot how strong you were."

Howler grinned, clearly basking in the attention. "You're still the most beautiful woman I've ever seen."

"Not the most beautiful person?" Isa waggled her eyebrows, giving Howler's sense of humor back to him.

"I'm sorry, baby, but that's got to be Levi. He's just lucky you've already locked me down."

"You're awful. Why do I love you, again?" his wife teased, not at all bothered by his comment.

"Because I'm strong." Howler winked, flexing the same arm she'd squeezed.

I rolled my eyes as his daughters came over to greet me. I patted them on their heads, while the more affectionate one got a hug.

"Hi, Uncle Levi," the eldest, a ten-year-old named Maya, greeted me before leaving to go over to Wraith and Boats, their favorite relatives. The younger two of the four stuck with me for a few extra minutes, filling me in on what they were studying and how their chickens were doing. At least I was still their favorite uncle.

But I wasn't a huge gift giver like their aunts.

"Auntie! Auntie!"

And there they went.

While Wraith wasn't known for being touchy, she did love to spoil her nieces. "I got something for each of you." The kids went down to the officers' quarters, leaving just Howler, Isa, Mae, me, and the baby in Howler's arms.

"And who is this?" Isa asked, gesturing to Mae still standing there like she didn't know what to do or where to go.

"Mae," she said, reaching out her hand. "It's nice to meet you. Howler has said so much about you."

Isa returned the handshake. "Nice to meet you, too, Mae."

Then she glanced over at her husband like she wasn't sure if she was supposed to know who Mae was.

"Resident stowaway. Saved my life. Runaway princess. My friend," Howler supplied.

His wife nodded. "Well, any friend of my husband's is welcome for dinner. You could stay for the card game."

"Oh, I couldn't impose," Mae said, her cheeks still that hue of red.

"Nonsense." Isa waved her hand. "You will come to dinner."

"Oh… okay," Mae mumbled. "Then I will. Thank you."

Howler kissed Isa one more time, passing their boy back to her. "I still have some work to do here. Keep me company?"

"Always, baby," Isa agreed. "We'll see you two later."

I nodded as they disappeared under the deck. Mae and I stood there in silence before I asked, "Do you want me to show you around? You'll get lost if you don't know where you're going."

She was quiet, fiddling with her fingers before she decided. "I'd like that."

22
MAEVE CROSS

I'd never seen anything like Anchorage Cove before. The blue water lapped gently against the pier, and brightly colored little fishes were swimming in the shallows. As Leviathan and I walked along the pier to the dirt path lining the fishermen's huts, I couldn't help but notice how at ease he seemed.

The light flickered off the water, reflecting and dancing on his face.

I supposed it made sense. On *The Ollipheist*, he was at work. It was his job to keep his sailors safe, fed, and paid. But here, it was apparent he was home.

The slow swagger of his steps and the dimple indented on one side of his mouth. The way his eyes seemed to glimmer more than usual. They showcased a comfort that Levi didn't have on the ship.

Various sailors and fishermen greeted him like a friend, not a superior, as we passed them. They threw out their fishing lines and reeled them back, overflowing with catch. No shortage of food here.

My feet tapped against the wood in the pair of boots

Boats had given me. I was lucky she was the same size as me or I would've gotten a nasty splinter by now.

"So what's the plan, Mae?" Leviathan asked, gazing down at the crown of my head. His voice rumbled.

I rubbed my arm in an effort to keep my skin from prickling. "What do you mean?"

"You're free now."

I was quiet for a moment before I noticed a loose plank and reached for his arm without thinking. He let me pull him out of the way. "Watch your step."

"Thanks," he murmured, his eyes lingering on my fingers curled around his forearm.

My face boiled as I let go. Rubbing my hands together, I avoided catching his eye as we stepped down onto the dirt path that ran along the edge of the water.

"But, erm, to answer your question, I haven't given it much thought. I don't have anywhere to go. All I care about is not going back to Farlight."

He made a throaty noise. "For someone who was willing to duel me for her freedom, I'm surprised you don't have a plan."

"I didn't think I'd make it this far, if I'm being honest."

He stopped, folding his arms. "And are you?"

I looked up. "What?"

"Being honest."

I laughed nervously under my breath. "Well, you'd be able to tell if I was lying. So what's the point?"

Leviathan's mouth turned up in both corners, nearly knocking me dead with those dimples. It was still unfair that despite everything, my knees never ceased to wobble around him.

"What about you? What happens next?" I asked, eager to get his attention off me. But his eyes didn't leave me as he sat on a boulder overlooking the part of the water that dipped off into a deep darkness.

"Right now? Shore leave. Then we careen the boat—"

"What's that?" I interrupted. "How do you do that?"

He was quiet for a moment before he indulged my curiosity. "Everything not bolted down gets taken off the ship, and we tilt it on its side to scrape barnacles off the bottom. Treat it for wood rot or worms if necessary. Just another step in caring for the ship." He smiled again. "Treat it right, and it'll treat us right."

I tiptoed over to him, feeling his presence thicken the air around me as I sat on the other side of the boulder. "How long have you had *The Ollipheist*?"

He hummed, leaning back. I gulped hard, my eyes dipping to the parting of his shirt that exposed his skin and the taut muscles that elongated and bunched with every movement. "Almost twelve years. I must've been eighteen, determined to make a name for myself," he said. "When my mother was captain, our ship—*The Reaver*—was blown to smithereens. *The Ollipheist* was the ship that destroyed it. We took it over. Found an elf kept as a prisoner in the pit."

"Is that how you met Wraith?"

Leviathan looked up at the ceiling of the cavern like it reflected a fond memory. "I didn't think I'd make a friend for life, but here we are."

"What about the twins?" I wondered, just enjoying the conversation.

"That's a... more difficult story." It was apparent that this memory was painful by the way he didn't answer right away, visibly swallowing like he had a mouthful of nails. "Their father hid my mother and me under their dock when the guards came."

My lips parted, but he didn't give me time to ask anything

else. It was a vulnerable statement, and he threw his guard back up almost immediately.

"Doesn't matter. It was a long time ago. What about you? Have any friends in the castle?"

"Ha," I scoffed. "No one really cared about me. Not my mother—"

"Varric's wife, Katherine?"

I blinked, trying to ignore all my internal suspicions. "Yeah. Of course. Who else?"

He waved his hand dismissively. "I interrupted. Continue your statement."

"It doesn't really matter. But it really felt like my father did everything in his power to keep me from the public eye. I had never even met any of the guests who attended my wedding aside from a handful of spoiled nobles."

Leviathan looked at me from the corner of his eye, a peculiar expression on his face, but it was gone as soon as I noticed it. "Sounds lonely."

"It was. But—" I stopped myself, my cheeks darkening.

"But what, sweetheart?" For once, his voice was soft. The pet name didn't come across like he was teasing me. It sounded genuine.

I gave him a nervous smile as my face became hotter, the heat now coloring my ears. "It might sound silly, but I... I don't feel so lonely anymore."

The way he looked at me caused flutters to erupt in my belly. "There's nothing silly about that."

He clearly meant it. A breeze ruffled my hair, making it stray all over the place.

A big hand came into view as he brushed my hair out of my face, his rough fingertips scratching the skin of my cheek softly. Warmth brewed in my belly. He cleared his throat, pulling away completely, but even I didn't miss the pinkness forming on his cheeks under his beard.

The moment felt so incredibly tender that my heart pounded harder as I fought the desire to look at his mouth.

I wanted to kiss him again.

"Since you don't have a plan, you…." He made another throaty noise. "You can stay with me until you figure it out."

Stay with him?

In the same house?

In the same bedroom?

Don't get ahead of yourself, Mae.

"You don't have to do that," I replied.

He stood up from the boulder. "I have a spare room for my mom when she wants to visit. Or when Wraith wants to be alone. I don't see why you can't use it. Besides, what kind of man would I be if I threw you on the streets?"

"Well… thank you, Leviathan," I said.

"You can call me Levi." He paused. "If you want, that is. I'm not your captain." He shuffled his feet, the small tell of his own nervousness surprisingly endearing.

A small smile curled the corner of my mouth. "I thought pirates didn't do favors."

I watched his face darken, feeling satisfied that I wasn't the only one who was starting to feel nervous. "But we reward good work," he reminded me. "And I'm repaying a favor. Howler would kill me if I let you sleep on the streets."

He was quiet for a moment, counting on his fingers.

"At least Howler." Levi turned, holding his hand out to me.

I laughed a little under my breath and took his hand, letting him pull me off the boulder to my feet. Sparks flew up my arm, but I didn't try to hide my reaction this time.

I liked the way his hands felt as I looked up at him, mouth going dry at his proximity.

We hadn't talked about what happened in his cabin a few days ago, but I couldn't help but wonder if he'd push me away if I did it again. But the way he now completely pulled away from me told me that he also viewed it as a mistake.

"Listen, Mae," he sighed.

"I know," I interrupted. "I don't want to kiss you either."

His chuckle caught me off guard, as did the two prominent dimples. "I was going to say that we should make our way to Isa's here shortly."

Oh Gods, my face *boiled.* "Oh."

"But if you're so eager to talk about how you shoved your tongue down my throat, we can do that."

I huffed, mainly out of mortification. "Don't act like you didn't reciprocate."

He dipped his head down, that scent of seawater and cedar more potent than ever before. Then his hot breath fanned over my lips, and I had to fight the urge to slide my tongue over my lower one.

"I never said I didn't." His eyes darted down to my mouth, then back up to my eyes. "But we both know that shouldn't have happened. Not under the circumstances."

I gulped hard. "Yeah. I mean... you and me. Could you imagine?"

I could.

He lingered for a moment or two longer before veering back, giving me space so my knees could regain a little strength. "Let's not complicate this more than we already have."

"No... definitely not," I agreed, even though my legs wobbled underneath me the more I imagined what he'd look like between them. I was about to ask him why it had to be complicated and probably stick my foot in my mouth again.

Out of the shadows by the pier, I noticed Lieutenant Commander Lazlo saunter down the planks, clearly looking for his favorite person.

Thank the Gods, a distraction. "Hey, Lieutenant Commander Lazlo," I greeted, crouching and holding my hand out so I could pet behind his ears. I'd learned that Lazlo never responded unless you recited his full title.

After he had gotten his pets from me, he hopped onto the boulder and then onto Levi's shoulder, where he curled up comfortably. If I were a cat, I'd probably be pretty comfortable on his shoulder too.

Levi chuckled, rubbing Lazlo under his chin before he hopped down to go do whatever it is cats do. "Come on. I'll show you the way to Isa's."

23
MAEVE CROSS

LAUGHTER FILLED Howler and Isa's house, a modest and homey cabana on the cliffside. Chickens and goats ran amok in a fenced enclosure while the youngest two girls, Ellie and Dina, fed and played with them.

Howler's other two daughters, Maya and Lissy, sat at the long table with the adults, chatting up Wraith, who had an uncharacteristic smile on her face while she listened to the two young girls. It caught me off guard at first because I'd never seen one on her before. A grin broad enough to show all her teeth. I felt wary around her still, expecting her teeth to turn as razor sharp as her blade.

Howler was tossing his little boy into the air while the baby giggled with absolute glee.

Seabird, Boats, and Levi were helping Isa in the kitchen and brought out a steaming pan full of roasted vegetables and chicken.

Everything smelled divine. I didn't know Levi could cook. Every time I learned something new about him, it revealed another layer I never knew existed.

He was wearing an apron over his clothes while he skillfully chopped more vegetables for a side dish covered with ground salt and seasonings. I stole more glances at him than I should've, but I couldn't help it.

The kitchen was open to the main dining area, so I could clearly see him chatting with his mother and Boats and bumping hips with Isa. There was so much freedom in how he interacted with them like they were all family.

The cool ocean air wafted in through the cabana from the cliffside. All the windows were open including a huge one that led to their backyard for a perfect view of the coastline. Gods, it was beautiful here.

While most of the common area was open to the outside, draped with colorful fabric that danced in the wind, it wasn't hard to notice a hallway leading to an enclosed area. Probably the bedrooms.

"What do you think?" Howler asked, sitting his son on his lap. "Different than Farlight Harbor?"

I smiled and nodded. "The sky is clearer here. Not foggy with industry. It's beautiful."

"Glad you think so," Levi said as he came into the room and placed a final tray of golden-brown bread on the table. "It's our little slice of paradise."

"How do you get all your supplies?" I wondered as the other adults joined us at the table.

"Shipwreck Bay's harbor isn't far. The port town is about a mile or so walk if you know where you're going," Howler replied. "If we need supplies, we take the horses."

"What's that pirate safehold like?" I wondered.

Wraith laughed. It sounded so unnatural to me that I jumped. "It's loud. Sometimes you can hear the revelry from here."

"It's very different," Levi said, taking his apron off and then sitting next to his mother. "I'll take you sometime if you'd like."

My cheeks warmed as I said, "That sounds nice."

I noticed Seabird look over at her son with the most incredulous expression.

Isa called her other two daughters in. "Ellie! Dina! Dinnertime!"

And as expected, dinner was delicious.

"Roasted chicken, Isa?" Howler commented as he sliced off a few pieces for his kids before taking another for himself. "You know how to spoil me."

Isa's eyes glimmered with mischief as she spooned roasted vegetables onto her children's plates. "If I don't spoil you, you'll run off with Levi. How could I possibly compete with your best friend?"

This wasn't the first time she'd made that joke. But, just like last time, Levi rolled his eyes. "I'm never going to live that one down, am I?"

Isa giggled. "Never."

"Well, I don't know how you stayed with Howler all this time. He's a terrible kisser," Levi replied.

What?

Howler cracked up as he noticed me looking between the two of them. "Oh, Mae. Sweet, sweet Mae. Don't look so concerned."

"I'm not concerned," I argued, but my face was bright red. I could feel the heat of my telltale flush.

Boats joined in the laughter, taking pity on me. "We were playing cards, drunk off our asses, and we ran out of coin. So whoever lost would have to kiss Howler. Except for me, of course, because I had all the money. That, and I'd sooner burn in one of the Nine Hells than kiss my brother."

"Like kissing a dead fish," Levi added, the corner of his mouth turned up in a smile, one dimple proudly on display.

Isa nodded along, taking a sip from her glass of water.

"Hey, hey," Howler interrupted. "You like my fishy lips!" He made a face at his daughters, pursing his lips together like a fish and earning another fit of giggles from his girls, wife included. His son just stared blankly up at him like he was unsure how to react. Then he started to fuss.

Isa stood up and kissed Howler fondly on the mouth. "Oh, my lovely husband. Always so wrong. I *love* them." She scooped her son up. "Someone is ready to nurse. I'll be right back. Those who didn't cook are on dish duty."

She took the baby in the direction of the bedrooms, and I glanced over at Levi. "So that's why you insisted on cooking when we arrived."

The other side of his lips curved to match, and both dimples dented in his cheeks. "Perhaps. Or maybe I just like to cook." His eyes traced the brightness of my cheeks down to my throat and back up again. "I'm sure at some point during your stay, you'll experience it firsthand."

"Oh. Well, there's no way to tell if you're any good at it until I experience it, hm?" I teased, leaning on my elbow and across the table toward him.

I liked how light it felt. How easy it was to poke fun at each other.

Is this flirting? Are we flirting right now?

As soon as I realized that, my face got even hotter. I reared back in my seat.

"Is Mae staying with you?" Seabird asked, the same incredulous look on her face as earlier.

Levi took a drink of his rum, followed by a bite of chicken. "Mm-hmm."

"She could stay with me," Howler offered before meeting

my gaze. "We'd never turn you away."

"Oh, that's nice of you," I said, nervously twisting my fingers together.

Levi swallowed and cleared his throat. "Mate," he started. "You have five kids. Boats and Wraith stay here. Mama is also staying to help Isa with the kids. You don't need to worry about an eleventh person in your house."

Howler then looked over at me and repeated, "We'd never turn you away, Mae. If he annoys you, we'll find someplace to put you."

"I appreciate that." And I did. Just like on the ship, I felt like I fit in here. I never fit in at the castle. Not once. But here… it felt right. Like I was among friends. I didn't feel lonely. I felt accepted.

Howler and Wraith got up.

"To the dishes," Howler said dramatically, pointing ahead. "And you, kiddos, come with me."

His four daughters grumbled among themselves before they followed to assist with the chores. He scooped the youngest one up, propping her over his shoulders as she released a gleeful giggle.

I also followed suit, gathering the empty dishes to take outside.

Even washing dishes was pleasant if the view was this beautiful. The sun was setting, painting the sky and the sea a myriad of colors. Orange, purple, violet.

It took my breath away.

I dunked the dishes in the water with the older kids before handing them over to Howler and Wraith, who sudsed and dunked them again. The youngest two dried and laid them out on the rack.

Together, despite the mountain of dirty dishes, we made fast work of it.

Of course, it felt faster because Howler's daughters were telling him all about the adventures they'd had while he was out at sea.

Maya had taken up writing and had dreams of being a novelist.

Lissy loved music and would go down to the common cabana to play on the piano.

Dina liked planting and caring for the flowers in the garden.

Meanwhile, Ellie only cared about the chickens and could tell us which one laid the most eggs.

Howler beamed and praised them the entire time they were telling him about their studies and hobbies. They were wonderful kids. Nothing like the snotty ones I'd been around at fancy gatherings back at the castle. When we came back inside, the sun had gone down and the other four adults had set the table for cards, a bottle of rum, and money to gamble. Howler took his kids off to bed, but they didn't leave without telling me that it was nice to meet me.

Seeing Howler's kids and how much he adored them made me feel… confused. I never had that, and I wondered what my childhood would've been like with an attentive father. Sure, Howler was gone a large part of the time, but he made sure to make it up to them as much as he could. And not with buying them gifts.

With time.

That was more precious.

"You ready to play, sweetheart?" Levi asked me, breaking me out of my thoughts.

I supposed it would do me no good to wonder what could've happened all those years ago if my father gave me his time. Instead, I was going to be happy that I made it this far.

"I don't have any money to play with," I pointed out, tucking some hair out of my face as I looked at him settled in his seat. "I can watch, though."

The corner of his mouth turned up, weakening any resolve I thought I had. "Do you *want* to play?"

I nodded. "I'd like to."

"Then I'll spot you. Come. Sit." Levi scooted over, making room for me on the bench.

His form shadowed mine, and my belly coiled again. Even though Boats, Wraith, and Seabird were making conversation while they waited on Howler and Isa to put their kids down, it felt like Levi and I were alone.

I knew that being attracted to him was pointless. It would never be long-term. After shore leave was over, he'd go back to sea, and I'd move on somewhere else, far away from Farlight. I'd probably never see Levi again. But that didn't make the desire go away.

"Drink?" he offered.

"Please." The burn of the rum didn't scald my throat as badly anymore, as I'd started to get accustomed to the taste. I didn't drink a lot of it, only a few sips, and with a full stomach, I doubted I'd feel much of the effects.

Howler and Isa returned, and the game began.

"Are you sure she's not cheating?" Boats demanded, swallowing down rum as I, once again, trumped her hand.

Levi grinned, nearly out of coin. "She's not. Can't lie. Certainly can't cheat."

I giggled, excitedly taking another hand. Isa and Wraith watched, neither interested in playing, but they loved listening to all the banter. Seabird had turned in for the night, and it was our job to keep it down.

But we were terrible at it.

"Gods, we should take you to the tavern at port. Maybe we could win back all the money we've lost there," Howler said, dealing another hand.

"It's just beginner's luck," I objected. "I'll lose all my luck out there."

"Maybe, maybe not," Levi added, his presence absolutely swallowing me.

I could blame the heat under my collar on the drink, but I knew I wasn't drunk.

He reached into his pocket and threw something else into the pile. "I raise."

It glimmered, looking very familiar. "Where did you get that?" I asked, looking up at him and then back down at my wedding ring. "I threw it off the boat."

Levi nudged me with his shoulder and leaned over, whispering, "I find all sorts of shit at the bottom of the ocean."

His breath tickled my neck, deepening the color in my cheeks. "Do you do that often? Scour the bottom of the ocean?"

Levi hummed. "I need the ocean like I need the land. Man and sea serpent. Both and neither."

My eyes widened with interest. "Can you shift on land, then?"

"Not recommended. It takes a great deal of energy that gets depleted faster on land. I'd only be able to hold that form for a few minutes at most," he answered, tipping his glass back so I could watch his throat bob when he swallowed. His tongue swiped over his lower lip to collect a stray golden droplet.

My mouth ran dry, my thighs tingling as I gazed at the strong cords of his neck. I yearned to take a bite out of him.

"Maeve," Howler interrupted. "Are you going to raise or not?"

"Oh, right." I glanced at my cards and said, "I raise."

Soon enough, we called it quits, each of us going home with a little money, but I definitely cashed out the most. I gathered the obnoxious ring and offered it to Levi.

"You can take this."

He glanced down at the stone and back up at me. "You won it. Fair and square."

"But I don't want it."

He shrugged, and his lips curved into a sideways smile. "You don't have to wear it, Mae. You're not his property. Sell it. I'm sure it's worth a decent sum. Trade it for clothes, supplies, what have you. Certainly a nice start to your new life."

I lowered my hand and felt my mouth quirk up. "You're right."

"Usually am," he agreed, tossing me a wink before waving at his mates. "Good night."

Boats came over and gave me a friendly side hug, and Wraith tipped her broad hat at me before saying, "We'll see you tomorrow."

I beamed, happy that I didn't have to say goodbye just yet. I wasn't ready to. "I like the sound of that."

"Come," Levi said, dipping his head toward the door. "It's a bit of a walk."

"Night, you two. See you later." Howler wrapped his arm around my shoulders in a fond squeeze before socking Levi in the arm.

Then together, under the light of the moon and oil lanterns along the dirt path, we were on our way to Levi's cabana. I didn't know what would happen when we got there, but I knew one thing.

I wasn't afraid of the future.

I wanted to live in the moment.

24
MAEVE CROSS

The moon lit up the path back to the cove. The symphony of insects and ocean waves made me smile with a sense of peace settling in my belly.

At least, it would've been peaceful if I didn't keep looking up at Levi to ogle his back. He wasn't wearing his coat anymore and had it draped over his arm. That thin linen shirt clung to the muscles of his back, stretched taut over his shoulders.

My heart beat a rapid tattoo inside my ribs. My hands felt all clammy. And the closer we got to his cabana, the more I realized that we would be alone at his house. It excited me just as much as it terrified me.

It wasn't so much that I thought Levi would make advances on me. Despite his rude attitude on occasion, he'd never made me feel uncomfortable. At least not in that way. It was my own thoughts of climbing his body that made me hot under the collar.

I cleared my mind. "You live in the cove?" I asked.

We stepped through the mouth of the cave and descended down the pathway to the pier. Gods, the view was spectacular. The moon reflected off the water, glowing with blue light. Most of the water was shallow until it dropped down into an abyss-like darkness.

"I do," he replied. "Up there."

He gestured to an incline lined with golden-hued oil lamps that led up to a modest cabana on the edge of a drop-off hovering right above the deep part of the water.

"Let me guess, you like night swims?" I commented, half serious, half teasing.

Levi looked at me over his shoulder, a dimple in his cheek. "You guess correctly."

"So do you have to shift often? How does that work?" I wondered, following him up the steep incline.

"You're full of questions, aren't you?" It wasn't a jab. Levi sounded more amused at my curiosity than annoyed.

Slightly out of breath, I said, "I can't help it."

He hummed, a deep growly noise that I almost didn't hear under the chirping of insects. "Well, I've never been away from the sea. Ever since I was old enough to shift, I've needed to be close to the water. I don't know what would happen if I couldn't be." He rolled his shoulders. "I'm not interested in finding out."

I nodded, finally reaching the part of the incline where it flattened out. "This is charming," I commented, gesturing to the small but homey cabana. I also noticed that there weren't many other houses in the cove. Maybe a few fisherman huts or supply caches, but no homes. "Don't you get lonely out here?"

"I like my privacy. It's quiet," he replied. "Do you want to chat out here all night, or do you want to go inside?"

I flushed. "Inside is nice."

His door didn't have a lock, showing me just how much

he trusted his crew. Leviathan held the door open for me. I walked in beside him, just barely brushing him.

But that brush sent a shock wave all through me.

He closed the door and lit a few lamps with a matchbook before twisting the dial to make them brighter. He tossed his jacket onto a table next to a few small trinkets.

His cabana was very similar to his cabin on the ship. Except there was a small kitchenette in the corner opening to a modest dining area with a sitting area nearby. There was a bedroom loft above the common area and what looked like another room off to the side.

His common area included a large bookcase and a fireplace. I could imagine settling here after a long voyage.

"I'm sure you're exhausted," he commented.

It was hard to be tired when my pulse roared in my ears. I was hyperaware of his body only a few feet from me. "Yeah. Very tired," I agreed even though it was a lie.

"Mm-hmm, okay," he said, and by his tone, it was clear he didn't believe me. He sidestepped me to point out the private room under the loft. "My mother has spare clothes in here, but you should buy your own sometime soon."

I tucked some hair behind my ear. "Do you know a good tailor?"

"I do." He paused. "Siggi has to patch some of my garments anyway. I'll take you there."

"Thank you."

He made a noncommittal noise. "The head is in the hallway. You can get fresh water in the kitchen."

"Okay, then. Good night," I said, passing him again to go into the spare room.

"Yeah. Good night."

The door shut with a soft *click*. His footsteps moved away

from it. But even though he got farther away, I could still smell him.

Still feel his presence.

Gods, it was intoxicating.

I sat down on the cot that had been made comfortable with a few furs laid across the top. The window to the side let in a little moonlight. I was used to seeing moonlight from the officers' quarters, so I didn't pull the curtains closed.

My body buzzed, achy for touch. Between my thighs, I felt heat pool, moistening the fabric.

I yearned to feel his big hands stroking up and down my inner thighs. Parting them to ease the desperation aching inside me.

He said we couldn't complicate matters between us, but why did it have to be complicated? Why couldn't it just be two people fulfilling a physical desire?

Damn it.

I buried my face in my hands, and it felt hot to the touch. Now that I was alone, all I could think about was that night in his cabin. The way his hands felt. How he tasted on my lips. His cock notched up against my pelvis, bumping and grinding into me.

The love bite on my neck had haunted me for the entire night before it disappeared the next morning. Maybe if he'd sucked a little harder, it would've lasted longer.

He'd slid his hot tongue against the skin of my throat, but I couldn't help but want it where I burned. *How would Levi look on his knees in front of me?*

My entire body tightened at the image. I was hot to the touch. Unbearably aroused. I'd never been this pent-up in my entire life.

I wanted Levi.

Even if it was only for a night.

I shook my head, took my boots off, and lay down on my back.

Just go to sleep, Mae.

I didn't know how much time had passed after I squeezed my eyes shut. But I was restless.

Worked up and restless.

I needed a drink of water. Something cold.

As if that will quench my thirst.

Deep down, I knew it wouldn't. But I needed to do something. Would he be asleep yet? Probably not, but I felt fidgety. I needed to get out of this room.

I tiptoed to the door and opened it as softly as I could to keep from waking Levi if he'd gone to sleep. Just as I stepped out of the room, I heard something.

A growly breath whispering, *"Fuck."*

Heat ignited everywhere. The repressed desire flooded back to the surface, washing away any denial I hid behind. I stood under the loft, listening closely.

Unable to help myself.

Levi groaned softly, though I wished he was a little louder. My mouth watered as I listened, hot lust curling in my belly. My breathing deepened, my face boiling. I couldn't help but imagine what he looked like in the throes of pleasure.

Did his face get all hot?

Did his breathing get uneven?

Did his pupils devour his irises like they had when we were in his cabin?

"Sweetheart," he murmured, making me that much wetter.

Is he thinking of me?

I chewed my lower lip as desire moved through my body like a poltergeist, arching my back, blazing for him. There was nothing I wanted more than to watch him break for me as I broke for him.

To dissolve into nothing, lose myself in my desire with his arms caged around my head.

At the castle, my worth was tied so intimately to my chastity. It was indecent to want sex. Shameful to feel lust.

I'd started to think there was something wrong with me the few times I'd felt desire and then was ashamed of it. Time and time again, I was told that I'd lose all my value the moment I let myself experience pleasure.

That I *wasn't supposed to feel pleasure.*

I was a body. A vessel to be used for *Nathaniel's* pleasure and not my own. But now... after the night in Levi's cabin where I discovered the way a mere kiss rumbled me like a thunderclap, I realized those lectures were simply another way to control me.

No.

I was going to take control of my body.

The ache inside intensified as Levi released another guttural groan and muttered another curse.

I liked it when he cursed. I liked how his hands felt on my hips, the way he controlled our kiss, giving as much as he took.

Did he want me as badly as I wanted him?

My throat bobbed as I swallowed, trying to keep up with how much my mouth watered. I hadn't even touched myself yet, but just listening to Levi pleasure himself tightened me immensely.

Gods, I want him.

But was I bold enough to say anything? Do anything?

My knees wobbled as I took another step, making sure he could hear me this time. The floors creaked. The noises stopped, and I heard Levi stumble out of his bed in the open loft. "Mae? What're you doing up?" His voice was deep, out of breath.

A small part of me was satisfied at how nervous he sounded.

My face burned and my thighs tingled. "I was thirsty," I murmured, not yet working up the courage to look up at him as I opened a few cabinets to find a cup.

"The one to the left," he said.

I still couldn't find where he kept the cups. "Um... I... uh...." I didn't know what to say, the nervousness settling in.

Gods, what am I doing?

Repressing the urge to flee back into my room, I felt my face blaze even hotter.

I heard footsteps behind me as Levi walked down the stairs, my insides tightening more and more the closer he got. The smell of his skin sent heat down my spine as his thick arm reached next to my head to open the one cabinet I'd missed.

"Here," he said, handing me a cup.

My hands shook embarrassingly hard when I accepted it. My eyes darted up, desire coiling as I raked over his bare chest and up to his flushed face. "T-Thanks."

"Are you all right?" Levi asked, leaning against the countertop.

I turned open the tap and filled the glass with water while I tried to figure out what I was going to say. It was overwhelming being next to him. My knees buckled. Having him barely a few feet in front of me dialed the budding heat up into a full blaze.

"Why does it have to be complicated?" I asked, then took a gulp of water to silence myself before I could say anything else.

Levi blinked. "What?"

"You. Me. Why does it have to be complicated?" I swallowed a lump in my throat, my face no doubt red like the sash he'd wear to house his weapons. "I... I...." My words abandoned me. "No. Never mind."

I put the glass on the countertop and attempted to flee. Mortification felt thick in my throat.

Until Levi caught my arm. "Say what you're going to say, Mae."

I couldn't look him in the eye. "Do you want me?"

He released my arm. "What gave you that idea?"

Slowly looking up at him through my eyelashes, I murmured, "I heard you."

"Just because I was pleasuring myself doesn't mean I was thinking about you," he said, looking away from me completely. But the way his cheeks pinkened in the darkness wasn't lost on me.

The mortification was gone, replaced with irritation. I straightened up, crossing my arms. "Now who's lying, Levi?"

He whipped around, towering over me as he eyed me down the bridge of his nose. An intimidation tactic. He wanted me to drop it.

Unfortunately for him, I was just as stubborn as he was.

My eyes flickered down to the half-done laces and the tenting fabric at the front of his trousers. He could fight it all he wanted, but his body betrayed him. And my own responded in kind, getting hotter as wetness pooled between my legs.

"If it makes you feel any better, I liked listening," I commented, thinking that would get him to let his guard down a little.

It didn't.

"Well, I'm flattered, Princess, but I have more interesting people to fantasize about than you."

I pressed my tongue against my inner cheek. "Who else do you call *sweetheart*, Levi? I'd love to meet her."

His face darkened, but he doubled down. "Can you just leave it, Mae? Must you insist on being so fucking *infuriating*?"

"I think you like it." I took a step toward him, but he stood his ground. I placed a hand on his chest, feeling his heart hammer. His pupils were blown to the Hells. "Admit it. You want me too."

He moved, switching our positions so I was pressed against the countertop. A bolt of pleasure cascaded through me again. I liked this. I liked it when he towered over me close enough that I could feel his breath.

"Too?" he asked.

No taking it back now. "Answer the question."

"And if I did… what then? After shore leave, I'm gone. You're gone. What's the point in any of this? I'm never going to fall in love with you."

I almost laughed. "Do you think I want love? Do you think I want to preen under every compliment and wait on you hand and foot? If I wanted that, we would've never met."

The corner of his mouth turned up, denting a dimple into his cheek as his intense eyes fell to my mouth. "That doesn't sound like you at all."

His smile was infectious, enticing one of my own. "It doesn't have to be complicated."

"Then what? Do you want me to fuck you?" Levi put both arms on the cabinet behind me, caging me between them.

I shuddered. "I want to get you out of my system."

"Likewise, *sweetheart*," he replied cheekily, swiping a tendril of hair from my face. "I'd like to never think about you again."

My tongue shot out to moisten my lower lip, and Levi's

eyes followed the motion. "I want to forget about you the moment you leave."

"Good," he nearly growled, grasping the nape of my neck.

Our eyes locked, both pairs half lidded with desire. My fingers ached with the need to touch him. I never dropped his gaze as I stroked the skin on his chest, tracing the blue ink of his tattoo, trailing lower and lower.

The goose bumps prickling across his skin gave me all the encouragement I needed to feel bold.

I pushed down my nerves and stroked his cock through his trousers.

The thick hardness throbbed against my fingers, and through the fabric, I could feel how hot his skin was. I shuddered again, pushing myself against him. His chest was so solid, and there was no mistaking the power in his body.

All it did was make me that much more eager.

Levi threw his head back, groaning a swear as his hand tightened in my hair. Pinpricks of pain ran up my scalp, but the bite only made the pleasure that followed more intense.

He looked down at me, pinning me with his eyes, and dragged me into an all-consuming kiss.

25
MAEVE CROSS

I'D FORGOTTEN how good he tasted.

I rose on my toes and threw both my arms around his neck, kissing him back with everything I had.

There was nothing soft or exploratory about this kiss. It was all ravenous, burning lust. He pulled my lower lip between his teeth and nipped it, earning a gasp of surprise.

I could feel his lips curve as he took the opportunity to lick his way into my mouth, stroking my tongue with his. I mimicked the motion, and I knew he liked it based on how his hand tightened in my hair, the other wrapping around my waist.

His cock thickened against my belly. The ache between my legs got worse until it hurt. I moved restlessly, wanting to kiss him until my lungs burned, but I couldn't focus on anything but my own desperation.

"Please," I murmured against Levi's mouth.

When he pulled back, I couldn't see any color in his eyes, only the inkiness of his pupils. He looked as desperate as I felt. My hands fell to the side, and I grasped the countertop.

A wild gleam hungered in his eyes as he panted hard. His

mouth was swollen in the darkness, but it wasn't nearly swollen enough for me to be satisfied.

"Please what, sweetheart?" he asked, his voice low and gravelly. "Tell me what you want."

My face felt hot. My heart hammered. My breath came out in heavy gasps. "Touch me." My hips wriggled against his body, seeking out sensation. Pressure where I wanted it.

He groaned, the hand at the nape of my neck falling to grasp my hip, stilling my movements. "Stop that."

My lust-lagged brain took several moments to understand why he said that, but as soon as I did, my eyes widened, my mouth curling up in a mischievous smirk.

I wanted to get him writhing as badly as I was.

I wanted him desperate.

I wanted him to say *please*.

Not once had he ever said please.

Before he could stop me, I reached down to press my palm firmly against the bulge in his pants. His hips punched forward, grinding against me without any control.

"*Fuck*," he hissed, grabbing my hands and pinning them both down to the counter on either side of me.

My pulse jumped. I liked that. I liked that a lot.

"You're such a brat," he said, his breath fanning my mouth.

"I think you like that about me," I rebutted, pressing my hips forward to grind against him again.

He growled in the back of his throat, his eyes fixed on me. His cock pulsed against my belly, somehow getting even thicker until I thought he'd tear the seam in the front of his trousers.

"You do, don't you?" I continued to prod, liking how the power dynamic between us was changing.

Levi seemed to realize that, too, but instead of trying to

physically seize control back for himself, he released my hands. "I won't deny that I enjoy it when you misbehave," he hummed, looking down at me from the bridge of his nose.

That same intimidation tactic he'd used on me several times before just made the fabric between my legs even damper. I arched my back, my eyelashes fluttering as his hard body rocked against mine.

He watched me closely, trailing his hands over the front of my blouse. "But the more you misbehave, the more I'll have to punish you for it."

His mouth fell to my throat, fanning the flames in my belly. My mind went blank before I could ask him what that meant. In an instant, those big hands fisted my shirt as he ripped it open, buttons flying and pinging all over the place.

I gasped, "Levi! This isn't my shirt."

"Don't care," he murmured against my neck, nipping the sensitive flesh. "If you want to stop, tell me to stop."

I moaned as his hands curved around my bare waist, the calluses scratching my skin. "I-I guess the damage is already done." My voice broke midsentence when he cupped my breasts, squeezing them as his thumbs rubbed rough circles around my nipples.

My knees wobbled, my pulse racing against his lips. My core throbbed, blood rushing to the apex of my thighs where the shy little bud cried out for his touch.

"Oh... *damn it*," I swore breathily. "Touch me. Touch me right now."

He drew back, looking awfully pleased with himself. "Where, sweetheart?"

My mouth felt dry. I wasn't sure what to tell him. "I-I don't know."

Those deviant fingertips rubbed my nipple even harder,

causing a spear of pleasure to shoot between my legs. "Yes, you do."

Again, my words escaped me.

He pressed a kiss against my neck again. "There's nothing to be nervous about."

"Is it that obvious?" I panted, overwhelmed as butterflies erupted in my belly.

"You're shaking."

I am. I didn't even realize it until he mentioned it. My hands shook violently against the countertop. My heart was in my throat. "I… I don't know what to do," I admitted.

He drew back, and instantly my entire body cried out in rejection. "Come here."

I followed as he led me by the hand over to the sitting area.

"Sit down," he ordered softly.

The shaking got worse when I sat down, both my legs rocking back and forth. My shirt was torn, hanging off me, making me feel completely naked. I crossed my arms, but that didn't help.

The chaise lounge dipped as he sat next to me. "Have you had sex before, Mae?"

I couldn't look at him. "I have. Just some stable boy. It didn't mean anything."

He gripped my chin, gently pulling my face up to look him in the eye. "Why are you still lying to me?" His voice was incredibly low, soft. It sent chills down my spine.

I gulped. "I don't want to be treated any differently."

Levi's gaze never left mine. "I don't care about that, Mae. But I don't want to hurt you."

"Sex is supposed to hurt," I replied automatically. "I don't know what the big deal is."

"No. It's not. Discomfort at first? Sure. But pain? No." He sighed, stroking my chin with his thumb.

I leaned into it, disappointment starting to unfurl inside me. This was why I lied. I didn't want to stop. Maybe my frown gave me away.

After a pause, he asked, "Do you want this?"

My insides tightened, excitement lighting up my system again. "I do."

He could see the honesty in my eyes. A devious gleam shone in his as he slid off the chaise lounge and onto his knees. He put both hands on my thighs, spreading my legs so he'd fit between them.

A wash of heat flooded over me. "What are you doing?"

"Giving you what you want."

"Y-You don't have to if you don't want to," I murmured, feeling equally embarrassed and aroused as he toyed with the laces of my trousers.

"Don't worry about me, sweetheart. I'll enjoy it just as much as you will."

My voice was uneven. "Enjoy what?"

"Foreplay." On his knees, he was still tall enough to kiss me while I sat down. He slid his hand behind my head, eyes darting between my lips and my eyes. "If you want me to fuck you, I need to get you nice and wet."

My insides tightened. "I'm already wet," I whispered as I squirmed on the chaise.

A dimple punctured his cheek. "Oh, are you? Then let me see how wet you are, pretty girl."

I shuddered, the words breathing a new confidence into me. "O-Okay."

He unlaced my breeches, and I raised my hips so he could slide them down. Then he tossed them off to the side.

Before I could snap my legs shut at the breeze tickling my

bare skin, Levi cupped my inner thighs, keeping them spread for him. "Don't hide the view from me."

I gulped thickly, my face red and hips wiggling in a desperate attempt to get him to touch me. But he still hadn't done it yet.

The bastard.

He groaned under his breath. "Look at you. Good enough to eat."

I nearly jumped out of my skin when he pressed a kiss to my thigh. He held me down as he left torturous kisses along the sensitive skin, pausing to nip it every so often.

"Levi…."

"Is this all right, sweetheart?" he asked, his lips moving even closer to my core. His breath whirled out against my skin, adding a new sensation.

"Y-Yes," I murmured. My insides throbbed, clenching around nothing. Gods, every moment was drawn out, leaving me hanging on each breath.

But I think he preferred it that way.

His eyes flickered up to me as he slowly leaned in and slid his tongue up my thigh, giving me time to move, to push him away. I didn't want it to end. My legs were trembling in anticipation, and I quivered with bated breath.

"*Please*," I whispered.

I felt him groan as he glided his hands up my thighs, carefully using his fingertips to part the delicate folds of my sex. A gasp fell from my lips, my eyelids fluttering when he finally touched me. Heat welled inside me as he watched my reactions to each exploratory touch as if he was committing everything I liked to memory. A soft cry came next when he stroked upward, smearing my own wetness across my clit.

Oh Gods….

Gods….

My hips punched upward. "Oh…."

Levi rubbed a circle with his thumb, and my inner walls started to flutter, and a completely new sensation swelled in my belly. I looked up at the ceiling, slapping my hand over my mouth to stifle the embarrassing whimper.

"Watch," he ordered. "Eyes. Me. *Now.*"

My eyes rolled back as I fought the burning desire roaring through my veins to look down at him. His hand was drenched with my arousal, the noise of my heavy breathing filling the air as he slid his fingers down to play with my slit while pressing his thumb harder against the swollen bud. The image was so incredibly erotic that my belly clenched again.

"Do you like that, sweetheart?"

By the smirk on his face, he already knew the answer. I couldn't speak. It felt like too much, yet not enough. Somewhere in between.

"Look at how you soak my hand. It's nothing compared to how you'll soak my cock. I'll make sure of it." He pressed a wet, smacking kiss against my thigh.

He groaned as I saturated his hand. I was sure I'd ruined the chaise by now, but I couldn't find it in me to care. I parted my legs wider, needing more.

I needed so much more.

"Will you let me taste you?" His gaze was locked on me, devouring me spread out in front of him in my vulnerable state. "Hm? Will you let me taste that pretty little cunt?"

That mouth.

That *filthy* mouth.

I gasped, the lewd words injecting more fire into my veins. "Yes."

Without a moment's hesitation, he tilted his head down to

glide his hot, wet tongue across my swollen clit. He made a noise of pleasure at the same time I did.

"*Fuck*," I cried out as the potent sensation of lust came over me, the word nearly getting stuck between my teeth.

He chuckled, the vibration making my legs shake more. I felt his thumb join his tongue while one of his fingers pressed gently against my entrance. I sobbed when it sank inside me, instantly clenching around it.

"Mmm, that's right. Strangle my finger like you'd strangle my cock."

His breath blew against the sensitive, hot flesh, and I could feel something unfurl inside me. Heat pooled at the base of my spine, and my breath got all uneven.

"Levi… *Levi*…," I begged even if I didn't understand what I was begging for.

I felt so hot.

So desperate.

So close to liberation.

I could hear how wet I was as he slid his finger in and out of me, curling it slightly to brush against a bundle of nerves that had me chasing stars behind my eyes. I rotated my hips, pushing against his face, demanding more of his tongue.

And he was more than willing to give me whatever I wanted.

I cried out, my heart pounding so hard, I thought it would combust in my chest. Tears welled in my eyes, my entire body shuddering like I was about to *break.*

He pressed another finger in to join the first, adding increased pressure against the bundle of nerves just inside. My eyes rolled back as I released a noise of guttural torment.

I was close….

So close….

How do I let go?

My vision blurred as I looked between my legs at him. I didn't know this amount of pleasure was attainable. My belly clenched, my inner walls fluttering more rapidly around his fingers. I knew I was about to come, but I didn't know how.

A sob burst from my chest as I started to feel inadequate. Vulnerable.

Levi veered back, watching me with hungry eyes. "Are you going to come for me, Mae? Or do I need to work a little harder?" His face glistened with my arousal. He licked his lips, thrusting his fingers firmly against that spot inside. The circles he rubbed on my clit were unrelenting.

My eyes rolled backward, my body spasming as I reached the precipice of pleasure.

"Come on, baby. Give it to me," he murmured.

Baby?

"Show me how sweet you look when you let go. I'll drink up every last drop of it."

With one more firm lick, he brought me right up to the edge and shoved me over. My orgasm moved through me like a force of nature. Torrential downpours and rough waves. It swallowed me whole, throttling me under the waves until I lost my breath. A rush of heat flooded out from me.

Then I was free of my body. Of all the cresting pain and stresses. I fell slack against the chaise, trembling and panting. When I could see again, Levi was staring at me from the floor, both dimples proudly on display.

"Good, huh?" he asked.

I nodded, giggling a little under my breath, though I replied by saying, "Mediocre."

My head felt light, like a burden had been lifted from my shoulders. He rolled his eyes at my comment, moving back so I could close my legs.

He stood, crooking a fingertip under my chin so I'd look up at him with my eyes all glassy. I was hyperaware of his cock pressed against the placket of his pants. I curved my spine inward, pressing myself against his hand.

I wanted to return the favor. My insides had started to feel sore from how roughly he'd fingered me, but if he wanted to have sex, then I'd bite down the pain and take it.

My eyes became half lidded as I asked, "Are you going to *fuck* me now, Levi?"

He released a sharp breath and muttered, "No," through his teeth.

The rejection felt like a blow to the chest. "What? Why not? I can't even get pregnant until my wedding tonic wears off."

Levi sighed. "It's not that. I couldn't sire children with you even if I wanted to."

"Then why?"

He didn't let me look away. "It's not that I don't want to, Mae." He groaned under his breath as his gaze flitted over my naked body and back to my eyes. "*Gods*, I'm hard as a godsdamn rock just looking at you."

"Then why?" I repeated, feeling vulnerable again.

His voice turned all soft. "You wouldn't possibly be able to take me right now. I'd hurt you. There's no way in the Nine Hells I'm going to make you bleed because I want a quick fuck."

I looked away, freeing myself of his hold, slightly ashamed but also oddly relieved. His concern about my body touched me, sending a pang of something new through me. It wasn't lust. Or guilt. Or doubt. It was something much more tender.

"You should go to bed. Especially if you plan on going to Shipwreck Bay tomorrow."

Without another word, he turned to leave, but I had one more thing to say.

"Let me take care of you."

He paused, his rigid back tensing. "You gave me ample material to take care of myself."

"But I want to. Show me how to…." I trailed off as I found the courage for my words again. "Show me how to touch *you*."

He looked at me from over his shoulder as if considering it before he decided. I was even more aware of my nakedness as I felt his dilated pupils run across my skin like they were his fingertips.

Then he turned back around and headed toward the loft.

"Not tonight. Good night, Mae."

Quietly, I acquiesced, saying, "Good night, Levi."

26
CAPTAIN LEVIATHAN

What the fuck was I thinking last night?

I gulped down a scalding sip of breakfast tea, but even that wouldn't get the taste of Mae out of my mouth. All night, it haunted me. I could've drunk her up until the sun rose and fell. Taken her straight from one euphoric climax to another.

All I could think about was how pretty she was when she broke.

Her flush washed down her entire body, painting her peachy skin a lovely shade of pink. Freckles speckled everywhere, enticing me toward where I could kiss her next. Her brown eyes were wide, glassy, hazed over in ecstasy.

Gods, she was a sight.

What I wouldn't do to watch her fall over that edge over and over again. I'd make her come until she cried. Until she couldn't take any more. Until her legs were trembling so hard, she wouldn't be able to stand by the time I was done with her.

I sighed, hanging my head down.

I was fucked.

Although Mae had given me plenty of material to get myself off, it didn't help one bit. I'd ended up somehow more sexually frustrated than I was to begin with. I had to go for a swim to cool off.

I wish she'd actually fucked a stable boy instead of lying to me about it.

Then I wouldn't have to be so damn careful. I enjoyed rough sex, hair pulling, and a little spanking. Perhaps some restraints if my partner was up for it. I'd rut her like a fucking animal if I had my way, and I wasn't exactly known for reeling it in.

That was the biggest reason I didn't let her finish me off, even if my cock had argued with me the entire way back up to my loft.

That thin strand of control would snap like a fishing line, and there was no way in the Nine Hells I'd be responsible for hurting someone who wasn't ready for it.

I never messed around with virgins.

But, to the *Gods*, I *really* wanted to mess around with Mae.

With another grumble, I sipped my tea. At least we were on the same page. We'd fuck about a bit, then go our separate ways. I'd get her out of my system. Give her the experience she wanted before going out on her own. Simple enough. Though I couldn't be sure the next bastard she fucked would be as thoughtful toward her well-being. She'd spent her entire life with the expectation of being used up and spat out.

I didn't want her to think that was normal.

People weren't items to use.

My mouth turned into a frown, a bitter taste invading my mouth at the thought of anyone touching her. I didn't like the idea of her muttering someone else's name. Someone else seeing her vulnerable and flushed with pleasure. Someone *using* her.

Get the fuck over it. Mae does not belong to you. Or anyone. End of the fucking story.

I just wanted to fuck her. She was going to use me, and I was going to use her, and that was going to be the end of it.

I heard my mates striding up the path, embroiled in some exuberant conversation. Rubbing circles on my temples, I braced myself for their overbearing energy first thing in the morning.

Didn't make me love them any less, though.

Regardless of that, I couldn't let them suspect anything. After they'd given me such a hard time for fancying Mae, I wasn't keen on proving them right. And considering both twins were in long-term commitments, they made it quite clear to me that I couldn't fuck around forever.

But I'd fuck around as long as I wanted to.

I hadn't trusted any of my former relationships enough to consider anything long-term. My priority was keeping the crew safe, and my lovers wanted to be my first priority. That would never happen.

Howler threw my front door open, and the twins strode in like they owned the place. They were dressed in an array of colors—Boats in rich purples and greens while Howler favored oranges and yellows. Both of them were armed with cutlasses and flintlock pistols at their waists. Boats usually also wore a dagger tucked between her colorful corset and her blouse.

And in her left shoe.

And somewhere in her trousers.

And there was a long, thin needle in her locs, hidden among refreshed beads and cuffs. It stuck out slightly from the side of her tricorn hat.

Necessary in Shipwreck Bay. Not that any of the locals would try to screw around with us, but better safe than dead.

Boats and Howler chatted up a storm, hauling a bushel of fruits in a basket and a bag full of damaged clothing that needed repairs. Their boots clapped against my floor, and if Mae hadn't already been awake, she was now.

Both my eyebrows went into my hairline. "Would it kill you lot to knock every once in a while?"

They blew off my comment. "Hope you're hungry! Conway picked this for us this morning." Boats lifted the basket to emphasize her point.

"That man could grow a pygmy pecan tree in a drought," Howler added, taking a glistening elderwood cherry and popping it happily into his mouth.

Boats plopped down on the chaise lounge, and I couldn't help the warmth that found my face as I thought about everything I did to Mae on that chaise last night.

They can't find out.

I can't complicate things more than I have already.

Putting on an air of indifference, I took another sip of my tea to quell my thoughts. A twinkle on the floor caught my eye. One of the buttons I hadn't picked up yet. "Merrows are notoriously good gardeners. I don't know why this keeps surprising you," I commented as I subtly kicked the rogue button under a cabinet.

Howler waved his hand dismissively, joining his twin. "Whatever. Where's Mae?"

"I imagine she's still sleeping," I said, sitting on an accent chair across from them. "At least before you two clambered in here like drunks."

Boats kicked her feet up onto the side of the lounge, not wasting any time sharing her cheeky comment. "Kept her up all night, did you?"

You have no idea.

"Please," I scoffed. "Nothing happened."

Howler leaned forward. He had his favorite orange scarf tied around his head. He never wore it on deck—only when he came to town. Isa bought it for him as their first anniversary present. A decade later, and they're still just as smitten as they'd always been.

If only my life was that easy. At least they knew each other's birth name. The second I told anyone my name, they'd know who I was, and Varric would hunt me down.

"You mean to tell me that you flirted with Mae during the entire card game, then insisted on letting her stay with you... *to not make a move?*" Howler asked and pinched the bridge of his nose.

"I've told you once and I'll tell you again, but only because you're my friend. There's nothing going on between us." I brought my tea back up to my lips, mildly disappointed that it was the last sip.

Howler and Boats exchanged a look before turning back to me. It was as if they could read each other's minds. I'd always hated that about them.

"Whatever you say, Levi," Boats replied.

I didn't give a bilge rat's ass if they believed me or not.

The door behind me clicked open, and my entire back stiffened. I looked over my shoulder at a barely awake Mae. Hair sticking up everywhere. Pillow creases on her cheeks. Her face as pink as ever. She was fully dressed in ill-fitting clothes that she'd rolled up to make them fit her better.

But even so, she looked well rested with the most relaxed smile on her face.

I guess that orgasm did help her sleep.

I repressed a sideways grin and instead said, "Sleep well, Mae?"

Gods, she was so lovely when she blushed. "I did. Did you?"

"Not as well as I could have," I answered, making my best attempt at remaining neutral as I turned back around. "The water should still be hot if you'd like tea."

"Thanks," she said softly, that sweet voice of hers sending chills up my spine. "Good morning, everyone."

"Hey, Mae!" Boats greeted. "Come have something to fill your belly."

That sweet scent of hers clung to her hair, a combination of fresh berries and cinnamon. I'd noticed it before, but with how incredibly worked up I still was after last night, I was hyperaware of how much I liked how she smelled.

Her not-so-delicate hands reached forward to grab one of the peaches from the bounty, and she sank her teeth into the juicy flesh. Out of the corner of my eye, I watched the juice drip down her chin. She giggled when she realized how messy it was, her tongue darting out to catch the trickle.

I'd never wanted to be a peach so badly in my entire life.

Howler laughed and got up to toss Mae a hand towel.

"Thanks," she said, still giggling. She wiped her face, and I had to tear my gaze from her and over to Howler, who crooked an eyebrow at me.

"No Wraith today?" Mae asked.

"Elves have a rite they perform when they return home. It's a very private thing," Boats answered fondly.

"Oh, you've never been?"

Boats shrugged. "She misses her home. I don't need to be involved in everything. It felt wrong to inject myself between her and her people."

Mae furrowed her brows. "The Gullies aren't too far to visit."

Wraith wasn't from the Gullies.

She kept her cards close to her chest, always convinced that if the wrong people knew she was Algarian, they'd kill the few things she'd learned to love here. I knew how that felt.

We understood each other. More than Boats or Howler ever could.

"I get that you're curious, but it's not my story to tell," Boats replied. "If my wife wants you to know, she'll tell you. Until then, you best respect her privacy."

I almost expected Mae to backpedal defensively, but instead, she said, "Heard. So what's on the itinerary today?"

Howler lifted the sack of clothing. "Paying a visit to the tailor at the port. You're welcome to come. We'll get a drink."

Mae practically beamed. "I'd love that! I could use some clothes that fit." She turned to me and asked, "Do you know where I can sell that ring?"

"Keep it here. I have an account with Siggi." If Mae walked around with that ring, she'd get robbed before she even stepped foot into the bank. Like fuck I'd let that happen.

"You don't have to do that."

"If you want to buy something so badly, bring a small coin purse and buy us a round of drinks from your winnings last night."

Her lips parted, but I wasn't in the mood for banter. At least not when my mates were here. They were too suspicious of us already. I just hoped Mae kept up with the ruse.

Before she could argue, I sidestepped her and placed my mug on the table. "We're burning daylight."

As we walked down the dirt path to the port town, the bustling noise of business got louder. Mae trailed behind, staring down the cliffside like the sight mesmerized her. Her eyes were bright, and she had a smile on her face. She practically buzzed with excitement.

Lovely.

The way she looked at everything with a sense of wonderment made her naivety more obvious, but it also made her incredibly endearing. I had to fight the urge to wrap an arm around her to make it clear to other pirates that she was under my protection.

I'd seen too many innocent lights get snuffed out by bastards who saw an easy target. I couldn't let that happen. Mae wasn't armed, but I wouldn't leave her defenseless.

Fuck with her and you're fucking with me.

However, if I did that, she would get the wrong idea. We set a boundary last night. This relationship was physical. That was it. She didn't need me to stake a claim when our agreement was temporary.

"Keep up, sweetheart," I said. "I'd hate to leave you behind."

Her wide eyes darted over to me, her cheeks pinkening slightly as she picked up the pace to stay in line with us.

Boats scoffed. "We wouldn't leave you behind, Mae."

"Speak for yourself," I retorted. "Stay close. They'll rob you if you look like you're alone."

Or they'd do worse.

Next to all three of us, Mae was considerably smaller. Boats was the closest to her size, but even so, she had several inches on Mae. Don't get me wrong—after a month of hard labor, Mae was visibly stronger than when I'd first seen her.

But she was still a lamb entering a den of wolves.

As usual, the port teemed with sailors and merchants alike. Nothing like the sounds of haggling to remind me where I was. Working women were already walking the streets, ready to meet the ships coming into dock.

Didn't matter what time of day, the brothel was always booming.

I noticed a few of them eyeing us up, putting on their best seductive faces, but none of it ever appealed to me. I preferred having sex when my partner was using me for pleasure, not business.

The crown of Mae's head came into my peripheral as she stepped next to me, doing her damnedest to keep up with me. If Howler or Boats noticed, they didn't say anything. Almost immediately, the working girls stopped looking at me.

Is she glaring at them? How adorable.

I chuckled under my breath, turning the corner toward Siggi's shop. "Right here," I said, pushing the door open.

The bell on the top corner of the door chimed loudly. His shop was humble, nothing more than a desk and a few pieces on display. The door to his back room swung open, revealing an elven tailor with pointed ears and an incredibly deep complexion that was almost violet with all the blues in his undertone.

As soon as he saw us, he grinned broadly, revealing two extended canines. "Ah, Levi! Twins!" His Skadi accent deepened as he recited a common greeting in Skaditung.

I repeated it back to him before adding, "It's good to see you too."

Howler came forward and placed the damaged clothes on the desk. "Have a few things that need fixin'."

"That all?" Siggi asked. "You aren't going to introduce me to your friend?" He didn't wait for a response as he took several steps forward, outstretching his hand. "I'm Sigurd, but everyone calls me Siggi."

"I'm Maeve," she answered, taking his hand and giving it a firm shake. "Or Mae."

"Aren't you just adorable?" He looked down at her ill-fitting clothes. "You, Mae, are in desperate need of a new wardrobe."

"Put it on my account, Siggi," I said. "Do your worst."

His mouth broadened into an excited grin. "Fantastic! I have so many pieces." His eyes glinted as he looked back at Mae. Then he whisked her away into the back room where he kept all his premade designs.

I chuckled to myself, leaning on his desk to wait for her. "I'll wait if you two want to run those errands."

Howler narrowed his eyes at me. "You're acting odd. Odder than usual."

"I'm always on edge when we're at port." I had to be. If that guard went down, I'd be risking the safety of my crew.

"No, not that. You've been awfully cold all morning," he pointed out.

Boats interjected. "If he doesn't want to talk about it, you won't get anything out of him," she said. "Come on. We'll meet up at the tavern later."

I waved my hand dismissively. "See you then."

Howler hated it when I hid anything from him. But he didn't need to get involved in whatever it was Mae and I were doing. He scowled, but he knew Boats was right. If a torturer could tear my fingernails off without a peep from me, a glower from Howler wouldn't do shit.

The door chimed again when they left, and I kept myself busy eyeing Siggi's display pieces.

Siggi and I went way back.

It was almost six years ago when I wandered into his shop to see a handful of bandits trying to rob him. Safe to say they never bothered him again, and now I got a discount.

Siggi was quite a character. Elves weren't common in

Farlight Isles, especially those hailing from Skadi, one of the Four Kingdoms of Algar.

Traveling from Algar to Farlight Isles didn't used to be so difficult, but nearly a century ago, the Isles drifted farther and farther into the ocean. Now no one could travel the distance easily. Not even nomads.

Varric Cross's hostile takeover only made it more difficult. Citizens who didn't support the crown were considered traitors. The pirate safehold quickly became the only safe place for free thought.

But it won't be for long.

Not once Cross and Pike enact the siege.

I tried not to think about it. The fact that the demon from my childhood, the monster who stole everything from me, wasn't even close to being finished terrorizing the world. But how would capturing Shipwreck Bay help him? Cross was a strategic thinker. He didn't do anything on a whim.

I sighed deeply, rubbing the fabric of a doublet between my fingers.

The back doors swung open, and Siggi ushered Mae out of the back room, always in a hurry, no matter what. I glanced over, appreciating how the color crimson looked on her. The silky material of her blouse hugged her frame.

Even her breeches didn't have to be rolled at the ankles, as they tapered perfectly down her legs. Her waist was adorned with a violet sash where I imagined she'd wear her weapons.

I couldn't picture Mae in gowns. I couldn't picture her dancing at balls. Not when this attire suited her so perfectly.

"Where are Boats and Howler?" she asked.

"Out running errands," I answered, enjoying her new state of dress.

Siggi came up to the front and pulled out his logbook. He

jotted down a handful of numbers. Frankly, I didn't care how expensive it was. I wasn't a big spender, so I'd accrued a healthy amount of coin over the years. "Okay, I'll bill your account."

"You really don't have to buy me anything," Mae said, shifting from foot to foot.

I waved my hand dismissively. "You did the work, and considering I can't pay you from the ship's wages, I'll handle it. Consider it payment for working as a cabin boy."

"You pay your cabin boys this well?"

I did. It was only a matter of how well they spent it. "Sailors far and wide want to work for me, sweetheart." Before she could open her mouth again, I added, "At least you don't look like such an easy mark anymore."

Mae's cheeks flushed that hue I liked, and she scoffed, "Would it kill you to compliment me once in a while?"

"Yes."

She snorted a laugh. Gods, it was adorable.

I grinned, tilting my head at her. "You want a compliment, sweetheart?"

Her reaction was immediate, her eyes going all wide with a gleam of playfulness, her breath deepening. She looked at me through her thick, dark lashes.

I hated it when she did that. My cock, on the other hand, loved that expression.

"I don't think you're capable of common flattery."

Leaning down, I brushed her chin with my thumb. I whispered in her ear, "You look better underneath your clothes."

"*Scoundrel*," she breathed, but I didn't think for one moment that she meant it.

Her cheeks bloomed even brighter, the heat flooding all

the way up to her ears. She drew back, suddenly realizing Siggi was still here. Just as I had.

He gave Mae a sideways grin, revealing his canines. "Just a stowaway, huh?"

"Say a word of this to Howler and I'm taking my business elsewhere," I threatened. Half-heartedly, of course. Siggi knew how to keep his mouth shut, especially since I brought him business from not just my crew but all the sailors who wanted to use the same tailor as *the great Captain Leviathan*.

He laughed. "You'll never find a better tailor this side of the Algarian Sea. But your secrets are always safe with me. Have a nice day, you two." He then recited a goodbye in Skaditung, and I repeated it back to him.

The phrase was akin to "May the snow not be too cold."

An amusing phrase for a tropical climate, but Skadi was a frozen nation.

Siggi didn't have many people he could speak in his native language to, so I took the time to learn a few phrases for him. There was very little I wouldn't do for my friends.

I signed his logbook and then guided Mae out the door.

27
MAEVE CROSS

I FELT like I fit in.

The right garments did wonders for my confidence. Levi was dressed considerably well in jewelry and a vividly colored waistcoat. He looked like a captain, exuding a powerful atmosphere that dared anyone to get in his way.

Even Boats and Howler dressed to show off their status. Meanwhile, I had been wearing linen pants a few sizes too big and a shirt that hung off my shoulder. I'd looked like a little boy who hadn't grown into his breeches yet.

It was discouraging, especially when I noticed countless women eyeing Levi. Who could blame them, though? He was incredibly attractive, and it wasn't like we were courting. Our arrangement was temporary.

That didn't mean I had to like the attention he was getting.

I didn't want to think about what would happen in a few weeks when we went our separate ways, but that wasn't any of my business. I'd always been quite confident, but I was out of my element here.

Shipwreck Bay was nothing like Farlight Harbor. No one

knew my status. I was nothing more than an easy mark. My earlier state of dress only aided my insecurity, but when I saw myself in the mirror at Siggi's shop, dressed in properly fitted garments, I felt amazing.

I didn't look like a little boy anymore.

I looked like a woman. My confidence soared. And when I saw Levi again in the main shop, it reminded me that my attraction to him wasn't one-sided. It excited me. I felt like I belonged at his side.

I wasn't suffocated by his presence. I was a part of it.

While we waited to meet Boats and Howler for a drink, Levi showed me around the port. Pointed out places I shouldn't go after dark, especially alone. Merchants had set up various stalls along the port, selling fish, jewelry, books, fruit, and all sorts of trinkets. I even saw Gunny laughing with a sailor from another ship.

He caught sight of me and gave me a friendly nod, waggling his eyebrows in a playful way at my new clothes. Levi didn't notice Gunny pursing his lips in a teasing kissing gesture. Probably for the better.

Was it that obvious that I was getting involved with his captain?

Gunny's lack of a verbal filter would likely inspire him to tell me, "Aye, birdie. The sun gets hotter the moment you two walk into the same room."

I had this inherent need to prove him wrong, but he was absolutely right. Gunny and I would probably make plans to get a drink with the gunnery crew when I joined them for careening. I understood it was hard work, but I didn't want to miss the little time I had left with my friends.

"I need to pick up a few loaves from the bakery," Levi stated. "They have pastries if you want any."

"Are you still offering to buy me things?" I asked, half

teasing. "If I didn't know any better, I'd think you were trying to spoil me."

Levi made this throaty noise. "Then fucking starve for all I care."

I swear every other word out of his mouth is a curse. "Has anyone ever told you that you have a filthy mouth?"

He stopped walking and looked down his nose at me. His eyes glinted deviously, a dimple puncturing his cheek. "Oh, sweetheart, this is tame in comparison to the things I plan on saying to you tonight."

Oh.

"Is that a promise?" I demanded before I could stop myself. My face blazed, but that only made him grin even wider.

"I never promise. I suppose you'll just have to wait to discover that for yourself."

"I look forward to it," I whispered, shyly looking up at him through my eyelashes.

His eyes darted down to my lips, but he didn't do anything about it. "Once they sell out, they don't bake anything else for the whole day. If you make me miss out on fresh bread, I'm going to throw you off the pier."

"I can't swim," I said, continuing to tease him.

"Then you drown, and I don't have to worry about missing out on fresh bread for the rest of my shore leave."

I stifled a little laugh and replied, "Fine. Fine. Let's get you your fresh bread."

The bakery was warm inside with ovens firing left and right as they brought out their last batch of bread for the day. It smelled absolutely divine. Sugar and yeast. Berries for the turnovers. Crusty bread. Cheeses baked into savory loaves.

Smelled better than anything I'd ever been given at the castle.

"Oh my Gods," I moaned in delight, inhaling more of that decadent scent. "Will you still get me a pastry?"

Levi arched a brow, obviously amused at my comment. "Only if you agree to go on a swim with me when we get back to the cove."

"But I can't swim," I repeated. He'd already heard me once.

"Mae, you need to learn how to swim if you're going to be a sailor or if you're going to live on an island."

Can't argue with that. "Fine. I want something with sugar."

"Heard, sweetheart. You can sit at one of the tables. I'll be right over." Levi shooed me over to the sitting area, where numerous sailors and merchants were devouring baked goods like they'd never had dessert before.

Though, after being on a ship for a month, I could relate. You don't get to enjoy luxuries like sugar at sea. Or bread. The closest we got were those stale sea biscuits that Butcher would prepare before they left shore. So fresh baked goods were a nice treat.

Speaking of, I saw Butcher sitting at a table. He had his aids—simple devices he attached to his arms with leather straps to offset his missing leg—resting on a bench. He was missing one eye, the wound old and scarred over, visibly lighter in color than the rest of his face, which was deeply tanned from a lifetime of work at sea. I knew it affected his depth perception, which was why I'd never catch him with a pistol.

I caught a glimpse of a slender man sitting across from him who I didn't recognize.

Butcher's eye lit up when he recognized me, waving me over to sit with him.

I smiled in return, joining them for a little chat.

Butcher reached over to squeeze the man's hand. "Aye! This is my favorite lassie, Mae!"

The man was visibly younger than Butcher, dark haired and fair complected. His skin was nearly the same shade as his uniquely milky, pale eyes. He turned his head in my direction, and though he didn't meet my eyes directly, he followed my shadow as I moved to the other side of the table where Butcher was sitting. "'Ello, Mae. Pleased to meet you."

Butcher continued, his sea dog accent deepening the more excited he got. "This is my husband, Conway. Apple of my eye." He lifted Conway's hand to kiss it tenderly.

"Oh! It's nice to meet you. Thank you for the fruits this morning," I said, sitting down next to Butcher.

"Anytime. I have more than I know what to do with." Conway chuckled to himself, revealing a jagged line of teeth that I hadn't noticed right away.

"So how did you meet?" I asked.

"Conway saved me from dancin' with Jack Ketch. I thought an angel rose from the water." Butcher rattled on like it was a fond memory. His sea-speak was so deep that I wouldn't have known what he was saying if I hadn't already gotten used to it.

"From the water?" I wondered quietly.

"Long time ago," Conway interrupted. "My shoal used to live in Fisherman's Gully. I don't know what happened to the other merrow when the Farlight soldiers came for us."

Merrow?

Fisherman's Gully?

A flash of a memory seeped into my vision, briefly drowning out what Butcher was saying as he continued his story.

A hand around my ankle.
Blood saturating the soil.

Bleeding into the water.
The coast was red from the slaughter.
A sword glinted in the sun, coming right toward me.
Then it was over.

I blinked, coming back to reality. My heart hammered painfully, and I breathed hard through my nose to keep calm. A vision right from my nightmares.

A hand came into my view and gripped mine gently. Pale skin with silvery flecks in the light. Nails coming to a slight point. Nothing like a siren's claws.

I knew merrows were nothing like sirens.

Sirens hunted. They were apex predators of the sea. They devoured sailors.

Merrow cohabitated with sailors. Worshipped Cliohde. Evolved to grow legs as a gift for their loyalty. Protected lost ships at sea. Their songs didn't hypnotize—they soothed. I remembered how the song soothed me to sleep when I cried, too little to know how to calm myself.

How did I know that?

How?

"Are you all right, Maeve?" Conway asked, the low hum of his voice nothing short of comforting. I was thankful for it.

"I'm fine. Thank you."

Butcher seemed oblivious to my thoughts. "Oh, ahoy, Cap!"

"Butcher," Levi greeted, seemingly coming out of nowhere. I glanced up at him, trying to hide how shaken I felt. "Come now, we're meeting the twins at the tavern."

"Right," I murmured, standing up. "It was nice to meet you, Conway."

"Likewise, Mae."

Levi guided me outside, keeping his voice low. "Are you all right?"

"I will be after a drink or two," I answered. I kept my head down, trying to keep it clear. But Levi wouldn't let it go that easily. He was just as stubborn as I was. He stopped, pinching my chin between his fingers to keep my eyes on him.

"What happened?"

It felt too intimate to say it out loud. "Something Conway said just reminded me of something that happened in my nightmares."

Levi was quiet, considering his response before he asked, "Were you afraid of him? Merrows are nothing like sirens."

"Nothing like that, Levi," I replied, cupping his hand to pull it away from my face. "He seemed lovely. It's just…." I looked away. "My nightmares really scare me."

He didn't push the subject. "We can get a drink with the twins another time."

I shook my head. "No. It's okay. I'd rather not be in my head right now." Then I looked back up at him and tried to change the subject. "Now, stop being kind to me. It's odd."

"I can toss the turnover I got you into the ocean. Would that be mean enough for you?"

"What's with you and throwing everything into the ocean?"

He chuckled. "Easiest solution for me." He reached into his bag of baked goods and pulled out a berry turnover, all golden with crunchy sugar around the edges. "Or I can eat it for you."

"Don't you dare. Hand it over."

Levi maintained eye contact before taking a bite out of it. It sounded perfectly crunchy as it flaked, leaving a crumb on his lips. The berry filling steamed.

Still warm.

"You monster."

With a laugh, he reached into his bag and pulled out another one. "You're lucky I'm taking pity on you."

I repressed a grin and got up on my toes, taking it from him before he could take a bite out of it. *Gods...* it fell apart in my mouth, coating my tongue with a tangy, syrupy fruit filling.

To die for.

"Thank you," I said, munching on it as Levi showed me the way to the tavern.

And I was right. A few drinks later, surrounded by Howler's rumbling laugh and good conversation, my spiral at the bakery was a thing of the past. I used my handful of coins to buy us a round.

Boats and Howler didn't stay, insisting that they be back before the sun went down with the goods they'd gathered from their errands. And when they left, it felt like the right time to accompany Levi back to his cabana.

Fishermen were scarce that time of night. Sailors were either gallivanting at the port or home with their families. All I could hear as we got closer to the pier was the creaking of *The Ollipheist* as it bumped against the dock and the distant chirping of insects. But the silence never did me any good. It sent me right back to my flashback in front of Conway.

I was lucky the man was blind, or he would've seen how shaken I got.

Though, oddly, he seemed to be able to feel it.

A complete stranger witnessing me at my low felt mortifying. It didn't bother me so much with Levi, not after seeing how low he got after seeing my coat of arms the first time.

I followed him down the pier to that boulder we'd both sat on yesterday, just at the mouth of the abyss-like chasm of dark water.

Wait a moment.

"We aren't swimming here, are we?"

He glanced at me over his shoulder, shrugging off his jacket and discarding it on the boulder. "There's nothing interesting down there, if that's what you're worried about."

"Why do I have the feeling that you and I have very different definitions for the word *interesting*?" I rebutted, crossing my arms suspiciously.

I caught a glimpse of his grin as he said, "You'll be fine, Mae." He continued to get undressed, kicking off his boots and pulling his shirt clear off. His weapons joined the neat pile shortly after.

As usual, his body distracted me, a bolt of heat churning in my belly. "How can you be so sure?"

He tapped his chin in a mocking gesture. "Because nothing natural to the water is dull enough to fuck with a sea dragon."

"Are you going to turn into a dragon right now?" My eyes rounded with excitement.

"N—"

"Ooh! Ooh! Can I ride on your back?" I interrupted, completely intrigued by the idea.

He coughed, though it sounded suspiciously like a laugh. "Mae... I'm not a fucking pony."

"So I can't ride you?"

"Not on my back."

Instantly, my face darkened. "You're awful."

He took a thin strand of fabric from his pocket and used it to tie his hair up. "I only answered your question, sweetheart." He unlaced his breeches, no care in the world that I was behind him.

He pulled them down, but I only had a few moments to eye up his naked backside before he jumped into the dark water. He resurfaced, floating there, his eyes twinkling in the moonlight.

"Are you going to join me, or do you just want to watch me?"

"Uh…." I glanced down at my nice new clothes, then around the pier to see if I caught anyone watching us. We were in the open. Anyone could see if they wanted to. I chewed on my lower lip, twiddling my fingers.

"Only us out here, Mae," Levi stated. "You don't have to get undressed if you don't want to, but I'd hate to see you ruin those new clothes."

I arched a brow. "Nothing to do with wanting to see me naked?"

"Of course I want to see you naked." Even through my clothes, his eyes felt hot against my skin. "But you're free to do what you wish."

I thought about it for a moment. It could be fun floating around with Levi's big hands on my waist. Goose bumps rose up the back of my neck. I wondered if those hands would wander. Lust started to bead up under my skin like thick drops of honey.

I untied the sash around my waist, then undid the buttons of my jacket.

Interest lit up Levi's eyes as he watched me undress. Temptation roared in my blood as I slowed my movements, enjoying how he seemed to devour the image of me. He'd already seen me naked once, but this didn't feel any less exciting.

The crimson blouse found a place on the boulder, followed by my breeches. Levi hadn't said a word the whole time, but I knew his attention was solely on me.

I played with the hem of my undergarments until I eventually pulled them down, baring myself completely under the moon. It shone in from the wide mouth of the cove, painting all the rocks and shacks a shade of silver.

Levi made a throaty noise, his eyes incredibly dark. "Come here."

My knees quivered. "You'll make sure I don't drown, right?"

"I guarantee that you are much more interesting alive."

I jutted out my hip, crossing my arms. "That doesn't sound like—" I gave my best impression of his voice. "*Of course, Mae. I'd never let you drown.*"

He looked up at me, visibly amused. "Of course, Mae. I'd never let you drown."

"There! Was that so difficult?"

"Yes." He had both dimples on display. The cheeky bastard. "Now come here, sweetheart. Or I will come up there and *get you myself.*"

Was it a bad thing that I liked the sound of that? But I relented. "Fine. Fine." I walked to the edge and sat down on the ledge of rock before dangling my legs into the abyssal water.

I feel like a worm on a fishing line. Come get me. I'm mighty tasty.

My apprehensiveness flittered away as Levi floated over to my side. He seemed so at ease. And if he could be relaxed like that, then I could too.

Then his hand closed around my ankle, and he pulled me in.

My heart jumped into my throat as the water swallowed me up to my neck, but I didn't sink any farther. Levi's arms were caged around my waist, keeping me afloat while his legs did all the work under the surface.

His hands felt so hot in comparison to the water. I gulped

thickly, settling my arms around his neck. My legs mindlessly wrapped around his hips to anchor me.

Gods, he felt good.

His skin slipped against mine; I loved the feel of his hard chest pressed into me. Those dark eyes bored into mine. My gaze dropped down to his mouth, his lush pink lips beckoning me. He was so close that I could feel his breath fan across my lips.

I didn't want to wait for an opening. I leaned forward, parting my lips as I kissed him. His groan rumbled against my chest, making my thighs quiver on either side of his hips. He released my waist to grasp the rock above the water.

He moved forward, pressing me against it as we devoured each other's mouths. I forgot where we were. My eyes closed, and I gave myself over to every kiss. I pressed against him, and he reacted in kind.

A gasp flew from my lips when I felt his hardness briefly touch my sex. My insides clenched even though it was barely more than a ghost of a touch. My eyelids fluttered open, the sensation nothing short of divine. I arched my back, opening myself up to him.

I wanted *more.*

He pulled back, his eyes half lidded and mouth a deeper shade of pink. "I thought I was supposed to be teaching you how to swim."

I panted, now completely worked up. "Aren't you?" My hips started to move of their own accord, seeking out what I'd just barely gotten a taste of.

"Sweetheart," he murmured, capturing my lips again in a much softer kiss. "If you keep that up, both of us are going to drown."

Heat flooded my face, and my eyes widened as I realized

we were floating on the surface of a trench. "Can't you breathe underwater?"

"Not like this."

I couldn't hide my disappointment.

He rolled his eyes, amused at my frustration. Then he leaned in and whispered, "You're an impatient little thing, aren't you?"

My cheeks pinkened, proving him right.

"Good. More fun that way." He pulled back. "But I think teaching you to swim is a little more important than getting you underneath me."

"Teach me later, then."

"No." The corner of his mouth pulled up, weakening my knees. "There won't be a later, and I can't always be there to resuscitate you."

"Why are you so concerned with whether or not I survive after you leave? It doesn't affect you at all."

He was quiet for a long moment as we floated. "Maybe because you've come this far, and it'd be such a shame for you to die so easily." He stroked my chin with his thumb. "And perhaps I don't want to be the man who leaves you defenseless on an island full of scoundrels."

"Worse than you?" I teased.

He chuckled. "If you can believe it."

I stared up at him for a few beats before relenting. "Fine. Fine. Teach away."

I regretted saying that the moment a devious glint lit up his eyes and he released me into the deep water.

But he kept his word and didn't let me drown.

28

MAEVE CROSS

CAREENING WAS DIRTY, backbreaking work.

But I didn't mind the labor.

My time aboard *The Ollipheist* had made me stronger. I now had toned muscle on my arms where there previously wasn't any. Even though I made sure to protect my skin from the sun with long, lightweight garments and a wide-brimmed hat, I noticed a healthy brightness to it. A few new freckles here and there. Without chambermaids constantly brushing and pulling on my hair, natural curls had developed. The sea air did wonders for the texture. Some of the strands had lightened from the sun exposure too.

The ship was already on its side, pulled onto a beach and secured to two sturdy trees to keep it from snapping up and crushing anyone working beneath it. Boats had explained that the type of trees they used was important. If their roots didn't go deep enough, then they wouldn't be strong enough to hold the ship. The line they used also had significance. A weak line meant fraying. There was no room for failure.

Safety was everything.

The ship crew had spent the past two days scraping what

they could and were now getting some much-needed rest. Howler and Boats were at the hull, scraping away and working up a sweat. A handful of cabin boys were helping, but they weren't required to.

I'd only gotten here a little while ago. Levi told me that I didn't need to be here, but I insisted. I didn't have much longer until the entire crew went on another voyage, and I'd have to start over again. At least I had Siggi to keep me company while I figured myself out.

Wraith and Levi headed toward his cabana to make plans for which merchant route to take as well as what supplies needed to be loaded on board for the duration of the trip. To my knowledge, it was going to last a month or two.

The ocean beckoned me once again, and I desperately longed for Levi to ask me to join his crew. Accompany them. He knew I'd do whatever needed to get done on board, but that would also violate the terms of our current agreement.

But *damn it*, I wanted to go.

I rolled up the bottoms of my baggy trousers, tying them at the knee. Thankfully, not my nice new breeches. Careening damaged clothing, and I would hate to bring Siggi a damaged blouse right after getting it from him. This linen shirt would do. Then I tied my hair up before putting a cap on to protect my head from the sun.

All set.

I started making my way down the beach.

"Aye, birdie," Gunny's voice called out from behind me, stopping me in my tracks. "You just love getting your hands dirty, don't cha?"

I laughed to myself, turning around to greet him as he showed up with most of the gunnery crew. "You know me, Gunny." I caught a glimpse of his assistant and greeted Spider too. "I love to torture myself."

The head gunner came down to the beach and tossed an arm around my shoulders. "Well, it's good to see you. I expected you to be halfway across the Isles by now."

"And miss out on the chance to say goodbye? Never."

Gunny grinned, revealing that twisted tooth. "And it has absolutely nothing to do with my captain?"

My cheeks blazed. "I don't know what you're talking about. Don't we have work to do?"

I shrugged out from under Gunny's arm, and he barked a laugh before passing me and greeting Boats and Howler. Then he grabbed a few scraper tools, and the rest of his volunteers joined him.

Time for work.

Barnacles didn't come off wood cleanly. The tougher ones would leave sizable divots in the hull, and occasionally after I'd scrape one off, I'd find the end of a shipworm getting cozy in the planks. I'd uncovered one just then, its translucent body wiggling around in the wood.

I tapped Boats on the shoulder.

"Termites of the sea," she muttered. "I hate the buggers."

She took out a knife and dug it out. It was surprisingly long and had a small shell buried in the wood. She tossed it into a barrel where she'd collected a few others.

"When we're done scraping, I'll apply an extra layer of tar. That should help keep those damn things away."

"Does it happen a lot?" I wondered, getting back to my task.

"I've seen ships sink because of these little mollusks. But thankfully, I take extra precautions to keep them away." Boats hummed as she worked next to me. "Oh, and Mae…."

"Mm-hmm?"

"If you ever get on a ship and they say shipworms are a poor man's problem, get off the ship. If you don't, I'll pull you up from the grave and kill you again if I hear you've done something so ridiculous."

I nodded, laughing under my breath. "I hear you."

After a few hours, Gunny dismissed his crew for the afternoon, staying behind with the twins and me to get a little more scraping in. Even after all that work, there were still so many barnacles and weeds to pull off the hull. We'd barely scratched the surface!

Good Gods, how did they do this every shore leave?

A hand closed around my shoulder, and I saw Howler absolutely dripping in sweat. "Come on, Mae. Seabird's coming down to the beach with refreshments."

I hadn't realized how tired I was. "I think I love her."

He chuckled. "Oh, we all love her." He dipped his head toward a few sideways logs where Gunny and Boats were sitting and chatting.

I took a load off, my feet aching something awful. Boats gave me a grin that looked just like her brother's. "Thanks for your help today. We made some good progress." She offered me a cup of fresh water from the reserve.

With a nod, I took it, gulping greedily. "Happy to help."

In the distance, Seabird came along the sand, holding a canvas bag full of wrapped sandwiches. I definitely loved her. She distributed them, and we all munched happily, not saying a word while we enjoyed the sound of the waves lapping and leaving seafoam across the sand.

"Got any shipworms?" Seabird asked.

"A basketful of the buggers just for you," Boats answered.

Curiosity piqued my interest. "What do you want those slimy creatures for?"

"I like to chop them up and throw them into a pot of rice," Seabird said casually, taking a bite of her own sandwich.

Gunny clapped his hands together. "Mind sharin' a serving with me?"

"You're welcome anytime, Gunny. You know that. You can come join me."

He beamed.

I made a face, my lip curling up in distaste.

Seabird laughed. "They're just fleshy clams, Mae. Quite tasty if seasoned properly. It'd be a waste to throw them away."

I dropped my expression and shrugged. "I suppose."

"That's why they call me Seabird, Mae. I know how to find what's useful in what others find mundane," she commented. "Like a bird finding a crustacean by only the tip of its claw poking from the sand."

I wonder what they'll call me if I ever become a pirate.

"I best be on my way. I just couldn't let my kids go hungry," Seabird teased, getting up to kiss both Howler and Boats on the cheek and offering me a kind smile. The sentiment made me feel warm inside. Nothing like how my mother made me feel.

She left with Gunny in tow carrying her basket of mollusks.

"How about some drinks, eh? Rewards for a job well done?" Howler asked, pulling a bottle of rum from the supply cache next to the log.

"You know, Mae, someone sharing the history of their moniker is a personal thing," Boats said, accepting a drink as well. "Means Seabird is starting to trust you."

"Not an easy feat. She's suffered a lot in her life," Howler added.

I took a sip of my rum. "Levi told me how you all met. It must've been terrifying."

"It was," Boats said. "I remember our father staring down

the guard. Guts of steel. He didn't need time to consider whether or not he was going to hide Seabird and Levi. He just did it. Next thing I knew, we had a new brother and a mother. It took a while, but eventually she became our stepmother too."

Howler leaned back, tipping his cup. "Our father was a mean motherfucker, but Gods, did I respect him for it."

"Is he still around?" I asked, though I thought I already knew the answer.

"No. He was keelhauled."

My blood ran cold. Keelhauling was an awful way to go. Dragged under the ship while it was in motion, back and forth until the barnacles tore them apart. "That's horrible."

"Life at sea isn't easy," Howler said wistfully. "Especially not when you have a paranoid captain who thought the crew was after him. They weren't... not before then. Not until Seabird gave him a murderer's death."

"Is that how she became captain?"

"One of the best damn captains on the open sea," Boats stated.

I rubbed my hands together, looking away. "Levi never told me about any of that."

"The man lost two fathers. Can you really blame him?"

"No, I can't." I couldn't imagine losing one father just to lose another. And Seabird.... Gods, the pain that woman carried with her. I wished I knew how to help her. "How does Seabird handle it all?"

Howler took another drink. "She takes care of us. Our mother died in childbirth, but we never felt like we were without one." He chuckled to himself. "She gave me my nickname, actually."

I perked up. "Really?"

He nodded. "My birth name is Wesley Rhys, but Seabird

always told me that I howled like a banshee when I had something I needed to say." He grinned, thinking back on it fondly. "One day, it stuck."

"Suits you," Boats jested. "Especially since you also howl like a *baby* when you're drunk."

He scoffed. "That was one time. At least I have a good one. They just call you Boats because you're the bosun."

"At least *Alessandra* sounds better than Wesley." Boats glanced over at me and winked. "They used to call me Andra."

I watched them tease each other like any good siblings. A smile found its way to my face. I was feeling warm inside.

Bit by bit, I found myself getting closer to the crew. This was the only time in my entire life that I felt like I belonged. It didn't matter if I was a misfit everywhere else. They liked me for who I was. My chest started to feel empty as I thought about how bitter that goodbye was going to be.

I didn't want to say goodbye.

"Hey, look. It's lover boy," Boats snickered, gesturing up the slope to Levi and Wraith.

Warmth flushed through my belly when I saw him, remembering a few nights ago when he showed me how to stay above water. We were in the water for at least an hour or two, and he wasn't interested in making anything easy on me.

By the time the swimming lesson was over, I flopped onto dry land like a fish, and Levi left me there to catch my breath. When I finally struggled up that hill to get inside, I couldn't feel my damn legs.

And again, *no sex*.

Which led to me being pent-up and frustrated for the next few days. *Bastard.* He knew what he was doing. But I was still determined to get Levi to make the next first move, not the other way around. I'd been making it too easy for him.

Not anymore.

I was going to have fun this time.

Howler chuckled. "So it is." Then those mischievous eyes fell on me. "Is anything going on between you and Levi?"

I coughed on my drink, my hands shaking instantly. "No… of course not. What makes you think that?"

He threw his head back and released a bellowing laugh. "Oh, Levi is such a better liar than you."

"There's nothing!" I insisted. "We're friendly. That's all."

"Mm-hmm," Boats teased. "*Real* friendly."

Now I know why Levi doesn't want them to know anything.

Howler put his finger to his lips. "Shh. He'll get really touchy if we tease him again."

Again? How often had Howler and Boats teased Levi about me?

"Shut it," Boats giggled as Wraith and Levi came into hearing distance.

"What are you lot whispering about?" Levi asked, brushing the tail of his jacket back so he could take a seat next to me.

My cheeks were still warm. "Nothing important."

I knew he didn't believe me, but he also didn't pry. He would the second we were alone, though. "Pass me the rum and tell me something important, then."

29
MAEVE CROSS

I stood under a lukewarm spray of desalinated water, scrubbing dirt and salt from my skin after a long day of careening. My hands felt raw after scraping barnacles, but I felt a sense of accomplishment. Just another good day of hard work.

The washroom in the cabana was small but still slightly bigger than the one on the ship. On land, I could take longer than a three-minute shower, and *by the Gods*, I needed it.

A knock sounded at the door, and I knew it was Levi. We'd grown surprisingly used to each other the past few days. I liked it when he was around, and I think he liked my company. Not that he would ever admit it out loud.

And I wouldn't either.

I rinsed soap from my hair, shouting, "Yes?"

"I'm making myself something to eat. Do you want anything?" His voice carried into the room, and it elicited shivers despite the comfortable water.

"What kind of question is that?" I shouted back like the answer should be obvious.

"Never fucking mind," he retorted. "You get nothing, you godsdamn brat."

"No, wait!" I called out. "Come back!"

He didn't reply.

Damn it. Served me right for picking a fight instead of just saying, "Yes." But the banter was way more entertaining than giving him a straight answer. I enjoyed all the back-and-forth, and I *knew* Levi liked it too.

My stomach rumbled. I shut off the water and dried off with a towel before tying it around myself. I opened the door to shout, *"If I'm such a godsdamn brat, why don't you do something about it?"*

But as soon as I opened it, my retort got caught in my throat when I saw Levi standing there, looming over me.

"Oh, hello," I said sheepishly.

He ran his tongue over his teeth. "What were you going to say, Mae?"

I repressed the snarky smirk that pulled the side of my mouth. "Nothing interesting."

"I sincerely doubt that." He pinched my chin between his thumb and pointer finger. "Go ahead. See what happens."

Tingles erupted down my legs, warmth spreading at the base of my spine. He was baiting me, and there was nothing I wanted to do more than call his bluff. "Fine. I was going to say that you should teach me a lesson if I'm such a *godsdamn brat.*"

"You love to provoke me, don't you?"

His eyes darted down to my lack of dress, and I watched them darken. Excitement beaded inside me. I got up on my toes, keeping eye contact. "You're all talk."

He was quiet for a moment, the side of his mouth curling into a disarming smile. "You're so lucky you don't mouth off to me in front of the crew."

"Why? So you wouldn't reveal how soft you are?" I baited.

He released my chin, that arm coming up to lean on the doorframe. I fought the urge to shrink down even though every nerve wanted to retreat. "Sweetheart, *nothing* about me is soft right now."

My cheeks flared, and I pulled my lower lip between my teeth. "I don't believe you."

His eyes glinted, and that amused smirk turned into a full-blown wolfish grin. Before I could backpedal, he tugged on my towel, and I let it fall to the floor with absolutely no fight at all.

"While this would be a great opportunity to do something about that mouth, I'd rather listen to you scream when I sink my cock into your cunt."

Oh my Gods, his *mouth*.

Instantly, a rapturous heat enveloped me. That small bead of lust grew until all I could think about was how good Levi would look on top of me.

How good he'd *feel*.

I swallowed thickly, tightening my hands into fists so he wouldn't see them shake.

"Does that sound like something you'd want, sweetheart?" Levi spoke in an incredibly condescending tone, but the question was a serious one.

I couldn't speak. Words evaporated out of my mouth before I could say them.

He lowered his head and whispered in my ear, "All you have to say is yes. I can be patient."

My heart hammered in my ears, a rapid drum that drowned out almost everything else.

Except for him. I was completely tuned in to Levi.

"If you want to fuck me, Mae, I need you to say yes. I'll back off if you don't want me."

I didn't want him to back off. I wanted him closer. My eyes became half lidded as I murmured, "I want you. Do you want me?"

"Fuck yes."

"Then take me."

He made this mouthwatering throaty noise as he stroked my lower lip with his thumb. Without wasting another moment, he grasped me by the throat and dragged me into a kiss.

Electricity.

It fried all my nerve endings like a bolt of lightning. Anything else went up in an all-consuming blaze.

I moaned against his lips, losing myself in the feeling of his hands, the taste of his mouth. I fisted his shirt, jerking it roughly in an indication that I wanted it off. He groaned, pulled back, releasing my throat to tug his shirt over his head.

I wanted him to be as naked as I was.

"Trousers. *Off*," I demanded breathily.

The sash around his waist fell to the floor, but he wasn't unlacing his trousers fast enough. We moved toward the sitting area to the chaise where he gave me my first real orgasm. I reached down, my nipples beading up as I found his waistband.

"You want to do it for me, sweetheart?" he asked, just as out of breath as I was.

I nodded, pushing his hands away to loosen the laces and unbutton the top so he could push them down. I barely had time to process what he looked like fully erect and aching for me before I pushed him backward onto the chaise.

He cursed again as he collapsed onto the lounge.

My chest heaved as pure lust whirled through my veins, controlling every single action. His eyes devoured me like I was the most sublime creature he'd ever seen. It felt very gratifying to watch his cock thicken even more. He was unable to hide how badly he wanted me too.

My eyes widened as I wondered briefly how it'd fit. But if I knew anything about Levi, he wouldn't have me—*fuck me*—if he didn't think I could take it.

"Upstairs. Now. I want you in my bed."

"I want you here." I pushed him back again, approaching him slowly to straddle his waist and attack his mouth again. I'd become a bundle of need. All the teasing. All the repressed lust we'd built up the entire time we'd known each other bubbled over the top.

I knew without a doubt… *I was ready.*

I wanted this.

I wanted *him*.

He tossed his head back, making a loud noise as I felt the silky skin of his cock brush my sex. My eyelashes fluttered. It felt nothing like it had in the water the other day. This was pure heat, not an accidental brush.

He pulsed against my thigh, throbbing and hot.

"Fuck, you're wet," he ground out between his teeth. "*Gods*, the things I want to do to you."

"Show me," I encouraged.

Without any more preamble, he hoisted me into his arms. My legs wrapped around his waist instantly, earning a guttural noise of pleasure from the both of us. I wriggled, trying to push my hips forward to feel more of him.

"Keep that up and I will bend you over the fucking railing," he growled.

My inner muscles clenched around nothing as his words made me wetter. I wanted to tease him. Wanted to bait him again, but it would be a shame for this to be over so quickly when we'd only just started.

When we made it to the loft, Levi tossed me on top of his bed. I gasped as I bounced before settling into his pillows, my hair splayed everywhere. The smell of seawater and cedar swallowed me as he controlled that sense as well.

He was all I could taste.

All I saw.

All I heard.

All I felt.

And I still wanted more.

I wanted him to consume me until there was nothing left.

"*Leviathan,*" I murmured, my eyes locked on him as he watched me from the stairway. A strange look washed over his face momentarily, but he didn't say anything as he approached me like a predator stalking their prey.

I arched my back. "*Please,*" I whimpered, overwhelmed by how intense everything felt. "Please take the ache away."

The begging visibly affected him. Satisfaction coursed through me as he shivered, the tremble giving away how intense this was for him as well. But he didn't move any closer, almost like he wanted to watch me squirm and writhe in desperation.

"Levi… please," I pleaded softly.

I stroked my breasts, feeling how heavy they were. I caressed my trembling stomach. My thighs. Slowly, I parted my legs so he could see just how much I needed him.

His nostrils flared, his chest rising and falling erratically. He looked like a man holding desperately on to his control before it snapped.

His eyes raked down my body to between my legs where I knew I was drenched. This noise of utter anguish fell from his lips, and my body reacted to it.

"Please touch me," I muttered. "Please, Levi—"

"That's not my name," he said roughly.

My eyes rounded as he came closer, my body buzzing the nearer he got. He knelt at the foot of his bed, both his hands stroking circles on my thighs.

That was almost enough for me to break apart.

"Wh… what do you want me to say?" I asked, my breath catching as he hovered over me, his thick arms caging my head against the pillows.

He didn't say anything right away, but I didn't miss the vulnerability that flashed through his dark eyes. Plush lips brushed my throat, making my back arch up more as he laved it with his tongue.

He leaned on one arm as he stroked my belly with his other hand. He sent erotic, featherlike touches all the way down my torso. *"Ronin,"* he murmured against my throat.

For a moment, I broke out of the haze clouding my mind.

Ronin was a very unusual name in Farlight. Especially after my father enacted the coup and killed the line of Royal Leviathans and their youngest son… Ronin.

Ronin.

Oh shit.

"Ronin as in… Prin—"

"It doesn't matter, Mae. Just Ronin."

Before I could ask him anything else, his thumb brushed over my needy clit. I whimpered, mind going blank as pleasure ripped through me. "L—"

"No." He pressed down even harder, making me whimper. *"My name."*

My eyelids fluttered. *"Ronin,"* I panted.

"Good girl," he groaned, goose bumps rising all over his body at the sound of his name. He brought the fingers he'd used to tease me up to his mouth and slid his tongue across them.

My insides tightened.

"Now scream it." Two of his fingers sank into me as I threw my head back and cried out a warbled noise of pleasure.

He curled his fingers, repeatedly stroking the bundle of nerves that had tears streaming down my face. I screamed his name as he moved his fingers harder, faster, making stars burst behind my eyes.

Then right as I was at the edge of oblivion, he stopped, withdrawing his fingers altogether and sliding down so his mouth was positioned right in front of my trembling body.

"Please," I cried, unable to say anything else as my body shook in desperation. So close, just to have it torn away. I fisted the bedspread, desperately needing something to grab on to.

"You'll come when I sink myself into you, sweetheart. Not a moment sooner," he growled, dipping his head between my legs to lick my soaking slit up to the throbbing pearl aching for attention.

The teasing was agonizing.

Heat tightened at the base of my spine as another orgasm threatened to bring me over the brink before he tore it away. I wanted to cry.

"Please. Please. Please," I begged.

"Tell me what you need," he demanded, leaning back to watch me quiver. "I'll give you anything you want."

My inner walls clenched, needing something to fill this awful emptiness. "You. I want you." I reached down toward his cock that was nearly purple from how swollen he was. At least I knew I wasn't the only one he was teasing.

He grabbed my wrist, pinning it above my head. I moaned, belly tensing as it sent a surge of lust directly into my bloodstream.

Pin me down.

Take me.

Make me yours.

I was too aroused to dwell on the fact that I would never be his. He would never be mine. This was purely transactional. I had to be at peace with it.

"Last chance to say no, Mae."

"I don't want to say no," I murmured, looking up into his eyes so he knew I was honest. "I want you, Ronin."

He groaned, stealing another kiss. It felt different, full of everything he couldn't say. I gave in to it, letting him take what he needed from me. I spread my legs wider so he could settle between them, his cock notched up against my wetness.

Pulling back, I watched, mesmerized as he took his cock into his hand. He stroked it a few times, moaning in the back of his throat. I knew I'd carry that visual of him long after we parted ways.

"If it hurts, tell me."

"I don't want you to stop," I panted.

"I don't like to repeat myself," he warned, pressing the blunt head of his cock against me, sliding it up and down, saturating himself in my arousal. "Look at how soaked you are."

The lewdness of the gesture set me on fire, my insides clenching uncontrollably as the beginning of an orgasm started to move through me. Before it could take root, he pinched my thigh, stopping it right in its tracks.

My body shook with desire. I couldn't think about anything else.

"What did I say earlier, baby?"

I whimpered. "I can come when you're inside me."

"That's right."

He reached for my hand, heat boiling my face as he made

me grip his cock. Slippery and smooth, he felt so good just in my hand. He tilted his head back, clearly enjoying how my touch felt.

"Now, if you want me so badly, do it yourself."

Gods, I wanted him.

The nerves I'd started to feel slowly disappeared as he gave me complete control. He leaned in, letting me press him against my core. I murmured his name, my heart throbbing loudly in my ears.

At first, he slid in easily, gently pressing farther and farther. It felt like nothing else. Better than his fingers. Better than his mouth.

Oh Gods....

I whimpered, discomfort starting to tense my belly. Not pain. Discomfort. I gazed up at him, the tic in his jaw, the utter agony written across his face.

"Mae." His voice shook, his arms trembling on either side of my head. "You feel like fucking paradise."

I cried out, my thighs quivering. "Gods, I feel so full."

He groaned, swearing under his breath.

It wasn't enough. At the same time, it was too much. I didn't know if I needed to pull him in or push him away. Tears spilled down my cheeks.

"Are you all right?" he asked, brushing the tears away with his thumb.

"It's… it's a lot," I warbled. "Don't stop. Please…."

One of his hands slipped down to the apex of my thighs, and my walls clenched around him as pleasure hit me hard. He slipped the rest of the way in with little resistance, and my head fell back as I fluttered around him desperately.

I gasped, stars crossing my vision. His head dropped down to my throat, and he uttered a curse when I squeezed him again.

"Oh… damn it," I moaned. "*Ronin.*"

"Mae," he returned, his voice so deep, I almost didn't hear it.

I rocked my hips back and forth. "Gods, give me more."

"More?" he asked, nipping my shoulder.

"*More,*" I demanded, my legs falling open. I cried out as he pulled out slightly to push all the way back in.

Gods, that felt amazing.

He swore, playing with me harder, sliding the sensitive pearl between two of his fingers, slick with how badly I wanted him. He rocked his hips back and forth, and that discomfort completely ebbed away into ecstasy.

My hand fell over my mouth to stifle another cry as the denied orgasm welled in my belly, cresting higher and higher. My eyes rolled back, and Ronin grabbed both my hands and pinned them above my head with one of his, pumping his hips back and forth.

"When I say I want to hear you scream my name, I fucking mean it."

My eyelashes fluttered, that delicious sensation surging inside me, building and building. The inferno inside me burned recklessly, my heart blazing with how hard it pounded. I watched him thrust into me over and over again. I could hear how wet I was. See it on him every time he pulled out to push back in.

"Oh, sweetheart, I need you to come." I could feel him get thicker, throbbing as I clenched around him.

All that fell from my mouth were moans. Pleas. His name. I didn't know how to articulate how amazing it felt to have him inside me.

He groaned loudly, tipping his head back as if he was losing himself in how good I felt. The cords of his neck strained. Sweat glistened down his chest. His muscles clenched and bulged with every thrust. I ate him up with my eyes, loving how he looked on top of me.

"Baby, *please.*" His voice broke, his eyes rolling to the back of his head. "I can't…. Fuck, I *can't.*"

His cock pulsed, and my body reacted, fluttering helplessly around him as that heat inside me built. I liked it when he begged. How desperate he sounded.

My orgasm hit me like a tidal wave.

I reached up, grasping the back of his head and dragging him down into a scorching kiss. He moaned into my mouth, his hips losing their rhythm as I clenched around him, demanding him to finish with me. He swore loudly, thrusts getting sloppy. Harder. Faster.

He swelled, and I felt it when he burst, prolonging my orgasm with shallow thrusts. I could feel his warmth coating my insides, making me curl with absolute satisfaction. We kissed a few more times, moaning and sighing as we rode out the waves.

My head felt light, my body heavy and relaxed.

He pulled out, leaning back to stroke the side of my face with the back of his hand. His pupils were blown wide from his release, but even so, I saw the tenderness in his expression.

I stared up at him, feeling comfortable under his hands.

"How do you feel?" he murmured.

I couldn't help the smile that stretched across my face. "Good."

"Not mediocre?" he teased, both of his dimples puncturing his cheeks.

"A little better than mediocre," I admitted, reaching up to brush some of his hair out of his eyes. "Thank you."

"For what, sweetheart?" he asked.

"For taking care of me."

His smile faltered, and his hand lingered on my cheek. His lips parted with something he wanted to say, but then my stomach grumbled, and he smiled again. "Do you want something to eat?"

"Yes," I answered instead of making a fuss like I usually did.

"Go hit the head, and I'll make you something." He stood up, and I got chills the moment he wasn't shadowing me anymore. "I'll even let you eat it in my bed."

I started to feel warm inside. "I'd like that."

I fell back on the sheets, giddy and satisfied, before I got up on shaky legs to go relieve myself in the restroom.

30
RONIN MURDOCH

I DIDN'T REMEMBER FALLING asleep.

The last thing I recalled was Mae lying next to me. We were talking about something unimportant, a plate of crumbs next to us on the floor. She was flushed, her mouth swollen, eyes glassy. Her entire body was slack against my pillows, and she'd surrounded me with the smell of her hair.

I remembered rubbing circles on her trembling thighs, pressing tender kisses against her soft stomach. Mae unconsciously pushed toward me. She sought comfort. Touch. It had been a long time since I'd let someone share my bed. Maybe I craved it too.

In the middle of the night, Mae shot up next to me, tears streaming down her face. Panting like something was chasing her. Her heart was racing when I placed my hand on her back to ask if she was all right.

I knew it was a nightmare. I'd had plenty.

Pain ruminated in my chest. I hated how afraid she looked.

"Mae…," I murmured as I sat up, smoothing my hands down her arms. "You're safe. Shh, you're safe."

"Ronin?" she asked softly.

My name still sounded foreign to my ears. But finally, I'd begun to like how it sounded. I used to hate it for so long. Hated how intertwined my name was with my history. One day, I'd like to claim it again.

But I couldn't. Not with the dragon hunters and Varric sniffing around for more draconite.

"It's me, sweetheart," I replied. Her eyes gleamed, the tip of her nose red. I brushed her hair back from her eyes so she could see me better. Almost instantly, her breathing slowed.

"I-I'm sorry. I didn't mean to wake you."

"Come here," I coaxed, guiding her back down onto the pillows with me. Her back pressed against my chest, and I enjoyed how well she fit in my arms. "Just go back to sleep. I'm here."

She practically melted in my embrace, sighing as I kissed the back of her neck. She nodded, breathing slowly until it evened out into a quiet wheezing.

It wasn't long until I fell asleep again to the smell of her hair and the feel of her soft skin against mine.

I want this every night.

GENTLE FINGERTIPS ROUSED me from my dreamless slumber. Mae's leg was thrown over my hip, her small hands tracing the threads of my tattoo and a few scars here and there that had mostly faded over time. I'd had my fair share of injuries, but nothing too serious. Nothing I never bounced back from.

Her lower lip sandwiched between her teeth, she was seemingly focused on whatever design she was drawing on my chest. The sun cast its rays through the windows, showering her in a golden light and climbing over her mussed hair like a halo.

Dear Gods, she's lovely.

"Morning," I rumbled, my voice still thick with sleep.

Her eyes shot up to my face, her cheeks brightening with that pink hue I liked. "Oh, good morning."

"What're you doing?"

"This tattoo," she started. "It's magnificent."

Magnificent. That's a word I'd never heard used to describe me before. It made me weak inside. "I'm flattered."

"How does it work?" she asked.

Always so full of questions. I found it quite charming, even if I preferred to tease her about it.

"Has anyone ever told you that you ask a lot of questions?"

Mae looked away, her lips turned downward. "Yes. No one ever liked answering them."

I stroked her jaw, trying to wipe away her frown. "I was born with it."

She looked up, those wide eyes never ceasing to take my guard down.

"Faded, of course. It came into its full coloring around puberty. Then I could shift."

Her soft fingertips felt wonderful as she traced it again. "How do you shift? Is your dragon different than you are? Or are you the same?"

"I'm both and neither," I countered. "As far as shifting, it just happens."

"Are you always so vague with your answers?" she asked.

I chuckled, running my thumb over her cheek. "If you're dying to know, I suppose leviathans are like merrow. Evolved over time to coexist with people on land." I sighed. "There is so much I don't know about my people. My mother is human. She could only tell me so much." My jaw grew hard, but I tried not to let the subject spoil my morning.

Mae was quiet for a moment before she asked another question. "Your mother is Queen Enya?"

"She *was*. That life is behind us."

She nodded, getting back to tracing. Mae understood this was a sensitive topic, and she knew when to stop asking.

"You do know that this must stay a secret, right? My name. My history. All of it."

"Yes, I do." She looked me in the eye and said with conviction, "You saved my life by letting me have my freedom. The least I can do is save yours."

She meant it.

"And I promise I'll only use your name when we have sex."

A dimple punctured my cheek when I smiled. "Who's to say we'll have more sex? Unless… you haven't had your fill yet."

The way her face darkened to a rosy blush told me everything I needed to know. My hand slipped from her jaw to walk along her side. Her hip fit perfectly into my palm. Goose bumps prickled all over her skin as she released a shaky sigh.

So receptive.

"Is that it, baby? You want more?"

Her fingers began trailing downward toward my cock, which was already stiffening against her thigh.

"Don't play this game, sweetheart," I warned, noticing how warm she was getting, her nipples beading up and begging for my mouth. If I slid my hand between her thighs, I bet she'd be wet too.

"Why not?" she asked, her pupils devouring those deep-brown irises. "What if I want to play?"

When she grasped me, my head tilted back, and a guttural groan crawled out of my throat. "I don't want you climbing on top of me if you can't take me."

"I can take you."

I rolled us over so I loomed over her. She was spread out beneath me, her hair absolutely everywhere. Her eyes were wide, excited, her legs parted to reveal her swollen cunt.

Lust sparked through my system.

I needed to feel how wet she was just waiting for me.

"Let's see if you can take my fingers first, baby," I ground out between my teeth.

Her hand tightened around me, pumping up and down. Warmth filled my belly, flooding to the base of my spine. But if she kept jerking me off like this, I was going to get a friction burn.

I pulled her hand off me, and she whined, "I'm not done."

"Brat," I teased, bringing her hand up. "I'm not letting you whack me off dry."

Her eyes widened when I slid my tongue up her palm, getting it nice and wet. "Oh."

"Yeah, *oh*." I pulled her hand right back down, and her palm glided around me. A moan fell from my lips when she stroked up and down. "That's better."

Her legs parted farther, and I could see how much wetter she was getting. I lay down next to her, putting two fingers in my mouth before sliding them against her cunt. She made all these maddening noises, stiffening my cock painfully.

I played with her hard little clit. Sinking two fingers inside her, I could tell she was swollen from last night, but that only made her feel tighter. She rocked her hips up and down, trying desperately to fuck my hand.

"*Please*," she begged.

That *damn* word. I'd do anything to hear her beg.

"Please what?" I urged, my teeth gritting as her strokes became sloppy. Overwhelmed. My cock didn't care how rough they were.

She released me, using both hands to push me onto my back. My fingers slipped out of her, soaking wet. It didn't matter how satisfying it felt last night to have her. I wanted her just as badly now.

I sat up with my back against the headboard as I watched her come toward me with hungry eyes.

Sexiest thing I've ever fucking seen in my entire life.

This was a temporary thing, but there was no harm in another go at it. Maybe this time we'd both get our fill, and we could be done with it.

My breathing deepened when she straddled me. "You gonna ride me, sweetheart?"

Her face brightened, her chest heaving. I watched her tits bounce when she ground her cunt against me. She felt so slick. Fucking perfect.

"Please," she whimpered.

Do whatever you want to me.

"Then take me if you want it so badly," I replied, putting my hands behind my head to watch her fall apart the second she put me inside her. "Go on. Show me how good you are at riding my cock."

A sob bubbled up from her chest. The only time I ever wanted to see her cry was when she was this desperate for me. "I want to."

"Then line me up with that pretty little cunt and sink down on me."

She was shaking when she got up on her knees and took my cock to slide it between her folds, saturating me in her arousal. I watched the crown glide back and forth, getting visibly wet. The silky sensation had me white-knuckling the headboard.

Only a little bit at a time, she swallowed me, tilting her head back and moaning loudly. Gods, she felt tight, squeezing the life out of me as she took me down to the hilt.

Mae cried softly, and I bit down on my tongue to keep from releasing a slew of curses. Her thighs trembled on either side of my hips as she rose up to sink back down again. She controlled the pace, the depth, everything, keeping herself comfortable.

Gods knew that if I was in charge, I wouldn't have been as gentle as I needed to be. Her tits bounced in my face, and I couldn't fight the urge to take one of her stiff nipples into my mouth.

She moaned as I sucked, moving up and down to match her rhythm.

"*Oh….*" Her eyes rolled back as we went even harder.

"That good, baby?" I growled, kissing any piece of skin I could reach.

"Yes…. Oh, *yes*," she nearly screamed.

I loved how loud she was.

"Faster. Please. I want to go faster."

My hands fell from the headboard and I gripped her hips, helping her bounce faster and faster. Her walls fluttered, and my cock throbbed in response. Gods, I could rut her all morning if she wanted to.

Forget food.

Forget sleep.

Forget anything but her perfect cunt.

Mae cried out my name, and I nearly burst right on the spot.

"Kiss me," I ordered. "I need to taste you."

She whimpered before our lips crashed together. We kept going, building each other toward our highs. The bead of fire in my chest grew and grew, suffocating my heart as my pulse raced. Her cunt clenched down on me when she hit her peak, and I held her hips down, feeling her spasm and writhe as the waves washed through her.

"*Fuck*," I swore as she dragged me over the edge shortly after and milked me for everything I was worth. The pressure in my belly burst, washing a potent sense of relief all through me. Mae rocked back and forth, grinding down on the last few thrusts to prolong our mutual liberation.

Her head dropped against my shoulder, her body trembling. I embraced her, kissing her throat while we slowly came back to reality.

I was just about to pull away and kiss her breathless when my front door slammed open. I jumped, instantly on edge until I made direct eye contact with Howler from the overlook on my loft.

Shit.

Mae squeaked, falling off me to burrow under the covers. Howler was standing there, repressing the need to grin when both Boats and Wraith walked in behind him.

"Would it *fucking* kill you lot to *fucking* knock every once in a *fucking* while?" I shouted.

"So… who's up there with you, Levi?" Howler asked, both my other mates laughing under their breaths behind him.

I hated them.

"Get *the fuck* out of my house," I demanded.

A myriad of giggles followed as they left, closing my door behind them.

Maeve was a deep shade of red, looking up at me with those adorable doe eyes. "Cat's out of the bag, huh?"

"Seems that way. No point in hiding our arrangement now. They gossip worse on land than they do on the boat," I commented.

"What do we do now?" she asked.

I shrugged. "Enjoy ourselves. I don't see a reason why anything should change. My mates will just be extra irritating."

"I suppose not. It would be a shame to cut this short just because of them," she added, looking up at me from under her lashes. "Besides, we'll likely never see each other once you leave."

It felt bitter to hear it out loud, but she wasn't wrong. "It would also be a shame because I'm nowhere near finished with you."

Her eyes twinkled. "I haven't forgotten about you yet, so I can agree. You're not out of my system."

"I'm still thinking about you, so I must've not fucked you hard enough yet."

She giggled, making me smile. "Give a girl a break to recover."

My dimples punctured my cheeks as I replied, "If you insist." I gestured down to the kitchen. "I'm going to bathe and make us some breakfast. Take your time getting up."

"Okay," she agreed.

I got out of bed and leaned down to press a chaste kiss on her lips before leaving her to start her morning.

31
MAEVE CROSS

THE NEXT FEW days went by too quickly. Afternoons in port. Drinks with the mates. Nights with Levi doing nothing more than getting each other off. Even if I wanted to have sex, it was nice to have a break. We'd drink, talk, and enjoy each other's company instead.

I genuinely liked listening to him tell me about his excursions on *The Ollipheist*, and he would listen to me talk about what I wanted my future to look like.

Not that he would ever be a part of it.

Every day I was reminded of our limited time together. The mates had already restocked the ship with the shiphands.

Levi met with associates who had potential contracts. Inside information on what certain merchant ships would be carrying. How many vanguards were on staff. If the ships were insured. Intel that could mean life or death to a pirate.

I'd join Wraith and Boats while they took stock requests from Gunny and Butcher. Occasionally, if they were unavailable, I'd check in with Isa and Seabird. Keep the kids busy so they could have some time to themselves.

As much as I adored spending time with Howler's kids, I couldn't imagine having any of my own. Not with my father and Nathaniel in the back of my mind. Even if I eventually fell in love and started a family, nothing would stop them from taking it away just as cruelly as my father had done to Seabird.

I hoped they'd forgotten about me, but I doubted it.

I was a shiny toy for Nathaniel to play with, and without me, I believed my father's treaty would fall through and he'd lose his army. His final push to gain power and numbers.

For what?

I still didn't know.

Maybe that was for the better, but I couldn't be sure. The uncertainty left this pit in my stomach.

The beach beckoned me, and even though I'd spent a month at sea, I missed it. I missed the open water. The wind in my hair.

The freedom of it.

My mouth tasted bitter. Once Levi and his crew left, I'd be alone again. Without *The Ollipheist*, I didn't know what my purpose was. Being a shiphand made sense to me. I enjoyed it. I felt at home among the crew. But at this point, asking to go with them would be overstepping the boundary Levi and I made together.

Once we'd gotten each other out of our systems, it'd be over.

Still hasn't happened yet.

If anything, I wanted him more than I did to begin with.

I want more with him than sex.

"Aye! Birdie!" Gunny's voice carried from behind me.

I straightened up, pretending I wasn't in my thoughts. "Oh, how're you doing, Gunny?"

He continued forward, that same friendly grin on his face he always wore. His sash was loaded with weapons. Two cutlasses. A flintlock pistol. A dagger sticking out of each boot. A little overboard for a beach stroll. He even moved like it was heavier than he'd expected. "Cap said I'd find you out here."

"Oh yeah? What for?"

"Told me to tell ya it was my idea, but it's more fun to tell you the truth," Gunny admitted. He cleared his throat and imitated Levi's voice the best he could. But even so, I noticed a slight warble in it. *"I want you to give Mae a cutlass and show her how to use it."*

My eyebrows came together. "Are you serious?"

"He told me he'd be mighty disappointed if you died in a knife fight."

That sounds like him. I tried to hide my smile. "Apparently he'd be disappointed no matter how I died."

"All of us would be," he teased. "He'd never admit it out loud, so I will. I like you, birdie, and I'll miss having you around the ship to poke fun at." He pulled a cutlass out of his sash.

"Aw, I'll miss you, too, Gunny."

His smile turned sad, trembling at the corners. "So as a goodbye gift, I picked out some pieces from our armory. No one will miss them. Even Wraith signed off on it for me."

"That's nice of you," I said, thickness forming in my throat.

"You're my friend, birdie. Now, I want you to practice these moves every day, and then maybe you'll be an expert swordswoman one day." Gunny offered the cutlass to me, shined and sharpened to perfection.

I accepted it and took a step back to practice a slash. It cut through the air easily. Gunny was comfortably adept at swordsmanship. I'd seen him spar with Spider. I'd also seen him shoot a bucket off the mizzenmast when Howler wagered that he couldn't.

"I've taught you upkeep and basic repair for pistols and blades, but you have yet to use them."

"Hey," I interrupted. "I tried to fight off a siren one time."

"You never hit flesh, birdie," Gunny countered. He took a stance and demanded that I replicate it. "Now remember, this isn't nobleman sword fighting. This is a cutlass. Made for slashing, not for fancy poking."

I put my feet slightly closer than shoulder width apart for maximum stability. Rotating my wrist, I got a feel for the weight of the blade. Something about it felt… *right*.

"Most of fighting is defense. You'll be useless if they lop something off," Gunny instructed. He crossed his cutlass over his chest. "Block like this. Hold it if you have to. If running is an option, do it. Don't try to play at being an expert swordswoman. That'll only get you killed."

I stayed in the defense position.

"Hold it. I'm going to strike."

Gunny's cutlass slashed toward me, contacting mine so I could understand how hard a normal hit would be. Excitement flared inside me. I wanted more. "Show me how to strike."

He understood and demonstrated how I should be swiping the sword to keep the most control over it. Both of the cutlasses were sharp, so we proceeded with caution.

I struck his block, the sound of metal clanking and scraping together filling the air.

"Not bad!" he encouraged, his eyes widening as I performed exactly how he showed me. "I didn't expect you to catch on so quick."

I blocked while he struck, going back and forth through the moves he'd illustrated. For something I'd only ever seen, it felt natural. I altered my stance automatically, accounting for the weight of the cutlass.

When I started to feel comfortable, he allowed me to show a little flair, moving like the sword was an extension of my arm. As soon as I had the cutlass in my hand, I couldn't imagine not having it. How had I gone so long in my life without it?

"Gods, Mae. Where have you been hiding? Did they teach you some form of fencing in the castle?" he wondered, putting his cutlass away.

"Fencing was for boys," I said, remembering how horrible it felt when I heard that as a child. Instead of teaching me fencing, they taught me which spoon was for the soup. A waste of time for a girl who wanted to do something with her hands. "Etiquette classes were for girls."

"Their loss," Gunny pointed out.

My eyes dropped to his pistol. "Am I getting a pistol too?"

He laughed. "Oh, Mae, I adore you, but these are more trouble than they're worth." He took out his flintlock pistol. "Can't aim for shit. A pain in the ass to load. Unless you're shooting a target on a rival ship too far away to slash at, it's not worth it."

"Then why're you carrying one right now?" I wondered.

He rolled his eyes, tucking his pistol away. "I can't brag about being a head gunner if I don't have a gun on me."

"Fair point," I chuckled.

Gunny ducked down and grabbed a dagger from his boot. "Just in case, it's always nice to carry one in your boot."

"Thanks, Gunny." I took it, accepting the gift with a smile.

"You can call me Silas," he offered, showing off that crooked tooth. "Silas Hawke."

His admission brought tears to my eyes. My throat started to get thick again. "This really is a goodbye, isn't it?"

"Afraid so, birdie." He hesitantly reached out to pat me on the shoulder. "I have a lot to do before we leave dock."

"Did Levi really send you down here?" I wondered.

Gunny rubbed the back of his neck, looking away from me completely. "I wanted to give you a gift before we left, and he told me where to find you… and that I better show you how to use it. Then he said that bit about the knife fight."

I laughed a little through the thickness. "Well, now I'll know better than to *stick 'em with the pointy end*," I joked.

"That you will," Gunny tried to jest, but it didn't quite reach his eyes. He wrinkled his shallow nose and looked at the setting sun painting the horizon a variety of oranges settling into purples. "It's not too late to join the crew, you know. We could always use another gunnery assistant. Always the chance to get your hands dirty. You know you'll never sit still."

It broke my heart to say no. It'd be easy to say that Levi made those decisions, but I didn't want to point fingers. We both came up with this agreement. "I can't."

"I thought you'd say that." He kicked the sand. "Good luck out there, birdie. I hope you find what you're looking for."

"Me, too… Silas." I paused, rubbing my hands together. "And thank you for welcoming me. You really made me feel like a part of the crew."

He looked down at the sand. "I better hear great things about you, Mae. I'd love to point at a wanted poster and say, '*I knew that birdie.*'"

"You'll hear about me. One way or another."

We stood there in silence for a few moments as if there was so much to say, but we weren't sure what that was. As

Gunny left, climbing up the slope to the dirt path, I waved one more time, and he ducked away.

I sat back down on the log, staring out at the sea.

Despite the sun shining on my face I felt... cold.

32
MAEVE CROSS

"Do you remember the time Mae fell overboard?" Boats asked, taking a drink of her rum, Wraith's arm draped around her shoulders. Wraith glared at every single tavern patron who merely looked in their direction.

Howler leaned back in his seat, slapping a hand over his face. "We thought you were a goner." He jabbed Levi in the ribs a few times. "Until my brother pulled quite the feat bringing you back from the dead."

Levi stole a glance at me before returning his gaze to Boats. "Most people don't survive taking on that much water. You're lucky." A dimple punctured his cheek. "Next time someone tells you to back away from the edge, listen."

"I'm not a great listener," I murmured, taking my own sip.

Levi chuckled. "Don't I know it. Aren't great at respecting authority either."

All three of the mates laughed, signaling to the barkeep for another round. It was the last night of shore leave. What better way to spend it than sharing stories over drinks? As tempting as it was to drown my thoughts in alcohol, I also didn't want to forget it.

This was our last night together. But I wasn't ready to say goodbye.

I swirled the liquid in my glass, repressing a smile as I insisted on teasing Levi again. "I was perfectly respectful to your mates... just not to you."

"Keep talking, sweetheart," he warned quietly, his eyes flashing with promise. My belly curled, heat flushing down to my toes. "Remember that time we got becalmed off that Gully island?"

Boats slammed her hand down on the table. "And Howler got dragged off into the woods?"

I blinked, taking a moment for it to sink in. "What?"

"We're making fun of *me* now? Can't we go back to making fun of Mae?" Howler objected.

"Sorry, mate, you're an easy mark," Levi replied. He leaned back in his seat, his eyes on his friend. "Howler likes to wear bright colors."

To add emphasis, he gestured over to Howler, who was indeed dressed in bright yellows and oranges and interesting patterns. While his sister wore more jewel-toned items of clothing, he was decked out in vivids.

"And a bright yellow bandana," Wraith chimed in, clearly amused.

"Yes, yes. We all know this." Howler crossed his arms. "Can we talk about anything else?"

Levi wasn't interested in changing the topic. "You see, that island was home to a few flocks of harpies. And what are harpies attracted to?"

"Bright colors," Boats laughed. "They swooped in and carried Howler off to their nest."

My mouth fell open. "How did you survive that?"

Wraith cleared her throat. "Beast hunting is somewhat of a sport where I'm from." She took her hat off to put it on top of Boats's head, then cupped her wife's chin. "I think that's what finally convinced this pretty lassie to accept my favor."

"Saving my brother from certain doom is very sexy," Boats concurred, catching Wraith's hand to press a kiss against her palm.

"I could've saved myself!" Howler argued.

Wraith leaned over the table, clearly challenging him. "Oh? You mean those baby harpies weren't about to peck your eyes out?"

"I'll have you know, Wraith, those baby harpies were very close to calling me Mama."

The entire table erupted with laughter. Wraith picked up a handful of nut shells and threw them at him, the ghost of a smile on her face. "Full of it."

"Your beloved is just as bad as I am." Howler pointed at his sister.

"She knows how to make it up to me."

Howler gathered the remnants of the crumbs to throw them back at her. "Disgusting. That's my sister."

Levi chuckled, watching his friends with fond eyes.

I'll never have this....

Push it down. Push it down. It's over after tonight.

I had to be at peace with that.

Levi hadn't asked me to join the crew, and as badly as I wanted to keep this special feeling, I *couldn't* cross that line. I had to enjoy what it was. I couldn't strive for more.

I'd *never* have it.

Gulping down those thoughts, I tried to bring myself back into the moment. "What a story," I murmured, brushing away all the reminders that time was fleeting. I'd be alone again soon. Just as alone as I was in Farlight.

"We have loads," Boats said. "Though most of our time is spent staving off boredom between shifts."

Those were the best moments.

My favorite parts of being on board were all the moments in between. Helping Butcher in the kitchen. Making up games with the gunnery crew. Talking with the mates in the bunks after a long day.

It may not seem important in the long term, but those little moments made me feel like I belonged.

"The best stories happen when we're bored," Levi added. "How else would we know Spider is deathly afraid of cats?"

An image of Lieutenant Commander Lazlo scaring the dickens out of Spider came across my mind, earning a quiet giggle.

As the drinks kept coming, so did the stories.

It had to have been another few hours until I was pulled into a hug by Howler. He told me that if I ever needed anything, Isa wasn't far away. I was always welcome in their house.

As sweet as it was, I couldn't put that on Isa, especially while Howler was away.

Boats gave me another hug while Wraith nodded at me, wishing me luck on my journeys… whatever they may be.

I still didn't know what I was going to do after tomorrow.

But that was tomorrow's problem.

"Are you ready to go?" Levi asked.

I nodded, leaving a half-finished glass of rum on the table. "You didn't have to wait for me if you didn't want to."

"And leave you here after dark? No."

"I've got a cutlass now, though."

An amused breath left his lips. "And it looks very charming on you, sweetheart."

A red-hot spike of anger shot through me. I crossed my arms. "I can't stand you."

"Good thing I prefer it when you're angry." Levi stood up

and gathered coins from his pockets to pay the barkeep. He left a stack of them on the table.

I followed him out the door and onto the street. I hadn't been to the port at night, but I didn't feel as if I was in any danger with Levi with me.

"You can either fight me or fuck me. There's not enough time for both."

"Or I can simply say, '*Fuck you*,' and go to Isa's."

He stopped to loom over me, his calloused hand scratching my chin as he drew my face up to look at him. "Your choice. At least I'd let you sleep in."

I narrowed my eyes. "I'd rather fight you tonight."

Both eyebrows rose as he continued the banter. "You wanna play that game, sweetheart? We can play."

I shrugged, pretending not to know what he was talking about. "I'm awfully tired, Levi."

"Still a terrible liar."

The corner of my mouth quirked up, and just as I was about to say something, we were interrupted by the sound of whistling. Levi ran his tongue over his teeth, and I got the feeling that he knew exactly who it was.

He released me, turning completely toward the disruption. He didn't say anything, just rested one hand on his cutlass. I followed his gaze to another man.

Older than Levi was. Probably a little older than Seabird too. Dressed in a myriad of colorful, expensive fabrics. Jewels glittered in the yellow hue of oil streetlamps. His skin shone burnt umber in the light, his coarse dark hair twisted along his scalp. He had pointed ears and sharpened canines.

Once his uniquely violet eyes locked on to Levi, he grinned widely. "Captain *Leviathan*. I didn't think I'd see you here. Where are your mates?"

"Captain Lucky Bartram," Levi greeted, with not one ounce of friendliness in his voice.

"It's *Commander*."

"Oh?" Levi asked even though it didn't sound like new information. "Buy yourself another ship just for the chance at a title?"

Lucky pressed a hand against his chest in mock offense. "Don't be envious of a man with money, Leviathan. You could've been something if you'd joined me. Instead, you'll always be captain of a cut-rate ship with a promotion given to you by your mother."

"Not all of us want to rule the world, Lucky."

"And not all of us have the gall to lead the world. Do we, *Levi*?" Lucky's eyes drifted over to me. "Where are my manners? Who's this lovely little lass?"

Levi got between me and Lucky. "None of your fucking business. That's who she is."

"Testy," the older man chuckled. Despite Levi's hostility, he still peered around him to look at me, grinning widely. "If you want to put your colors behind a *real* captain, my sailors could always use entertainment."

Entertainment? That bite of anger whirled in me again. My cheeks darkened, but I sidestepped Levi, my hand on my blade. "Say that again."

Levi's hand shot out, catching me. "Maeve."

The older man put both his hands up, chuckling. "Oh, she's precious. I said, *darling*, my sailors could always use a pretty lassie to entertain them on long voyages. Not like you can use that thing anyway. Play to your strengths."

Piss off.

I drew my cutlass, breaking away from Levi's hold. Though, oddly, it wasn't very tight.

Lucky's eyes widened in surprise but not dissatisfaction. "Let's dance, lass." He drew his own weapon, an infantry sword. Designed for fancy swordsmanship, it was long and straight like naval weaponry, not curved like mine.

I was supported by the noise of Levi's cutlass being drawn behind mine. Tingles erupted down my spine, and I didn't know why the idea of fighting alongside him appealed to me so much.

"Sheath your sword and you can walk away, Lucky," Levi warned, but I was aching to test out my cutlass. I wanted to see how it fared outside of sparring. Put the things Gunny showed me into practice.

"I've been waiting for the opportunity to cut you down, Leviathan. Not as satisfying as meeting Albatross again in battle, but damn well close enough."

Who was Albatross?

Levi struck first. "You have some stones, saying his name."

With a sharp swing of his wrist, Lucky deflected. "I would've died happy if it was by his blade. Shame it was either him or me."

The older man moved with fancy footwork, while Levi moved with strength. He had grace in his movement and the swings of his blade, but Lucky had years on him. I stood there, cutlass in hand, trying to find my opening.

I watched intently, absorbing the moves. Strategizing how to swing my blade and what angle to hit to deliver maximum power. Lucky hit Levi's blade hard enough to spark, and something moved inside me.

Get in front of him.

Without thinking, I swung out, connecting with Lucky's blade and drawing his attention directly to me. Exactly like Gunny had shown me, I deflected, bracing myself and waiting for an opening.

Between Levi and me, we moved with amazing precision. A new rhythm rose in our swings, making Lucky back away with every intense swipe of our blades. The older man's eyes widened before he lost his sword.

Upon disarming Lucky, both of us backed off. Levi pointed his sword down at Lucky. "Unlike you, I would never kill an unarmed man. Now fuck off."

Lucky accepted his defeat, gathering his sword and sheathing it in the sash around his waist. "You've gotten better. Albatross would be proud of you." The older man cleared his throat and gave me a sideways glance. "My offer stands. Though I think you'll be more useful as a vanguard than entertainment."

I didn't put my cutlass away until Lucky was out of eyesight. My heart was beating fast, excitement running hot through my veins. "Still think I look charming with a cutlass?"

Levi was flushed, panting slightly, both dimples on display. "Absolutely." He slid his cutlass into the sash, one of his big hands cupping the side of my face. "Fucking precious."

I tilted my head back and released a long, exasperated sigh.

He laughed. "I can think you're lovely and be impressed with you, Mae." His voice turned serious. "As well as you performed, I never want you to get between me and a sword ever again."

"You're leaving tomorrow," I murmured, ignoring how it made my gut turn. "Provided that we don't get attacked on the walk back, I think I can keep that promise."

"Good enough. Come now, before Lucky decides he wants another fight." Levi pulled away, still slightly out of breath as we walked down the dirt path headed toward Anchorage Cove.

"So what's the story behind that man?" I wondered.

He shrugged. "Lucky and I go back quite a way. He was my stepfather's mate."

"Albatross?"

Levi went quiet for a moment before he said, "The Seabird and the Albatross. He was a fisherman, but over the years, as draconite started to dry up and the incentive to turn in leviathans grew, Lucky was the one who recruited us for piracy. The twins and I worked as cabin boys. My mother was a shiphand with my stepfather."

"Does… does he know?" Concern turned my mouth sour. Lucky did not seem like the type of man you could give a secret to.

Levi laughed. "Fuck no. He's always been self-serving. Lucky didn't know why my stepfather wanted to get away, and he didn't ask."

"I heard what happened to him…. I'm sorry," I murmured.

He hummed. "We didn't see anything, the twins and me. We were under the deck when it happened. But… with him, we got closure." It didn't seem as raw a wound as the one he had over his own father. "I can remember him as he was. A mean motherfucker who loved me like one of his own."

Howler said the same thing.

"And Lucky?"

Levi pulled a tree branch up so I could walk under it. "Lucky got his name because he was marooned by the same captain who killed my stepfather. Lucky that he wasn't keel-hauled too. Lucky that he found treasure on that island. Albatross and Lucky were constantly switching between being rivals and friends. They had an odd relationship."

"Do *you* have any rivals?"

He chuckled. "Of course I do. What kind of pirate would I be without rivals?"

"Well, go on. Do tell," I urged. "Tell me who I should make my enemy." I grasped my cutlass for emphasis, and Levi grinned, both dimples puncturing his cheeks.

He grasped the front of my shirt, completely taking me by surprise when he backed me against a tree, my chest flat against his. My cheeks flared, my breath catching in my throat. His eyes were on me, darting between my mouth and my eyes. "I'd start with me."

"You want to be my enemy?" I breathed.

"I want to be your rival." His fingers brushed my jaw. "A lass who can best me in cards, pull a sword on a siren, and has the guts to fight those who disrespect her? That's a woman I want as my rival."

Heat burned my face as I became hyperaware of how his body pressed against mine. "I don't appreciate you saying nice things when I'm supposed to be forgetting about you."

"You'll forget them by the time I'm finished with you."

My tongue darted out to moisten my lips, drawing his gaze back down to my mouth. "Promise?"

"I never promise anything."

I narrowed my eyes and placed both hands on his chest, pushing him off me with little struggle. My heart raced, adrenaline firing through my veins. "Then you, *Ronin*, are going to have to catch me."

His lips quirked to the side, his eyes becoming sleepy with desire. "Then you better run, sweetheart. Because the second I catch you, I'm going to make you forget every nice thing I've ever said."

I chewed on my lower lip, excitement flaring within me. A bead of lust burned in my chest, flowing down my legs like warm water. He didn't make any move toward me, his eyes locked on mine.

I kept his gaze, slowly stepping away from the tree before I turned around and sprinted through the woods in the direction of the cove. Giggles erupted from me as I ran as fast as I could.

But he was faster.

33

MAEVE CROSS

IT FELT like my insides were vibrating, a constant thrum of excitement in my ears. The farther away I got, the more impatient I was for him to catch me. I could hear his footfalls pounding against the ground.

But my breathing got heavier and heavier.

His cabana was just up the hill, but my legs were getting tight. Burning with exertion. My lungs started to hurt with every breath I dragged into them. I giggled uncontrollably, pumping my legs harder to climb up the hill.

A squeal left my lips as two broad arms encircled my waist, scooping me up and tackling me down onto the ground right outside his cabana. Levi grinned, his eyes gleaming, his chest rising and falling rapidly on top of me. He breathed hard, slightly out of wind from that damn hill.

His body shadowed mine, but I wanted it to crush me.

I grasped the collar of his jacket, pulling him down into a kiss. It didn't matter that we were in the dirt. I was going to enjoy every last moment.

He groaned against my mouth, one of his hands fastening around my throat while the other supported his weight. The loss of air excited me as I arched my neck up to give him full access to it.

We pushed and pulled each other in, a passionate haze settling over us. I shuddered, needing more. I ached for his touch. I slid one of my hands down to his waist, anchoring it in his belt, slipping my fingers under the material.

He released my throat, stroking down my chest while we kissed. I parted my lips, eager to let him devour me while his roughened fingertips caressed the opening of my blouse. Every passing second grew more intense.

Hungrier.

Overwhelming.

"Here?" he murmured against my lips.

When I'd first shed my clothes outside for a dip in the water, I was worried someone would see me. Now, that was the last thing I cared about.

"Here." The thought of stopping to go inside felt like agony. I needed him right then.

He pulled back, untying the sash around his waist to discard his weapons. I followed suit, desperate to rid myself of any and all layers between us.

To my disappointment, he removed his sash, but everything else stayed on. His coat, his linen shirt, his trousers. Gods, I wanted him *naked*, but instead, it was only me baring myself under the moonlight.

His mouth fell to my neck, and he sampled my throat and shoulders with soft, wet presses of his tongue. My hair started to get mussed in the dirt, but I still didn't care. I grabbed a handful of Levi's hair, earning a mouthwatering groan as he let me pull him to my lips again.

I parted my legs, drenched and eager. "Take your blasted clothes off," I demanded.

The corner of his mouth pulled up against my lips as he uttered, "No."

"Please?" I whispered. I knew that word made him weak, and I would use it every opportunity I got.

He drew back again, unlacing his trousers. My heart jumped into my throat as my body started to move on its own, seeking him out. The achy bud at the apex of my thighs needed attention. I was turned on beyond belief.

"No. I'm going to take you fully dressed while you writhe for me in the dirt." He nipped my shoulder, making me cry out softly.

I squirmed underneath him, both aroused and angry. "You monster," I whined.

"Keep whining and I'll fuck your mouth so you can taste yourself," he warned, pulling his cock out.

My insides tightened at the sight, the crown of it glistening with proof of his own desire. "How do you know I won't like it?" I panted, unable to keep myself from mouthing off even when he had all the power between us.

He stroked himself once, making this throaty noise that turned my knees to pudding. "Do you want me to fuck your mouth, sweetheart?"

"I want you to shut the fuck up and take me already."

"Such a brat."

"You like it."

He narrowed his eyes, though there was no mistaking the utter delight glimmering in their inky depths. Without another word, he tucked himself back into his pants, dragging me up to my feet to bend me over the back of the chair just outside his cabana.

I gasped when his hips pressed against my rear. All sorts of pleasurable sensations fired all over my body. "Ronin," I panted, the back of the chair cutting into my ribs.

"Is this all right?" he asked. However, he didn't have to because I couldn't stop backing up against him. He grabbed my hips tightly, stalling my movements. "Answer the question, sweetheart."

"Yes. Yes, it's okay! Damn it, just get on with it!" I complained, fighting his grip to grind into him again.

"You're infuriating," he said, and I knew he was rolling his eyes at me.

"*You're* infuriating. I clearly want you to take me. What else do you need?"

"I'm definitely fucking your mouth when I'm done with your cunt."

"Then get to it." I wriggled, the ache growing to the point of pain. I looked behind me to see him bathed in silver light, gazing at me with such intense lust that it made me even wetter. One of his hands left my hip to stroke my rear, slowly sliding down between my legs.

My knees shook as his fingers caressed my inner thighs up to my core. My eyelids fluttered, my shoulders trembling. At this point, all I'd need was him to brush my clit and I'd fall apart into a million pieces.

"Are you going to miss me?" he asked.

Yes. "N-No. I'll forget about you the moment you leave." My heart pounded, vulnerability rearing its head inside me. "Will you miss me, Ronin?"

Instead of answering, two fingers sank into my core. I cried out, my inner walls fluttering helplessly. His fingers weren't enough. No matter how talented they were, I needed something bigger to fill the cavernous ache inside me.

I heard him part the gap in his breeches so he could pull his cock out with one hand while the other pleasured me. His thumb stroked my clit, and my entire being throbbed. Every other thought left my head aside from seeking release.

"This position can feel more intense," he murmured, dipping to press his mouth against my bare shoulder. "If you tell me to stop, I'll stop." His fingers stroked a mind-boggling chord against a bundle of nerves.

I tried to whimper his name, but it didn't quite form in my mouth. Pleasure stole my tongue, hazed over my eyes, clogged my ears. My senses were stolen from me as Levi's cock nudged my insides.

"Or if words are hard for you, tap my thigh. I *will* stop." He nipped my shoulder. "Nod if you understand me, sweetheart."

I gulped, heat cascading under my skin like molten sugar. "Please," I murmured, nodding as I parted my legs a little farther.

"Good girl," he muttered against my shoulder as he pushed forward, sliding deep inside me with little trouble.

A mutual noise of pleasure fell from both of us. He was right—this position was more intense, a new incredible angle to explore. He palmed my rear, groaning as he drew out to push back in.

Oh... Gods....

"I want to paint your ass pink, Mae," he grunted, finding a rhythm that had me shivering and quaking against the chair. Any discomfort where it cut into my ribs was gone. All I felt was Levi rocking back and forth, his hips slapping against my rear.

It took me a few moments to register what he was asking me. "You—*oh Gods*—want to spank me?"

"Yes," he ground out between his teeth. "Can you take six of them?"

I wriggled my hips, eager for anything he wanted to give me. My head lolled back as he grabbed my hips harder, pounding against a tender spot inside me before slowing back down again. "Y-Yes," I whimpered.

"Count them."

Before I could comprehend what was happening, a sharp sting shot through me. I squealed in surprise before the sting ebbed away into a thrumming warmth. Everything inside me clenched, and I realized *I liked that*.

He made a throaty noise. "Are you going to choke my cock every time I spank you, baby?"

I whimpered, "I don't know."

To test the theory, his hand came down again, harder than the first time, and I cried out, my insides fluttering helplessly.

A curse fell from his lips. He slowed his thrusts, and I could feel him pulse inside me.

My body trembled in response. "*Ronin*."

Then he started moving faster, earning a shrill noise of surrender with every powerful snap of his hips. "I thought I told you to count. I won't repeat myself again, no matter how good you feel."

Smack. I cried out, my eyes rolling back as I shakily whispered, "Three."

He hummed. "Good. So fucking good."

Four. My clit started to tingle, heat licking the base of my spine. "F-Four."

"You're getting wetter. Are you going to come for me, Mae?" His hand came to my front, slicking circles around my clit.

I nearly screamed. My hips bucked forward desperately, stars erupting behind my eyes. Everything felt so intense. He played with my clit as his other hand came down even harder, cracking out another sharp pang of pain, only for it to disappear, replaced by a lightness in my head. A building inferno in my belly.

"Five," I squeaked.

Gods, I'm close. So close to teetering over the edge of something nearly unexplored. This felt different than the other times we'd had sex. More forceful. More vulnerable. He had all the power, and I gave it over wholeheartedly.

"One more," he said, stroking my clit harder. "I want to feel you squeeze the life out of me when you come."

His hand came down in one more final *crack,* and I shattered. I sobbed as the orgasm unfurled in my belly, washing through all my muscles. I spasmed around him, squeezing him desperately. He stopped touching my clit before it got overstimulated and grasped my hips to fuck me hard through my orgasm.

My eyes rolled back, tears streaming down my face as Levi released a final groan. His chest pressed against my back, and he let himself go, swelling and bursting inside me. He held me close, thrusts growing sloppy, his face buried in the back of my neck.

He brushed my hair to the side and kissed my throat when it was finally over, both of us slack with relief.

"I think I'll miss you, Mae." It was so soft, I almost didn't hear it.

Or I could've imagined it.

He pulled out and tucked himself back into his trousers. He held me up so my weak legs didn't shake so hard beneath me. "Let's get you inside."

The relief didn't last long before lust rekindled in my belly, sparking to life again.

"I'm not finished," I panted, twisting my fingers in the waistband of his breeches.

"Neither am I," he murmured, capturing my swollen lips as we stumbled into the house together.

All my nerve endings were on fire with a desperation I thought I'd never escape from.

The passion between us flared even brighter. It was blinding. *Blazing*.

We became two bodies seeking out pleasure. I wasn't sure where I ended and he began. Our skin was feverish as his touch suffocated me.

I could only hear the noises of our breathing. Panting quiet, desperate pleas for satisfaction. Liberation from the crushing weight of tomorrow.

I wasn't ready to say goodbye.

I palmed at his shirt, leaving a trail of clothing. I needed to feel his body pressed against mine. No barriers.

"Get into the water with me," he demanded, guiding me backward to the shower. "I'm not letting you into my bed caked in dirt."

My back was grimy where he'd pressed me into the ground. "Whose fault is that?"

"I take full responsibility." He reached behind me to twist the dial to release the valve of water above our heads. I backed into the wall, cornered by his broad body under the lukewarm spray. "Now shut the fuck up."

"Not unless you make me."

His eyes flashed, hooded and dark. "Gladly." He fisted my hair, sending sparks of pleasure all over my scalp. "Get on your knees."

My neck was craned back so I was staring up into his eyes. "Say please."

The corner of his mouth twisted up. "*Please* get on your knees and put my cock in that smart mouth."

He pushed my head down, his hand tight in my hair. I

liked the sting—it made everything more intense. I settled on my knees, my eyes never leaving his. I panted, rubbing my thighs together. "What do I do?"

My head was caged between his pelvis and the wall. Nowhere to run.

Not like I would.

I actually quite liked this.

His legs were shaking in front of me, his cock completely erect. It looked like he hadn't gotten a release at all when we were outside, but the proof of it was still sliding down my thighs. His desire for me gratified me beyond belief.

Maybe whatever was between us wasn't completely one-sided.

"Open your mouth as wide as you can, sweetheart," he coaxed, his voice strained but soft. "Do whatever feels natural. Pinch my thigh hard if you need a break."

Pearlescent arousal beaded at the crown of his cock, leaking uncontrollably. I leaned in, wanting a taste. I slid my tongue along it, and his grip on my hair tightened, a swear on his lips. While the water had washed a lot of it away, I could still taste myself on him.

Water rolled down his chest, moistening my face.

He made a guttural noise of agony, and it encouraged me to continue his torment. I sucked and explored. While I'd gotten him off with my hand, I had yet to put him in my mouth. Usually, he was relatively quiet with his pleasure, but in this position, strings of curses and throaty noises of pure ecstasy fell from his lips.

All of it worked me up.

I whimpered, pressing my thighs together as my head rested back against the wall, his cock pushing farther into my mouth, gagging me. My throat constricted around him a few times as he writhed above me. I held out for as long as I could before I pinched his thigh. He pulled back, a thin string of saliva connecting us as I drew breath into my burning lungs.

"Come here." Using my hair as a handle, he pulled me up onto my feet. At once, he captured my lips, lifting me into his arms to press me against the wall. Both of us were slippery and wet, which only made it easier for him to push himself into me again.

I damn near screamed, and it was only the beginning of our night together.

"Again?" he asked.

"Again."

When we were done in the shower, he pinned me down on top of the chaise. I bounced on his lap on the stairs. He bent me over the banister. Every time we reached the pinnacle, it wasn't enough. I pulled him closer, and he left fingerprints on my hips.

I never wanted it to end.

Once sleep came, it would be over.

I wasn't ready for goodbye.

So...

Again.

Again.

Again.

Until we couldn't take it anymore.

THE SUN ROUSED me from my slumber. I was still naked and curled up in Levi's bed. I could smell him, but I couldn't feel him around me anymore. I reached for the spot next to me to find it cold.

I bolted upright.

"Ronin?" I asked softly, holding the bedspread up to my chest to not feel so painfully vulnerable. My eyesight was still bleary, my body aching and sore.

My heart was in my throat.

Surely he wouldn't have left without saying goodbye, would he?
Not without asking me to go with him?

Right?

Thickness formed in my throat as I got up from bed, looking around for him, but he wasn't…

He wasn't there.

Pain squeezed my heart, tears welling in my eyes even though I tried to swallow them down into my churning stomach. I found one of his shirts and pulled it over my head to stop myself from feeling so *naked.* I padded down the stairs, holding in my hope that he was still here.

That he wouldn't have left without goodbye. Not after last night.

But my heart fell the moment I noticed a piece of parchment on the kitchenette counter.

No….

Hesitantly, I picked it up, tracing my name on the folded letter. I opened it, tears streaming from the corners of my eyes as I read Levi's penmanship.

Dearest Maeve—

You were sleeping so soundly that I didn't wish to wake you. If you're reading this, I've set sail. I will not return for several months.

Tears dotted the parchment.

Thank you for the past few weeks. I enjoyed our time together. Take it as it was. Do not wait for me. I will not wait for you. You can use my cabana as long as you need. Good luck, Maeve. I wish you the best.

—Leviathan

My lips trembled.

That *bastard*.

"'Good luck'? 'I wish you the best'?" I repeated through watery breaths. "Yeah, fuck you too."

Maybe it was one-sided after all.

I sank down to the ground, fighting the urge to sob as my heart cracked in my chest. I was always going to be alone, wasn't I? The pain inside crested. I buried my face in my hands and let myself cry.

34
RONIN MURDOCH

"Pull the anchor," I ordered once the rest of the crew finished saying goodbye to their families. The shiphands lifted the gangway while Boats gave the order to untie the ropes from the pier. We started to drift away from the cove as I glanced up at my cabana, rubbing at my chest.

The image of Mae curled in my bed, her mussed hair all over my pillows, the soft pink of her cheeks, and the steady rise and fall of her chest with a quiet *wheeze* would haunt me. I remembered looking down at her, wondering whether or not to wake her.

But if I woke her, I'd never leave.

It was easier to leave a note.

Though she would likely hate me for it.

Nothing irritated me more than my mates watching me from the corners of their eyes, whispering among themselves. Boats nudged Howler in the ribs as the shiphands got to work on the rigging and Plankwalker maneuvered around jagged rocks and reefs in the shallow water.

Plankwalker didn't ask questions. One of the things I liked about him.

We'd kidnapped him off a merchant vessel, and he decided to stay once we'd docked because the pay was better. He wasn't chatty, but he was loyal.

My arms were crossed, my mouth pulled down. I rubbed at my chest again to relieve myself of this awful feeling of heaviness. But it wouldn't go away.

"Hey, Levi?" Howler asked hesitantly as he stepped up the stairs to the helm.

"What?"

"Is Mae not coming?"

My belly squirmed like it was full of knots. "No. Why would she?" I turned away from the cove completely, ignoring the gnawing feeling of emptiness. I opened the door to my cabin, trying to get away from Howler's incessant questions.

But retreating never worked. He followed, closing the door to the cabin behind us. "I just thought—"

"Good thing I make the decisions, then."

He frowned. "I hope you weren't this much of a dick when you said goodbye to her."

I sat at my desk, trying to busy myself with merchant routes. "I didn't."

Howler's hand slapped down on the piece of parchment, drawing my gaze up to him. "What do you mean, *you didn't?*"

"I left her a note. She was sleeping," I said, no emotion in my voice. I wasn't in the mood to be interrogated.

My first mate made this look of utter disgust as he turned away from my desk. "Are you fucking kidding me?" He pinched the bridge of his nose. "She's going to hate you."

"That's the point. It was just a spot of fun, all right? Leave it," I muttered.

"I doubt she thought it was just a *spot of fun*. I saw the way you looked at each other. You liked her, Levi."

"I'm not in the fucking mood. Get the fuck out of here. You have work to do."

A tic formed in his jaw, but he threw his hands up in defeat. "Fine. Romances aside, she would've been a great addition to the crew, and you know it. All of us liked her. It's not all about you."

"But I'm the one who made the final decision. Now leave it. You might be my brother, but right now, I'm your *captain*." I flipped through the pages, familiarizing myself with our mark. "If anyone asks me about Mae, they're joining the cabin boys and swabbing the deck. Do I make myself clear? I don't care what rank they are. I won't have my sailors ask me about personal matters."

Howler didn't reply, but I did hear him slam the door behind him.

Good. I wanted to be alone.

I sighed deeply, running my fingers through the ends of my hair. Another memory from last night came into my head. The sensation of her soft skin. How good she felt. How badly we wanted each other.

I told myself I wouldn't think of her again when I left port, but here I was, thinking about how her wide eyes shone with vulnerability every time I buried myself inside her. The way she trusted me to take care of her.

Gods, I miss her.

I shook my head. *It's over.*

My chest tightened with an overwhelming longing to turn around. Beg Mae to come with me while we started our own adventures together.

Not only would she likely slap the shit out of me for saying goodbye with a half-hearted letter, but it would be overstepping the boundary we'd made to keep it casual.

Fuck the boundary.

A little late for that. I'd just give it a little time… and then I'd forget about her.

I just needed time.

After a few hours, the pain in my chest didn't go away. If anything, it kept getting worse. I made a huge fucking mistake, didn't I? It didn't matter. It was over. I had to live with it. But this bastard in my chest didn't seem to have gotten the message.

The door to my cabin flew open. "Levi!" Howler bellowed.

"I get it, Howler! I fucked up. I don't need another reminder," I snapped, my eyes shooting up to meet his. They were wide, nearly panicked.

This wasn't about her.

I stood up. "What's going on?"

"A man-o'-war on the edge of the horizon. Moving mighty fast."

"Naval? Merchant? Pirate?"

"Hunter. Come quick. Now."

Shit.

I snatched my spyglass from my desk drawer before following Howler out the door to where my crew was gathered along the side of the ship, watching the naval ship close in. This was never good.

But they weren't coming toward us. They were headed toward Shipwreck Bay.

Our families.

Our friends.

Our home.

I extended my spyglass to get a better look at the ship in the distance. Naval uniforms. Fully staffed. Swords and pistols drawn. A well-dressed man standing near the helm, giving a speech to his sailors. His sword glinted brightly in the sun, made with a unique sort of metal.

No... not metal.

Draconite.

Finding the main mast, I looked up, searching for the flag.

A barracuda.

The Pike naval ship.

I didn't know if this was Nathaniel Pike or someone under his charge. Either way, this was *not good*.

"Pike," I uttered. I glanced over at Wraith, whose hand was poised on her cutlass. "How far are we from land?"

"Three hours at most. With their speed, they'll get there faster."

I could hear the chatter among my crew. Pirate hunters within a day of their safehold. That meant Pike had the men and the means to take it.

And if they could take Shipwreck Bay, they wouldn't be far from Anchorage Cove. It wouldn't take much for them to find Isa and Howler's kids. Butcher's husband.

Mae.

"What are the orders, Cap?" Boats asked.

I closed my spyglass. "Prepare for battle. Plankwalker, get us between Pike's ship and Shipwreck Bay. We are not going to let them get past us. If they do, they'll go after our home."

Plankwalker dipped his head, twisting the helm. After hearing my orders, Howler took off to the lower deck, Wraith sounded the alarm, and my mother came up to the deck. Boats and the shiphands filed down to the armory for weapons, the vanguards were woken up, and organized chaos ensued.

The deadlights opened beneath us, and I heard the cannons being prepped under the deck.

"Raise the Jolly Roger."

A black flag adorned with the skull and crossbones was cranked up our main mast. I always gave ships the chance to surrender, naval man-o'-war included. I never flew a red flag. Not even for Varric Cross. If blood didn't need to be spilled, then I wouldn't spill it.

The man-o'-war turned its sights on us and came directly toward us. A flag rose up its main mast.

A white flag of surrender.

Instantly, my gut turned. It was a blatant lie, but it wouldn't feel right to fire on a surrendering ship either. I narrowed my eyes as the crew waited in a tense line on deck. "Bring us in," I ordered. "Be on your guard! I don't trust hunting ships to surrender."

Wraith stood behind me on one side, Howler on the other. Boats was at the head of her ship crew while Gunny waited below deck for the first order to fire. My mother stood on guard nearby.

She had more experience with the Pike family than I did. According to her, it was the Pikes who started turning in their neighbors on the suspicion that they were leviathans, single-handedly becoming the lead dragon hunters in the Isles.

Varric even gave them the Ivory Keys, an island that was home to both fae and leviathans, in reward. Nathaniel kept the legacy, hunting pirates in lieu of leviathan. I supposed it would be an outlet for his violence when he didn't have a wife to take it out on.

I ground my teeth together, remembering the marks that had been on Mae's neck when we met. What would've happened to her if she hadn't run? I couldn't let this ship get past us. I couldn't let them find her. And I sure as fuck couldn't let them destroy Shipwreck Bay like they'd destroyed the Gullies.

Murdered the merrow.

Hanged the elves.

Drawn and quartered anyone who disagreed with them.

It didn't matter who it was—or what they were—all Varric saw was an enemy. Those who kissed his rings were spared. Under the guise of freedom, he offered them the chance to be worked to death while believing that was the best treatment they could ever get.

I'd spent the twenty-five years since the coup avoiding the navy. Avoiding the Pikes and the Crosses. Staying alive and keeping my family safe. It was only a matter of time before all that luck ran out.

The man-o'-war glided alongside *The Ollipheist*. But this time… there were hardly any sailors on the main deck. Only the same well-dressed man and a handful of vanguards. Now that they were closer, I could make out the coat of arms embroidered onto his breast pocket with fine thread.

"This is an ambush," I muttered to Wraith.

She nodded, gesturing to Howler to get below deck to ready Gunny for attack. I'd sink them before they had a chance to sink us.

Their vanguards clattered a gangway between our ships. I raised one hand, silently urging my crew to stand back while I stepped forward, just in front of the gangway.

No way in the Nine Hells I'd let them rip that out from under me.

"State your business," I shouted.

The well-dressed man wearing the draconite sword stepped onto the gangway, and I didn't like how casually he sauntered onto my ship. "You're in my way."

I drew my cutlass and pointed it directly at him. "I said state your business, or I will cut you down."

He looked left and right, his eyes settling on the flag

underneath the Jolly Roger. The silhouette of a sea dragon. "I'd heard great things about *The Ollipheist*." He was too casual. For a man surrounded by a small army of pirates, he didn't seem remotely afraid.

"Our reputation precedes us. That means you're aware of what we do to those who challenge us. I'm going to give you one opportunity, and one only, to turn around and sail back to the Ivory Keys before anyone gets hurt."

He hummed, tapping his chin with his finger. He still hadn't drawn his sword. "I didn't think you'd be so accommodating." He paused, but I kept my eye trained on his other slimy hand, waiting for the sea slug to rear its filthy head and show me its true colors. "You know, there was word about two months ago that *The Ollipheist* was spotted at Farlight Harbor. Would you know anything about that... Captain...?"

"Leviathan," I uttered, baring teeth.

The man chuckled. "*Leviathan*. How amusing. Nonetheless, this ship was spotted at the same port that my wife disappeared from."

Nathaniel Pike. In the flesh. "I wouldn't know anything about that."

My hand tightened on my cutlass, ready to move at a moment's notice.

A sinister grin stretched across his face. "I thought you'd say that."

Underneath the ship, I heard shouting, gunfire. Metal hitting metal.

An ambush from beneath.

"Now!" I roared, and my crew instantly went on the defensive. Chaos broke out on board as Nathaniel drew his sword, the draconite whistling and hissing as it came into contact with my cutlass. I moved quickly, deflecting his strikes.

But every single hit stored kinetic energy inside his sword, each strike growing more and more powerful.

Fuck.

"Where is my wife, Captain Leviathan?" Nathaniel shouted, striking harder and harder while I braced my sword in front of me.

Behind him, my mother swung, but he was faster, a trained swordsman. His hand shot out, and he grasped her by her wrist, flinging her onto the deck while the hunters came up from the lower decks to fight my sailors.

I *needed* to shift.

But when I did, I'd have to kill every single hunter who came aboard my ship. After all, dead men keep their fucking mouths shut.

Nathaniel's eyes darted down to my mother's three-fingered hand and back up at her face. "Enya?"

Her eyes widened.

"It is you."

I straightened up, coming at Nathaniel with everything I had. His sword swung up, and the moment it came into contact with my cutlass, electricity shot from the draconite, shattering my sword completely down to the hilt. It knocked me onto my back, and I hissed loudly at the impact.

Nathaniel wasn't interested in my mother anymore. He shoved her into the arms of another hunter before whirling over to me while my sailors fought viciously in the background. Wraith was cutting through hunters, moving like a violent wind.

She was a force to be reckoned with during battle, but the draconite Nathaniel carried made him quicker, stronger, unafraid.

Wraith came toward me, but Nathaniel deflected her,

using his free hand to grip her red hair and knock her into the water.

Wraith. Fuck!

Pain gripped me by the throat as Nathaniel approached me, his sword a hairbreadth away from my chin.

"Luella!" Boats called out her wife's birth name, rushing over to the edge, only to be kicked behind the knees by another hunter. She screamed into the ocean, but it would be no use. Wraith would be dragged under the ship by the current, and she would drown.

Right before my eyes… everything started to fall apart.

Everything in me went cold as I was forced to look up.

Nathaniel's eyes gleamed with cruel satisfaction. "I know those eyes. Just like your father's." He looked up at his hunters. "We have our prize."

Before I could utter a response, his boot slammed into my nose, rendering me unconscious.

35
MAEVE CROSS

THERE I WAS, sobbing over a tankard of ale at the port tavern. I could feel every bar patron giving me a pitying look at every loud wail.

They'd left that morning, but it still hurt. My eyes were sore. After reading that note, I'd *desperately* needed to forget about it. So I marched down to the port with a ridiculous wedding ring in my pocket and a pouch full of gold coins.

At this point, I'd happily drink all my money away.

Fortunately for me, Siggi, my favorite tailor, happened to be getting a drink after work. The dark elf patted me on the back while I cried into my ale. Any other time, I would've been mortified at how pathetic it seemed, but right then, I didn't care.

"Who in the Hells does that, Siggi?" I demanded, tipping back my tankard. "Who leaves a note after all that?"

"There, there, lass," Siggi sighed. He gestured to the barkeep for another round. "Let it all out. We all need a good cry every once in a while."

I sniffled. "Thanks."

"Do you know what you're going to do now?"

"I guess I'll get myself recruited onto another ship. I want to be on the water… but Levi didn't ask me to join him." I huffed. "Did I do something wrong?"

Siggi shook his head. "Oh, no, Mae. Levi is just a fool. Don't get yourself all worked up over nothing."

"It wasn't *just* Levi." I paused, repressing more tears as my lower lip trembled. "All my friends are on that boat. I'm… I'm…." My shoulders slackened. "I'm alone again, Siggi."

"Come now, Mae. I'm here, aren't I?"

I gave him a weak smile. "I suppose you are. Thanks for listening to me bellyache, but you probably have other things to do."

He shrugged. "Perhaps, or maybe I'd prefer to listen to a pretty lassie bellyache about a foolish man who wrote a letter instead of saying goodbye." He paused as if he was about to say something he knew I wasn't going to like. "Did you not think that maybe he wrote that letter because if he saw your pretty face again, he wouldn't want to leave you there?"

I tipped back my drink. "Then he should've asked me to come. I wanted to."

"He's a foolish man, Mae." Siggi stood up. "Now, let's get you back home. A girl like you shouldn't be wandering around here at night."

I followed him, cupping a hand on the hilt of my cutlass. "Maybe I want to get into trouble."

"Then Levi isn't the only foolish one. Come now. I'll take you to my shop."

I followed Siggi out of the tavern. As usual, the port was bustling with trade. Always more exciting at night. "You don't have to let me stay at your shop."

"Do you want to go back to Levi's?"

"No."

"Then come, you stubborn woman."

"Fine. Fine."

We walked along the wooden slats of the port and headed to the back where his shop was.

Gods, crying took a lot out of me.

As we walked, rapid footsteps from the beach caught my attention. A raucous sound of shouting and urgency. That was odd. Something inside me tugged, and I stopped, turning to glance in the direction of the noise.

"Did you see…?"

"…washed ashore…"

"…the Wraith o' the Sea…"

I paused. *Wraith?*

"Siggi," I called out.

"Yes?" He stopped, turning to see that I wasn't beside him anymore.

"I think something is going on at the beach."

His eyebrows rose. "Why does that have anything to do with us?"

"I heard them say something about the *Wraith o' the Sea*," I said, not waiting for him as I went in the direction of the noise.

"Mae!" Siggi called for me, following me as I picked up my feet to run to the beach.

Something twisted inside me. My heart was racing. Something was *wrong*. I could feel it.

A circle of beachgoers surrounded something floating in the water.

The moonlight poured down on them, reflecting off distinctive red hair.

Wraith.

"Get out of my way!" I barked, startling the beachgoers as they dispersed. "Git! Go!"

Siggi saw it when I did and ran over to my side. "You

heard her! Move!"

Where she was floating face up, I could make out Wraith's pointed ears, her hair flowing like bloodied water. I dropped down, gripping her by the wrist and pulling her onto the sand.

"Gods," Siggi uttered. He shook Wraith's shoulders. "Hey! Lassie. Can you hear us?"

"Wraith," I urged. I felt for her pulse. Felt for the breath puffing from her nose.

She's alive.

Suddenly, she lurched up. *"Oh, fuck."* She coughed, water sputtering out of her mouth as she rolled onto her stomach, grabbing handfuls of the sand. "Oh… not again."

Again?

A question for another time.

"Wraith? Are you okay?"

She tossed herself onto her back, sand clinging to her wet skin and clumping in her hair. "Mae?"

I nodded. "It's me. And Siggi."

She breathed hard, clenching her eyes tight. "Shit." She lurched up again, groaning as she did. "They have my wife. They have Levi." Her legs wobbled as she tried to stand up.

"Slow down!" I urged, getting up to steady her. "What happened?"

Wraith grabbed my blouse tightly, her eyes blazing with panic. "Your fucking husband attacked us." She gulped thickly. "He knows, Mae. He *knows*."

My blood ran cold.

Nathaniel has Ronin… Enya….

No.

"Knows…?" Siggi murmured, completely out of the loop.

Wraith's gaze shot over to him, and he buckled under it. "I need to go. I need to go now. They're half a day in front of us.

I know he's taking them to Farlight Harbor. And he's got my fucking ship. If they strip *The Ollipheist* for scrap, I'm flaying every one of them."

She nearly collapsed on the first step. Her cutlass was gone. She didn't even have her flintlock pistol in her waterlogged sash.

"Whoa! Whoa! Slow down." I grasped her, keeping her upright.

She bared her teeth at me, snarling. "I *will not* slow down. Get the fuck out of my way."

I doubled down, grabbing her shirt even harder. "I'm coming with you."

Instantly, her guard went down. The violence in her intense gaze flitted away. "You're coming?"

"You are not doing this alone," I concurred. It wasn't even a question for me. I was going. "What's the plan?"

This time Siggi chimed in. "Lucky Bartram came into port last night with a whole fleet of ships. A few sloops...." He paused, looking around before adding, "You didn't hear that from me. Good luck."

I dipped my head. "Thank you." I wrapped an arm around Wraith's midsection to steady her. She was bigger than I was, but I'd do what I could to keep her from falling down. "Let's go. No time to waste."

Wraith panted. "They have two ships. A man-o'-war and *The Ollipheist*. That will slow them down. We are smaller. Lighter. Faster. We might be able to catch up. Especially if they get becalmed."

We staggered back over to port, eyeing Lucky's ships on the far side. I didn't see many sailors. The port was oddly quiet aside from the taverns and the brothel. We tiptoed over to that side of the pier as Wraith told me everything I needed to do once we got there.

"Untie the ship. Pull the anchor. Climb up into the rigging. I will man the helm. You need to be an extension of me."

"Got it," I promised, remembering the one time I asked Boats to let me work in the rigging, and she told me I wasn't trained for it. Guess I was getting trained now. Trial by fire. Best way to learn.

The sloops were small vessels. Perfect for a two-sailor crew. From the corner, I watched supplies get loaded onto the ship.

Look at them, getting it ready for us. How thoughtful.

When the sailors left the sloop, we snuck on board. Wraith stumbled over to the helm, and I untied the ropes holding it to the pier. I followed her instructions as I adjusted the sails and pulled the anchor.

Hopefully, I didn't run into Lucky again, considering how I'd dueled with him last night.

But luck was not on my side.

"Hey! That's my ship!" Lucky roared from the pier, a handful of men with him. I made direct eye contact with him as his men started sprinting toward us.

"Fuck. Go. Go!" Wraith demanded as I moved the sails, catching wind to pull us away from the pier.

The men filed into the sloop moored behind us, ready to chase us down.

There isn't any time for this!

I reached into my pocket for the expensive ring. "Sorry!" I shouted, throwing the ring as hard as I could.

Lucky's hand shot up and he caught it, a look of mild disbelief flashing over his expression as he glanced back up at me.

He barked another order to his crew, and they immediately stopped. Those mischievous eyes came up to look at me again as he waved the ring. Then he turned around and didn't look back at us.

"What was that?" Wraith asked, twisting the helm as she supported her weight on the banister next to it.

"My wedding ring. You know… payment."

She waved an exhausted hand. "Clever. We don't have the time to spat with Bartram. Come, take the helm."

36
RONIN MURDOCH

BURIED pain washed ashore on the surface of my mind. My eyes rolled to the back of my head, my temples pounding. A black spot was in the corner of my sight. I couldn't keep my eyes open as I slipped into unconsciousness.

I plummeted directly into my nightmares.

MY FATHER'S bloodied eyes were on the table. Crimson stained Varric's hands as he used an instrument to pull the crystals from his skull. Everything was blurred except for the amulet dangling from Varric's neck, no longer hidden under his robes.

I couldn't put the details together. I didn't understand what was happening. My lips parted to scream, but no noise came out. My limbs were heavy. I couldn't lift a finger. I couldn't cry. The only indication of my terror was the sensation of hot tears rolling down my rounded cheeks.

I was next.

I was next!

Varric dipped the draconite into a pinkened dish of water, and instantly, the crystal torn from its owner sparkled again, thrumming with power. His voice sounded contorted like a monster's when he murmured a word that made me cold.

"Beautiful."

"Open those eyes." Nathaniel's voice cut through my slumber worse than the kick to the ribs. I grunted, coughing and sputtering the blood in my mouth.

My eyes opened even as my head reeled.

Ropes confined my arms to my sides and bound my ankles. There was another one around my midsection to keep me upright against the ballast in my cabin. I tried to adjust, come to, but I…

I couldn't move.

Panic seized my heart as breath puffed hard out of my nose. Paralysis weighed heavily on my limbs. I couldn't lift a finger. I was only in control of the movement of my neck. I ground my teeth together and swallowed every indicator of fear. My eyes shot over to Nathaniel, letting that familiar sensation of rage melt into me.

I wouldn't be afraid.

But I would be fucking furious.

He sat at my desk, flipping through my papers, reading my captain's logs. Making himself at home in my fucking chair. He kicked his feet up onto my desk.

"About time you woke up. I was afraid my men gave you too heavy a dose." He didn't even look at me. "I don't have Varric's special blend, but I do have enough vitrophine on my ship to keep you paralyzed the entire trip to Farlight."

I gritted my teeth. "Better keep that syringe close, Pike."

He chuckled, glancing down at me. His eyes were cold, void of any sympathetic emotion. "Your threats amuse me."

"More like promises."

He put the papers down and got up to crouch across from me. If I had control over my limbs, I'd twist him into a headlock and snap his neck. Shifting like this was out of the question. Even if I wasn't paralyzed, I'd reduce the ship to splinters from here. At this point, I didn't know where my crew was.

I wouldn't risk them drowning.

Nathaniel swung his sword, the draconite gleaming. Thrumming with the power of dead leviathans. He noticed my eyes blaze the longer I looked at it. "Do you like it? Varric had it made for me after I brought him what we thought was the last leviathan. Twenty stones melted and forged into such a powerful weapon."

He laughed out loud.

"Amusing to think that we missed one. A Royal Leviathan at that. After all, your draconite is worth that of ten common leviathans."

I didn't answer, anger bubbling inside with nowhere to go.

"Where's my wife, Ronin?"

"I don't know what you're talking about."

Nathaniel sighed, stepping over to my desk to open a drawer. He pulled out a syringe of vitrophine and a small brooch.

Mae's brooch.

He set them down and made himself comfortable in my chair. "I'll ask again. Where is my wife?"

"Long gone," I replied. "You'll never find her."

"I don't understand why none of your crew wants to

divulge that little piece of information." He raised his sword to point it at me. "Unless you killed her."

"She drowned," I replied. "Fell off the ship when we hit rough water."

"Godsdamnit," Nathaniel groaned. "So the old man lied."

Lied about what?

Nathaniel didn't elaborate. "Varric has hounded me for her, saying I should never let the sea claim her. We both know how dangerous he can be if he doesn't get what he wants. No matter. You should be enough to make him forgive me. At least temporarily."

He waited for a reaction. His eyes glimmered, and I could tell that his next statement would be cruel. Designed to push my buttons.

"Shame I never got to use her. She really was quite pretty."

I fought the urge to bare my teeth. "You make quite the husband, Pike."

"I'll find another. Maeve is just as disposable as the rest of them." He tilted his head, watching me closely. As if I'd give him a tell. A way in. "I take what I want from them, and when they expire, I find another body to use. I just hoped she'd be the last."

I gave him *nothing*. "Where's my crew?"

"In the pit on my ship. Yours couldn't keep a pig confined."

"Really? Try it out yourself, then."

His icy blue eyes narrowed as he whipped a hand out to strike me across the face. I grunted, my head lolling back. "You're fortunate that I need you. You and your crew will give me quite the bounty. Enough to extend my rule to the far side of Farlight."

"It's never enough for you lot, is it? Always hungry for

more. Never sated. You and Varric are alike that way," I hissed.

"We have similar goals." Nathaniel was quiet for a moment. "I was nine when the coup happened. My father always told me that if we couldn't keep up, we'd fall behind. We'd lose our land. Lose our status." He hummed. "So we took the chance to get ahead. It didn't matter if we turned in our neighbors. They would be what we needed to rise to excellence. We became more than just the barons of a village. We are the lords of an entire island."

Scourge of the Sea.

"I never lost any sleep over it. And now I refuse to lose what I've built."

"You've built your legacy on a mountain of bones," I retorted. "It was sullied before it even began."

"At least I have something," he stated, standing up. "I've always been curious about the pirate lifestyle. Usually when we hunt them down, we sink the ships. I've never had the opportunity to really experience it myself."

Nathaniel started to run his fingers down the spines of my books.

"Especially not with the captain himself. I usually have their heads stuffed and on display by the time I get back to port."

He selected a book, pulling the leather-bound volume from the shelf. It was well worn, the leather softened and discolored by my fingertips. Flipping over a page, he didn't read it. He just tore it out.

"Get your fucking hands off my things," I uttered.

Nathaniel was trying to get a rise out of me, and he was succeeding. He tore out another page, followed by another. "I'm curious. Did Enya teach your crew to read like she used to teach in the schools? Or did she know better than to waste her time teaching the scum of society?"

I bit my tongue.

"Clearly those who can't afford it aren't worth the wasted breath."

That didn't get the reaction he wanted. He looked at the trinkets before passing them by and going into my side room. My teeth ground together.

He came back with his hand fisted around the neck of my freshly tuned violin, not a speck of dust on its polished wood. My eyes flashed, and Nathaniel had what he wanted. "Such a lovely instrument for a brute."

He took the bow and dragged it across the strings, scratching out an awful note. Then he hooked a finger under the strings and pulled, popping them one at a time. "I was never much of a musician. But I could always get the prettiest cries out of my wives."

Don't give him anything.

"Women are just like instruments, you see. Their tears are as lovely as a symphony. Pleasurable when you learn how to play the right chord. Earn the right cry. Some take longer to learn than others. Longer to wear down. But they all break eventually."

My upper lip curled into a snarl as he dropped the fragile instrument onto the planks and stomped down on it hard, splintering the wood with only the strings to hold the ruined violin together.

He leaned down to pick it up, discordant notes twanging together. "Once something is broken… the pleasure ends. Until you get another and do it all over again." He tossed the instrument behind him. It clanged off the wooden planks.

My heart pounded. White-hot fire balled inside me. This was the man Mae was given to. *Gods*, it made me sick. My fingertips twitched, and I'd never wanted to watch the light leave a man's eyes like I wanted to strangle Nathaniel until he turned blue.

"Are you done disrespecting my things?" I hissed. My legs started to tingle, a pins-and-needles type of numbness that signaled the beginning of gaining control.

"For now." He plucked the syringe from my desk and injected it into my thigh, all the numbness disappearing into nothing. "Don't worry, I'll grant you all the common decencies. I'll have my men spoon-feed you. Give you a bucket to piss in. I'll even have someone hold your prick for you."

I'm going to kill him.

"I can't bring Varric damaged goods, after all." He chuckled. "He might actually take my head for that." He tossed the syringe back onto the desk. "Until then, get comfortable. You'll be in good hands."

I'm going to enjoy *killing him.*

37
MAEVE CROSS

AFTER DOING everything in my power to run away, I almost couldn't believe I was going *back* to Farlight.

Back to my stone walls.

Back to my father.

I expected to feel anxious. That my heart would be in my throat. My hands shaking as I gazed at the ocean and pondered jumping into it.

But I didn't feel any of those things. I didn't want to turn around. I didn't want to run. I wanted to save my friends. I didn't need to think about it—the choice was obvious.

After rolling up my bedroll, I tucked it into the supply netting on the side of the vessel. The sloop was considerably smaller than *The Ollipheist*. One mast instead of three. Two decks instead of five. Shallow hull that made it much easier to fish if necessary. I could even go for a dip and pull myself back on board without help.

Most of the time, I didn't need to climb into the rigging. I could adjust it with a pulley and lever from the bridge. But surprisingly, this sloop was still completely armed. One cannon was located at the front. One in the back. A small armory of weapons. Enough supplies for ten sailors, so we'd have enough to last the whole month-long trip to Farlight.

The hatch swung open as Wraith crawled out of the lower deck, looking worse for wear but not as rough as she had when we left port.

"Good. You're up," she grumbled, rubbing her face as she made her way to the helm.

She was in a men's shirt and breeches, comfortably dry. Her other clothes were out on the deck, crusted with salt and sand.

"I am. Sleep well?"

"Adequate. I hope you know that if you want to go back to port, you're going to have to swim. I'm not turning around," she stated. Her hair was tied up, rough red tendrils everywhere. Her ears were poking through her mane. There was a bruise on her shoulder.

"I wouldn't ask you to." I approached the helm, gazing out at the open ocean. On such a small ship, it certainly felt like we were in the mouth of a giant. "Are you going to tell me how you wound up on the beach?"

"Fell overboard."

I blinked. "That's it? You fell overboard."

Wraith rolled her shoulder, giving me a sideways glare. "I was *thrown* overboard by your husband."

"Stop calling Nathaniel my husband." I rubbed my temples. "I never want to be associated with that man."

She looked away from me. "If you insist."

A woman of few words.

Gods, it irritates me.

"So, do you have a plan?"

"Yes."

"And that is…?"

"Save the crew."

I released a noise of frustration. "Wraith! For fuck's sake, can you give me a real answer? You're just as bad as Levi."

She made an odd noise. Took me a moment to realize she was chuckling. "Levi and I understand each other. It's not my fault that you and the twins haven't figured it out yet." Then the noise went away, and she frowned, nose wrinkling. "I don't have a plan. I just know the route."

"We should have a plan."

"Well, I'm all ears, Princess," she retorted, pointing at her extended ears.

Was that… was that a *joke*?

I can't deal with her right now.

I crossed my arms, gazing out at the water. Two women going up against a battalion of guards and pirate hunters in Farlight. The odds were not on our side.

"Wind is picking up," Wraith said. "I want full chase. This is our chance to crack on."

In common speech—catch as much wind as we can to catch up.

"Go on. My shoulder is still too mucked up to make the adjustments myself."

I stepped away from the helm to the rigging to make the proper adjustments. I tugged on the lines, fighting the harsh breeze as it slammed the canvas to and fro.

"You'll know it's right if you hear the rigging and sails crack under the wind."

Pulling them open and following her suggestions, I was rewarded with a sharp cracking noise as the wind hit the sails, drawing it taut.

"Well done, lass."

"How do you know so much about sailing?" I asked, tying the line into a knot and hooking it back in place so it wouldn't go anywhere.

She made a noncommittal noise. "You learn in the trade. I used to be a mapmaker."

"Oh?" Wraith never shared anything about herself, but what else was there to do when it was only the two of us?

She nodded. "Luella Peregrine—best Algarian mapmaker in the business."

Luella? Was that her name? It didn't suit her at all. In fact, it seemed much too sweet for the cutthroat woman I knew. But the longer I stared at her with the wind blowing her hair back, the less I saw her as that same woman who I couldn't turn my back on.

She trusted me to know her name and to go across the ocean with her to save our friends.

Luella seemed to fit her more and more by the passing moment.

But somehow that wasn't the most interesting part of her statement.

Algar? The continent of the Four Kingdoms?

"Algar?"

She didn't elaborate, just continued with her story. "Storms destroyed our ship off the coast. I fell overboard. The tide swept me away. I ended up washing ashore on one of the military-occupied Gullies."

That was how she ended up as a prisoner on a ship. "But Algar is… ages away. Our vessels can't carry enough supplies to even reach Algar."

A ghost of a grin pulled on her lips. "I always say that Cliohde was looking over me. Or that Lady Luck fancied me. Never thought I'd wash ashore twice."

"Lady Luck must *really* fancy you, then."

"She'll have to get in line. I'm married." Luella threw me a wink, turning the helm to the right. In front of us, all I saw was water, but it amazed me that she seemed to have a map in her head at all times.

I laughed under my breath at her joke.

"Enough talk. Go get me something to eat."

"Aye, aye," I said, padding over to the hatch. There was some produce in a box. That would spoil first. Unlike *The Ollipheist*, this sloop didn't have a greenhouse, so we had to get nutrients while we could.

While Luella ate, I practiced my cutlass skills at the bow of the ship. Footwork Gunny had shown me. Moves I saw Ronin make when we fought Lucky Bartram.

I didn't let my heart sink.

The letter he left me didn't matter. This wasn't about my feelings for him. It was about doing what I could to save him from the same death my father granted his family. Sickness stirred in my belly as I thought about how awful it would be to stand by while my father stole Ronin's draconite from him.

I'd never be able to forgive myself if I knew and did *nothing*.

"Do you think we'll catch them?" I shouted, swinging my cutlass in a controlled manner, practicing strike after strike.

Luella rolled her shoulder again. "We'll make good time. We'll move faster than them." She stepped away from the helm once she set us on course. She scrunched one eye, looking up at the sun and then back down at the water.

Satisfied, she approached me.

"When Pike caught us, it was early afternoon. You found me on the beach at night. I don't think we'll beat them to

Farlight, but I do think we'll only be a few hours—at most—behind them."

I nodded, stepping forward and slashing at the air.

"Get me a sword."

I stopped. "What?"

She outstretched her hand. "Sword. Now. Your form is weak. Too pretty."

"Gunny showed me these moves."

With a wave of her hand, she said, "Gunny is a gentleman. He doesn't have a mean bone in his body."

She was right on both counts. "And how is that a bad thing?" I opened the supply cache tied onto the half wall and retrieved a cutlass, handing it to her.

"You're small. Men in this world overpower those who are smaller than they are. Gunny doesn't need to fight dirty —nor would he. Too honorable for that. I don't have honor for those seeking to kill me." Luella grasped the hilt and gave it a swing, testing the weight. "People don't see you as a threat. Use that."

I blinked. "I hate the fact that I'm not threatening."

"That is a good thing, lass. When I walk into a room, I put people on edge. Their fear makes them predictable. You walk into a room and people relax. They become loose-lipped and easy to manipulate." She smiled, and for once it seemed genuine. "Neither is better or worse than the other. You just need to know how to use it."

I furrowed my eyebrows. "Can you show me?"

"I would love to, Princess. Take a stance. I'll show you how to strike where it hurts."

Straightening my shoulders and assuming a defensive stance, I readied myself for her strike. "I'm ready."

"We have honor where it's necessary. But if honor is

standing between life and death… fight dirty. Especially with men like Pike. They haven't earned honor."

Her cutlass came down, sparking where it made contact with mine. I gasped, digging my heels into the ground as the metal ground together.

"If all else fails, strike them in the groin or throat, but right now… *try to keep up.*"

38
RONIN MURDOCH

Nightmares.

I couldn't escape them. The days bled together. A vicious cycle one right after the other.

Eat.
Sleep.
Vitrophine.
Numbness.
Nothing.
Eat.
Sleep.
Vitrophine.
Numbness.
Nothing.

Every shred of dignity I could hold on to was stripped from me. I was trapped in my body. The only sensation was the brewing rage simmering in my belly. It fueled me.

As I lay there, Lieutenant Commander Lazlo came crawling up the space between the shelf and floorboards. He'd curled up at my side, and even though I couldn't stroke his ears, he'd purr and press his nose into my limp arms.

My only source of comfort.

Until one of the pirate hunters caught him nuzzled into my side. My cat yowled and hissed, scratching them with all his might. They kicked him and he screeched, limping while sliding as fast as he could under the shelf.

I feared the worst.

And when I didn't see Lazlo again, I believed the worst.

My wrists chafed from the ropes. My muscles slowly weakened as I was confined to this motionless heap on the ground. It enraged me.

I could feel myself wasting away.

But there was nothing I could fucking do about it.

Nothing.

The pirate hunters spoon-fed me porridge, wiping the corners of my useless mouth. Everything I used to be capable of was taken from me as Pike's men laughed about who would assist me in relieving myself.

I didn't want anyone to touch me. Every day was torture. I was reliving the same helplessness I felt when I was five years old, watching my father die over and over again.

I was going to kill every hunter on this ship. I was going to take great joy in holding Nathaniel's head underwater until the bubbles stopped. And when I was finished with them, I was going to burn Farlight to the ground.

All I needed was one lapse in the vitrophine. Then I'd kill them all.

MAEVE CROSS

The days dragged on.

Between our daily duties, I practiced with a cutlass. We

drank stale water from the reserve, rationing it since the sloop wasn't built for desalinating seawater. The produce lasted about two weeks before it became mush.

Luella and I survived on sea biscuits and fish jerky. No livestock on board, so no fresh eggs. The galley was small and barely operational, though it was functional enough to let me cook up the fish she caught in a net.

I'd wash clothes and scrub the deck. Even though this wasn't *The Ollipheist*, I knew that if I treated this sloop well, then it would treat me well.

Every free thought was consumed with strategizing a plan. What would we do when we got to Farlight Harbor?

Where would we dock?

Every little detail had to be planned out.

If the guardsmen saw me, I'd be taken inside, likely to a physician. I could slip away from there, sneaking down to the dungeons where I knew the crew would be.

I'd release them, and I would have friends at my back when we went for Ronin.

I just prayed that I wouldn't be too late. I didn't know how long it'd take for my father to extract the draconite. I didn't know if I'd be stopped by the guards before I went down to the cells.

But with all the things Luella was teaching me, my skills were developing fast. I wouldn't let anyone get between me and my friends.

Between me and Ronin.

I didn't know what was happening to them on Nathaniel's ship, but I'd make Nathaniel suffer for it. Even if Luella never said it out loud, I knew she was worried about her wife. Her family. Everything she'd built for herself so far away from Algar. All of it so close to being stolen from her.

At least we weren't alone.
I'd never be alone again.

39
MAEVE CROSS

Back in Farlight Harbor.
But this time, everything felt different.
I wasn't afraid.
I wasn't hiding.
I grasped the hilt of my cutlass.
I wasn't *defenseless*.

Just past noon, the sun was high in the sky. The port was flushed with merchant ships. Military vessels. At one of the docks, I caught a glimpse of a man-o'-war with a flag flying.
Barracuda.
All teeth.

Luella extended a spyglass, scanning the port. She hummed, passing it over to me. "Look."

"What am I looking for?" I asked, peering into the telescoping spyglass. I scanned from the flag down to the pirate hunters, watching a straight line of our crew being transported off the ship. Irons around wrists and ankles.

"See our crew?"

"I do. Remind me of the plan."

In front of them, I caught a glimpse of Nathaniel,

draconite sword on his hip. Two of his hunters dragged a man behind them. He didn't seem able to stand on his feet, a dead weight. His shoulders weren't as wide as I remembered them being, but his frame was still unmistakable.

Ronin.

What did they do to you?

My insides twisted, teeth grinding. Determination flared in my blood, warming my entire being. Suddenly all the exhaustion from travel didn't matter. I wasn't hungry. I wasn't tired. All that mattered was getting the crew out of there.

"Next to Pike's ship is *The Ollipheist*," Luella stated.

I swung the spyglass over, watching pirate hunters strip down wood paneling. Bringing out books and supplies. "They're breaking her down into scrap."

Luella growled. "My fucking ship. I will handle readying it for sail, but you need to get the crew. When you find them, I need you to send half of them here. Then save Ronin. I imagine the guards will be on your tail."

I nodded, noticing a dock bay open on the main pier. I closed the spyglass and tucked it into my pocket. "Pull into that dock."

"Do you have the papers?"

As soon as we docked, we'd need to prove we were here on business. Especially since it looked like they'd bolstered security since the last time I'd seen the harbor. Two women on a ship would garner plenty of suspicion. So we dressed in the clothes we found below the deck: tricorn hats and men's shirts.

"I do," I replied, pulling the papers from my sash. Lucky Bartram's seal of approval. A quality forgery.

"Good. Be ready. I'll do the talking. You can't lie for shit."

We pulled into the open bay as the harbor watchman

came over to inspect our ship. Dressed in a vibrant tailored uniform and wearing the Cross coat of arms, he had a clipboard in his hand and was ticking off boxes with a quill. He was an older man, but jovial in his appearance.

This was a man who loved his job.

"Good day. What is your reason for coming to Farlight Harbor this fine afternoon?"

"Supply run. Collecting for Commander Bartram." Luella kicked my shin. "Cabin boy, give 'im the papers. What do I pay you for?"

I managed to not shoot her a glare as I handed them over, trying not to look him in the eye. The hat shrouded my face, but if he looked any closer, he'd be able to tell that I wasn't a boy.

The harbor watchman glanced over the papers, humming a happy tune. "Everything looks in order. When will we expect your departure?"

"Shouldn't be more than a few hours. We won't stay long."

He nodded along, not once looking Luella in the eye. "Good. Good. The half-day fee is fifty coins. You can pay upon departure. With the pirate hunters taking up twenty dock bays, I need all the space I can get. Have a good day, now."

The harbor watchman turned on his heel, off to another bay.

Under her breath, Luella uttered, "That was the most pleasant harbor watchman I've ever met." Then she cleared her throat. "Now, time for the hard part. I secure the ship and our escape route. You save my wife, the crew, and our captain. Think you can handle that, Princess?"

"Can you handle taking *The Ollipheist* alone?"

She released a full belly laugh. "Do you know why they call me Wraith o' the Sea, lass?"

I shook my head.

She leaned in, an utterly terrifying gleam in her eye. "Because when I reveal myself, rising from the sea, it's already too late." She chuckled at the horror in my expression. "Good luck. I'll kill you if you fail."

It was a serious threat. As if there wasn't enough riding on me.

The main gate to the castle wasn't far from the port, always protected by at least ten guards. I needed a way in. If they saw me, it would cut into my time, and I wasn't sure how much time Ronin had.

The busy walkways. The loud chatter from sailors. Everyone dressed like me.

I fit right in.

I hung back, analyzing the entrance, racking my brain for every possible way to get in without being noticed, but I didn't think it was possible.

I could play the long-lost princess card, but I didn't think the guards would believe me. I didn't have my brooch. I was filthy. I looked like a cabin boy.

Nothing about me screamed *long-lost princess.*

How in the Hells am I supposed to get in there?

Think, Mae. Come on.

Suddenly, the gate opened and Nathaniel exited, holding a bag full of coins, numerous pirate hunters behind him.

Oh, hello.

That was my way in.

I glanced down at my outfit. I needed to look pathetic. I needed to appear like I was groveling. Nathaniel would *eat it up*. I tossed my hat off toward the bushes, followed by my cutlass. But my knife stayed in my boot.

Time to test out Luella's advice and try some manipulation.

I turned the corner and waited for Nathaniel to pass by it with his men. I could hear his voice, the familiar tenor of it making revulsion bubble in my belly.

Push it down.

"Not enough coin for all the warrants, but at least King Varric will finally put the whole losing-his-daughter situation behind us," Nathaniel chuckled. "Start a proper political relationship without the burden of women."

"It shouldn't be too difficult to find another virgin, sire."

Ugh.

"Maeve was going to be different. More durable."

Durable?

My hands tightened into fists as I thought of all the strikes Luella had taught me on the journey. I'd take great pleasure in practicing them on Nathaniel.

Nevertheless.

I took a deep breath, pretending like I'd been running as I turned the corner, purposefully bouncing off Nathaniel and crashing backward onto the dirt.

"Watch where you're going, peasant!" He whipped around, his eyes widening when he recognized me. "Maeve?"

With rapid breaths, I scrubbed my eyes. "Nathaniel?" I whimpered.

His facial muscles went slack in pure shock.

I pretended to sob, getting to my feet and grasping at his shirt. "Oh, Nathaniel! Nathaniel! It was terrible."

He was completely still as I threw myself into his arms. He made no move to embrace me. No move to comfort me even as I was *really* throwing myself at him. "I…. How are you here?"

Damn it, he was suspicious. I couldn't lie… so I didn't. "I… I fell overboard on this pirate ship. And I thought I drowned, but I survived."

"Huh." His arms slowly closed around me, but I could feel the tension across his entire body. He glanced over at his pirate hunters. "Quite durable."

Nathaniel was taking too long to get me inside.

"I'm so... so tired." I buried my filthy face in his neck. "I thought I wanted adventure... but I... I don't."

My voice broke, but he didn't notice.

"I just want to see my father, Nathaniel. Please."

"He's indisposed at the moment, but let's have the physician take a look at you."

The physician was farther from the dungeons than my chamber. My blood ran cold. I leaned back, widening my eyes as far as I could in my best attempt at innocence. "Could I just be alone with you? In my chamber? Please. I need...."

Am I about to seduce him?

Ugh.

I glanced at his pirate hunters. There was no chance that I'd be able to fight all three of them. So yes, I was about to seduce him.

Leaning in, I whispered, "I need to be alone with my husband. Have my servants prepare a bath for me, but I only want to feel your hands. We never... consummated our marriage."

I shook as I stroked the neckline of his shirt. Luckily, it was easy enough to pass it off as exhaustion and not rampant lying. He narrowed his eyes, but I think he wanted to believe me enough to bypass all my shakiness.

Nathaniel brushed my hair back, but it made my skin crawl. It felt nothing like Ronin's touch. But I forced myself to lean into it, feigning faintness to fall slack in his arms.

He scooped me up, moving with urgency.

I doubted it was for my gain. My disgust for him grew,

but I repressed it. I'd pretend as long as I needed to for Ronin.

For the crew.

For everyone this false monarchy had wronged.

Nathaniel spouted out orders, and doors opened for him. I closed my eyes, letting him do all the work for me.

"The princess is back!"

"Quick, prepare a bath."

"Call the physician."

"Inform the king."

I knew where we were going. The familiar pattern of the staircase. The sound of my door. He was alone with me. Gently, Nathaniel lowered me onto my bed, and my eyes fluttered open.

"What… what happened?" I asked, dialing up the pitifulness of my tone.

"You're in your chambers, Maeve," he said. The bed dipped as he sat next to me. "Your disappearance was marked around the same time this pirate ship left port. Did those scoundrels touch you?"

The only scoundrel who touched me was you.

He gripped my chin, and my hand fell down on my boot. I kept his gaze.

"Is your chastity still intact?"

"I've been gone for three months, and you care about *that*?" I narrowed my eyes. "Is that how you see my value?" Every word was laced with venom. "Whether or not I've bedded anyone?"

"There's the Maeve I remember. I was beginning to think you'd lost all your bite." His fingers tightened on my chin. "And yes. I will not be wed to a woman who was used by another man."

A humorless laugh slipped from my lips. I gazed down at

his draconite sword. A deep distaste welled inside me, disgust churning like bile.

"Did you know those scoundrels were harboring a monster? A leviathan. Filthy creature." Nathaniel's eyes were locked on mine so intensely that he didn't see me slip the dagger from my boot.

"You want to talk monsters?" My blade nipped his ribs.

His eyes went completely wide. "Maeve? What are you doing?"

Satisfaction warmed my blood with the spike of adrenaline. "I only see one monster, Nathaniel. But you see him every time you look in the mirror." I jabbed him hard, but not hard enough to draw blood. "Now get your *fucking* hands off me."

40
RONIN MURDOCH

"Ronin Murdoch."

A familiar voice roused me from a deep slumber. My head lolled side to side, ice flowing directly into my veins.

Varric Cross.

My eyes flew open, and I came face-to-face with gray eyes. They were dark like a brewing storm. A white-gold crown was embedded among graying curls, almost as if it didn't fit quite right. Elegant silken robes were hanging behind him off the back of the chair where he was sitting.

A draconite amulet hung from his collar as he rolled up the sleeves of his tunic. I saw a wide array of instruments rolled out on the desk. I could smell the old blood, cold and musty like a cellar.

The smell almost shot me back into my childhood, but I grasped onto reality.

Now is not the time to spiral.

I bit down on my tongue hard, the spike of pain and taste of metal enough to keep me grounded. Just like on my ship, I had no use of my hands. No twinge of numbness or pins and needles in my limbs.

Trapped in a suit of flesh.

"You look just like your father," Varric mused, his fingers tracing over an array of gleaming instruments that had been polished and sharpened. Some I recognized. Others I didn't. He seemed to be taking inventory of them. "Hard to believe you were nothing but a sniveling child the last time I saw you."

"You got old," I replied.

Varric paused his ministrations before caressing them again from first to last. "When we found Enya's fingers clinging to the sewage grate under the castle, we thought you both had been washed to sea. It would've been such a pity to lose a valuable resource to the trenches."

"Where's my mother?" I nearly snarled.

"With the rest of your traitors. Scheduled to hang at dawn." He chuckled. "You have quite the roster of criminals under your command."

"Necessary under a tyrannical rule."

He gripped a needlelike instrument, whirling around to stab it directly into my shoulder. I didn't feel it bite into the skin. I didn't feel it dig into the muscle. I didn't even feel the blood pooling from the wound. The only indication that it had been jammed into my shoulder was the wet sound of blood and flesh.

"You're familiar with vitrophine," Varric started. "But I've grown more adept with herbs. The addition of cane ivy slows the blood, prolongs extraction, but the goldenglow watercress prevents shock. Pain. You won't expire until I'm finished."

"Do you want me to say *thank you?*"

"I assumed you'd appreciate the anesthetic. After all, your father and your brothers felt every single cut."

My pulse pounded in my ears, fire spewing in my belly.

My hands ached to rip this godsdamn needle out of my arm and drive it into Varric's eyes. "How can you take so much pride in killing children?"

He continued his preparations calmly. His back was to me, his shoulders set in a relaxed slope. "Like when dealing with any invasive snake, sometimes you need to smash the eggs."

Bile rose in my throat. "When you take my eyes, will that finally be enough for you? Or will you always seek more?"

He peeked at me from over his shoulder. "Do you know the origins of Farlight Isles?"

I did, but I didn't answer.

"It's fine. I doubt Enya does either. You Royal Leviathans do like to bury history." Varric sat down in his seat. "How about a history lesson? Hm?"

I thinned my lips. I needed to indulge him. Needed time for the medicine to wear off. "Why not?"

"One hundred years ago, Farlight Isles wasn't much more than a cluster of islands off Algar. Home to the leviathans and several fae. That was until a guild of sorceresses came together to push Farlight far, *far* into the sea. Making it nothing more than a prison."

I narrowed my eyes. "And *why* did they turn it into a prison?"

He fiddled with his amulet, going off on a tangent. "I had a friend once while studying off the Gullies as a sorcerer's apprentice." Varric grew interested in the instruments again. "You see… my family didn't have anything to their name but a hovel. A hovel and disjointed memories."

The adrenaline in my veins slowed, my extremities growing cold.

"That doesn't matter now, but I was alone, spending my time

studying the flora and the fauna. Until a leviathan washed up on shore. Injured. Bleeding. I'd seen them in the water but never on shore before. So I hid behind a boulder, hoping that when the thing died, I could analyze its corpse. It was a little gangly creature, not like the Royal Leviathans, but you know this."

I gulped hard, the lump refusing to go down.

"Until… I watched it shift. From leviathan to man. More boy than man. He collapsed onto the sand, and I wanted to help him."

"Help him or study him?"

Varric slowly turned his eyes to me. "I'm not a monster, Ronin."

"We have different definitions, then."

"That young leviathan was so grateful for my help. I slipped vitrophine in small amounts into his tea to ease his wounds. A larger amount would paralyze him. As I tended to him for weeks, he told me how eager he was to be a Guardian of Farlight Isles."

No. My upper lip curled into a snarl. "That's a fucking lie. We would never tell a stranger."

He tilted his head back, looking at me from down his nose. "But you would tell a friend, wouldn't you?"

My mouth tasted bitter. "What about the draconite? Tell me about the draconite."

"Don't be impatient. I want to savor this, Ronin."

"Then continue."

"This guardian was quite a talker. He told me about the *Fifth* Kingdom of Algar. The exiled kingdom. That the royal family—*my family*—had their memories stolen and were forced to live in a hovel. My grandparents were supposed to pass away surrounded by luxury, yet they died in their own filth. An ending suitable for a commoner, not nobles."

Varric's nostrils flared, the storminess in his eyes growing.

"I knew then that there was no way I'd ever defeat the leviathans. Not only did they possess a dragon form, but they ruled the land and the sea. I'd never win. Not if I didn't have their power. But soon enough, I learned that leviathans were most vulnerable in their human state, no stronger than the rest of us." He held his amulet, admiring the intricate spotting of the crystal. "The key to my freedom was *inside* my warden. I slipped a large amount of vitrophine into his tea, rendering him paralyzed, as he'd told me his magic was useless if he died."

My stomach churned. I was disgusted.

"I could only harvest one stone before he died. Never fear, I got much better the more I practiced."

"That's not the whole story," I stated. "You left out the part where Farlight Isles would join Algar again once hate left your hearts. That was the only stipulation the kingdoms gave you. They could've executed your family and their followers, but they gave you a chance to redeem yourselves."

Varric chuckled. "And what then? Hmm? Live in filth? Stay poor and hungry? No… no, I will take what was owed to my family. The rulers of Nyland."

"And what was owed, Varric?" My fingertips twitched.

"Algar. With your draconite powering our ships, I will finally finish what they started a century ago." He smiled fondly as if he wasn't suggesting war with the Four Kingdoms.

"The Kingdom of Nyland lost. They committed *war crimes* on civilians. They convinced the *Grand Sorceress's* daughter to set herself on *fire*. The Grand Sorceress was merciful, and instead of killing them, the Guild of Sorceresses mustered all the power they could to send Farlight Isles far into the ocean."

Varric shrugged, unbothered. "The Kingdom of Nyland didn't go far enough, Ronin. I will do whatever it takes to finish it. Take back my history. Reclaim my kingdom."

"You have no honor," I uttered, flexing my toes in my boots.

With a chuckle, he stood, tracing his fingers across the sharpened tools. "What has honor ever gotten you? Trapped in a chair. Paralyzed. Weak. You will be nothing… but I thank you for your sacrifice."

I needed more time. My arms were still numb. "What of Maeve?"

Varric paused. "Maeve? What do you know of my daughter?"

"She was a guest on my ship." I gulped. "Until she fell overboard and drowned."

"Drowned? She's dead?" Suddenly, he started to laugh. This awful grinding noise that sent horrible chills down my spine. "No, she's not."

How would he know that? "I pulled her corpse back onto my ship. She's dead."

"You're a good liar, Ronin." He paused, twirling a pointed instrument around in his hand. "I don't know why you're protecting her, but she's of no use to you. She's as good as gold to me."

I frowned, unsure what he was getting at.

"I had been looking for something else that day, but instead, I found her. It was perfect. This little fae girl could pass for my daughter. Give me the opportunity to choose my heir. Boys are so hard to gauge as they get older, but with a girl, I could simply marry her off." Varric was interested in the conversation again.

My mouth went dry, the knowledge that my suspicions were correct. Mae was not Varric's daughter. "Her ears are tipped."

"You not only know my daughter, but you were close enough to see the scars on her ears?"

I didn't answer.

"Marrying her off wasn't easy. After spending twenty-odd years with the little thorn in my side, I felt a sort of fondness for her. She was also somewhat of a mystery." He grinned. "Fisherman's Gully. The merrow shoal cared for the little orphan."

Fisherman's Gully was a massacre.

Every word put me on edge. Twitchy. A tic formed in my jaw as I thought about the little girl snatched from her home by a power-hungry tyrant. Conway survived the assault, but the majority of his shoal painted the reefs red.

And Mae was *there*.

Oh Gods... her nightmares.

My heart slammed against my ribs. Everything was stolen from her, like it had been stolen from me. And... I left her behind.

I had no time to feel guilty.

"You never loved her," I muttered.

"Love is a fickle thing. Can't say the same thing for my wife. Katherine had to be constantly reminded that Maeve wasn't our daughter. That I'd get what I wanted from her eventually."

My fingertips twitched again my toes growing numb. "And what did you want, Varric?"

"You're awfully interested. Why does it matter? I'll find her, rid myself of Nathaniel, and then not even the Four Kingdoms united will be able to stop me."

He believed every word.

"Nevertheless. You don't need to concern yourself with those details. You won't be around to see it." Varric turned to sanitize his instruments. "Not that it's necessary, but I don't want you to succumb to infection before I'm finished. Sometimes the extraction can take hours."

A dull ache throbbed in my shoulder where the needle was.

Feeling was returning.

Fucking finally.

41
MAEVE CROSS

Nathaniel tried to grasp the knife and disarm me, but I was faster. I kicked a leg up, twisting it around his back and wrestling him down to the ground. Trinkets fell from my vanity. Chairs toppled over during the struggle.

He knocked it away. My dagger went flying across the room, my wrist aching.

He didn't call for the guards.

He didn't see me as a threat yet.

Good.

I locked my arms around his neck as he thrashed, pushing me over, taking control.

Damn it.

"You can't fight me, foolish fucking woman," he ground out between his teeth. He grasped my arms, using brute force to separate me from him altogether. I shouted as he flipped me over his shoulder, the air knocked out of me as my back collided with the unrelenting ground.

His foot slammed onto my rib cage, pinning me flat. I wriggled under it, the heel of his boot digging bruises across my midsection.

"Though it's quite adorable to watch you struggle."

Fuck you.

Frustration had tears streaming from the corners of my eyes. I was failing. Nathaniel was stronger than I was. He'd overpowered me just as he did in that carriage several months ago.

But I didn't freeze. I wasn't afraid of him like I was then.

I was afraid of losing my friends. Not getting there in time to save Ronin. Nathaniel was just in my way.

Fight dirty.

I remembered Luella pinning me down similar to this. Her voice echoed in my head.

"How can you expect to fight if you can't get out of a hold?"

"How can you expect to fight if you can't take a hit?"

"If all else fails, Mae, remember how other people see you. A delicate little flower. Use that."

I sniffled, struggling under his boot. This was where I'd be right now even if I hadn't run away. Only I'd be broken. I wouldn't have anything worth fighting for.

"I'm sorry," I cried, letting myself sound as pathetic as possible.

I had no room for dignity. Nathaniel wanted to strip me of it. The blue flecks in his sword gleamed more brightly the longer I looked at it.

I need to get that sword away from him.

"Beg for my forgiveness, wife."

"I'm sorry. I'm sorry. I'll stop fighting. I'll let you take me away. Please just let me stand up," I begged as convincingly as I could.

Take the bait, Nathaniel. Let me stand up. Get me out from under your boot.

"Wasn't so hard, now was it?" he hummed. He lifted his boot, letting me up. But before I could get up all the way, he grasped my hair, keeping me on my knees. "How about you show me how grateful you are? Show me how badly you—"

I grabbed his prick through his pants *hard*.

The weakest little cry left his lips as I fisted it even harder. "Enough with the damn power play, Nathaniel. I don't have time for this shit." I yanked hard enough to crumple him to his knees.

When I released him, both of his hands came down to cup his thoroughly bruised shaft. I grasped his head and drove his face down onto my knee, shattering his nose.

Instantly, he lost consciousness. He collapsed, and I felt the most satisfying twinge of delight.

"Pig," I uttered, loosening his belt and sheath.

The draconite sword was heavier than the cutlass, but it would give me enough power to get down to the dungeons. I pulled it from its sheath, holding it like I'd seen the guards practice all those months ago.

All I could do was watch between meals.

I stared down at Nathaniel's motionless body, debating whether or not I should let the sword cut into his body.

I should kill him right now.

My lips pressed into a tight line as I lifted the sword, but it felt too heavy. I'd never killed anyone. The longer I looked at him, the more I realized that it would be wrong to take advantage of his unconscious state.

I'm better than that.

When I killed him, it would be because I *won*, not because I took the easy way out.

I threw the door to my chambers open and swung the sword. It whistled, thrumming with stolen power. It felt wrong to wield it, but I had every intention of returning it to the water when I was finished.

Nathaniel certainly wasn't worthy of wielding it.

No one had the right to steal power that didn't belong to them.

"Princess?" a servant gasped when she saw me striding down the corridor.

"You didn't see me. Go," I ordered.

She nodded, turning to go into one of the several chambers to continue her duties.

I heard the next round of guards coming down the corridor. I turned the corner, sneaking around them.

I knew that eventually Nathaniel would come after me. The guards would ring the bells, and I would be out of time. Luckily, I had the rounds committed to memory. One of those little things I hadn't thought about until it was important.

The stairs.

I moved down…

Down…

Down….

The lights slowly got dimmer. The sun was unseen beyond the stone walls. I could hear chatter. Loud shouts. Familiar voices.

The crew.

The closer I got to the dungeons, the more guards I had to dodge. It wasn't incredibly difficult with all the shadows in the corners. And the guards had never been particularly good at their jobs either. My father was a firm believer in quantity over quality.

He always needed more.

More gold.

More soldiers.

Never satisfied.

I ducked around the corner, getting a glimpse of the

watchman's desk. A group of soldiers stood outside, chatting. And of course, I eavesdropped.

"…morning?"

"Yes, hanging. It should be an exciting gathering. It's been a while since we had an event in the gallows."

Sickness churned inside my gut. From inside one of the cells, I heard Seabird—Enya—shout distantly, "Get your filthy hands off my daughter!"

My grip on the sword tightened. Time to put all the practice to good use. I stepped out of the shadows, and the guardsmen all turned to see who was there.

"Princess Maeve?" one of the guards asked, his eyebrows creased in confusion.

The sword whistled as I took a defensive stance. "I need you to get out of my way."

"We… we can't do that. You should be with the physician in your chambers."

"I'll repeat myself only once. Get out of my way."

They looked at one another as if they weren't sure if they were allowed to fight me or not. The watchman snatched the keys from the hook, and two of the three other guards put their hands on their swords. "We can't let you pass, Princess. Now, we don't want you to hurt yourself—"

With a sharp swing of the sword, I silenced them. "Shut up and fight me, then."

Two of the guards looked at each other. "I'm not fighting her."

"I'm not doing it either."

"The king would kill us."

"What does the handbook say about this?"

"There is nothing in the handbook about this!"

I did not have time for them to bicker. My lips parted to silence their bickering, but then the watchman slammed the keys onto the desk in front of him. "I do *not* get paid enough for this." He took his sword out and pointed it directly at me. "But I know my job. You are not permitted in the dungeons. Now back away, or we will throw you into a cell."

They had made up their minds. I was the enemy.

But their hesitance was the boost I needed. The draconite sword's power crawled up the hilt and into my hands, whirling in my blood. I moved faster, every blow stronger than the last. Fighting felt right, as if I had tapped into my purpose. When I threw the sword up to deflect a hit, the kinetic energy inside the blade pulsed outward, forming a circle around me.

The hilt felt warm in my grasp, nearly thrumming as it connected with me. It was more than just a sword. I was wielding the power of a leviathan. The *soul* of stolen power. This time it didn't fill me with dread. Bile didn't rise in my throat.

Deep inside, it didn't feel stolen. It felt borrowed, as if the soul inside was giving me permission as long as I kept up my side of the promise.

I will return you to the sea where you belong.

At my silent vow, power pulsed more forcefully around me, rolling like a wave of thunder. All four of the guards were thrown across the room, knocking them senseless against the walls.

I moved forward, flinging the door open to the dungeons.

Down the dark, musty corridor, I saw Enya reaching out for Boats—Andra. The guards were dragging her out of the cell. They were being kept far enough down in the dungeons that they hadn't heard much of my fight.

Several of the cells were filled with crewmembers, their gasps rising up as I made myself known through the cellblock.

"Let go of her!" Enya screamed. "Unhand my daughter this instant, or I will *gut* you."

Indignance spouted up inside me. "You heard her!" I shouted, the sword becoming an extension of me, breathing a new rush of adrenaline into my veins.

The guards dropped Andra, their eyes flashing over to me. The crew followed, cheering rousing up from the cells.

"Mae!"

"Hey, it's Mae!"

"Birdie!" Gunny shouted from one of the cells. Though I guess it was Silas now, since we were friends.

A sense of pride bloomed in my chest. My friends. They were here.

Silas started to pound on the bars. All the other crew members followed. They shouted and cheered for me.

Pure encouragement.

There were four guards in the cellblock. "Princess… you're with these scoundrels?" one of them asked, shock lacing his tone.

"I'm with my friends." I charged toward them, readying my sword. I came down slashing and blocking. Spinning with all my might. Every hit built up a reserve of thrumming power within the sword. I knew the next hit would release it, so I slashed the lock on the cell door.

The blade cut through it like butter, releasing the crew from their confines.

The guards shrank, backing off now that it was nearly twenty against four.

Andra grabbed the keys and got to work releasing crewmembers from the irons binding their wrists and ankles. Spider helped her, unlocking cells and releasing more crewmembers and whoever else was stuck down here.

A few elves, humans, and fae mixed together.

They got up, moving with the same urgency.

Looks like they're crew now.

Howler—Wesley—threw the guards into an unoccupied cell.

Enya grabbed my shoulders. "Mae, Levi is down the corridor. Follow me. I know where."

I placed a hand over hers. "Most of you need to get to *The Ollipheist*. Wraith is there, but she needs help."

"Luella?" Andra's eyes twinkled.

"Yes. Go," I ordered. "Howler and Gunny, with me."

Enya pointed down to the opposite end of the cellblock with her three-fingered hand. "Down the sewers. It'll take you to the dock. Careful of the tide."

Then we were off. Enya led me down a long corridor, my friends at my back.

Outside a side room, there were two guards by the door, muttering, "Who should tell him his daughter is here?"

"I don't know. No one is allowed to interrupt the extraction."

I scoffed, getting their attention. "Don't worry, I'll tell my father I'm here."

My friends grabbed the guards, holding them back while I kicked the door open, sword at the ready. The first thing I saw was my father gripping Ronin's chin, an instrument barely inches away from his face. My father sat in his chair only a few feet away, an array of tools arranged on the table behind him.

My entrance startled him. His eyes flashed over me, the sword in my hand, and then Enya at my side. His lips curled into a frown. Ronin's eyes widened slightly as if he couldn't believe I was there.

I extended the tip of the draconite sword. "Unhand him at once, Father."

Suddenly, my father looked between me and Enya, his head tilting back in a chilling bout of laughter. He spoke in Antediluvian—the words of magic. The amulet around his neck pulsed as Enya was blown back into the hallway. The door clicked closed.

I could feel the magic wash over me, but it didn't shove me away—it moved *through* me.

An icy chill settled over me as fists started slamming against the door that was now completely immovable.

My father blinked, a brief glimpse of something akin to surprise coming over his face. Then it was gone. His amulet glowed with power, but where it had been once shiny and well cared for... I now noticed the smallest crack form within the black crystal.

"Nice of you to make an appearance, daughter," my father uttered, bringing his attention back to Ronin. He flicked his fingers over the instruments, turning his back completely to me.

Ronin didn't say anything. Dark shadows under his eyes told me how horrible the past month had been. He was thinner, sallower in his complexion. Looking worse for wear, but just as magnificent as I remembered him.

"I said unhand him!" I slashed the sword down onto my father's desk, scattering his instruments all over the floor.

He grew completely stiff, a tendon rigid in his neck. His eyes flashed over to me. Cold. "Your temper tantrum will not distract me from this, child."

The blue glints in Ronin's eyes gleamed as he uttered. "Varric is not your father, Mae."

My grip on the sword faltered. "What?" My voice shook.

Ronin's eyes directed my attention to a syringe on the desk, unused and filled with a blue fluid. My father blew out a sharp breath before he slammed a sharp scalpel onto his desk. His knuckles were white as he grasped it.

The pounding on the door got louder.

Panicked breaths sounded on the other side.

"Tell her, Varric. Tell her all about Fisherman's Gully. How you murdered the entire village and stole her." Ronin's words were sharp, cruel, designed to get a rise out of my father.

No, *Varric*.

Varric didn't deny his words, didn't beg me to believe that he was my father.

He... he stole me.

My nightmares.

My hands went up to my ears, feeling the subtle roughness of flesh there. They were scars. Everything started to make sense, shattering everything I'd thought I was.

"I'm not human, am I?" I whispered, barely able to form the words.

Varric leaned back in his chair, his amulet pulsating the longer the spell kept the door closed. But his eyes, the gray color that used to be filled with something I couldn't place—I now knew what it was. They were cruel. *He* was cruel.

The marriage.

The tower.

Every little piece of my life I cared for that he'd taken from me.

It wasn't out of protection or concern.

It was out of control.

"You never cared for me at all?" I gulped hard, tightening my hand around the sword, finding my vigor once again. The defiance I'd always been too afraid to show for fear he'd take something else away.

"Care?" Varric asked as if the word felt odd on his tongue. "No."

I didn't understand. Why did he want to have me in his possession? "Was I just a bargaining chip, then? Just something to sell off?"

"Oh, Maeve," Varric sighed. "Pretty, *pathetic* Maeve. You were so much more than that."

I didn't understand what he meant. But while his attention was on me, I watched Ronin's fingers move. Whatever they'd given him was wearing off.

I bit down the pain Varric's words had caused. I couldn't let that pain... that *betrayal* cloud my judgment. "Then why?"

Varric hummed, tapping his chin with one hand, his other gripping the instrument tightly. It unnerved me, but he needed Ronin alive, and he wouldn't kill me. Not if he needed me. But *why* did he need me?

"You really don't know?" Varric asked.

"Know what?" I whispered, a cloying sense of cold in the air as if everything inside me was on the edge of freezing.

Fight.

Flight.

Or freeze.

My survival response was bubbling up, begging me to do something, but I didn't understand why.

"This will be fun, then." Varric glanced over at Ronin with a slow smile on his face. "You care for her. That's why you kept asking me all those questions. I can see it now. How your eyes soften. That's good. It's the same way your father softened when he looked at you. When he looked at your mother. It'll make the magic stronger."

My heart pounded in my ears, adrenaline flaring. "What are you talking about?"

"I don't know what you are, Maeve." Varric stood up, the scalpel tight in his grip. "But I can't wait to find out."

Before I could comprehend what he was saying, one of his hands flew into my hair, pulling my head back as the scalpel slid across my throat. Blood spat out from the wound, the sword clattering on the ground as a soundless cry fell from my lips.

I collapsed onto my knees, grasping my throat as everything grew cold. Hot crimson poured from my fingertips, saturating my shirt. It was all I could see.

Blood everywhere. Caked around my neck.

Pain erupting from my ears as they took the tips away.

My small body resting against a black amulet with flecks of blue....

Ronin shouted my name, utter horror in his voice as his face paled. Darkness flooded my vision, curling at the edges like burning parchment. His voice grew distant, and everything around me crumbled into darkness.

Then I heard Varric's laughter. "Just wait. This is the best part."

A punch of adrenaline fired in my system.

My eyes flew open, wide with animalistic terror as I searched for something, a pool of crimson around me.

Breaths flooded into my lungs.

My neck was still slick with wet blood. Slippery like oil, it crusted around my fingernails.

I was... *alive?*

Tears cascaded down my cheeks as I slowly looked up from the floor, confused and terrified as Varric grinned at me before glancing over at Ronin. "I didn't want a fae daughter. I cut her down next to the merrow caretaker. Imagine my surprise when this little girl stood back up."

"...more durable..." What Nathaniel said about me rang through my head.

He knew.

"As much as I wanted to test the extent of your viability, Katherine had reservations about experimenting on a child. She couldn't have any of her own, and she wanted to care for Maeve so badly."

Varric looked at Ronin, who was angrier than I'd ever seen him before. His eyes promised violence.

My chest couldn't stop rising and falling. The tips of my fingers were numb. I was in shock.

That explained my mother's—*Katherine's*—distance. Tears fell harder as everything around me fell apart. I could've had a mother, but Varric was so intent on torturing me. So intent on using me that she pushed me away to protect herself. And after all that… she still wanted me to have a *chance*.

"But I relented. Decided to take a ward. And when Nathaniel Pike reached out, searching for a new wife, I knew his reputation. I promised him a more durable woman in exchange for what he could give me."

Varric hummed, glancing over at the draconite blade that I didn't know if I had the strength to wield anymore.

"Do I still have to worry about Nathaniel, Maeve? Have you taken care of him for me?" He chuckled. "It would've given me great pride to watch you kill him."

A myriad of confusing emotions assaulted me. "He… he's alive," I croaked, feeling for the slit in my throat but finding none.

Varric's lips formed a pout as he stood up from his seat, his back to Ronin. I watched him quietly struggling to remove his feet from the metal cuffs, wriggling his wrists from the rope.

Focus, Mae.

Give him time.

Then we can get out of here.

My throat felt thick, mouth gummy with dryness.

"What a shame." Varric smiled wide. "Well, once I finish with Ronin, how about we find Nathaniel, hm? I have my army. I have no use for him. You and I, Maeve, we could go to Algar together. Or better yet… I could send you there in place of my assassin. You'd finally get that freedom you wanted so badly."

He grasped my chin, and I didn't have the strength to fight it. Ronin slipped out of the seat and grasped the vial of vitrophine.

"They wouldn't be able to kill you. They wouldn't be able to stop you. You could be what I need to shatter their kingdom to make it that much easier when I take it for myself. *For us.* You can be my daughter again." He tilted my head to the side, manipulating the corner of my mouth. "Come on, Maeve. Show me that *smile*."

Indignance flared inside me as my eyes shot up to Varric's, a snarl on my lips. "Fuck you."

Ronin drove the syringe into Varric's side, shooting him full of vitrophine.

His eyes flared open as his hand grew slack. His body slipped down to the floor as he lost all mobility. His amulet glowed once, twice, before the power ceased altogether.

Ronin reached up and tore the needlelike instrument out of his shoulder, groaning a little under his breath. "One month of being fed vitrophine over and over again. I built up a bit of tolerance." His legs were shaky as if he was still figuring out how to work them properly.

The door slammed open. Both Silas and Wesley sprinted over to me, helping me stand up in a puddle of my own blood. I grasped the sword, determined not to let anyone in that castle wield it. I needed to keep my promise.

Enya ran in to grab her son and pull him into a back-breaking embrace.

He flinched.

"You're okay. You're okay," she nearly cried.

She ruffled his hair, and he kissed her on the cheek. "I am," he replied, his eyes flittering over Varric's body. Enya's gaze turned downright murderous as Ronin crouched down to speak to him. "I'd never kill a man who can't defend himself. Not even you."

Enya's lips turned downward. "Ronin. This is our chance. Right now."

"No," he insisted. "We need to get out of here and regroup."

Wesley and Silas stood there, visibly conflicted by Ronin's decision.

"This is a mistake." Enya ground her teeth together.

Varric laughed. "The biggest mistake a fool like you will ever make."

"Killing you now would be easy, Varric. Besides, I'm not foolish enough to leave an opening for someone worse than you to fill." Ronin stood up. "After all, that's how you came into power. You took advantage of a situation very similar after you murdered my family."

In the distance, I heard the warning bells ring. Nathaniel must've come to. Or they'd found him knocked unconscious in my chambers.

"Besides, there's not enough time to *enjoy* killing you," he continued. "When I kill you, and I will, I'm going to take my time. I'll grant you the same decency you granted my father and brothers. You'll *feel every cut*."

"I *will* come for you. I *will* take the draconite from the last

Royal Leviathan." Varric's eyes rolled over to me. "And one day, Maeve, I'll figure out what's behind your eyes."

Ice flooded my veins again at his threat. It wasn't empty.

"We need to move," Silas said. "The guards are on their way."

"Out the sewers," Enya declared, supporting her son as she guided us out of the room and down the corridor to a grate big enough for us to crawl through. It didn't take a lot of investigating to realize that this was how she'd escaped with Ronin all those years ago. This was where she'd grasped on to something and lost her fingers when the current washed her into the sea. If those memories were running through her head, she didn't show it.

We were crawling through the muck, trying our damnedest to ignore the smell. Every step brought us closer to the light at the end of the tunnel where it let out to the ocean. We climbed onto the wooden slats, pulling Ronin with us as his legs gave out.

Guards were flooding the pier with their swords drawn. They were clearly hunting for pirates. We ran as fast as our legs could take us. A shout got my attention from *The Ollipheist*. Andra was already untying the line and pulling the anchor.

"Run!"

"Come on, run!"

"Move your asses!"

The crew cheered us on as the ship started to drift away from the pier, the gangway scraping as it moved along. Ships were destroyed as *The Ollipheist* crashed into them, breaking them into scraps and demolishing half the pier.

A big mess for the harbor watchman to clean up.

I felt a tinge of guilt for ruining his good day.

Enya and Ronin were first on board, followed by Wesley

and Silas. Right before the gangway dropped into the sea, both Wesley and Silas grasped my arms and pulled me on board before I tumbled into the water.

I flopped down onto the deck, panting, my legs throbbing. The smell of blood was sickening. I was still coated in it.

A boot kicked me in the side, and I looked up to see Luella grinning down at me. "Looks like I don't have to kill you."

"I didn't need to die again today." I glanced around, taking in the ship. Last time I saw it, it was being broken down into scrap, but now, it was practically good as new. "How'd you pull this off?"

"Sara the barmaid owed me a favor." She winked. "I cashed in."

Vague as always, but I'd be content with it.

Plankwalker was manning the helm, maneuvering us off into the sea. Our massive ship left a trail of wooden planks, the crew adjusting the sails to catch the most wind. Thankfully, all the damage left by the pirate hunters seemed to be cosmetic.

Andra held out an arm to help me back up, wrapping me in a huge embrace when I was on my feet. Luella clapped me on the back. Ronin hadn't said anything to me yet, but he was immediately stopped by his crew, each of them voicing their relief that he was alive.

I grasped the draconite sword, eyeing the intricate detailing. But it was time to return it to where it belonged. When the water was deep enough that I couldn't see the bottom, I tossed it in to be lost among the waves.

Back home.
Like I was.

As the wind blew, I swore I heard a whisper caress my

ear. A gentle "Thank you, *Sentry*." My heart jumped into my throat as I whipped around. The crewmen were carrying on with their duties like normal. The beating in my chest started to slow.

Sentry?

The same thing the siren had called me.

42

RONIN MURDOCH

Every muscle in my body ached from exertion. I was exhausted, and I'd barely had control over my body for more than a few hours. Atrophy was apparent in my arms. My legs. Obvious in my face where my eyes had sunken in.

My hair was matted in some parts due to the lack of care. I felt dirty and disgusting.

Pathetic.

I needed to gather myself before I was ready to talk to my mother. My mates. My crew. My cabin was in disarray from Nathaniel taking liberty in destroying my things. I didn't have the energy to process that.

Nor did I have the energy to come to terms with the realization that I'd nearly met death the same way my father and brothers had. The same way my people had.

Standing under a spray of water, I cleansed myself of the trip into the sewers. Thankfully, I was alone. After being touched without my consent for the better part of a month, I needed to be.

I needed to have power over my body again.

My crew was bypassing the desalination process to wash

away the filth from the past month. Salt was better than sewage. There was a line for the showers, but everyone seemed happy to be home, the taste of freedom sweeter than before.

I'd lost people during the ambush. A foolish mistake that I should've seen from a mile away. But it was either that or let Nathaniel go to Shipwreck Bay and ambush the innocents living there.

After I turned off the water, I sank down against the wall, my head between my knees.

I watched Mae die today.

Seeing her brandish that sword, kick down the door to give me enough time to flush the rest of the vitrophine from my system... I thought I'd already died, and she was the guardian sent there to guide me to the afterlife. I never thought I'd see her again. I certainly didn't think she'd voyage across the ocean for me.

Then the pure horror of watching Varric slit her throat. I couldn't move my arms. I couldn't stop him. I had to sit there and watch her gargle her own blood. I watched it pool around her as the light left her eyes.

Every time I closed my eyes, I saw it over and over again. It terrified me more than my fate. More than that night when I was a child.

More than losing my second father because of a paranoid captain.

I lost the girl who'd traveled across the ocean for *me*. To save my crew from being hanged.

What the fuck was I supposed to say to her? Especially when I left without so much as a goodbye. I left her a note reducing what we had to a fling.

Gods, I was fucked.

A chirping noise from across the side room drew my

attention. Lazlo squeezed between a shelf and the floor, wiggling above the floorboards. The black cat was a welcome comfort. He trotted over to me to sit just outside the raised lip for the shower.

The cat purred, vibrating the floor.

A weak smile pulled at my lips as I reached over, unbearably tired as I scratched behind his ears. My heart soared with such happiness that my eyes brimmed with tears.

"I'm so happy to see you."

Wide green eyes blinked at me as he leaned into my palm. The purring comforted me, slowing my heartbeat and offering a moment of reprieve from my warring thoughts.

He nudged my palm with his nose and disappeared under the shelf again.

Then the anxiety came back. Buzzing in my ears. Restless and panicked.

I was so twisted inside, and without my violin, I didn't know how to regulate it.

I didn't believe that I was back on the ship. I didn't believe Mae survived. I needed to see her. To touch her. I needed proof that she didn't bleed out on the floor in that awful room.

It took all my strength just to get up off the floor. To get dressed. My hands shook just from not being able to use them for so long. It felt like I had to relearn my own body. Learn my new limits. Build myself back up again.

I didn't want any of my crew to see me like this. Whatever I had to do to regain my strength, I wanted to do it alone. Even the leviathan spirit inside me felt heavy.

Too heavy.

My knees nearly buckled when I dressed myself. But I had to pretend like I was all right. My crew needed to see me strong. Especially when I figured out what was ahead.

Varric was going to war with Algar. He had weapons of draconite. Ships powered by it. He had an army and was forcefully drafting anyone who disagreed with him into it. An assassin poised to go and shake up the Four Kingdoms from the inside so they wouldn't put up such a big fight.

I didn't know what to do.

All those unsuspecting innocent people on the continent. Cannon fodder.

I should've killed him.

I thought back to Varric on the ground, how easy it would've been to kill him.

But it wouldn't have been right.

Because while Varric was the head of the snake, cutting it off would've only left a power vacuum. Two would've taken its place. And there was no guarantee that it would've been any better.

When I opened my door, I wasn't surprised to see my mother and my mates waiting on the other side of it. Mae wasn't there.

My heart twisted in my chest. I *needed* to see her. "I need someone to get Mae. She should be here during the meeting."

Wraith nodded. "She's in the officers' quarters. I'll go get her."

Mama and the twins stepped into my cabin, seeing it in its full disheveled state. I repressed a pained groan as I sat at my desk, determined not to let anyone see just how off-center I felt. "You'll have to thank Pike for this fucking mess," I uttered, holding myself up straight.

It took *everything* not to crumple from how weak I felt.

"Are you all right, Levi?" Boats asked, concern glimmering in her eyes. She was freshly showered, but I noticed the bruises around her wrists like I was sure she noticed the needle holes in my arms from where I was constantly injected with vitrophine.

"I will be," I uttered.

"What happened in there? Did you learn anything?" my mother asked.

My cabin door opened, revealing Mae and Wraith. They stepped inside. Bruises lined Mae's arms, some of them the shape of handprints. They were already yellowing. Her cheeks were pink, and a sense of relief came over me because she was alive.

"The women of the hour," I stated, gesturing to them. "How the fuck did you two end up in Farlight?"

Wraith rolled her shoulder, glancing fondly at the smaller woman. "Mae dragged my ass off the beach of Shipwreck Bay and stole one of Lucky Bartram's sloops."

Mae blushed furiously, shaking her head. "I paid for it, but you should be thanking Wraith. She, uh, came up with the plan, and I just went along for the ride."

Wraith snorted, smacking Mae across the back of her head. "Bullshit. Mae was ready to go before I'd even finished spitting up seawater."

The pinkness of her cheeks spread to her ears as she rubbed her hands together.

Lovely.

"Thank you," I said, enjoying how her gaze softened when she looked at me. I turned my attention away from Mae to my mates. "Varric is going after Algar."

Wraith stiffened.

My mother's eyes widened. "You can't let that happen."

The legacy I'd run from. It felt like a hot breath on the back of my neck. "There's only one of me. There's no way I could stop an army."

"If Varric goes to war, the Isles will *never* join Algar again.

If he starts this, the Four Kingdoms will retaliate," Mama said. "Innocent people will die. Leviathans are meant to be the guardians."

"Innocent people have already died," I interjected. "I don't know what you want me to do about it."

"It's your responsibility to guard the islands and the people."

"You mean my *burden*." I sighed. "I can't have this conversation right now."

My mother's eyes narrowed, but then she nodded. "You'll make the right decision. You always do." She turned, leaving the room altogether.

"What do you want me to tell the crew?" Howler asked.

"Proceed to Shipwreck Bay. Let's go home. Spread the word on what's coming for us. But for now, we recover. I'll deal with the rest tomorrow." I buried my face in my hands, feeling so damn tired. "I need you to leave now."

My mates respected my privacy, all of them turning to leave.

"Except you, Mae."

She stopped, and the others patted her on the back as they left, then closed the door behind them. Mae turned around, tucking tendrils of hair behind her ears. "Pleasant weather today, isn't it?"

I pushed myself up from my desk, tendons and muscles whining. Something inside me ached to touch her. Hold her. Apologize for leaving her.

She looked up at me with wide brown eyes that felt so warm, then came toward me as if sensing what I wanted. I wrapped her up in my arms, burying my face in her hair. Her arms came up around my neck as she pressed her face into my chest.

Everywhere she touched left a wash of warmth. A tingle

of delight. "You came for me," I murmured.

Her shoulders shook. "Did you see Wraith? She practically begged me to come," she replied.

Still a terrible liar.

I drew back, brushing her chin to look at her face. The petal softness of her mouth. The roundness of her eyes. The pointed sharpness of her nose and ethereal quality of her cheekbones. Just as lovely as the first moment I saw her.

"Are you all right?" I asked.

She shook her head, tears welling in her eyes. I brushed them away with my thumbs, pulling her back in. "I... I don't know how to process anything from today. I want to laugh and poke fun at it. I want to sit down and cry. I just—" Her shoulders drooped. "I don't know what to do."

I brushed her hair back, adoring the way she melted into me. "I know how you feel."

My knees nearly buckled from merely standing. I felt frail, ashamed of any of that weakness showing through, even with Mae. But somehow, it didn't feel as bad.

She took a shallow step backward, subtly leading me over to my bed while supporting me enough not to let me fall over.

Her hands were fisted in my shirt, her forehead against my chest as we sat down together. My legs cried out in relief.

"You didn't tell anyone about me," she murmured.

"No. It's not their business."

"You knew Varric wasn't my father?" She leaned her head back, eyes still glistening.

"I suspected. That's not something you drop on someone," I replied, comforted by her touch. It felt different than the overwhelming sensation I'd get if anyone else touched me. It gave me peace. I accepted it, unsure how long I'd be able to tolerate it.

She nodded, pressing closer to me.

"You should be angry with me," I said. "After how I left things."

"You mean your lack of a goodbye?" she commented, leaning back to arch an eyebrow at me. "I'm very angry about that."

A chuckle slipped past my lips, easing some of the tension in my body. "Yet you still rescued me."

"A princess rescuing a dragon," she added, a small giggle following. "Seemed imperative."

The sound of her laugh made me smile.

Gods, I missed her.

"I missed you, sweetheart," I murmured.

"Missed me? I forgot all about you," she quipped, lips brushing the side of my neck.

I curled my fingers through her hair, breathing in the smell of salt from the strands. The ship swayed back and forth, and I just burrowed closer.

"Are you all right, Ronin?"

It felt odd to hear my name on her lips without the stipulation of sex. I liked it. "I've been running from my name for so long, sweetheart."

She drew back, wearing a tender expression on her face when she stroked the side of my jaw. What unraveled between us had nothing to do with how I craved her physically.

It was more than that.

"Then maybe it's time you reclaimed it," she said softly.

I sighed. "It's not that easy."

"Why not?" She paused, fingers brushing my jaw. "The man you've been running from knows you're alive. Knows about Shipwreck Bay. You're not hiding anymore."

She has a point. But I wasn't sure if I was ready to face that yet. I looked away. "Everyone will be in danger from associating with me. Including you."

"Look at me," she murmured, pulling my face over to her. And everything in me crumbled. My resolve. This wall I'd built around myself. I became soft the moment I saw the warmth in her gaze. "It's come to my attention that I'm not human. I'm not a princess. I'm an orphan, and I somehow can't die." Her voice warbled as if she couldn't believe the words she was saying. "But I made my choice. I chose this crew. I chose to stand with you. Danger be damned. It's more exciting that way."

Fuck, I love her.

Oh, fuck. I loved her.

This woman had shown me her bravery time and time again.

Stowing away on an unknown pirate ship.

Facing off against a siren.

Joining me to spar against Lucky Bartram.

Traveling across the sea to save me from a tyrant.

Brilliant, warm, beautiful Mae. Lovely as can be. Unafraid to jump into the unknown. I just didn't understand why she was here with me. The man who'd spent his entire life running away. The man who couldn't save her from getting her throat slit by another man who called himself her father.

I was weak. I could barely stand. I was so fucking *pitiful* right now, and she was still *looking at me like that*. Like she didn't care about any of it.

I stared into her eyes, searching for what it was that she liked about me. Why was she still here? She had her freedom. Why did she come back?

"I don't understand you, Mae."

She tilted her head to the side. "What's not to understand? I didn't want you to die."

I shook my head. "You didn't have to come. You could've stayed away. Been free. Forgotten about me."

"I'm free right now." She got up on her knees on the bed, rising to be eye to eye with me. "Maybe I'm here because I just so happen to care about you, Ronin."

My voice broke as I battled with myself, torn between hating myself and hating that she cared about me. "I'm weak. I can barely stand."

I'm not worthy.

She scoffed, and my face started to feel warm. She grasped my jaw hard, keeping me in place. "I still care about you, you foolish man. Now, stop complaining. Both of us could be dead right now, but somehow, we're still breathing."

A small smile curled the side of my mouth, and her eyes dropped to my lips.

"I missed your dimples."

"Not the rest of me?" I inquired, her words making me smile wider.

She shook her head, teasing me. "Only your dimples. Maybe your mouth too. I like your mouth." Her fingers walked down my arms. "Perhaps your arms." She stroked a tense cord of muscle on my neck. "I like this too."

I brushed her lips with my fingertips, and they parted under my touch. Her cheeks deepened their rosy hue, and I found myself once again struck by her loveliness. "Stay with me tonight."

She pulled my hand down from her lips. "Only if you promise not to bellyache about your weariness. A month of exhaustion and atrophy doesn't resolve overnight."

"I don't promise anything."

She sighed dramatically. "I can't stand you."

"Good thing we aren't standing."

With a shake of her head, Mae pressed both hands against

my chest and knocked me flat onto my bed. "You're infuriating." She threw a leg over my lap, straddling my thighs. Heat beaded under my skin, fueled by the intimacy of our conversation.

I ached for that connection. If I could go back to that last night in my cabana, I wouldn't have left. I would've held her and kissed her. Stayed in our bubble as long as we could've before Pike's raid.

My hair prickled along the back of my neck and arms as my desire for her built. I needed to feel her skin. I needed to feel okay. An expansive emotion filled my chest as my hands sought out the softness of her skin.

I needed to forget about the past month. I needed to forget about every awful thing that Varric said. Most of all, I needed to forget about how Mae looked when she died.

"I need you," I whispered, aching for her.

She stared down at me, her breaths shallow. She struggled to keep my gaze as she looked away and then back at me again. Her hand slid down my chest, lingering at the buttons of my shirt as if testing our connection.

Vulnerability flared between us, but I didn't feel ashamed of it.

I trusted Mae.

And she trusted me.

I reached up, stroking her warm cheek with the back of my hand, and she leaned into it.

"I need to feel alive," she murmured softly. "Remind me I'm alive."

Without another word, I nodded and guided her chin down so I could capture her lips. And everything felt right again.

43
MAEVE CROSS

Everything we experienced at the castle was intense. I hadn't even begun to process it. All I wanted to do was give myself a reprieve, a moment of peace. I wanted to bury myself in the sensations of Ronin's lips. His body pressed against mine.

I felt connected to him in a way I'd never experienced before. I knew it would take time before he was back to his full strength, especially when he still swayed under his own weight. He wanted to remain unaffected for the sake of his crew, but he didn't need to pretend with me.

Not after everything that happened.

Our mouths molded together as I tugged at his shirt, undoing the buttons. I needed to feel his skin, remind myself how good he felt.

Sex was probably not the best coping mechanism, but it was what we both needed.

I flattened my palms against his chest, loving how his stomach tensed under my touch. He groaned, swiping his tongue between my lips to taste my mouth.

He gripped my hips, guiding me to rock against his hardening cock. He swore, the veins in his arms bunching and throbbing.

I grasped his hands and pinned them over his head.

His eyes flew open, his irises only a thin ring of dark brown around his pupils. "Baby—"

"I'm doing the work. You don't get to have me until *I* think *you* can handle it."

I felt his chest rise and fall rapidly, his eyes hooded with lust. But also uncertainty. "What if I flip us over?"

"Then I'll hunt down those restraints you used to cuff me to that ballast and tie you to the headboard." I twisted my hips, rocking against his length with every word.

He cursed, his eyelids fluttering before he said, "Another time. I… I can't do that right now. I *need* to be in control."

I released his hands and brought one of them up to kiss the red marks around his wrist. His eyes softened again. "Tell me how you need me."

"Roll onto your side, sweetheart," he urged gently.

I obeyed, lying down and facing him. Ronin cupped my face, bringing me into a soft kiss. It wasn't hungry like it had been earlier. It was tender. Exploratory. He leaned back, discarding his shirt before reaching for mine. He pulled the white linen over my head. His mouth dropped to my neck, my breasts.

A moan slipped from my lips as he took a nipple into his mouth, sucking it softly and eliciting shivers everywhere. "Ronin," I murmured, tangling my fingers in his hair. Coarse and thick. Smelling like cedar and seawater. That scent that turned my insides to mush.

He grasped my waist, his thumbs drawing circles on my soft belly. I hooked one leg over his hip, pulling him closer until I could move against him. He released noises of pleasure against my chest, his hot breath blowing over my skin.

His noises made me wet, saturating the fabric of my pants.

I could feel him get thicker, the pressure dulled by the fabric separating us. "Please," I murmured. "Give me more."

He pulled the laces from my breeches, leaning back to wiggle them down my legs. I propped my hips up and was greeted by the cool air and Ronin's hungry gaze as his eyes settled where my legs were parted. "*Gods*, you're beautiful."

Heat flooded my face, my heart fluttering at the compliment. Playfully, I said, "Stop being nice to me."

"Not going to happen this time, sweetheart."

I rose up onto my knees to unlace his trousers next so he could kick them off. His cock sprang out. My eyes widened. I'd forgotten how much I liked the look of it. My mouth watered and I ached to taste him again. "Let me take care of you."

"Take care of me?" Ronin asked, flopping onto his back as he sighed deeply. "If anything, I should be taking care of you, sweetheart."

"I want to taste you again," I whispered.

He swore, tossing his head back onto the pillows. "You want to put my cock in your mouth?"

I blushed. "Yes."

"Then you get that pretty cunt over here and sit on my face."

Tingles erupted down my spine, my thighs slick with my own arousal. "Wh-What?"

He didn't repeat himself as his eyes gleamed with desire. "Come here. You can suck me off if I get a taste, sweetheart."

I pressed my thighs together, the room growing even

hotter. I crawled over to him, warm and nervous. Ronin licked his lips, chewing on the lower one as his eyes darkened even more.

"Now, baby. I can't be patient this time."

My heart slammed against my ribs. I got on my knees and into a position to hover above his face. His arms curled around my thighs as he forced me down to kneel with one leg on either side of his head.

My eyelids fluttered as I felt his hot tongue taste me. "Ronin," I cried out, my thighs already trembling.

He lifted me off him enough to order, "*Suck.*"

I lowered my head, opening my body up to a further assault from his mouth. He groaned, devouring me like he was starving. I shook, bolts of pleasure fluttering everywhere. His mouth was electricity. It felt like a lightning bolt igniting an entire sea. Cracking a tree in the middle of a clearing.

Pure destruction and fire.

I gathered the pearl of arousal on my tongue as he moaned against me. The vibrations made heat bunch at the base of my spine. I took the crown of him into my mouth and sucked.

He slid his tongue up and down my slit before closing his lips around my clit to give it some suction. I cried out at the onslaught of pleasure, and he slipped farther into my mouth. I laved it, enjoying the velvety feeling of his skin sliding against my tongue.

We devoured each other, moaning and whimpering together like everything was too much. I needed more. I needed to feel him inside me. My face steadily became slicker with my own saliva and his arousal.

He cursed as I bobbed my head up and down, hungry for more of his noises. He sucked on me harder before using his tongue to drive into me over and over again.

I gasped, gagging on him. He shuddered, going still as my throat spasmed around him. My body tightened, but his mouth wasn't enough. Never enough. I pulled off to cry out, "I need you. I need you now."

His grip on my thighs loosened enough for me to get up. "Then ride me. Look at me. I need you to look at me."

I turned around and settled my thighs around his hips. I was drenched. Overwhelmed. Hungry for more. I reached down to line him up with me.

I sank down, accommodating him easily.

He shouted a curse, his face flushed as he fisted the sheets.

I threw my head back at the feeling of fullness. "Oh... *Gods*," I nearly screamed.

His hand shot up to my mouth, stifling my cry of pleasure. "Not here, baby. Not here."

I bit my lips as I rose up to sink back down again. I whimpered, "Ronin... Ronin... I can't."

An uncontrollable tremor swept through my body as I clenched around him, painfully close to oblivion. He grabbed me by the throat, dragging me down into another kiss.

I could taste myself on his lips, and I was sure he could taste himself too.

I moaned into his mouth as his hips pumped up and down, rubbing against a mind-altering bundle of nerves.

My walls fluttered, and I felt him get thicker. I bounced up and down, messily kissing him as our bodies moved on their own, taking and giving gratification as we worked together toward the pinnacle of pleasure.

Tears streamed down my cheeks from how intense it felt. I bowed my spine upward, thrusting my throat toward the ceiling, both of my hands tangling in my hair. Ronin's hand was around my neck, a gentle pressure only adding to my euphoria.

My heart raced.

I watched him slide two fingers into his mouth to moisten them before bringing them down to my clit to rub the swollen pearl between two slick fingers.

A tingling surge climbed up my spine until it exploded all over my body. He took his hand from my throat to clasp it over my mouth before I screamed, erupting and shivering with elation. He groaned, swallowing his shout as he pumped upward.

His eyes rolled back, his body falling slack as he joined me in rapture.

I collapsed on top of his chest.

"Oh, *fucking Hells.*" He grasped my face and pulled me into one more kiss before I rolled onto my side and burrowed my face in his chest.

"I love you." He stroked my hair where it lay down my back, and I didn't think he realized he'd said it out loud. Until several moments later when his hands froze. Then he continued rubbing my back to play it off.

I leaned back and kissed him again. "I love you too. Don't overthink it. Just shut up and hold me."

Ronin's eyes widened. He didn't say anything, just pressed his lips against my forehead and held me. His arms were trembling. Shaking with exhaustion.

And I was too.

"What happens next?" I asked, lying on my stomach while he rubbed circles on my back with those big hands.

He hummed, relaxed and basking in the sex afterglow. My head felt light, my worries melted away. At least temporarily. Right now, it was only us. There was no impending war. No sorcerer after us. No worry about the fate of Algar—or Farlight Isles.

"That's a loaded question. I don't want to fucking think about it. Too much to do and not enough time for it," he replied. He sighed one more time before sitting up.

I followed him, pressing a palm against his back. "Then what do you need?"

"Don't touch me right now." His voice wasn't cold or cruel, merely voicing what he needed.

My hand fell to the side. It felt so drastically different to how open he was to touch a few minutes ago. But I understood.

"It's not you."

"I know. What can I do? Let me help," I offered. "I *want* to help."

He eyed me intensely, tilting his head to the side. "Now you're being too nice to me, Mae." He backed up against his headboard, grunting as he fell slack against it. "I'm one person. I don't know what the fuck my mother thinks I can do to stop an army."

I didn't say anything, biting my tongue. He'd never admit it, but I could feel how off-center he was. So close to falling either way when he needed to be balanced.

"Don't spare my feelings, Mae."

I gulped. "You want to know my thoughts?"

"I value your input. Besides, you've seen me at my worst and you're still here."

"I doubt that was your worst," I teased. "I still have yet to see you piss drunk."

He rolled his eyes, a dimple puncturing the side of his mouth. "Shut the fuck up."

I grinned, enjoying the moment of normalcy before I told Ronin what I thought. "I think the first step you take is claiming your name. Claiming your legacy. That's something no one has the power to take away from you."

Warmth filled his eyes as he gazed at me before he reached to brush some of my hair from my face. The anxiety he seemed to carry in his face melted, as if my words put him at ease.

"You're right."

44
MAEVE CROSS

We talked the entire night. I told Ronin about what happened with Nathaniel, and he slowly accepted the stroke of my fingers up and down his arm as he told me about what happened on the ship.

In the dungeon torture room.

About the history of Farlight Isles.

That Varric was a fanatic.

His obsession for power had been fueled when he learned the history of his family. The Fifth Kingdom. A family that I… wasn't a part of. Which was both a relief and another layer of confusion.

Ronin admitted that he didn't know much about the history of the leviathans. His mother was human. It was his father, Raiden, who was supposed to share that with him, but that history died along with the rest of his family.

Ronin and I were both products of an unknown past. I didn't know who I was… or *what* I was. But I knew where to start.

Conway would know—Butcher's husband. A merrow

from the shoal who took care of me. Perhaps he would know what a Sentry was.

The next morning, the crew greeted me with excitement. Appreciation. There were a few new faces from the dungeons. Some of them ran once they were freed, while some of them came along. They seemed grateful for the fresh air all the same. It felt good to be welcomed into open arms while Ronin figured out the next steps. He was still a private man, but I was thankful for the little moments when he let me in.

He trusted me.

I trusted him.

The in-between didn't feel like it mattered. We understood each other on an entirely new level than we used to. Whatever happened, I knew we'd have each other's backs. The mates and I had gained a new respect for one another too.

But still, Ronin kept my vitality a secret. As far as the mates and crew knew, I was still Maeve Cross. Varric's daughter. Heir of the fanatic.

The following two weeks went by slowly, but everyone had their job. It felt almost normal, like the month I was on the crew before we made it to the safehold. But so much had changed since then. And there was still this atmosphere of uncertainty.

Wariness.

Ronin still flinched when anyone touched him—me included. A subtle jerkiness in his muscles that he repressed as much as he could. But every day he seemed to hold his weight better. His shoulders were still narrowed, his waist thinned, but his face wasn't sallow anymore. His skin regained its color the stronger he got. Even his hair got glossier aside from the matted parts.

Not that he would let anyone help him. Not with his hair. Not with his training. He was as bitterly stubborn as I was.

I sat down in the mess with Gunny across from me. Even though he'd told me his name, he also told me that he preferred Gunny to Silas. So be it. We clicked our bowls together before bringing them up to drink down the porridge.

Still as delicious as the first time I tried it. Warm and substantial for sailor bellies.

In the middle of breakfast, Wesley came down to the mess, howling, "Captain has an announcement! Everyone is to get to the main deck!"

I perked up. This only meant one thing. He had come to a decision.

Gunny put his bowl down. "Do you know what this is about? You've been awfully secretive about what happened in Farlight."

"Not my place," I answered.

"Fair." He stood up and passed the bowls to a cabin boy. "Let's go."

Gunny and I went to the main deck alongside a bunch of different crews. The gunnery crew. The mess crew. The shiphands. And a handful of cabin boys, too, including Luther, who gave me a friendly wave.

The deck was full of eager shipmates chattering among themselves as Ronin stepped out of the captain's cabin. His name was still somewhat of a secret. Most of the time, it was only said aloud away from the main crew. He was isolated from them the entire journey back to Farlight and isolated when he got there.

All the crew knew was that he was a common leviathan, exposed and sentenced to death.

Ronin's back was ramrod straight, the air of authority

coming off him effortlessly. There was no question that he was the captain of the ship. Even though he was still in the early stages of recovery, his presence filled the air.

On either side of him, he had his mates and his mother. Plankwalker was still manning the helm while Ronin came down to the main deck. I noticed the tightness of his fists. The small tells of nervousness that he hid well.

But I knew him better than that.

The crew grew silent as Ronin's voice projected down the deck.

"We had a close call on Farlight Isles. If not for the courage of Wraith and Mae, we wouldn't have made it out alive."

Gunny slapped me on the back, grinning. "Ain't that right, birdie?"

I flushed as a few sailors hooted at me before quieting again for the announcement.

"I've spent a long time running from my name. From my legacy. But I'm ready to reclaim it." He straightened up, pulling his shoulders back to stand tall and proud. "My name is Ronin Murdoch. Son of Raiden and Enya Murdoch."

The silence felt loud as Gunny leaned over and whispered, "Does he mean the king? Our captain is the king? Oh Hells, he's a Royal Leviathan!"

I elbowed him in the ribs. "Shush! Just listen."

"A war is coming to the Farlight Isles. Varric Cross is sending an army to Shipwreck Bay. He's going to recruit soldiers to pillage Algar and hang anyone who fights back. He will send an assassin to Algar to weaken their kingdom so he can take over."

The crew erupted in chatter.

Wesley stomped his feet. "Eh! Quiet!"

Steadily, the chatter petered out.

"When we dock, you will have the option to stay or leave. This is my fight. I will continue to do it with or without help."

Uncertainty grew within the crew. It was understandable. It was a big ask.

"Fuck that!" Gunny shouted. "You have me, Cap! Silas Hawke!" He pushed past the bodies of crewmen to stand along the steps. "Where else can I be the best head gunner in the Isles?"

The gunnery crew cheered, shouting a myriad of "Let's fight!" or "Fuck Varric Cross!" or even "Stronger together!"

Gunny flashed Ronin a smile. "You got me, Cap. And my gunners."

Ronin blinked as if he wasn't expecting any type of backing.

Luella stepped up. "My name is Luella Peregrine. I'm an elf from the continent of Algar. Washed ashore and rescued by Cap. I know what's at stake. I know the families that inhabit the continent. We know the violence Varric is capable of."

"I'm Wesley Rhys," Wesley shouted. "My name is my story. I will not hide it anymore."

"Alessandra Rhys—or Andra," Andra chimed in. "We share our names out of trust."

Enya smiled, patting Andra on the shoulder. "My name is Enya Murdoch. My family was stolen by Varric Cross. My story is not unlike many of yours. Imprisoned or threatened. Trapped in the crosshairs of war. I stand beside my son."

Ronin's shoulders were stiff, but the shouting and hooting from the crew loosened them. "We stand with you!"

His eyes shone with determination.

You're not alone, Ronin.

"The pirate colonies are scattered. Ununified. Easy to take out one at a time," Ronin announced.

Wesley glanced over at him. "Are you suggesting what I think you're suggesting?"

"Two pirate monarchs. We get them on our sides, then we have a standing chance against Varric and his armies," Ronin said.

The energy around the crew changed, the wariness dissipating to reveal *hope.*

Unity.

We're in this together.

"There is work to do when we get to Shipwreck Bay. I don't know how much time we have, but if we stand together, we have a chance. Though, if any of you wish to leave, take your families and go. See Luella, and she'll distribute your cut, and you can leave honorably." Ronin's words were straight to the point. "Now get back to work!"

The crew disbanded, going to their designated positions or back to the mess for breakfast.

I slowly walked up to where my friends were all standing. "Quite the speech," I teased.

Ronin glanced at me, a dimple puncturing one of his cheeks.

"So the two pirate monarchs…. Don't you mean *three* of them? The Big Three?" Andra pointed out.

He shook his head. "No. Lucky Bartram and Bliss Thatcher." Ronin glanced over at me. "You've already met Lucky, but Bliss is anything but their name."

Wesley laughed. "We're going to need Violetta's help, too, Le—Ronin. It doesn't matter that you used to fuck her."

Ronin pressed his fingers into the bridge of his nose. "You forgot the part where she robbed me."

Gunny started to laugh.

"What're you laughing at, *Silas*?"

"I prefer Gunny," he pointed out before adding, "And *everyone* knows about your tryst with the pirate queen, Cap."

Everyone glanced over at me. My face bloomed several shades of pink. "Except me."

"Except for Mae, of course," Luella agreed, laughing under her breath. She whispered something to Andra but said it purposefully loud enough for all of us to hear. "He *definitely* has a type."

Ronin wasn't amused, but it was quite adorable to watch his cheeks subtly flush with embarrassment under his beard. "As your captain, I'm ordering you to go the fuck away. I don't care that you saved my life. I hate you right now."

Luella loved teasing Ronin. It was the type of banter that happened between siblings. "Aye, aye, Captain."

"Since you're a king, you're not gonna start being all snooty, right?" Gunny asked.

Both cheeks dented in with dimples. "I don't know how to be a king, so I'm just going to keep being a pirate."

Gunny and Wesley both seemed content with that answer as they left to get back to work.

Enya's hand curled over Ronin's shoulder, and I watched his entire body tense. She seemed to notice and removed it immediately.

"I'm proud of you, you know," she murmured.

Ronin softened. "It's not going to be easy."

"But it's the right thing to do. Varric isn't going to stop."

"No… he's not." He sighed.

Enya nodded. The knowledge of how far Varric would go created a somber moment they shared between them. "Now, we have some crewmembers who I promised to teach how to read. I should get going."

His mother gave me a fond smile before ducking away to go below deck.

Ronin turned away and climbed onto the upper deck above the captain's cabin. I followed, clambering up the ladder shortly behind him.

The wind tousled my hair, sending prickles up and down my arms. The sun beamed at my back, rising in the east. The cool metal of the ladder didn't feel rough on my calloused hands. I'd earned my calluses through hard, satisfying work.

When I crested the top of the ladder, using the half wall to steady myself, I saw him leaning over it, simply enjoying the moment of quiet as the morning chill swept over us. The sun bounced off his leather coat, bathing him in its light.

He might've told me that he felt weaker than ever, but I thought this was the strongest I'd ever seen him. More magnificent than before. A man who looked death in the face and still chose mercy.

My heart swelled with adoration.

I approached him and found a spot comfortably close to him so I could feel his presence but not touch him if he wasn't ready for it. I hooked my elbows over the wall to stare out at the cerulean water that went on forever.

I breathed in the salty air, a feeling of relief washing over me.

We had a plan.

Beyond that, the future was uncertain, but right now, I could enjoy the moment.

Fingertips brushed my hand as Ronin silently reached over. We didn't say anything as he laced his fingers through mine.

No matter what happened... I was ready for it.

EPILOGUE

Varric seethed—a rare type of emotion to wear so visibly on his face. He sat in his study, his jaw clenched, his hands balled into white-knuckle fists that dared one more person to defy him.

His wife, Katherine, was nowhere to be seen. Not uncommon. They were never in each other's company unless it was required. It was likely that love had long evaporated. The attraction gone with it.

The study had taken the brunt of Varric's violence. Charred books. Broken glass. His normally steady fingers shook with restrained rage. He grasped his amulet, staring at the draconite gem, stroking a crack in the black crystal.

It wasn't there before....

The enormous embossed wooden doors into his study were gently pushed open.

Varric released the amulet, throwing up an air of indifference. The guards stepped to the side, revealing an elven man. Not particularly old or young. Not attractive or plain.

Forgettable.

"Thallan," Varric greeted. "Leave us."

The guards obeyed, closing the massive doors behind themselves.

"You've called for me, sire?" the man asked, stepping close to the desk before dipping down to one knee, bowing deeply in a show of servitude. "I wasn't expecting to hear from you so soon after our last meeting."

"Change your face, Thallan. That will not get you beyond the walls," Varric demanded.

Upon the request, the elven man—or *whatever* they actually were—shifted, muscle and flesh molding into something new.

This time Thallan took on the appearance of a young woman, objectively pretty, but just as forgettable as the last. The same red hair cascaded longer, curling delicately around their shoulders.

"That'll do." Varric produced a stone of draconite and tossed it to Thallan's bowing form. "We don't have time to waste."

Thallan grasped the stone, rising to their feet, wearing an expression Varric perceived as confusion. "But sire... it's too soon. The ships aren't at the ready for invasion."

"Plans change." Varric stood. "I need Algar in disarray long before I arrive."

Thallan dipped their head. "And our deal? Will you still honor it?"

Varric's upper lip curled into a snarl, but he pulled it back, his face becoming a mask of thinly veiled violence. "Only if you succeed, Face-Stealer."

A flicker of fear crossed through Thallan's violet eyes before they flashed into a more neutral brown. "How long?"

"Two weeks," Varric determined. "Kill the heirs of Algar by any means necessary. That stone is only powerful enough to take you to Algar and back again. Fail, and your flesh and blood will bear the consequences."

Sensing Varric's tone of finality, Thallan used the power of the draconite to split open a portal to the mountains of Algar. The edges of the portal split and frayed. An unstable source of magic, it wasn't meant for this. As Thallan stepped through, the portal closed.

Varric returned to his seat and opened a drawer in his desk, pulling out a well-worn journal. The spine had been broken, the old leather discolored from fingerprints. A wax lip was sealed over the top to keep it closed from prying eyes.

When his fingertips glowed, the amulet pulsing with power, it snapped open.

Then he began to write, using a cipher only he would understand.

ACKNOWLEDGMENTS

I want to thank my husband, Joseph, for always pushing me to accomplish my dreams. I love you and couldn't have accomplished this without you. To my brilliant sibling, Kayla, who was always there to bounce ideas off. To my mom, Libby, and my mother-in-law, Carolyn, for reading my roughest drafts and giving me feedback.

To my family and friends who won't read my book but will still buy it, thank you for your everlasting support.

To the friends I made along the way. Especially to Aimee Ferro, Kendra Dawn, and Deana Van Cura for being so supportive through this journey. I adore you!

And of course, I want to thank Kristin and Becky for making my dreams a reality!

ABOUT THE AUTHOR

Anacostia Miller is a novelist and screenwriter with a background in filmmaking and prop creation. After ten years of writing and two years of ghostwriting, she found her niche in romantasy. She loves exploring different themes like found family and showcasing inclusivity.

World-building and developing intricate histories in her novels are some of her favorite things to do. She also grew up on classics like *The Lord of the Rings* and *Buffy the Vampire Slayer*, which have inspired her writing. Developing complicated lore and having moments of happiness are vital to the stories. Also, humor plays a big part. As dark as things will get, readers can always hold out for that moment of happiness to make it worth it.

During her days, you can find her trying out a new recipe to figure out how to describe it in her writing, daydreaming, or annoying her husband by telling him exactly how the lighting conveys emotion in every movie they watch together.

instagram.com/anacostiamillerauthor
tiktok.com/@anacostiamillerauthor

ABOUT THE PUBLISHER

Hot Tree Publishing loves love. Publishing adult romantic fiction, HTPubs are all about diverse reads featuring heroes and heroines to swoon over. Since opening in 2015, HTPubs have published more than 300 titles across the wide and diverse range of romantic genres. If you're chasing a happily ever after in your favourite subgenre, HTPubs have you covered.

Interested in discovering more amazing reads brought to you by Hot Tree Publishing? Head over to the website for information:

WWW.HOTTREEPUBLISHING.COM

facebook.com/hottreepublishing
x.com/hottreepubs
instagram.com/hottreepublishing

Milton Keynes UK
Ingram Content Group UK Ltd.
UKHW012249110624
443988UK00005B/301

9 781922 679819